Time Tree

THE EMERGENCE

Time Tree

THE EMERGENCE

LISA RAE MORRIS

Published by Author Academy Elite
P.O. Box 43, Powell, OH 43035

www.AuthorAcademyElite.com

This title is also available as an ebook and audiobook.

Library of Congress Cataloging-in-Publication Data available upon request.

ISBN 978-1-64085-691-2 (softcover)
ISBN 978-1-64085-692-9 (hardback)
ISBN 978-1-64085-693-6 (ebook)

Library of Congress Control Number (LCCN): 2019905765

Cover design: Elena Karoumpali, L1 Graphics
Back cover photo of Ecclesgrieg Castle by Barry Dominic Graham
Author photos: Leslie Fairman Photography
Interior design: Chris O'Byrne

Printed in the United States of America

To Gracie...
who fixed it.

Contents

Prologue

Ancient Scotland ~ 4,000 years ago

A hooded figure slowly made his way down a long-worn path in the dense wood. Bits of dried leaves and bracken clung to the hem of his moss-green cloak. He stopped before a craggy hawthorn tree, its girth so immense that, were seven men to stand in a circle around it, they could only just touch fingertips. Its emerald crown climbed fifty feet in the air, while its rugged elbows lay half buried, lifting thick, ivy-laden branches and tufts of greenery in every direction. Within its spiraled bark lay a city of hollows and highways where generations of creatures had settled.

He laid his hand on the bark, sensing the energy pulsing through it. The tree hummed faintly.

"It's almost over, Albion," said a second cloaked figure, who stepped lightly around the other side of the Great Tree.

"Indeed. Our last night. Tomorrow, our kind will retreat to shadow. The time of floods is past, and the new humans will soon arrive. The Great Trees must cloak themselves in secrecy, as this one has done." Albion patted the bark with great affection. "Although real hawthorns don't usually grow this large, I think the disguise suits it perfectly. Don't you agree, Caledon?"

"I don't think any disguise would suit," Caledon retorted. "I still recall the light which used to emanate from this place, before all creation fell into darkness. It would fill the sky with harmonious song, every fractal radiating in perfect symmetry as it touched every point in its space, connecting with every other Great Tree on earth, holding all of Time together. It was glorious! It was my appointed joy to be its Guardian. Now, it is a nest for squirrels," he huffed. "I wish it could be hidden away in the ether, as the First Tree was. Then I might be allowed to remain its protector. Instead, it must be costumed in lowly greenery, with humans as its Guardians. And I must look on helplessly and do nothing."

"Nothing? Hardly nothing, Caledon. We must protect and teach the Guardian families, as the Master has commanded."

"I will obey, of course," Caledon sighed. "He wills it, and therefore it will be done. But for my part, I see little logic in laying such an important charge upon men of clay."

"I, too, am anxious about the future of the Great Tree I have long guarded," admitted Albion. "I must pass its charge to a human mere hours from now. But, I believe the Master knows best. The human Guardians will do well. Fathers will teach sons. The Guardianship will pass from generation to generation as a legacy. We must do whatever we can to help the Guardians succeed so that the Great Trees remain safe."

"As the First Tree was kept safe? It was relegated to the ether and required a posted sentry before even the second generation of humans could draw breath!"

"That tree still lives, Caledon. The Master will replant it at the proper moment. Meanwhile, the Great Trees of earth haven't lost their beauty. It's just beauty of a...different kind now. The energy of Time still flows through their branches. Can you not hear it? The Master has brought the earth's forests back from watery death to conceal them. The Guardians will see to it that no one finds them. They must succeed."

"Yes, but why must these glorious trees even exist in a world where they have to be kept from sight?"

"To keep—"

"To keep the humans from exploiting them. Yes, I know. It was a rhetorical question. Yet it is those very humans who are now appointed Guardians. They, who abandoned their immortality so easily."

"I know," sighed Albion. "The universe is groaning under their foolishness, even as it is reborn. Time is thinner than ever. The humans' lifespans are but a fraction of what they used to be. They see so little of Time that they can't even agree on what day it is from one calendar to the next."

The two stood solemnly, listening to the rustle of leaves and the faint, melodic hum under the bark.

"The Master's ways are a mystery to me," said Caledon after several moments. "He could fold up Time like a useless old garment if He wanted to. He could be done with it. All of this," he gestured around him, "seems utterly unnecessary. Things were better before Time, when the Master's wild glory could rampage across infinity unveiled and unguarded, when the Three would shake the universe with their laughter. Now it must all be shrouded in secrecy, revealed in only tiny, digestible glimpses, in order not to overwhelm the soft little clay people. The Great Trees are only here anchoring the time fabric in the first place because mankind is too fragile to cope with the reality of infinity! Yet it is mankind who have driven the Great Trees to this lowly state and weakened Time itself. How could they allow it?"

"Indeed, they are too easily misled. The Master's graciousness to them defies understanding. Regardless, Caledon... the next Guardian arrives this night. You must teach him and then remain with his family, even from the shadows."

Caledon sighed and hung his head. "Why must the Three continue with humans at all?"

"Because He loves them," Albion said simply.

Chapter 1

A ngus Armstrong took a slurp of tea and frowned. He flipped back a page in his diary and scanned the column of numbers he had scratched there with his pencil over the past month. He flipped forward and looked at the sum at the bottom, willing it to be higher. He had checked and rechecked his arithmetic, so he knew the numbers weren't lying to him. Dad in the grave since winter and Mum in bed with a broken leg left him the keeper of the house now. And the keeper of this house needed at least six pounds more to pay the landlord by Friday, a mere three days hence. He'd already given the doctor most of the earnings from his last completed job · to set Mum's leg, and he still owed more. The gold sovereign that remained in his little leather pouch looked lonely indeed. His eyes darted to an intricately fashioned wooden box on the mantel. Dad and he had carved it together—their last carpentry project before Dad had taken ill. Inside it, a treasure that

1

the Armstrong family had passed down from one generation to the next as an inheritance. Angus shook his head. *I cannae sell her. She'll stay in the family. It's just the six pounds I need. Something has to turn up.*

The front door opened and a man of four and twenty with unruly, sandy blond hair peeked around it.

"Angus! Goin' down the pub. You comin', mate?"

"I'll come wi'ye, Patrick Dawson, but y'know I'm not drinkin.'"

"Aye, I'm well aware of you and your holy ways, ya big side o'beef," Patrick rolled his eyes. "Baps and bacon then, on me. I've a new job!"

Angus's eyes widened at his best friend. "You're nae fishin' anymore?"

"And I suppose I'll have to stand in your doorway tellin' you about it till I collapse into a pile of bones, dead of hunger?"

It was Angus's turn to roll his eyes. "Mum?" he called into the other room. "I'll be back in a while, arright?"

"Have a good time, son!" she called back.

The aptly named Village Inn Pub was a low-ceilinged affair, one of a few buildings left in the main street that had a thatched roof and flaking white plaster walls supported by ancient hewn beams of dark timber. The main pub could seat two dozen comfortably, but there were usually at least thirty men laughing over pints of ale in the evenings.

Gordon Mayfield, the proprietor, was always in the thick of it, polishing glasses with his smudged apron while shouting gossip back and forth with the patrons. His golden-haired daughter Gillian brought out plate after plate loaded with every combination of fish, sausages, bacon, baps, cheese, potatoes, and pickles to the hungry diners. Her melodic and slightly sassy voice could be heard ringing out above the din.

The pub was the only place in the village to gather besides the church. It was the best way to get the latest news, since St. Cyrus didn't have a newspaper, and only some could read one anyway.

Angus and Patrick claimed a small, round table that was only just vacated and placed their order with Gillian as she balanced a stack of dirty plates in one hand while wiping the table with the other.

"So what's this job then, Pat?" Angus asked.

"I'm a builder, mate!" Patrick beamed.

"A builder of what, besides earwax?"

"Y'know the old Mount Cyrus house?"

"Of course I know it. It's but two miles west. Everybody knows it."

"Well, the place passed down to old man Frederic's nephew a couple years back, though nobody ever saw the chap. Canadian gent, name of William Forsyth Grant." Patrick hooked his thumbs behind imaginary lapels and puffed up his chest importantly as he said the name. "It's his mum 'tis one of the Grants, but he's ta'en on the name, too. Gotta go about with *two* surnames if you're landed in a pile of money, I guess."

"The Grants have had the place for a couple o'decades arready. What of it?"

"Well, now he's actually here! He's set out to make a name for himself, so he's buildin' a bloody castle! He's renamed the place 'Ecclesgrieg' on account of 'Mount Cyrus' sounding too much like the name of the village. He'll be gettin' the plantation goin' again—aims to turn the place into a real money maker. He's even brought an architect all the way from Bath."

Gillian set down their plates, plus a pint for Patrick and mug of tea for Angus. She pulled a small paper-wrapped parcel from her apron pocket.

"For your mum, on the house. Tell her that Dad and I are real sorry about her leg, and sendin' up prayers that she'll soon be on her feet." She smiled shyly.

"Thank you, Gilly, that's a real blessing." Angus returned the smile. His cheeks reddened as his eyes followed her retreat.

Gilly. They were children when she said he could call her that. They had always lived within walking distance, and played together since she was old enough to run. She had been an agreeable friend, always up for fishing off the stone bridge over the River Esk, always up for a jaunt down the beach, easy to chat with. They'd both started working with their dads around the same time—she, a girl of twelve, learning to cook and run the counter at the pub with her father; and he, a boy of fourteen, learning the woodworking trade in greater earnest alongside his father. They'd not only had less time to take adventures then, but she seemed to have grown rather shy around him. He longed to run down the beach with her again, but as the months passed, it began to seem improper to ask. So he'd settled for chatting with her every Sunday after church.

It was around that time that it became evident to Mrs. Keith, the reverend's wife, that more of the children in the village should learn their letters and numbers, in order that they might better themselves in trades. Since the village had no proper school, she began a small class in her parlor. Angus was among the first to come, eager to read and write. To his delight, Gillian Mayfield was also in the group. She was her father's only child and desired to inherit his pub, but hadn't the skills to manage the business side of things. She had no one to teach her at home, because her mother had died giving birth to her, and her father was far too busy running the pub. Mrs. Keith's tutoring was a godsend to them both. They'd felt a bit sheepish, though, being the oldest pupils in the class, so Mrs. Keith had allowed them to work together while she helped the younger ones. Under her guidance, they had taught each other to read and write. Angus had looked forward to the time they spent sitting side by side, Gilly pointing with her slender finger at the words as he sounded them out, Angus watching her make funny squinty faces while she did her sums. He missed those days.

"Mate?" Patrick elbowed him.

"Eh?" Angus shook himself from his reverie.

"You wanna go back to the kitchen and wash some dishes? Polish her boots, perhaps?"

Angus punched Patrick's arm.

"Oi!" Patrick cackled. "So I've got on as a builder," he continued, tearing into his bread. "Today was my first shift. Could be a year at least till it's finished, maybe even longer. I finally get to do something with my hands besides slingin' fish about! And nae too soon. I was nearly ready to try the shipyards in Glasgow." He swigged his ale. "Didnae want to leave my sisters alone till they're old enough to go into service. Now it looks like the Grants could take us all on."

"Pat, that's tremendous!" cried Angus.

"And, they're lookin' for carpenters. No more fixin' furniture, mate. You might get to do some real work for a change. I spoke to the foreman after my shift today and he said I ought to bring you along in the mornin.' That is, unless you have a more pressing engagement?"

"To a real man's wage, and steady!" Angus lifted his mug. Patrick lifted his ale.

"Slàinte!"

The late spring day dawned misty and cold. Angus stirred a small pot of porridge over the fire, working hard not to burn it. Mum sat close, her foot propped on a small stool that Angus had made as a boy.

"My son, the carpenter," she smiled. "But four and twenty years of age, and already off to build castles. I'm so proud of you."

"I've not got the job yet, Mum," he reminded her, but couldn't help a smile.

"You must take these with you. I made them for you last night." She pulled three sheets of crinkled butcher paper from her pocket and handed them to Angus. "You must show Mr. Grant that he's hirin' the finest craftsman in all of Scotland!"

Angus unfolded them to reveal charcoal rubbings of his own intricate wood carvings. "Mum, these were just practice patterns I was messin' about with," he said. "I'm sure Mr. Grant has seen much finer."

"Sure he's not, and I'll lay a guinea on it! He'll soon agree that the elegant Mrs. Grant must have Angus Armstrong's works of art in her castle."

"And I'll lay a guinea there's nae a finer mum than mine, in the whole of Her Majesty's realm," Angus grinned as he leaned in to hand her a bowl of porridge and plant a kiss on her cheek. "I've got to get on. Pat'll be waiting." Angus hefted his sailcloth rucksack, clanking with tools. "Mrs. MacDonald said she'd look in on you this afternoon, arright?"

"I'll be fine enough here, son. I've got my lace and needlework to keep my hands busy. Go show those Grants what finery is!"

Angus and Patrick walked the two miles to the Ecclesgreig estate. The ancient 16th-century house, the face of which Angus had grown familiar with as a boy, was all but swallowed up by scaffolding. As they picked their way across the lawns and around newly trimmed shrubbery, they could hear the morning bustle on the construction site. Despite the chill, a dozen men had already shed their coats and were busy unloading bricks from wagons. Another half dozen huddled around a parked two-wheeled cart, helping themselves to baskets of bread, steaming copper jugs of coffee, a jug of fresh milk, and a pan of boiled eggs that had been set out under the maroon awning.

"Breakfast?" Angus marveled.

"Aye, part of the wages," Patrick enthused. "Two eggs, two baps, a cup of milk, and all the coffee you kin fit! Mr. Grant says, 'Hungry workers cannae be hard workers.'"

"I like him arready!" Angus said. He could feel his body burning through the last bits of his meager portion of scorched porridge on the walk here.

Patrick steered Angus toward three men hovering over a makeshift worktable propped on two sawhorses, studying blueprints and murmuring. In the center of the group was a man of forty, a striking figure in a top hat, cravat, and trimly tailored frock coat. He listened intently to the man on his left, who stood in stark contrast in his bowler hat and work trousers. They both burst into a sudden fit of congenial laughter. The third man, dressed in a simple but elegant brown suit, was the first to notice their approach.

"Mr. Dawson, isn't it?" he asked pleasantly.

"Aye, Mr. Goodridge, nice to see you again," Patrick replied, lifting his cap. "Mr. Grant." He nodded to the man in the center before turning to the man in the bowler hat. "Mr. Barclay, here's the chap I told you about yesterday. Angus Armstrong, the finest woodworker in Scotland."

Barclay's eyebrows lifted as he shook Angus's hand. "Is that so?" The corner of Barclay's mustache twitched as he suppressed a smile. "Bit young to have conquered the trade already, I'd think."

"Pat likes to exaggerate, but I do put my heart into every job, sir." Angus blushed.

"Well, that's reassuring. I suppose Dawson told you I'm the foreman on this site. This is Mr. Edmund Goodridge, our architect." The man in the brown suit smiled. "And this, of course, is Mr. William Forsyth Grant, owner of the estate."

Angus was suddenly unsure what to do... Tip his cap? Shake the man's hand? Bow at the waist, perhaps? He'd never made the acquaintance of a landed aristocrat before. Grant offered him a warm smile and a firm handshake. Angus was relieved.

"Happy to have you here," he said. "Did you have to come far?"

"Eh no, just a couple miles down the road," Angus replied, mildly fascinated at Grant's Canadian accent. "I live in a cottage not far from the church in St. Cyrus."

"It's a lovely little church," Grant commented. "If all goes well this summer, we'll do our next christening there."

"Och, congratulations, sir!" Patrick interjected.

"Thank you," he smiled. "Eueretta's hoping for a girl this time. Might be a calming influence with two boys about the place. Well, I'll let you two gentlemen discuss business while I continue with Mr. Goodridge here. Nice to meet you, Mr. Armstrong." He touched his hat brim lightly with one finger.

Barclay clapped Patrick and Angus on the shoulders and they broke away from the huddle. "Dawson, go stuff some breakfast in your face and get on the brick crew in fifteen minutes," he said.

Patrick trotted off.

"Now then, Armstrong, let's hear about you..." Barclay removed a small book and pencil from his trouser pocket. "Ye've brought your own tools, I see. Good sign. What sort of work have you done? I assume you're an apprentice?"

"I was," Angus began. "My dad was a master joiner and carpenter, and I've been workin' with him since I could hold a hammer. He thought it best that I learn from someone besides just him, so he set me up with an apprenticeship in Aberdeen. Never made it, though. Dad died of a fever last winter, and I've had to look after Mum. Been fixin' furniture, mostly, but I've made my own pieces here and there."

Barclay closed the little book with a snap.

"So what you're sayin' is, you're the best carpenter in Scotland because yer dad thought you had talent, and you've fixed a couple of broken chairs."

"Ye'll recall those were Pat's words, not mine," Angus bristled, stuffing his hands into his pockets. "But my Dad probably *was* the best master craftsman in all of Scotland, and he taught me everythin' I know."

"We can use a framer, I suppose," Barclay mused. "It's a pound a week. But without an apprenticeship, I cannae pay you a craftsman's wage."

"Fine." Angus attempted a pleasant expression.

"You'll report to Jameson over there," he said absently as he reopened the little record book and began to scribble.

"Thank you." Angus moved to touch his cap, but as he pulled his hand free of his pocket, his sleeve button caught the edge of the folded papers in his pocket, sending them fluttering to the dewy grass.

Barclay retrieved one paper that had landed on the toe of his boot. "What's this, then?" He examined the intricate charcoal rubbings. "Inspiration?"

"Nae, that's my mum's idea of showin' me off," Angus explained. "She made these off of the latest bits of carvin' I've been doin' in my spare time. I think she's not got a stick of furniture left in the house that I've not practiced on."

"This is no time to be modest, son!" Barclay's entire demeanor had changed. "D'ye realize how much trouble you've just saved me?"

"Trouble?"

"Aye! Trouble! Mr. Grant's been askin' me to find him someone to make some really stunnin' pieces. Y'know, fancy chairs, mantel surrounds, picture frames, and the like. There's nae a body within a day's ride of here to fit the bill, especially with the nearby village full of fishermen! I was about to advertise in the city papers. Then here you come this mornin' with your pockets full of secrets!" Barclay took him by the elbow and steered him back toward Grant and Goodridge, still clutching the papers in his rough hand.

"Mr. Grant, I'm sorry to interrupt," Barclay said. "But I've found just the master joiner you need to make those interior pieces the way you want 'em." He handed Grant the charcoal rubbings.

Grant eyed Angus's designs hungrily. "A master indeed! These are brilliant! Barclay, don't let this gentleman get away from us!" His eyes sparkled with intensity. "Mr. Armstrong, have you had breakfast? Feel free to help yourself."

"Thank you," Angus replied, head spinning at this sudden turn of events.

He and Barclay strolled to the food cart and filled their coffee cups. Angus added thick cream to his. It had been years since he'd drunk coffee with cream. Barclay was quiet, watching Angus intently, hoping for some outward sign that Angus had overlooked his brusqueness from earlier. But Angus's face was unreadable.

"Three pounds a week all right?" Barclay asked abruptly.

Angus spat coffee several feet, then turned his head slowly to look at Barclay's face. He seemed completely sincere.

"Three pounds a week?" Angus repeated.

"Aye, a master craftsman should make what he's worth. You give me sixty hours a week, that's the pay. Besides, you've just saved me figurin' out room and board for a Glaswegian import."

"Three and half, then," Angus countered, feeling suddenly confident.

Barclay's mustache twitched again as he suppressed another smile. "Three and two shillin's, and that's final. Dinnae push yer luck."

"Done." Angus took another sip of coffee, trying to appear collected. However, he had to tighten his grip on his cup to keep from dropping it.

Chapter 2

Vancouver, Washington, U.S.A.
Present Day

I ris Jacobs sipped her orange mocha with a look of deep concentration. She was oblivious to the swirl of chatter around her, and only vaguely aware that the smell of freshly roasted coffee was beginning to cling to her hair. She perched on a stool, her eyes scanning job postings on the screen of her dilapidated laptop. Her right foot began to tap, seemingly of its own free will, evidence of the amount of caffeine she'd ingested over the past hour of free wi-fi.

Her search had made her positive of two things. One, finding a job was going to be harder than she thought. She still had no prospects that didn't involve dodgy work-at-home schemes. Yet she knew she'd better find something this week, or face having to welch on her half of the rent. Her roommate didn't have both halves, that was certain. Two, she knew that her next job could not, *must* not, involve carrying liquids and hot foods balanced on trays lofted precariously over the heads of surly, demanding diners. *Not again.* She shuddered involuntarily.

A slow motion movie reel replayed on the screen in her mind... an impatient man tugging her elbow, upsetting her stride as she maneuvered past his table; five glasses of icy root beer, two dozen hot breadsticks, and a bowl of steaming marinara wobbling sideways... the look of panic on her face as she failed to right the tray, and instead dumping it on the wig, lap, and Sunday spaghetti special of an elderly lady in a wheelchair... the screams and gasps of every person within twenty feet...

Iris shook herself out of the waking nightmare with a sharp inhale through her nostrils. *Nope.* She was hanging up that crusty little black half-apron for good this time. She took another sip of mocha and realized it was long cold when she got nothing through the straw but fudge sludge. She made up her mind to savor it by adding plain coffee to it when she got home. Decaf, though.

Even though she had used up the very last of her Coffee Villa gift card, she had tucked the plastic card back into her pocket. She would need it soon. She squinted across the little sitting room full of cushy, mismatched arm chairs and peered out the window. The snow had stopped half an hour ago, leaving a half inch of frozen crust on her car. The sky was a bland, featureless gray, like a worn ceiling.

Iris stood and snapped her laptop shut. Time to face the inevitable biting cold, and make the trip to the temp agency. As she slung her bag over her shoulder, she glanced up at the community notice board. Sometime in the hour that she had been absorbed in the employment listings, someone had sloppily tacked up a flyer in the most nauseating yellow she'd ever seen.

HELPWANTED
Activitty Assistent, full time, will discus benafits, $$ D.O.E
Rookwood Senior Home

Although she had more questions than answers—*what sort of activities needed assisting at a senior home? Who proofreads these things? What is the actual name of this color?*—Iris pulled the flyer down with a quick jerk, and made up her mind to go immediately.

She checked the restroom mirror to make sure she looked presentable enough to do a job inquiry. The twenty-two year old ginger looking back at her was in need of a hairbrush and an eyeliner touch-up. She took out her eyeliner and leaned into her reflection, making the long, silly, putting-on-makeup face.

She hadn't wanted to start wearing eyeliner so early in life. She thought of several of her mother's friends who, when they were caught without makeup on, looked sickly enough to be on the verge of a cranky death. She wanted her natural coloring to be what people were used to, so she'd have the freedom to leave the house bare faced and not be asked whether she was feeling all right.

But last summer, when she had graduated from WSU with a history degree and started looking for jobs, nobody took her seriously in an interview. They all asked the same, not-funny-anymore questions: "Are you old enough to be driving? Are you sure you're 21?" Her ideal jobs of teaching, researching, and writing went to candidates who looked "more experienced."

She had asked her best friend and roommate, Charlie, who had just finished cosmetology school, for advice. Charlie (short for Charlotte) gave Iris a makeover that added trendy layers to her hair and five years to her face. Iris begrudged the extra time it took to tame her thick hair and put on makeup every morning, but she had to admit, she did look less like a high school junior and more like a twenty-something news correspondent. She still had no idea what she would end up doing with her life, but for today, finding a way to pay the rent would have to suffice. At least now she looked old enough to do it.

She finished her touch-ups and rearranged her plaid scarf to cover a coffee stain on her cream sweater. *Red hair, green eyes, and a tartan scarf? Am I trying to look Scottish?* she mused. *Well, I am Scottish. Just as well I look it.*

Her boots crunched through the snowy crust as she withdrew her spent gift card from her back pocket and used it to scrape the ice away from the lock on her car door. She could see her breath inside the car, but the dashboard lit up happily as the engine purred to life. She cranked up the defrosters and then slid back outside to continue scraping. She pulled out her phone with her left hand, dropped it in the snow, snatched it up quickly, and switched it to her right hand while the left continued to scrape the window.

"Navigate to Rookwood Senior Home, Vancouver, Washington" she shouted at it.

"Okay," the robotic voice answered. "Rookwood Senior Home. You are on the fastest route and your route is clear. You should arrive at your destination by 12:52 p.m."

Iris could see the blue line on her phone's map would take her twenty minutes north, to a part of the county she'd never had a reason to be in. *At least it's not too far.* She dashed off a quick text to tell Charlie where she was going. That way, they would know where to begin the search for her body if she didn't come out of this interview alive.

Rookwood Senior Home was an imposing gothic style manor, almost castle like, which burst suddenly into view as Iris emerged from a winding, uphill drive shrouded in towering western red cedar and sword fern. She eased her little white hatchback through the black, spear topped iron gates and into a visitor space as she took in the building and grounds. It was as if she had entered a scene from Bram Stoker's *Dracula...*

creepy and elegant in equal measure. How had she been living twenty minutes from something like this, and never realized it? *It must cost a fortune to live here*, she mused.

A school field trip came flooding back to her memory—she'd visited a place very much like this. She, an eight year old in her tartan skirt and navy blazer, had followed her mates along the grounds' wooded path, lush with snowdrops, through the box hedge maze, past urns and statuary, up the stone steps, and around crumbling castle walls. Though school tours weren't permitted to see the derelict interior, Iris had done her best to peer through the murky glass windows to catch a glimpse.

The once grand, high ceilinged parlor still haunted her memory. Floral wallpaper, ceiling joists, and dusty furniture were sagging with fatigue after over a century and a half of standing against gravity. A piano, white with dust and decay, rested upon the ruin of an intricate oriental rug that must have been outlandishly expensive. The instrument's broken grandeur was poignant and wretched, as though it was crying out to be heard once more. A delicate floral-framed mirror hung by a wire over a small nearby desk, tilting dangerously away from the wall, reflecting the piano's broken back.

Although she didn't know it then, it was to be her last school trip in Scotland. Her father's job would make an immigrant of her that very summer. Iris had fought it desperately, using every means available to an eight year old to persuade her father not to take her from her little village. She had even begged to go away to St. Leonard's boarding school, just to stay in Scotland. She could not imagine any place as magical as her home, with farmland stretching away in all directions surrounding the village, and the sparkling North Sea to the east. She could not imagine being away from her beloved beach, not seeing the church steeple from her classroom window.

Iris had had to adjust to life in Washington quickly. At first, she'd simply ignored her surroundings and dealt with the Americans as best she could. She missed her mates. She grew tired of being a source of fascination. Her accent drew attention that Iris had never anticipated—from adults asking her to repeat herself, to kids asking her to say silly phrases just so they could hear it in a Scottish brogue. Her parents had encouraged her to be a good sport, and she'd tried. But she had decided to lose the accent as quickly as she could. In the fourteen intervening years, it had almost entirely disappeared; although those with a keen ear could still hear how it bent her vowels just slightly. Only when Iris was truly emotional did it all come back, and she'd "go full Scottish," as Charlie was fond of saying.

Iris had also begun to appreciate the breathtaking natural beauty of her new home. Her awe grew as she hiked the Columbia Gorge with its diamond waterfalls and emerald fern groves. The rocky crags of the Washington coast had soothed the heartache of missing her beach. And now, on the grounds of this strange manor, she was transported. The architecture and landscape around her were unmistakably European in their influence.

She climbed the stone steps of Rookwood Senior Home and took a steadying breath. She gazed up at the rusting weathervane, creaking in a lazy circle on the nearest rooftop spire. She pressed her freckled lips tightly, as if to press away her imagination's nameless doubts, and gave the twisted iron door handle a confident tug.

A warm breeze wafted past her, filled with the scent of disinfectant, carpet shampoo, and cafeteria food. The lobby had the feel of a hotel and hospital combined. Its scattered groupings of brocade arm chairs and round cherry wood tables were populated with walkers, canes, and wheelchairs which had brought their bent owners for chess, checkers, bridge, and shouted conversation. A grand chandelier sparkled over lush carpets, high ceilings, and a bird cage the size of a large wardrobe filled with sweetly chirping yellow canaries.

A round lady with reading glasses on her nose, whose name badge said "Becky," clacked away at her keyboard behind the front desk. Iris pulled the heinously yellow flyer from her coat pocket and approached.

"Excuse me, where might I find a manager?"

"What's happened this time?" Becky huffed, looking over her glasses at Iris.

"Sorry? No, uh…" Iris produced the flyer. "I'm looking to inquire about this position. Activity Assistant?"

"Well. That was quick. James only put that up an hour ago." She went back to typing. "You'll want to talk to Candace Wood. Her office is down the hall, third door on the right." She returned to being completely absorbed in her work, and Iris doubted whether she'd heard her muttered thanks.

Iris soon discovered that "down the hall" could mean one of three different directions, since the building's main floor was neatly divided into two equal squares. She found herself at the center of a four way intersection with the lobby behind her. She glanced back at the receptionist and decided against asking for clarification, opting instead to take herself on a little tour.

She turned left and found that each door down this corridor was numbered with a neat brass plate which also bore the name of its resident on it. The floor gleamed with a high polish. It had a decadent marquetry pattern, forming a series of intricate medallions in a dozen colors of wood grain. The walls boasted a luxurious cherry wainscoting and paneling with brass sconces above every door, with a practical handrail stretching along its length. Iris suddenly felt underdressed in her jeans and coffee stained sweater.

She passed a large rotunda containing a stage and theater seating at the end of the first hallway, took a right, and passed a dining hall. She could hear clanking silverware and soft piano music. She caught a glimpse of a man in a wheelchair wearing a terry cloth bib while a woman about her mother's age spooned soup into his mouth. The white haired lady beside them raised a cup to her lips with a trembling hand. Iris pondered the quiet dignity of the scene, as she completed the left square by heading up the central corridor, seeing only more residents' doors. Back at the center of the intersection, she headed left down the other square.

Here it was, not twenty feet from where she'd begun, that the third door on the right bore a brass plate which read, "Candace Wood, Activities Director." The door was ajar. Inside, with her back to Iris, sat a woman in her late forties, with pixie cut, messy-on-purpose blonde frosted hair. She wore a velour tracksuit in a stunning shade of purple. Iris knocked.

The woman lifted her Converse-clad feet and whirled around in her office chair at such a velocity that she decided to complete an entire rotation and a half before stopping.

"Hi! What can I help you with…" As she took in Iris's appearance, her eyes came to rest on the yellow flyer in her hand. "Oh, gosh! Look at that! You saw the color of the flyer, and you came anyway!" She hopped up and extended her hand.

Iris was impressed with her glittering smile as they shook.

"I'm Iris Jacobs. I'm here about the assistant's position?"

"Well hello, Iris Jacobs. I'm Candace. Have you got a resumé?"

Iris produced two sheets, neatly stapled, which Candace speed-read.

"Tell me, Iris, do you like old people?"

Iris smiled. "I think so. I haven't known more than a few besides my grandparents, but they're pretty awesome."

"Well, I'm not going to waste time. Come on in, we'll make this short!" She gestured to a vinyl upholstered chair next to her desk.

Iris sat.

Candace continued, "Most of our residents are pretty awesome, too. But some of them are cranky, because getting old really sucks. A great percentage of our residents are here because they have more money than time. A few are here because they have no one left in this world to care for them. A lot of them are lonely. So it's our job to make Rookwood a fun place to be."

"*Our* job?" Iris asked.

"Yes. *Our* job." Candace smiled. "I can tell I already like you. And I'm never wrong about people."

She took out a bagel and began slathering it with pink cream cheese from her mini fridge.

"Now, you won't be cleaning up any accidents or lifting anybody. The nurses take care of that. We leave the hard stuff to the heroes. What this department does is give the residents something to look forward to each day. While the nurses give baths and meds on a strict schedule, we feel the same way about our activity schedule. It's gotta be predictable. These people love structure and consistency." She took a bite and continued to talk around it. "We keep a pretty full schedule. You need to think of yourself as something of a cruise director. Are you punctual, Iris?"

"Definitely," Iris replied. "It's one of my things."

"Excellent. Are you good with names?"

"Not so much."

"That's fine. Neither are most of the people here," Candace mused as she chewed. "Can you call a BINGO game?"

"I'm not sure."

"That was mostly rhetorical. Anybody can call a BINGO game. The real trick is breaking up the fights afterwards." Candace winked.

"You have to break up *fights*?" cried Charlie.

"I think she was kidding. I hope she was!" Iris giggled. She and Charlie lounged at their tiny dinette table, finishing the last of the lasagna Charlie had defrosted. Charlie was still in her black work uniform and smelled like perm solution. Iris was used to it. Charlie had also come home with a new hair color. Iris was also used to that. It was indigo blue today.

Iris sipped her cream soda. "I think the blue really suits you," she told Charlie.

"Really? Don't think it's too... Smurfy?" Charlie lifted a spoon and looked at her upside-down reflection. She fluffed her bangs and squinted.

"Nah. It's more of a violet-blue. Maybe a suffocating Smurf?" Iris grinned impishly.

Charlie gasped and feigned a look of deep offense. "Just for that, you're doing the dishes," she sniffed.

Iris looked over the disposable aluminum baking dish and paper plates, and let out a long suffering sigh. "Fiiiiiine. I deserve it."

"So what else is involved in this job besides spending a ton on gas and calling BINGO games?" Charlie asked as she dug through the freezer for ice cream.

"Hey, the Integra gets awesome gas mileage. And I don't know what else. I'm supposed to go in tomorrow and shadow Candace for an entire day. There's an activity going on just about every two hours while people are awake over there, and I have to learn them all." Iris stacked the dirty dishes and chucked them into the trash. "You should see that place, Charlie. It must have cost an ungodly fortune to build. It's basically a castle."

"Oooh, do you think there are secret passages?" she asked with sudden seriousness.

"Yes. I'm sure Colonel Mustard is sneaking from the billiard room to the conservatory with a lead pipe as we speak."

Chapter 3

Scotland ~ 1844

A ngus helped himself to boiled eggs, baps, and more coffee from the breakfast cart while Barclay scribbled his details into the record book.

"Mr. Grant's nearly finished with his meetin' over there, and then he'll go over with you what he wants," he said. "I can arready tell ye, there's goin' to be quite a mix of things to keep you busy. He's plannin' on importin' some of the furniture... y'know, for guest rooms and what not. But for the family, he's got specific ideas about how he wants things to look. We've got imported walnut and mahogany in the workshop o'er there," he jabbed his pencil in the direction of a large, whitewashed outbuilding about a hundred yards away. "And we've been bringin' in local pine and oak as well."

"So that's my work space, then?"

"Aye, you'll have the whole of it," Barclay said. "And it's locked up at night, so you'll have no need of luggin' your tools about."

Angus had just drained his second cup of coffee when Grant approached.

"Ah! Mr. Grant!" Barclay greeted him. "I was just beginnin' to tell yer new craftsman what he'll be doin' round here. Shall we show him the workshop, then?"

"Yes indeed!" Grant replied, and they headed off together. "Mr. Armstrong, I trust you had a good breakfast?"

"Aye, 'twas just the thing. Thank you indeed," said Angus.

"It's no trouble, no trouble at all. I think hearty meals are the best thing to keep one's constitution in top form. I've toured enough factories to see what fatigue and malnourishment can do to productivity. So I've resolved to show my employees kindness, provide plenty of food, and pay a good wage. All I ask in return is your soul."

Angus's eyes widened. Grant's laugh was genial.

"You'll get used to Mr. Grant's sense of humor," Barclay chuckled.

"Yes, when they gave pompousness training at aristocrat school, I must have fallen asleep that day," he laughed. "I only wear a top hat so Barclay here doesn't confuse me for someone else and start barking orders at me."

"I never bark," protested Barclay, feigning offense.

"You're right, it's really more of a bellow," Grant teased. "Ah! Here we are!"

He heaved open the workshop's heavy door to reveal a wide, airy space that used to serve as a barn. It still smelled of hay with a hint of cow, but even more strongly now of freshly cut lumber. There were stacks of wood piled in both back corners. In the center was a workbench, with an assortment of vices and clamps mounted on one end of it. On the other end was a new wrought iron lathe.

Angus could feel his soul lifting with optimism for the days ahead. A real wage, work he loved, and a generous boss. *Could this be real?* He set his tool bag on the bench approvingly.

"I can get loads done in this place!" he beamed.

"Glad to hear it!" Grant was pleased. "Now let me show you some plans." He grabbed a large roll of design drawings and smoothed them out on the bench.

"Excuse me, sir, I've got to go bellow at some people," Barclay interrupted.

"Carry on, Barclay!" Grant chuckled. "Now, Mr. Armstrong, as you're aware, I'm a married man. I've got to have my priorities in order. To that end, your first orders of business will be a rocking chair and a vanity mirror for my Eueretta. She enters her confinement in June, and I'd like to see to her comfort. Are these doable by then?"

Angus considered the drawings and nodded.

"Aye, sir. I believe I could finish 'em in that amount of time. This rockin' chair design is nae much different than one I made for my mum a year back. 'Tis a bit throne-like, yet curved just right for sittin.'"

"Indeed, it's much like the one my own mother rocked me in as a babe. I'm a bit sentimental, you see."

"Nae a thing wrong with that, sir." Angus smiled.

"But this mirror is a special request," Grant went on. "I have given my wife an exquisite gift after each of our children was born. With each one, I try to outdo the last. I think perhaps after giving birth a third time, she'll be in want of reminding how highly I esteem her beauty. A lovely mirror is just the thing, wouldn't you agree?"

"Well sir, bein' a bachelor and an only child myself, I'll have to trust your word on that. I cannae say I was much aware of my mum's frame of mind after I came into the world. And I dinnae ken if I've got any kinda gift for knowin' what a lady wants. But your logic is sound enough!" Angus smiled encouragingly.

"Good, good. I obtained the glass on special order. It's there in the crate marked 'FRAGILE.' I'd like you to use the finest wood, and make the mirror frame something truly unique... a work of art, if you will. The shape and measurements are

23

in the design, but as to the exact embellishments, I'll have to leave that to you. My wife is fond of roses and ivy, I know that much. I trust you'll make her the envy of all her friends."

"Aye, sir. I'll do my best!"

When Grant had gone, Angus set to work. The longer he studied the drawings, the more confident he grew about the rocking chair, but the less confident he became about the mirror. *Make her the envy of all her friends? What do I know about what highborn ladies envy?*

The frame was to be heart shaped. The design had a group of crudely drawn flowers at the top, and vines that curled down both sides of the heart. There were a few more small roses at the bottom. The thing wouldn't be very large. The design called for a piece of glass sixteen inches across. This was going to take some thought.

He wandered over to the lumber stacks and began pulling pieces suitable for a rocking chair. *Mahogany's what she'll be wantin.' Pine's quicker, but this chair's goin' into a fine nursery. Gotta have somethin' strong to be around the wee ones...*

He brought the pieces to the bench and began to sort them into stacks. *I'll make the back and seat first. That's the fun part anyway... then basically, it's two of everything after that...*

Angus continued to mutter to himself, and to the wood, as was his way when he was deep in his work. He loved the feel of transforming a plain piece of wood into something useful and beautiful.

This was the first time he'd had such a vast work space. He found that he moved more quickly when he wasn't worried about dinging his mum's table or having to sweep up his sawdust every couple hours. "I really ought t' get meself a workshop once I have the means..."

"Talkin' to yerself again, mate?"

Angus was pulled back to the present to find Patrick leaning lazily in the doorway, grinning at him, covered in brick dust.

"Or were you talkin' to the wood this time?"

"Patrick Dawson, it's downright unnervin' how close you watch me," Angus grumped.

"Maybe so, but if I didnae watch you, how would ya know you've nearly missed lunch?"

Angus's stomach growled in response.

"Good grief, you're right! I must've been runnin' on excitement!" Angus stood.

"Tatties and bacon today!" Pat said brightly.

"So I see. You've still got a bit on your shirt front," Angus pointed out.

"A bite for later. How goes your first day?"

"This place is amazing! I've arready made some progress on a rockin' chair, but I've got my work cut out, and no mistake." Angus laid his apron neatly across the bench and followed Pat out into the late afternoon sunshine.

"You'll prove me right, is all," Pat smiled.

"Right about what?"

"That Angus Armstrong is the finest woodworker in Scotland."

"You sound like my mother."

"Aye, well, your mum and I are obviously more clever than you, since we know what we see. Nae our fault you cannae take a compliment, mate. Me, I stand by you for two reasons... First, we've been near brothers, you and I, since we were wee bairns. Secondly, and most importantly, when you get rich and famous, you can take care of me in my old age."

The two men shared a hearty laugh.

"Pat, I live with my mum! I've yet to even think of takin' a wife. I cannae imagine old age!" Angus mused.

"Well, let's never get old, then." Patrick clapped him on the shoulder.

25

"A reasonable plan, if ever there was," Angus chuckled as he pulled a tin plate from the stack at the food cart.

"I know! I'm a genius." Patrick pulled out his remaining roasted potato, which he'd put into his pocket earlier, and bit into it like an apple.

"I hope you turn out your pockets when you do the washin,'" Angus laughed. "Lord knows what else you find in there."

The men found some shade across the grounds and sat in the grass. Angus took a few bites of potato and grew serious. "Pat?"

"Aye?"

"When's payday? I never got round to askin' Barclay."

"Every Friday, round quittin' time. Two days hence, this bein' Wednesday."

A pang of worry settled into Angus's stomach. In the excitement of finding work and finally setting his hands to challenging projects, he'd been able to forget. But the reality of Friday flooded back. The landlord had accepted a pound in earnest and given a week's extension on the remaining six pounds rent, due to Mum's condition. But that week was up in two days. He still had that lonely gold crown sitting in his box at home, plus the not quite two pounds he'd see this payday. *Not even close. Not even halfway.*

"Well, I'm back on the clock," Patrick said in a strained voice as he stretched his lanky arms out like an awkward scarecrow. He stood. "Och, Lord. My back..."

"Remember the plan, mate..." Angus warned. "No gettin' old!"

"Right!" Pat grinned and trotted off to lay more bricks.

The days were lengthening, and golden sunlight still spread across the ground after their walk back to the village. Patrick was eager to get to the pub and regale the men with his colorful version of today's events. But Angus's head was swirling with thoughts.

"I'm off home, I think," he said.

"Mate! How's it you've got the morbs after landin' your dream job? You artistic types ne'er make a lick of sense to me."

"Just tired, I suppose."

"You'll nae even come for a bit? You'll miss seein' Gillian Mayfield lookin' all impressed wi'ye!"

Angus punched his shoulder. "Will you *quit* with that? She's ne'er looked at me that way. She's got be'er suited, and, I might add, be'er lookin' men wantin' her attention."

"Aye, be'er lookin,' maybe. But I dinnae see her handin' out get-well parcels to anybody else's mums," Pat muttered.

"It's just kindness, is all. It's because we go back. As friends."

"I'm sure you're right, mate. Ignore the feelings. Die alone. It's for the best."

"You're a wee nyaff," Angus said good naturedly.

"And puttin' up wi'me is character building," Pat added.

"Truer words were ne'er spoken," he smiled. "I'll see you tomorrow, arright?"

"Tomorrow it is." Pat touched his cap dandily and sauntered away.

"And Pat?"

"Aye?" He turned.

"Thanks for today. For landin' me the job."

"You landed yerself the job, mate," he grinned. "And I cannae be held responsible for how factually I tell the tale!"

Angus peeked through the open front window and saw Mum sitting at the table with her back to him, chopping potatoes and chatting away to Mrs. MacDonald, the widow who lived across the lane from them.

"Hello, son!" Mum called without turning around. "How was it?"

"How d'ye do that?" he marvelled. "I didnae even open the door!"

"A mother just knows when her child is near," she said warmly, leaving out the fact that Angus's mop of dark, curly hair made a distinctive shadow on the wall.

"Well, you were right, as usual," he answered, pulling up Dad's old chair. "Mr. Grant and the foreman both liked my work enough to start me at three pounds and 2 shillin's a week."

Mum's mouth was agape.

"Och, you *were* right, Marjorie," said Mrs. MacDonald. "Congratulations, Angus!"

"That's astonishing news, my boy!" Mum cried. "Even your Dad ne'er saw such a wage! Soon, you'll be able to lay a bit aside for your future."

"In good time, Mum, but I'm nae thinkin' *that* far into the future. How about just lettin' me get you back on your feet?"

"You're a good son, Angus. I dinnae ken what I'd do without you. But my silly leg will be right soon enough. The doctor says a month. Then I'll be back to earnin' a wage, instead of bein' a burden."

"You're nae a burden, Mum."

"Fine then, I'll be less of a burden. Meanwhile, some of the ladies from the new Free Church stopped by to say the new building's underway, and the church meetings should be out of the barn before the weather turns. I suppose it's all right I gave to the Sustenation Fund? They say if everyone gives a penny a week, it should keep things goin.' Even Reverend Keith himself is donatin.'"

Angus felt a chill. Marjorie Armstrong had the most generous heart he'd ever witnessed. As a child, he'd felt proud to see her stretch out her hands to the needy with a plate of this or that, a neighborly helping hand, a penny or two. Even a pair of boots one time. Dad had loved her for it, and always found a way to let her do it.

How will I find a way?

Angus smiled and chatted politely with the women through supper, though he was only half aware of the conversation as Friday's deadline eddied just beneath the surface of his conscious thoughts. He managed his end of the talk as long as he could before excusing himself for a walk outside.

His feet led him, as always, toward the ocean. The thickening twilight was chasing the last shred of pink from the western horizon, while over the sea, the first three stars were beginning to twinkle.

God, if you've got any brilliant moves I've nae thought of yet, now would be a great time to tell me.

Angus scuffed his toes through the sand.

Three more measly pounds. Might as well be a million.

He sat down heavily in the cool sand, leaning his back against a driftwood log. He gazed out at the sea through the growing darkness. It never rested. Endlessly journeying, endlessly arriving.

I've nae got the heart to tell her the doctor's taken the last of Dad's money... or about the rent, either.

He mindlessly piled sand into a mound, letting it trickle through his fingers.

I dare not ask an advance. I've only been on the job for one day. Pat's got the odd penny for ale, but he hasnae any three pounds to be loanin' out, not with two sisters to look after.

He picked a piece of grass and poked the mound of sand.

The Deacon's Court doesnae give alms to the able-bodied, and it's unlikely they're meetin' anyway, since the church split last year... God? You wanna chime in here?

The thought came to him a second time in as many days, as if on the wind.

The Mary coin.

His mind turned to the little carved box on the mantel in the cottage. Inside it, an Armstrong family heirloom: a gold three-pound coin emblazoned with the bust of Mary, Queen of Scots. It was a piece of history, nearing three hundred years old. It had begun as a bit of insurance, according to the story... tucked away for a rainy day by eighth great granddad Christopher in 1555. It had become something of a good luck charm, always passing from one Armstrong to the next. And now it had come to Angus.

Eight generations, and I'll be the one to lose it. A fine heir I've turned out to be.

He squashed the sand mound with his boot and stood. There was nothing for it. He could keep a bit of history, or keep a roof over Mum's head. With any luck, he could catch the owner of the pawn shop before closing time tomorrow, and get a good price for Mary, Queen of Scots. He could make it if he ran.

Chapter 4

Vancouver, WA ~ Present Day

Iris wound her way back up the wooded road to the senior home the next morning while it was barely light out. Thankfully, the freezing rain had relented the previous day, turning to a constant splatty, slushy rain that was just warm enough to keep the roads from turning into a skating rink. Her early 90s front wheel drive hatchback maneuvered easily on the slick roads.

She glided into the employee lot this time. Pulling her hood over her freshly styled hair, she picked her way down the frozen walkways, past boxwood hedges crusted over with white shawls and statues with icy hats and blindfolds.

"Iris!" called a voice on the path just behind her. Candace huffed up to her in a flowered pink parka and polka dotted rain boots. "I was just out for my morning run!" she puffed.

"Really?" Iris tried to hide the doubt in her voice, eyeing the fat clouds.

"Of course not!" Candace elbowed her. "It's freezing, it's drizzling, and I don't have my running shoes. Also? I don't run. Unless there's a sale." She laughed. "I'm glad I caught you. I want to show you where we go in. The owners like us to keep the lobby looking nice, so we use the servants' entrance. That's where the time clock is, too."

"Servants' entrance?" Iris asked. "That sounds old fashioned."

"Well, it is. It's been called that since the beginning because that's where the servants' quarters used to be, when the castle was a home. Now it's offices, a break room, and a kitchen."

They rounded the corner past the modest boxwood maze, which was more for effect than for actually getting anyone lost. "It's just under there," she pointed.

Under the dripping portico, Candace shook out her yellow umbrella, folded it, and leaned it against one of the stone columns. "Had you ever been here before yesterday?" she asked, digging through her immense striped bag for her keys.

"Uh, no, actually," said Iris. "I was shocked to see a building like this sitting here in the middle of the woods."

"There's certainly nothing else like it! It's over a hundred years old!" Candace smiled as she pushed the door open. "Here, fill out a timecard. Punch it over there," she pointed at a silver box mounted on the wall. "And try to clock in and out within five minutes of your shift times. If you don't..." she trailed off ominously.

"What?" Iris asked.

"Forty lashes with a wet noodle," Candace wiggled her eyebrows.

Iris grinned. "You're wrong, you know," she said thoughtfully as she signed her time card with a flourish.

"Doubtful," Candace retorted. "Wrong about what?"

"There actually IS another place like this. It reminds me of a castle near the little village where I grew up back in

Scotland," said Iris. "It looked just like this from the outside. Even the garden is similar."

They stopped by a row of lockers on the wall of a modest eating area that had been converted to an employee break room. It stood adjacent to the massive kitchen. Iris could smell bacon.

"You grew up in Scotland?" Candace doffed her rain boots and slipped into a pair of teal high tops. "I can barely hear any accent!"

"Exactly," Iris said grimly.

Candace raised an eyebrow.

"Too many questions," Iris said simply.

"I gotcha. Well I hide my New Jersey accent for the same reason," said Candace.

"You really don't."

"What?"

"You just said 'New Joyzee,'" Iris giggled.

Candace's eyes widened. "Aaaanyway… Any empty locker is free for you to use," she said. "There's a box of padlocks in the cupboard. Pick a color. The combo's on the back, just make sure you peel that off and stick it somewhere you'll remember."

They stashed their coats and purses, and then began the trek past the kitchen and up a flight of stone steps to the main floor.

"Well, I think the original owner of this place was British or something," Candace picked up the conversation. "I don't really know the story, other than he loved architecture and spent gobs of money building the place. His family lived here for a few generations, but after the last one died, nobody else could afford to live in it. The historic preservation people were worried it would fall into disrepair, so they took pictures of the flooring and all the amazing craftsmanship around here and sent it to somebody with money. They managed to get a grant to make it into a nursing home. So now it's owned by a private trust. I know there's also some state funding involved, because five of our residents have social workers that I have to talk to. I don't know what the rest of the residents pay. That's not really my area. But apparently it's enough to keep the place running, and keep me in Converse."

They passed a few people in wheelchairs and one with a walker as they rounded the corner into the corridor where the Activities Office was located.

"Good morning, Irene!" Candace shouted cheerfully.

"Nine o'clock, it says here!" Irene shouted back.

Iris stopped by her walker to examine the printed calendar Irene was holding. Each day of the month had the day's activities listed, along with the time and location.

"Are you on your way to gardening?" Iris asked her sweetly.

"Well of course!" said Irene. "The people aren't there yet. I have to make sure I get Lois there on time. Only got fifty-four minutes."

"Good thing you've got a jump on it, then," winked Candace. "C'mon in, Iris," she said as she unlocked the office. "We've got a lot to do in fifty-four minutes."

The next forty-nine minutes were a flutter of activity as Iris learned the essentials of setting up a gardening activity, cleaning the colossal canary cage in the lobby, sanitizing tables in the Activity Room, setting up the chapel for a hymn sing, delivering the day's mail, and distinguishing a "call the nurse" situation from a "call the janitor" situation.

At 8:55, Candace announced, "Taxi time!" Iris had no idea what she meant, so she followed her down the hallway into the lobby.

"You look like you could use some dirt on your hands, Gladys!" Candace said to a prim woman in a pink chiffon blouse and string of pearls. "C'mon, we need your help in the garden."

"Oh, is that right?" Gladys chuckled. Without waiting for permission, Candace took the helm of her wheelchair and struck up a conversation with her as they breezed along toward the east rotunda, a Victorian style sun room filled with potted ferns and flowers. Iris followed.

"Let's bring Fred, too," Candace side whispered and pointed her chin at a dozing gentleman parked in his wheelchair just outside the door of his room.

"He's asleep!" Iris whispered in protest.

"Bring him anyway. He's used to waking up in strange places." Candace grinned.

Feeling more than a little awkward, Iris eased the chair forward and followed. Fred stirred slightly, then snored contentedly with his chin on his chest. Irene and Lois were puttering up with their walkers just as she and Candace approached the sun room.

A wide-eyed woman dressed in a pale blue polyester pantsuit came in behind Lois. She was holding hands with a man whose cane was painted slick black with orange flames shooting up from the bottom.

"Nine o'clock, it says here!" piped Irene, waving her calendar. "Got three minutes!"

"Three minutes it is!" called Candace over her shoulder as she and Iris breezed back toward the lobby to gather more participants. They found two more ladies who happily agreed to join. Candace pushed another man in his wheelchair, while Iris approached a tiny woman sitting in an armchair by the fireplace. She had a long, silver braid, and had clearly decided against wearing dentures today. She hummed peacefully to herself, working her jaw up and down.

"Would you like to come help with the gardening this morning?" Iris asked her cheerfully.

"Eh? Help the garden?" she repeated. "Well, huh. Is that today?"

"Yes, we start in just a couple minutes," Iris said.

"I'm waiting for him to come back," the woman said, and resumed humming.

"Who are you waiting for?"

"Hm? Oh, he said noon! I have to make coffee. He likes his coffee."

"Well it's only nine o'clock," Iris comforted her. "You've got plenty of time to help in the garden and come back here before noon."

"Hey? Yes, noon. That's right. Hmm, I can help if I'm not late. Hm, hmm, I can't be late for coffee," she half said and half hummed, rubbing her knuckles with her thumb.

"Do you know where the sun room is?" Iris asked.

The woman stopped humming and a look of panic swept over her face.

"Oh, it's all right! I can take you there," Iris reassured her.

The woman reached for her hand and stood.

Iris paused at the reception desk. "If the man she's waiting for comes while she's gone, will you let him know she's in the sun room?" Iris asked Becky, the receptionist.

Becky glared over her reading glasses at Iris. "Hilarious," she muttered, rolling her eyes.

"Sorry?" Iris was befuddled.

Becky ignored her and clicked away with her mouse.

Iris shrugged and continued to lead the woman by her child-sized hand. All the way back to the sun room, Iris's every effort at conversation was met with more humming.

"Irene!" beamed Candace as they walked in. "Nice you could come!" Irene smiled, flicked her long braid over her shoulder, and kept humming.

"What? Yes! Well, it's 9:02!" called the other Irene.

Fred snorted awake.

"Oh, *two* Irenes," commented Iris.

"Actually, there are five," muttered Candace. "Two of them, we rarely see, but it's still your best shot if you forget a name." She winked. "I even got away with calling Walter that once. But he thinks I'm a fox."

Candace led the group through forty-five minutes of painstaking effort. Even donning garden gloves wasn't as simple as Iris thought it would be, but fifteen matching pairs were found and sized, and 150 shaking fingers made to fit into the correct holes. The group scooped black soil from a bucket with little silver spades and potted tiny starts of maidenhair fern to take to their rooms and place on their ledges, sills, and knick knack shelves. Helping the participants wash up afterward was a wet affair. Iris decided that keeping a spare shirt in her locker wouldn't go amiss.

"It says here eleven o'clock!" said First Irene, referring to the calendar.

"Be there, or be square!" Candace called as Irene and Lois puttered away. "She's talking about BINGO, of course," she said to Iris. "We used to do it in the evenings, but the nurses didn't like us getting people all sugared up at bedtime. They won't stay off their call buttons."

With the garden tools stowed and the tile floor swept, Candace and Iris returned to the Activity Office to enter the morning's participants in the computer system's attendance log.

"We like to keep track so we can chase down the stragglers," Candace explained.

Iris giggled.

"No, seriously, we actually do like to see who participates and who doesn't. Sometimes it tells us when someone is losing their ability to function or in need of a friend. Some people never come to activities, and that's fine. But when someone

37

comes all the time and then we suddenly never see them, we like to find out why. This gentleman, for example…" Candace trailed off as she tapped one name with her mouse and scrolled back through a few weeks' worth of records.

Iris pulled her chair closer.

"He's been absent from all activities for a week now. Looks like the last thing he went to was a hymn sing in the newly renovated chapel. I went to see him a couple days ago, and he's okay, but he didn't seem in a good frame of mind. So I put him on today's visitation list. We'll go see him before lunch. In the meantime, let's go down to the kitchen and get some coffee, and see what Will's baking today!" She stood, grabbed her keys, and locked the office door behind them.

"You lock the office even while you're at work?" Iris wondered.

"Yeah, I've had one too many surprises upon returning," Candace answered. "Let's just say our dear residents can't always be relied upon to leave my bagels alone. Or not take my pens. Or not mistake where the bathroom is."

Iris's eyes widened as she tried to stop herself from imagining the last scenario.

Will, the chef, had baked blueberry muffins this morning. The kitchen was a buttery-fruity heaven. A lanky boy of sixteen was seated on a stool in the corner, scarfing down a soft, crumbling muffin over a paper plate. Next to him on the counter were two hideously yellow paper airplanes and a third in progress.

"Hey James, how's it going?" Candace greeted him. He gave her a crumby high-five. "Willy, what's cookin'? Do I get to approve this batch?"

A tall brown haired chef appeared from around a rack of cooling baking pans loaded with muffins. "Candy, you cheeky thing, of course you do. Except James has eaten through half the employee tray, so you'd better chase him off."

"You know you're the only one who gets to call me 'Candy,'" she flirted at him, while simultaneously sashaying across the room to slap James's hand away from a fifth muffin and snatch it up. "James, doesn't Becky feed you?"

"Would it matter if she did?" he groused. "You've tasted her cooking."

"Touché. But I've heard she types like ninety words per minute. So there's that."

"Yes, there's that." James rolled his eyes.

"Iris, this is Will Donovan, our head chef. He's my favorite person ever." She winked at him.

Will waved.

"And this is James, our Everything Guy: all-around assistant, errand runner, paper airplane engineer, doer of all things. His mad flyer skills brought you to us. And you must have met Becky, our receptionist. That's his mom. Guys, this is Iris Jacobs. She's my new assistant. She's lasted two whole hours so far!"

Iris shook hands with both and received a light dusting of flour from Will and a few crumbs from James.

"Nice," said James, who took in her appearance approvingly. Iris smiled. *Not a chance, kid. Can you even drive yet?*

"N-nice to meet you," Will stammered. Iris thought she saw a hint of color rise in his cheeks as he hurried back to his work.

"Guess what Will's making for lunch?" James changed the subject excitedly.

Candace looked at Will.

He lifted the cloth from a stainless steel bowl the size of a truck tire, to reveal a gorgeous lump of rising dough.

"Tomata pie!" Candace crooned.

"And 'tomata' soup for those who don't prefer chewing," Will added.

"Oh my gosh, it's pizza, Candace!" James retorted. "Nobody calls it tomata pie."

"What? Everybody calls it that," she sniffed.

"Your New Joyzee is showing again," Iris teased.

"Well I'm sure they've got some funny name for it in Scotland, too," she defended.

Iris switched seamlessly to a thick Scottish accent.

"Och, ye've naever HAD such luv'ly faer as ae pizza croonch! Wheer th'whool lot's been depped en batter'n deep frei'd!"

A long moment passed as the other three exchanged astonished looks, then burst into laughter.

"You're awesome, Iris!" James hooted.

"Might have to make yours a crunch, then," Will said shyly.

"Don't joke about that!" Iris warned teasingly. "Once I get that craving into my head, it's gotta be satisfied!"

"I don't make idle threats when it comes to food," he grinned.

❧

Coffee and muffins in hand, Iris and Candace trudged back up the steps to the storage closet where the BINGO supplies were kept.

"Oh my gosh, Iris! Did you see how Will was totally into you?" Candace beamed.

Iris's cheeks went pink. "Isn't he like... an interest of yours?" she asked.

"Oh, please. I'm old enough to be his mother. Well. Maybe his much more gorgeous and mature sister. It's all banter, my dear. He calls me 'Candy' and he gives me baked goods. That pretty much sums up our relationship. Obviously, if he became a chocolatier, I'd have to marry him. But so far he's safe."

"What makes you say he's 'into' me?"

"He went all shy and suddenly had no idea what to say. Do you know how rare it is for Will to be speechless? Not to mention he was going as red as a tomata!"

"I don't think I want to date anybody at work," Iris said, shuddering slightly as she thought of the last chef who'd taken a fancy to her. *Ugh. No.*

"I can respect that. But don't let that stop you from helping me approve his batch of doughnuts tomorrow morning."

"Sounds like a good plan," Iris laughed.

"Deal! Let's get this stuff to the Activity Room real quick and set up BINGO. We've only got 20 minutes before the Irenes descend to duke it out for the king sized Snickers bar!"

Chapter 5

Scotland ~ 1844

Angus's fitful dreams woke him before dawn. He'd made up his mind sometime around three o'clock in the morning that he would put aside enough of his wages to buy back the Mary coin as soon as he possibly could, and pray it was still in the pawnshop by then. Perhaps Mum could be spared knowing what he was about to do.

He slipped into his work clothes, tidied his bed, and tiptoed out to stoke the fire. There were a few orange-black coals slumbering in the ashes. They sparked in annoyance at being awoken so early. Angus fed them a breakfast of twigs and driftwood, and brushed his hands on his trousers.

The little carved box on the mantel waited, daring him to lift the lid. He inhaled some courage and reached for it.

"I thought perhaps it had come to that," said a voice behind him.

He spun around, sending the box, lid, and coin clattering to the floor.

"Mum! You're awake! Was I makin' too much noise?" Angus snatched the box and coin off the floor.

"I've been up near an hour arready," she stated calmly. "Just catchin' up on some light readin.'" She held up the diary where Angus kept his accounts. "Your Dad was the one with a head for figures, but I do know what rent costs, and I see we've not got it."

Angus hung his head. "Mum, I..."

"Angus, why did you keep this from me, son? I didnae realize there was such a lack!"

"I was tryin' not to worry you! I thought I'd have enough furniture repair to cover the rent, but... I just... I fell short." He sat down heavily in his chair by the hearth. "A couple of jobs didnae come through, that's all. And by then, I'd arready paid the doctor. He says y'ought to keep calm and peaceful-like. It's best for healin.'"

"I'm healin' just fine, son, whether I'm calm or not. I keep my worries in my head, not in my leg. And in the meantime, you've decided I'm not to share your burdens with you? I hate that I'm the cause of all this worry. Without my wages..."

"We would have been arright on Dad's savin's, but for the doctor bill."

Marjorie was quiet. She let out a little sigh.

"I see. And were you plannin' to sell off the Mary coin, then? Did you not try Reverend Keith?"

"Reverend Keith's just lost his stipend and is tryin' to build a new church. I'm not about to knock on his door askin' for loans. Besides, I'm an able-bodied worker, Mum. I've no need of charity. I can care for my own."

"Aye. But there's nothin' wrong with askin' for help when you need it, son," she said gently. "God often provides the way through others."

Angus clenched his jaw. "I was goin' to find a way. Dad always did."

"Angus! Son, you are not your father. There's so much on your shoulders arready. You're a grown man, a craftsman, a fine provider. It's down to you we've not gone hungry. Dinnae add chasin' your dad's shadow to your pile of burdens."

Tears pricked Angus's eyes. He and Mum didn't often speak of Dad this way. His presence had been ripped away from them only three months ago, and it had left a sudden and breathtaking wound. John Armstrong had been larger than life, full of wisdom and kindness. He'd had a keen mind, a booming laugh, and broad shoulders. Next to him, Angus had felt like a sheltered sapling. Now he stood alone, bending in a bitter wind. The gold coin felt heavy in his hand.

"I'll find a way," he repeated, blinking back his tears.

"Well, then. You'd best put her in your pocket."

He turned to look at his mother's lined face in the early dawn light. Unshed tears glistened in her eyes, ready to spill over. "Do what you feel is right, Angus. I trust you."

⁓✤

Angus slipped out of the cottage, mind churning. He closed the door behind him and leaned against it for a few moments, his head bowed against the rising sun. He was already tired, and the day was only beginning. *She trusts me, she says. God, I dinnae even trust me. I can barely keep my head above water. Dad would've had this handled weeks ago. He always knew what to do.*

Angus could feel a stirring in his soul, gently shushing him. Mum's words echoed back to him… *"Dinnae add chasin' your dad's shadow to your pile of burdens."*

Arright, God. I'm not him. I admit, I'm ne'er going to measure up to Dad. I'll have to settle for being his second-rate son.

Then, like a leaf floating on the wind, a line of a psalm they often sang in church came drifting into his mind and settled there: *"I will lift up mine eyes unto the hills, from whence*

44

cometh my help. My help cometh from the Lord, which made heaven and earth."

Angus closed his eyes and considered the depth of this truth. *My help never did come from Dad, did it? It's always been You. Dad was young once. Maybe he was as scared as I am. And his help came from You, too.*

"Arright, Angus?" a soft voice asked. Angus opened his eyes, and there was Gillian, her golden curls haloing her face in the dawn light. She looked at him with concern.

"Gilly." Her name sounded more like a high compliment than a greeting, the way he spoke it. "Aye, I'm arright. Just gettin' my heid on straight." He smiled. "What're you up to, so early?"

"Off to buy fish, of course! Nothin' but the freshest in my kitchen!" She grinned.

"*Your* kitchen, is it now? Finally shoved your Dad the rest of the way out the door, have you?"

"Och, I'm the be'er cook and everyone knows it. Takin's prove it. He ne'er sees the till so full and the fish flyin' out the pan so fast when he's doin' the cookin'!"

"Well, I've no complaints. I've ne'er had a bad meal at the pub. O'course, just about everyone cooks be'er than I do. I cook to survive. Mum's been havin' to eat what I call porridge, the poor dear woman."

Gillian's laughter was like music.

"Sounds like I ought to send home more parcels! Now Angus, be a dear friend and dinnae be stubborn with me about it. When you come back from work, stop by the pub and get some decent food!"

"I wish I could, Gilly, it's just…" Angus kicked the dirt with the toe of his boot.

"Are you really that stubborn, Angus Armstrong?" she challenged him.

"Nae, it's just that…"

"Just what?"

"I cannae pay you, arright? There, I said it. I'm flat out, Gilly, and I'm resortin' to drastic means just to make the rent." Angus blushed and stared at the ground, his head whirling with emotions from sharing so embarrassingly much, and from being so near her at the same time.

She was brought up short by his confession, and stood quiet for a few moments. Then he saw the edge of her blue skirt come into view as she set down her basket and gently laid her hand on his arm. Her touch warmed him to his core.

"I had no idea, Angus. I'm so sorry for vexin' you. I didnae mean anythin' by it. Course it's gotta be hard... with your Dad gone, and your Mum laid up. Now listen..." She gave his arm a gentle squeeze and he met her blue eyes. "It'd be my honor if you'd come eat with us, anytime. That's an invitation. After all, you're nae a customer, you're a friend."

"Thanks, Gilly, but I cannae impose on you," Angus protested.

"Angus, you stubborn ox! Will ya just say *yes*? I just..." Her hand tightened on his arm.

"Just what?"

"I *care* about you, alright? Now you've made me say it! I care for you!" Color rose in her cheeks. "And your mum, of course..." But she'd added that part too late for it to be an effective distraction.

Angus covered her hand with his and searched her face. "You... care for me?"

"Aye..." She broke her gaze and looked down at their hands. Tears sprang to her eyes. "I've cared for you since I was twelve, maybe even before that... it's felt like always."

"I thought you just outgrew me, or somethin'..."

"I just dinnae ken what to say around you!" Her cheeks were glowing.

Angus pulled up her chin and looked her full in the face. "You dinnae have to say anythin' fancy... it's just me." He wiped a tear from her cheek with his thumb.

"Exactly. It's *you*."

"Why d'you care for me, when so many be'er men want to catch your eye?"

"Because you're *Angus*. There *is* nobody be'er."

He couldn't believe she was saying these words... out loud! To *him*!

"I care for you, too, Gilly. More than I know how to tell you. I just... well, I never thought I had a chance wi'ye..."

Gillian impulsively wrapped her arms around his neck and held him, so glad, so relieved to hear that her years of hoping were not in vain.

He returned the embrace, the sweet scent of her hair all around him. His stomach leapt as he considered finally speaking aloud the words that had been building up inside him since he could remember.

"I love you, Gilly," he whispered.

She released him and stepped back in shock, staring at him in wonderment.

"There, you made me say it," he said, with a sheepish grin.

She stepped toward him and took his hand, still unable to speak through her amazement. He raised her hand to his lips and kissed it. Her shocked face began to spread into delight. Angus stroked her fair, freckled cheek with his fingertips and leaned toward her. "May I?"

She looked deeply into his eyes, which were only inches away now, and made a firm decision which sparkled in her eyes. "Always," she replied, and closed the distance to their first kiss.

Angus was quiet on the walk to the estate while Patrick reenacted the facial expressions and reactions of everyone in the pub last night who'd heard him tell that Angus Armstrong, the finest craftsman in Scotland, was being paid "nearly as much as a barrister" to make furniture "fit for the queen herself."

"Gillian Mayfield told me she's not surprised in the slightest to see you a success." Patrick grinned, and did his best Gillian voice: "Angus is too good for this town, so I'm going to marry him before Buckingham Palace calls for a new furniture maker!"

"She did not say that!" Angus protested, but cracked a tiny smile. *If you knew half of what she did say...* Her freckled nose and soft lips rose up in his memory. The walk (or was it the memory?) was making him warm, so he shed his coat and draped it over one arm.

"Ah, maybe she did say it. Who's to know?" said Pat mischievously, and continued in his piping Gillian impression: "I want Angus to make ME a rockin' chair!"

Angus swung his coat at Patrick playfully. A small white rectangle flew out of the pocket and landed in the road next to a puddle.

"Oops! I hope it didnae land in the..." Patrick picked it up. "Nope! It's fine." He handed it back. "Your mum havin' you carry the post?"

"Aye. Picked this up yesterday and forgot to give it to her. She and my aunt write each other once a month or so."

The envelope was addressed to his mum in flowing script, from her sister in Stonehaven, and had a neatly trimmed one penny red stamp in the corner. He tucked the letter back into his coat.

"What's on the workbench today?" Patrick asked. "Goin' to keep on with the rockin' chair, then?"

"Eh, no. I'm still dryin' out the bends in the runners. I thought I'd start on that li'l vanity mirror Mr. Grant ordered. I've been thinkin' it over, and I'm going to try green carvin' it. It's a risk, but I think it'll pay off. All that fine detail wants a softer wood, but I dinnae want to use a soft wood, so green hardwood's the ticket. Dad showed me once. The wood grain really dries out nice if you do it nice and slow."

"Mate, I hav'nae the foggiest idea what you're sayin,' but I'm glad you understand all that. Me, I just do what I'm told."

"Ha! Since when?"

"It's somethin' I'm tryin' out lately," Patrick said. "I'm startin' to see why people recommend it!"

Angus sorted through the lumber stacks in the workshop. He had spent almost the entire walk to the estate with thoughts of Gillian swirling through his brain. Thankfully, it took considerable effort to concentrate on a plan for making the roses and ivy that Mrs. Grant loved into a frame for a mirror. And it was a relief to focus his mind on other things besides the centuries-old coin weighing down his pocket.

He remembered a number of roses he'd seen growing in the garden of the parish manse where the Keiths used to live. Mrs. Keith had planted and cared for several varieties. His two favorites were the large ones with soft petals, and the tiny ones that seemed to grow an entire bouquet on one stem. He decided to do a combination of the two, in a handsome three-dimensional bouquet at the top of the heart shaped frame. *God knows beauty, so if I arrange 'em the same way He does, how can I miss?*

However, he found few options in the lumber that would suit his idea. He dismissed the oak and mahogany straightaway, remembering a few detailed carvings he'd done as a teenager, only to see them split and crack. Dad had shown him how to dry the wood in stages to minimize the chances of that happening, but oak and mahogany had never cooperated with him in this regard. The planks of pine were too soft, all the wrong sizes, and held little visual interest. *Time to go a'hunting.*

Angus emptied the last few tools from his rucksack, leaving only his small ax, and slung it over his shoulder. As he emerged from the workshop, he noticed that the late morning sun was now shrouded in gray, and a chilly breeze had picked up. He ducked back in and donned his coat. Back outside, he peered around for either a top hat or a bellowing foreman. He spotted the former sipping coffee by the food cart and he made a beeline.

"Good morning, Mr. Armstrong!" Grant greeted him cheerily.

"Morning, sir," Angus replied. "I wondered if I might walk about the estate, and find some green wood for carvin'?"

"Oh, is there nothing in the workshop to suit your purposes?"

"Aye, sir, there's a lovely bit of mahogany turnin' itself into a rockin' chair at the moment…"

"Good, good! I can't wait to see it!"

"Aye, it's comin' along well. But the mirror frame is another thing. I've a good idea what I'd like to do, but I need to find somethin' the right shape and hardness. If I could look about…"

"Say no more, good man. My entire estate is at your disposal. Will you be felling an entire tree? Or…" Grant smiled.

Angus chuckled. "Nae an entire tree, sir. Just a wee limb. I'd like to find an ash, or perhaps a rowan. Somethin' interesting that'll take shape and then dry up nice and even."

"Well, there's plenty to choose from in the wood beyond the fields. Take what you need."

"Thank you, sir. I should be back in a couple hours." Angus took a roasted potato from the cart, wrapped it in his handkerchief, and stuffed it into his rucksack.

"Not at all. Oh, and Mr. Armstrong, I should make you aware that there's a man who lives in the wood, in a little cottage on Woodstone Hill. Members of his family have always lived there… for centuries, even. May sound strange, but it's been the tradition that lords of this estate provide them a stipend and just leave them be. He's a gamekeeper, of sorts. He hunts at will, so you may run across him. He's rather opinionated, but harmless. Just beware." He winked. "And try not to look like a deer."

Angus headed northeast past the sluice, cut through a field, and trekked into the forest at Woodstone Hill. He welcomed the excursion. Although the chilly breeze had blown away the warmth of the day, he was sheltered amongst the trees. The forest was newly awake, and springtime had coaxed the bright green leaves, buds, and blades out into the open. Bluebells carpeted the forest floor, while bees busily attempted to visit each little blossom. A slender red squirrel darted up and down tree trunks, looking for pine seeds. Angus breathed in the scent of moss and sap, loving the feel of the trees enveloping him from sight.

After several minutes' walking, he took a direction that led him into a denser, older part of the forest. Here, he was sure, he would find the right sort of tree. He paused and looked all around him, for he could faintly smell smoke from a chimney. Seeing no sign of the gamekeeper, he pressed on.

He suddenly found himself on a worn path through the bracken. It made the going much easier. He paused briefly to consider an ash tree, but moved on after deciding its branches were too skinny. Another five minutes' walk led him into an oak grove with trees so immense in girth that they seemed to have lived forever. Angus whistled with appreciation, making mental note of a knobby burl protruding from one of the trees. The whorled pattern inside it would make a richly artistic tabletop.

In the center of the grove stood an ancient hawthorn. It was larger in stature and girth than the surrounding oaks, and it had a peculiar beauty that made it seem both lonely and commanding. It held him transfixed. He had seen a lone hawthorn here and there in the countryside, which had grown at the mercy of the wind. This one, however, was the largest and oldest he'd ever seen. It had grown into a perfectly symmetrical city of branches that spread along the ground before reaching toward the sky. It was as if the old fellow was leaning on his elbows, but in every direction. The surrounding trees had given him a wide berth, full circle.

As Angus drew nearer, he began to feel his ears ringing. He shook his head and swallowed, but that did not diminish it. In fact, the sound grew slightly more pronounced, turning into a light humming as he reached the tree's center. He ducked under a low branch and touched the tree appreciatively. The twisted bark was full of mossy hollows, and tiny white flower buds were beginning to stand out like freckles against the foliage. In a few weeks, this tree would be lavish with pink-white blooms.

He recalled a story that Mum had read to him often as a boy, from a dusty copy of *Thomas Keightley's Fairy Mythology*, about two ladies who had seen a troupe of fairies on tiny white horses ride out from under such a hawthorn.

"Their tongue when they sang was like the sound of a far-away psalm…" he remembered aloud. *That would explain what I'm hearing… if I actually believed in fairies.* He wondered if Mrs. Grant believed in fairies. Those who did considered it extremely unlucky, even dangerous, to disturb a "fairy-thorn" tree except in the month of May when it was in bloom. *Would she mind havin' a piece of hawthorn in her house?*

Angus was unsure how long he'd stood there, staring in fascination, but he knew he needed to get moving. He considered the budding branches. *Eh, only a couple weeks early. Near enough. Besides, there's somethin' special about this tree. It would surely be a thing of beauty to carve.*

He moved away from the center of the tree to where the limbs were a bit straighter and more tender, and found the perfect one, about shoulder height off the ground and six inches thick. He took out his little ax and poised it over the branch, but was suddenly overwhelmed with doubt. He lowered the ax and looked around him, wondering. He took in the entire tree once more, gazing along its height and circumference, trying to judge whether the loss of this one branch would harm it in some way. He was certain it wouldn't. It would barely even make a dent, visually. The branches were so numerous and so proportionally spaced, that this one would scarcely be missed.

He lifted the ax a second time, fighting the urge to hesitate, and chopped. The faint hum grew to about the same volume as a person singing in another room. He stopped and peered around him again.

Perhaps the gamekeeper's got a wife who's singing nearby?

With several more strokes, he freed the limb. The humming grew suddenly quieter, still steady, but almost inaudible, as it had been at first. He chopped the foliage away from the opposite end of the branch, keeping only the thickest section, about four feet long. This, he cut into two foot segments, and then stuffed them into his rucksack along with the ax, being careful to remove his roasted potato first. He hefted the sack onto his back, untied the handkerchief from around the potato, and began the trek back to the workshop.

His first few bites of potato tasted a bit like tree sap. He wiped his hands on his trousers, then on his handkerchief, but to no avail. The sap had a strange quality. It bonded fast to his skin, leaving a dark stain, yet it wasn't sticky. He took a few more swipes at it with the handkerchief before giving up and going back to his potato.

He thought it best to walk back the way he had come, since he'd made an obvious enough trail that any gamekeeper worth his salt could tell it wasn't made by any deer.

Just as he reached the place where he had smelled chimney smoke, he heard a rustle in a thicket far to his left. He stopped.

A man with a grizzled beard emerged from the trees. He wore a simple tan work shirt and brown trousers with braces. His white hair was long, but neatly brushed and tied back with a bit of twine. He looked to be about seventy years old.

"Hello!" Angus called out. "I'm just here on an errand for Mr. Grant!"

"Time has changed," said the man in a startled tone, approaching Angus with cautious steps.

Angus stared blankly, unsure of his meaning.

"Aye, there's a new owner on the estate," Angus offered.

"Somethin' is *different*," the gamekeeper insisted with a shaky voice.

"Well… There's a new castle bein' built…"

"There's a hole, I can feel it."

"Oh, ehhh…" Angus faltered. "Were you huntin' weasels?"

"It's widening every second! Excuse me, there's something I really must check on," he interrupted.

Angus tipped his cap, but the old man didn't see. He was already hurrying off in the direction from which Angus had just come.

"That chap's been livin' in the forest too long," Angus muttered.

Chapter 6

Scotland ~ 1844

An anguished cry arose from the ether, echoing across the sky. Albion, who was perched on the roof of a small cottage, lifted his eyes to the afternoon sky. His senses tingled with a strange feeling of disruption and foreboding. He glanced down through the roof slates, which were transparent to him, to the cottage's occupants. The Guardian of the Oak was writing in a large book, while his infant son slept on his shoulder. His wife was chopping potatoes. *Good. Still safe and busy.*

Albion checked the perimeter, but seeing no threatening beings or physical dangers, he turned his attention toward another being who was passing just above him, and waved him down.

"Albion? Is everything alright?" he wondered. "I heard something just now…"

"I heard it too, and I think I recognized the voice," Albion replied. "Are you free to stand watch here for a bit? I must find out what's happened."

"Tree Guardians really aren't my specialty, but I can handle sentry duty. Go."

Albion streaked into the sky like a comet, toward the eastern shore of Scotland, toward the sound. As he drew nearer, his sense of dread deepened. The atmosphere was thick. He dropped into the dense forest below and darted noiselessly among the trees until he saw his old comrade.

Caledon stood beside the Great Hawthorn, his forehead against it, groaning.

Alarmed, Albion rushed to him. "Caledon, what's happened?"

Caledon looked up with a horrified expression and said nothing for several moments. He finally took in the fact that Albion was standing there and spoke at last.

"Albion. Why have you come? Where's the Guardian of the Oak?"

"He and his family are safe, and Sherwood is quiet. What's going on? Why is the gravity so strange here? Where's the Guardian of the Hawthorn?"

Caledon pointed to the oozing stump where a branch of the Great Hawthorn had been chopped off.

Albion sucked in a breath. He approached the gaping wound, careful not to touch, and stared in horror at the dark energy seeping from it and trailing away into the distance. The hum coming from the cut, though almost inaudible in the physical world, was pained and pronounced. Albion looked back, wide eyed, at Caledon, who had returned to groaning.

"Caledon, *what* is going on here?" Albion's voice was strained with horror.

"The Guardian of the Hawthorn has failed! That's what's happened!"

"Failed? What has he done? Surely, he hasn't..."

"No. This is the work of a young man. See him there?" Caledon pointed through the trees, which also appeared semi-transparent to them as they stood in shadow. Albion could clearly make out the outline of a muscular young man half a mile away, trudging out of the forest with a bag on his back, eating a potato. Behind him stretched a narrow band of darkness, a rip in the delicate time fabric, ever stretching and widening.

"He's got to put the branch back!" Albion cried.

"I KNOW THAT, Albion! He shouldn't have even *gotten* this close! The Guardian of the Hawthorn is as deaf as a squid! He should have passed the Guardianship to his son a decade ago! I've done everything I can think of for that hard headed man! I even let him fall down once, though it was against my nature, just to remind him he's not getting any younger. Still, he judges himself fit for this task! When that carpenter came into the wood, I did everything I could to get the Guardian's attention, and still he didn't hear the ax!"

"Caledon, you must try to get the branch back! If it isn't returned, the Tree will grow a new branch in the wrong place and a portion of Time will be rewritten!"

"Well, how am I supposed to do that? Hm? I'm not the Tree Guardian anymore, remember? We're both pushing our limits as it is. I'm not supposed to let Ré MacCrann out of my sight. Although I can see him from here. He's weeping in his bed at the moment. Maybe he's finally getting a clue."

"This is dreadful," Albion moaned. "I've never heard of a Guardian failing this badly." He looked toward the young man hiking cheerfully away from them. The dark rip had widened around him, and a swirl of dark energy seeped from the bag on his shoulder, enveloping him. "He's almost outside of Time."

"And the longer he stays in that hole, the more likely he is to fall right through it and be lost," Caledon finished.

"Go to Ré, and remind him to visit his son," Albion said.

"Much good it has ever done," snorted Caledon, "but I'll try again."

"Good. I'll see where that young man is going."

They streaked away in opposite directions.

Albion came upon the swirling darkness of the rip. The young man was blissfully unaware as he tried to dab away the stain of dark energy sap from his hand, then shrugged.

"It's getting worse," said an eight foot being walking beside the young man on the other side of the rip.

"Are you his guardian, Aimsir?" Albion asked.

"Yes," Aimsir replied. "I did all in my power to stay his hand in the forest, but the Great Hawthorn held such allure for him. I will hold the breach closed for as long as I can, but it won't be long. Perhaps I can keep him on this side of the rip long enough for Caledon to rouse the Guardian to repair the Tree."

Albion took in the stretching, widening gap, and thought of Ré MacCrann, Guardian of the Hawthorn, weeping pitifully in his cottage. He shuddered. The young man began to whistle a lively tune. He was as good as lost.

Vancouver, WA ~ Present Day

BINGO at Rookwood Senior Home was an Olympic scale event. When Iris saw the extent of the setup, she realized why the residents looked forward to it every week. She lined the tables with extra large print BINGO cards and bright green ink daubers while Candace festooned the head table with patriotic bunting. The shiny brass ball cage was set on one side of the table. On the other side stood a miniature winner's podium. The lower two steps were piled with a variety of candy bars, and on the top step was the infamous king sized Snickers bar.

"If this game is based on luck, then how does someone win the king size bar?" Iris wondered.

"Ah, yes. That bar goes to the person who gets BINGO twice in a row," Candace explained as she taped balloons to the table corners. "Every winner gets a regular bar, but on your second consecutive win, you get to go up a size. Also a pants size."

"Must be pretty easy to do," Iris mused.

"Actually not as easy as it sounds, with twenty people playing. One of the Irenes was so close last time... missed it by one number. She actually turned in her first candy bar in protest. And by 'turned in' I mean I had to duck."

"Wow! Now, was this the Irene who's really punctual, or the one who likes to sing?" Iris asked.

"Neither. It was a third Irene you'll meet today. She never misses. Three things that never change... the Rock of Gibraltar, Stonehenge, and Third Irene at BINGO."

"She uhh... she sounds very committed," Iris giggled.

"I believe the word you're circling around is 'stubborn,' but I like 'committed.' Oh! Iris, I left the sugar free candy in my office. Would you run and grab that before taxi time? It's in my bottom desk drawer. I'll finish setting up here."

Iris had almost returned with the candy when she heard a faint voice.

"Excuse me, Nurse?"

Iris turned and looked around for the source. She realized it was coming from an open door she had just passed.

"Nurse?"

She saw no nurses nearby, but didn't feel right walking past. Perhaps this lady couldn't reach her call button. Iris decided to help her find the call button, and move on. The brass plate on the wall read "Eva Thomas." Iris peeked her head in the door.

"Eva? My name's Iris. I'm not a nurse, but is there something I can help you with?" She approached the frail woman who sat up in the bed.

"Not a nurse?" Eva sighed and flopped back onto the pillow. "It's like they just don't care about me any more," she moaned.

"Who doesn't care about you, Eva?"

"Nobody here does! I've been calling for an hour, and nobody comes. I missed breakfast because nobody came to get me. I hurt myself trying to get out of bed to get to the bathroom because the nurses don't answer the button any more. I can't find my wedding ring, either. I think one of the nurses stole it."

Iris was stunned. "I'm sure there's got to be some mistake," she reasoned.

"Well I'm starving and about to mess m'self because everyone's forgotten me, so that's a mistake if I ever saw one," Eva grumbled.

"I'll go call a nurse for you myself, okay?" said Iris.

She hurried to the nurse's station at the end of the central corridor.

"Eva Thomas says she's been calling you guys for an hour and nobody's answered. Sounds like she really has to pee," Iris said, out of breath.

"You're new," said a nurse in lavender scrubs.

"Yes, but could we focus on Eva?"

"What's your name?"

"Iris. Iris Jacobs."

"I'm Kathy. Well listen, Iris... Eva doesn't have to pee, okay? I know this because she has a catheter and I just emptied the bag about ten minutes ago."

"Oh..." Iris faltered. "I'm sorry. She just seemed so insistent, I was afraid she was miserable or something."

"Well you're sweet to want to help her. She is kinda miserable, but it's her mind that's miserable. She has Alzheimer's, so it's hard for her to think clearly about what's going on around her."

"She said nobody came to get her for breakfast…and that a nurse stole her ring!"

"Yep, she says that to everybody, pretty much every day. It's because she has no memory of breakfast, and no idea what time it is. She assumes she's hungry because she missed breakfast, not because it's almost lunch." Kathy smiled. "And she gave the ring to her daughter years ago, because she was afraid she would take it off and forget it somewhere. It's okay. You'll get used to the people at Rookwood. They're sure of what they think, even though their minds are somewhere else. It's best not to correct them… just kind of… help them around it."

"Well… thanks for the advice," Iris said lamely. "Sorry again."

"Anytime, hon."

Feeling sheepish, Iris made her way back to the Activity Room.

All these people have dementia? No wonder Becky reacted the way she did when I tried to leave a message at the front desk for Irene's husband. Did she think I was trying to be funny? I can be really thick sometimes.

Iris plopped the bag of candy onto the head table and dropped into the nearest chair.

"What's gotten into you?" Candace asked as she dumped the last of the BINGO balls into the cage.

"I feel like I've got to be the stupidest person in the building."

"How so? And by the way, I know a few people in this building who'd give you a run for that title."

"Rookwood Senior Home. I mean, there's nothing in that name to imply anything other than the fact that old people live here. I had no idea what sort of old people they were!"

Candace raised her eyebrows.

"Is that a fact? And what sort of old people are they?"

"I didn't know they *all* had dementia," Iris said quietly.

"A few, maybe, but…"

"Ohhh. Oh dear, that's my fault." Candace smiled sadly. "I should have made that more clear. I'm sorry. I've been hanging around here so long, I sometimes forget they have memory loss… hm, that's a bit ironic. Anyway, I've seen their personalities come out so much over the years, that to me, they're just quirky people in need of a cheerful face."

"I'd say a complete break from reality is a bit more than quirky," Iris smirked.

"Well, that's a fact. I'll lead with that next time I interview you for a job, I promise," Candace replied with a grin. "Am I forgiven?"

"I suppose," Iris smiled back, "as long as you keep your promise about the doughnuts in the morning."

"Oh, there *will* be doughnuts!"

"Excellent. So… I pretty much can't trust anything anyone says around here?"

"Pretty much not. Unless you see physical evidence of a complaint, you can safely assume the complaint isn't based in fact, or at least anything very recent. By the way, how'd you figure it out?" Candace asked. "Did Walter ask you to hide him from the cops?"

"No, but that sounds like a story I need to hear."

"Most definitely. Whoop, it's taxi time! Gotta go!"

The two of them gathered participants from all corners of the building. Without being asked, First Irene was acting as the town crier, waving her calendar in the air as she puttered along with her walker, with petite Lois shuffling close behind her.

Iris went to the lobby and announced to each little table of cribbage and chess players that BINGO was on in five minutes. Several players rose shakily and began making their way to the Activity Room. Iris saw Second Irene in the same chair she'd been in earlier that morning, playing with her long silver braid, swinging her feet and humming to herself.

"Irene, do you play BINGO?" she asked.

"BINGO? Hmm, I'm not much of a gambler. I've got a couple shoes, is all. Hmmm, hmm, hm. And a hat."

"Well it's your lucky day," Iris assured her. "There's no buy-in. You can play for free!"

Irene offered her tiny hand to Iris and they began to walk. Irene was swaying to the tune she hummed, swinging their clasped hands like a schoolgirl. Iris began to recognize the song, an old tune that she knew to be American, but her dad sang it often while cheering on West Ham, his favorite football club.

"I'm forever blowing bubbles…" Irene hummed and sang.

"Pretty bubbles in the air…" Iris joined. Irene's grip on her hand tightened slightly and her face beamed with recognition, admiration, and delight.

"They flyyyy so hiiiigh, nearly reeeaaach the skyyyy…" they sang together. Irene stopped and pointed to Iris.

"Then, like my dreams…" Iris sang.

"They faaaade and diiiiiiieeeee!" Irene continued in a clear, confident voice, pointing to herself. They resumed their frolicking walk.

"Forrrtune's alllllllways hiding!" they belted so loudly that people began to peek out from their doorways and join in.

"I've looked everywherrrrrre!" sang everyone in the hallway. "I'm forever blowwwwing bubbles, pretty bubbles in the aiiiiir!" They all broke into applause, and Irene began to giggle uncontrollably.

"You're wonderful, mm-hmm!" She patted Iris. "Wonderful!"

Once the players were assembled, a small dispute broke out over who would sit in the far right chair at the front left table. This, apparently, was Third Irene's "lucky seat" and Betty thought she should sit there due to the fact that being in any other seat would cause her to have to turn up her hearing aids to such a volume that she "may as well be down a mineshaft."

"What makes that seat lucky, Irene?" asked Candace.

"That's the seat where I win the most!" Third Irene huffed.

"Well actually, that's the same spot at the table, but the chair itself was moved today," Candace whispered.

"Oh?" Irene perked up. She whispered back, "Where is it now?"

"It's that one there," Candace pointed to the far left chair at the front right table.

Third Irene turned to Betty and shrugged. "Sit there if you like, I guess. It's all the same to me." She sauntered to the new "lucky seat."

Betty sat and straightened her BINGO card at a perfect right angle to the table. She placed her ink dauber precisely on the upper right corner of the card. Then she took out a bag of trail mix and began to sort its contents into piles.

"I've got 10:59!" hollered First Irene from the back row.

"Thanks, Irene," Candace called back. "Iris, you're going to run this, okay? Just turn the cage handle until a ball falls into the little chute…" she pointed. "Make sure you yell the letter and number clearly, *twice*, and *only* twice, then put the ball in the tray there. Whatever you do, do NOT call the wrong number, and do NOT mumble! No pressure! Good luck!" She gave Iris a double thumbs-up and left the room with a wink.

Iris was suddenly nervous, like she was onstage at a school play and had forgotten her lines. "Everyone ready?" she croaked.

"Eleven o'clock!" announced First Irene.

"What number did she say?" Walter, with the orange flame painted cane, asked.

"Oh, I didn't say a number yet!" Iris blushed.

"I said ELEVEN!" First Irene repeated loudly.

"Have we started yet?" asked Doris, her hand on Fred's knee.

"Would you quit flirtin' with that guy?" Walter groused at her.

"What guy?" Doris asked, wide-eyed.

"Okay, we're starting now!" Iris called out.

"I think I've missed two numbers already!" Walter complained.

"N! 44!" Iris called out. "N! 44!"

A few people dabbed ink on their cards.

"Ennnnnnnn thirty-fourrrrrrrrr... four four four..." mumbled Fred.

"No, Fred, it's N, forty-four," corrected Iris.

"You said that one already!" yelled five different players. Iris flinched and snatched another ball. "B! 4! B! 4!"

"Beeee foooooouuuurr, before, before, before..." Fred muttered.

"Before what?" yelled First Irene.

"That's never funny!" Walter shot back. "Wasn't funny the first time, and it's not funny now!"

"Shhh!" said Third Irene.

"I! 17!" called Iris. "I! 17!"

"No, you not seventeen, chicky! You eighteen and legal!" Walter elbowed Doris, who giggled.

"O! 69!" Iris yelled, hoping to stop Walter from going any further with his train of thought. "O! 69!"

"Oh! Me too, baby!" Walter hooted. Iris's eyes widened and she quickly drew another number.

"G-54! G! 54!" That seemed a safe number. A few more people dabbed ink.

"What is *that*?" wondered Betty, examining a piece of trail mix. "I don't even know what that is, but I ain't eatin' it." She tossed the tidbit backward over her shoulder.

"Hey! Who's throwing peanuts?" demanded Fred. He tossed the nut back.

"B! 12!" called Iris as the peanut bounced off her forehead. "B12!"

"I took mine!" said Doris. "And vitamin C, too."

"Shhhhhhhhhh!" Third Irene was getting exasperated.

"Shhhhhhhhhhhhhh!" Gladys, sitting next to Third Irene, shushed her for shushing so loudly.

Irene dabbed ink on Gladys's BINGO card. Gladys dabbed ink on Irene's. Irene retaliated by dabbing ink on the back of Gladys's hand.

"Okay ladies, let's keep our ink to ourselves," Iris said diplomatically. Second Irene turned up her hearing aid, which began to squeal.

"I don't know what that is, either," said Betty, eyeing a raisin suspiciously.

"G! 50! G! 50!"

"What's the big idea?" growled Walter, throwing back a raisin that had landed on his BINGO card. The raisin whizzed past Iris's ear. Second Irene, who hadn't inked a single number, began to hum in the middle row.

"Shhhh!" Third Irene and Gladys shushed together.

"O! 71! O! 71!"

"Binnngooo, bingo bingo!" sang Second Irene, waving her blank card. Iris had no idea what to do next. Nobody was looking at her, so Iris tiptoed over and slipped her a candy bar.

"Congratulations!" she whispered, then hurried back to the head table and continued calling. Second Irene giggled.

"I! 25! I! 25!"

"BINGO!!!" Gladys yelled frantically. She did indeed have an actual BINGO, so Iris announced her the winner and presented her with the first (official) candy bar of the day.

"I'll give you a kiss for it!" Walter offered. "Double or nothin'!"

"Oh! What a nice offer!" Doris crooned.

"That doesn't even make sense!" griped Third Irene.

"Are we ready for another game?" Iris asked loudly.

She was answered by a mixed chorus of "Yes," "No," and "What?"

"How bout we raise the stakes this time?" challenged Fred. "Loser buys everyone a scotch!"

Candace returned an hour later to find Iris standing at the doorway of the Activity Room, saying goodbye to the players as they filed out.

"So how'd it go?" Candace asked, as Third Irene emerged with several green ink blotches up her arm, followed by Gladys, who was sporting a fashionable green circle on her forehead. "Never mind, I see it went well!" she laughed.

They pushed everyone in wheelchairs back to their rooms before returning to sort out the mayhem.

"I think I'm losing my voice from all that shouting," Iris rasped. "Also? Betty should really sit in the back." She began brushing bits of trail mix into a trash can. There was some on every table.

"Looks like it was a real party! I'm glad they had a good time," Candace gathered up the inked BINGO cards. "Ah, and I see the king size Snickers remains unclaimed."

"Third Irene wouldn't really 'jump' anybody, would she?" Iris asked incredulously.

"Nah, she'll forget," Candace reassured her. "Okay, once we've got this cleaned up, we have a few room visits to do in the next half hour. I think it would be most efficient to split up. You take one name, I'll take two."

"Okay, a room visit sounds relaxing after this. Do I just chat with them about whatever?"

"I'll actually give you a list of things to check in with him about, but largely, yes. Just get acquainted, get a feel for how he's doing. Have a nice conversation." She riffled through some papers in a folder she'd been carrying, and handed one to Iris. "Here you go. I think you'll like this guy."

Chapter 7

Scotland - 1844

The walk back to the workshop seemed shorter than the walk to the wood. Angus's feet made quick work of the trail. His mind was filled with inspiration. The exquisite beauty of the wood he carried in his rucksack energized his thoughts until he had no thought left for anything else. He didn't speak to anyone, nor did he stop, until he reached his workbench and laid the magnificent wood before him. He tossed his cap onto the bench, tied his apron, and set to work. He was like a man possessed, overtaken by a thousand possibilities.

He gave the ends of each wood segment a quick, vigorous coat of wax to stop them drying out, then laid out his hammer and chisel. He turned the thickest piece in his hands, marveling at its unusual growth pattern and luster. As he removed the bark, he envisioned how he would shape it. Like Michelangelo standing before a solid block of marble, he could see an image emerging in this mind. This piece would become a three dimensional bouquet of large-petaled roses, with bunches of leaves and tiny roses shooting out both sides in two scallops, forming the top of the heart shape. The second, more curved piece would be cut into two lengths and become the sides of the heart, with ivy vines cascading down them, into a cluster of roses at the bottom.

He looked briefly at his pencil and sketch pad which sat at the other end of the bench. He'd been planning to draw out a design and transfer it to a flatter piece of wood than this, then carve from there. But that idea annoyed him now. That was childish stuff, like what he did on Mum's kitchen chairs as a lad. This wasn't going to be any relief carving. This was going to be a bouquet so real you could smell it.

He picked up his chisel... and hesitated. Once again, he was brought up short by the same feeling he'd had in the forest, some strange instinct of warning. Yet his mind fought back with the image of what this piece could become. He shook his head to clear his thoughts. He closed his eyes and brought up the most stunning roses he'd ever committed to memory. He gritted his teeth and began to chip away at the wood.

Around seven o'clock in the evening, Patrick banged on the door of the workshop. He waited.

"Oi! Angus!" He banged again. "You in there, mate?"

Hearing no answer, he heaved the heavy wooden door open and peeked inside. Angus was nowhere to be seen. Wood chips and shavings lay strewn about, evidence of the work he'd been doing on the rocking chair pieces drying in the corner. His apron was draped neatly across the bench, as it always was when he'd taken his leave. His tools were stacked on the bench beside the apron, but his coat, cap, and rucksack were gone.

"Angus Armstrong, ya numpty, did you make for the village without me?" Patrick muttered, shutting the door. He headed back across the grounds, hoping to see Angus talking to Barclay. Instead, he saw Barclay talking to Grant.

"Pardon if I'm interruptin', Mr. Grant, Mr. Barclay, uh... sirs... but would you happen to have seen Angus roamin' about the place?" he asked.

"I saw him this morning," Grant offered, "when he came to me about looking around the estate for some green wood to carve." He opened his pocket watch. "But that was over eight hours ago. I haven't seen him since."

"Aye, I saw him saunterin' off into the wood as well," said Barclay. "I just assumed he was holed up in the workshop the rest of the day."

"Well, he's nae in there now..." Patrick looked around distractedly. "Thanks anyway, sirs, but I'll start home and likely spot him on the road."

Patrick was unsure whether to worry just yet. It could be that Angus had answered the call of nature and he'd just missed him. Perhaps he was absentmindedly mulling over his projects and had started home without him. Wherever he was, Angus could take care of himself.

Hour after hour, petal by elegant petal, the bouquet sculpture took shape. As Angus brought each bloom to life, he could see where the next one, and the next one, and the next, would emerge from the wood. His left hand had grown strangely numb from the constant impact of hammer on chisel, but he held his grip. He switched to a finer chisel, which didn't require a hammer, and began to dig out space beneath one of the roses.

In an instant of careless motion, he caught the tip of the chisel in a burl and it sprung haphazardly toward his hand. A quick stream of red flowed from the fleshy part of his thumb.

In a panic, Angus shoved himself backward from the carving, anxious not to spoil the wood with blood stains. He held his hand out over the straw-littered floor and examined the wound as it dripped. It was fairly deep, judging by the amount of blood, but not worrisome. He'd had worse. He tied it up in his handkerchief with the aid of his teeth, and carefully resumed his work, but with even more intensity.

When at last he had finished the bouquet, he felt more relieved than triumphant. It was exquisite. He was sure of that. He had never created something of this magnitude before. He covered it with a cloth to slow the drying process and prevent cracks from forming. He rested his hand on top of it for a moment. His fingers trembled, weary from the constant hours of effort.

He turned his head from side to side, trying to work out the stiffness in his neck. His shoulders felt heavy, as though he were sitting under a yoke laden with water buckets. His breath came in labored puffs through his nostrils while his mind raced ahead to the next step of the work. This piece alone, for which he'd allotted at least a week in his mind, was now sitting in front of him after just a day, ready for drying and sanding. How, he had no idea. Yet he did not stop.

He pulled out the second piece of raw wood, once again overcome by its alluring vibrance. He quickly began preparing it to become the two ivy-laden curves that would finish the heart shape. He found that he couldn't talk to this wood as he usually did when he worked. Indeed, he could not imagine the presumption of doing so. Instead, he listened. His focus was surreal, as if time itself had stopped. He was so preoccupied that he hadn't the space in his mind to form words. The wood surrendered to him, though it seemed to bend unwillingly. It was not so much a physical resistance as a feeling that Angus kept having, such as one might experience while eating stolen sweets with a parent's footsteps approaching.

Patrick walked at a breakneck clip the entire two miles home, his brow furrowed, squinting as far into the distance as he could manage, both in front and behind him. There was no sign of Angus. Bypassing the pub, he headed straight for the Armstrongs' little cottage and knocked on the door.

"It's open!" called a woman's voice. Patrick peeked in.

"Hello, Mrs. Armstrong," he greeted her.

"Ah, hello, Patrick! You're the same size as him, but not the man I was expectin' to see at this hour."

"Is Angus not here, then?" Patrick frowned.

"Why no, I was thinkin' he'd be walkin' back with you. Have you not seen him?"

Patrick shut the door behind him and sat on the edge of Angus's chair by the hearth.

"Nae… not since this mornin.' The bosses said he went off into the forest to look for wood, but nobody noticed whether he'd got back or not."

Marjorie went pale. "Nobody bothered to check on him? The whole day?"

"Well, he's kind of a crew unto himself. He's got the workshop and all, and he comes and goes when he needs to. They're happy with that if he produces what they want. I checked the workshop, though. He'd left his apron and taken his coat."

"Well, he's got to be… Oh…" Her eyes widened with recollection. "He did have an errand to run today, and he said it'd be a tight squeeze to get there before closing time. I'm sure he ran there."

"Oh right, to pick up the post or something?"

"Well…"

"Must have been dreadful urgent. I hope everythin's arright?"

"It is. It's…" Marjorie closed her eyes. "Lord, I am a terrible liar."

"Liar?" Patrick raised an eyebrow.

"I feel if Angus didnae tell you about it himself, then it may not be my place to say," she began, "but I'm terribly out of practice at makin' up cover stories. So I'll just tell you straight out, and ye'd best keep mum, Patrick Dawson."

"Of course!" he assured her.

"Well Angus is a proud boy… er, man. He's been tryin' so hard to keep things together since his Dad passed. But what with the doctor bills from his dad's illness, then my broken leg, and my not earnin' wages whilst I heal, he's been shoulderin' a heavy burden. We've rent due tomorrow, and we hav'nae got even half. The last bit of wealth to our names is Angus's inheritance… a coin issued in 1555, during the reign of Mary, Queen of Scots. Perhaps he's mentioned it before?"

"Aye, he showed it to me once when we were boys. He thought it was lucky that every Armstrong who'd ever had that coin had kept it tucked away for a rainy day, and never ended up needin' it."

Marjorie gave him a pointed look.

"He… he ended up needin' it, then." Patrick understood.

"Aye, but he was hopin' to get it back before I was aware of the situation," she sighed. "He tries to protect me from worry. But I'm not blind, am I?"

Patrick gave her a rueful smile. "Well if he's gone to the pawnbroker's, then I'm sure he'll be back soon…"

"And I'm equally sure he'll be in want of a friend," she said.

"My honor," Patrick said, giving her arm a gentle squeeze. "I'm just going to pop home and look in on my sisters, then I'll come back and harass him until he tells me everything himself." He grinned.

Returning his smile, she patted his hand. "He's lucky to have someone like you, who cares enough to meddle."

Angus put the finishing touches on the ivy, blowing away the last of the wood shavings. He set the two curved pieces aside to cure under a cloth. Once dry, they would be glued together to form the bottom point of the heart. He noticed again, absentmindedly, that this second stage of the project was finished in record time, though it was something he'd estimated would take him at least three to five days.

Despite the relative cool he'd felt earlier in the day, Angus noticed that the air had been getting progressively hotter and thicker in the workshop. He could feel a drop of sweat trickling down his back and another trying to get in his eye. He used his sleeve to mop his face, eyeing the newly carved bouquet sitting under a cloth at the end of the bench. He knew it would need several days to dry before he could lightly sand it and begin adding coats of shellac. But he couldn't resist peeking under the cloth to admire it.

He was astonished to find, as he ran his fingers across it, that it was completely dry. Not only dry to the touch, but seasoned all the way through, as though it had been sitting years in the sun. He had never carved a piece of hawthorn before, so perhaps it had an unusually short drying time? His subconscious mind produced the word "*nonsense,*" but just as quickly, the idea blew away like smoke.

He lifted the piece to the middle of the bench and worked over it carefully, first with fine-grit sandpaper, then with a fine bristle brush, and finally with a homemade tack cloth, to remove every bit of dust.

He idly wondered what time it was as he carefully measured and mixed flakes of shellac into a jar with alcohol. His paintbrush felt heavy in his hand, like an iron bar. He gripped it tighter and expertly dabbed the mixture into every crevice, bringing out a golden shimmer in the wood. The roses gleamed under the shellac, looking both beautified and smothered, as though the same finish which would preserve them had also imprisoned them. He felt a little glum as he pushed the thought away.

By the time he'd finished shellacking and turned his attention to the ivy-laden pieces of the frame, he was unsurprised to find the wood completely dry, ready for gluing and sanding.

His injured thumb had begun to throb, so he rested his left elbow on the bench and held his hand near his face to slow the blood flow to it. His hand grew cold and white almost immediately, and his fingers began to tingle. Startled, Angus lowered his arm to a horizontal position across the bench. Color returned to his hand in seconds. He ignored the pain. He still had shellac left, and it was expensive stuff. He was determined not to let it go to waste.

Now that his artistic vision was fully underway, his mind echoed with quiet. Occasionally, he had to make a decision, such as determining that the back of the frame would have turn buttons to make the glass easily removable, should it ever need replacing. But for the most part, he worked mechanically and without his usual mental noise. His limbs felt heavier every moment, yet he pushed himself to the next task as though stopping would be the end of him.

Patrick returned, as promised, to find Marjorie sitting rigidly in Angus's chair, her hands clasped tightly over the Bible in her lap. She'd been attempting to read, but comprehended nothing as her mind wandered to places a mother never wants to visit when her child is missing.

"Is he not here yet?" Patrick's tone was alarmed.

"Not a sign, not a word," she gasped. The words began to rush out. "The pawnbroker's closed two hours ago and there's nowhere else he'd go! Not without at least checkin' in on me first. He's been so worried to be away, with me in this state, and now? Gone since dawn?" Her voice shook. "Somethin's terribly wrong, Patrick. I feel it. What shall I do? Suppose he ne'er did return from the wood?"

"I'll get Reverend Keith and Mr. Mayfield and whoever else I can find, and go see Mr. Grant. We'll find him." He latched the door softly behind him, but darted off at a sprint.

Marjorie's heart lurched with fear as hot tears spilled onto her cheeks. She pressed her palm over her mouth and stifled a sob. While she had sat alone in uncertainty, it was easier to believe that she'd imagined all the worry, that Angus would be home at any moment. But seeing the look on Patrick's face just now, and realizing he was about to summon a search party, made the nightmare real. Her son was missing.

Angus repeated the sanding and shellacking process for the second part of the frame and then joined the two pieces together, forming a perfectly symmetrical heart. The joints slid together with absolute precision and the glue set almost instantly. He set the specially cut glass into place carefully, holding his breath. It fit without needing a single bit of sanding or adjustment.

He lifted the heart-shaped wood backing to fit in behind it like a puzzle piece. As he spread his fingers wide to hold it, he felt the sharp sting of the wound in his hand reopening. A warm trickle of blood oozed out from under the makeshift bandage. He finished placing the wood quickly and snatched his hand back, but too late. A drop of blood fell on the wood and spread into a circle.

Angus thought he could hear a strained cry, like a faint moan of sad music, which died away quickly. He shook his head and tightened the handkerchief around his hand, letting out a frustrated sigh. The piece was no longer perfect, but at least this blemish would always face the wall.

With the last bits of hardware in his bandaged hand, he readied a small mallet to tap them into the back of the frame. He glanced out a high window, feeling sure it must be getting dark soon, and that Patrick would shortly be coming round to walk home together. But the sun was still blazing high in the sky, near its peak. Angus froze, mallet poised over the very last tack.

His mind, which had been quiet for several hours, suddenly awoke, as if from a dream. All sorts of realizations came flooding into his consciousness. He finally comprehended what he'd just done. He looked at the volume of work in front of him, and then back out the window. Somehow, he'd just completed nearly two weeks' worth of labor without a break, and it was... what? He didn't even know. Not yet noon, by all appearances. He shifted his weight uneasily. Sweat soaked his skin. His boots squeezed his feet like they were a size too small. His hands shook. His body felt heavy, like he was buried in mud. Every movement was burdened. The mallet in his hand had the weight of an anvil. Yet, he had only to tap this last tack into the wood, and the entire thing would be finished.

Finished? But how? Found, cut, designed, carved, dried, sanded, buffed, glued, shellacked, glass installed, made ready to hang... finished? He was bewildered beyond words. *Have I been kidnapped by fairies?*

For the third time that day, Angus was overcome with hesitation and foreboding, as if something didn't want him to finish this. *But I must finish it. I've come this far...* With one last befuddled look out at the sunny midday, he swiped with his sleeve at the drops of sweat that were racing toward his eyes. He tapped in the last tack, his trembling hands causing him to miss every other stroke. Without pausing, he grabbed his pencil and signed his name to the back with a heavy hand. He turned the mirror over and laid it on the bench as gingerly as his shaking arms could manage. It was a shimmering, golden explosion of blooms. His masterpiece was finished.

Caledon streaked through the wood, skirting the edge of the black rip that trailed out of the tree line all the way from the Great Hawthorn. He was careful not to even put a toe near the bleeding darkness. He fought the desperate frustration welling up within him as the pained hum echoed through the forest.

He reached the tiny cottage of Ré MacCrann. The ivy-covered stone wall was transparent to his eyes, and he crossed through it with little effort. The Guardian of the Hawthorn was kneeling on the stone floor by the simple wooden bed, his face buried in his hands. Caledon softened as he remembered how the Three felt about this man and his kind.

Ré drew a ragged breath. "God, what's to be done?" he gasped.

Caledon waited. Instructions would come. He could see that the Master was dealing with this man. Already, the stubborn square of his shoulders was bending.

Open the door. The Master's voice came to him in a whisper of a thought.

Caledon blew toward the cottage door, generating enough force to knock the latch loose and swing it halfway open.

Ré jerked his head up at the squeak of the rusty hinges. He processed this development for a few moments, and decided against it being a coincidence.

"Of course…" he mumbled. "I should go, I should do something… what? How can I? Maybe… " He reached for his boots, which he'd kicked off in a muddy heap near the bed earlier. "Aye. I should see to the tree."

Not yet... Danger...

Caledon lifted his hands and shifted the atmosphere around the cottage to amplify the pitiful hum coming from the Great Hawthorn, just long enough for Ré to hear it. His eyes widened as he took it in. Foreboding settled over his spirit.

"Nae..." He shook his grizzled head. "I cannae go near it." It began to dawn on him what he needed to do. "I must go to Éamon. He's the only one I can talk to." He finished yanking his boots on and struggled to stand as his aging knees wobbled and ached. Caledon lifted him to his feet, imperceptibly, and sped him on his way.

The mile and a half to his son's cottage in the village usually took him the better part of an hour to walk, but today he made it in forty minutes. The fishing boats had docked for the day, and the streets were bustling. He got more than a few strange looks as he passed the villagers, for he hadn't bothered to check the looking glass before setting out. But the stray leaves and twigs in his hair and his dirty, tear stained face were of little consequence to him. All he could think about was the fate of that young man if he didn't set things right.

Angus gazed at his finished work and sighed. A strange feeling began to take hold of him, as if he had been stretched to his very limit. His body, spirit, and soul were wrung to the point of exhaustion. For the first time since he'd returned to the workshop, Angus listened to his surroundings. He heard nothing but his own labored breathing. He heard no workmen outside, no sound of tools. Nothing. Not even birdsong. The air around him felt thick. A profound weakness gripped him. *I must need some fresh air...* He tried to stand, and collapsed to the plank floor. Pain shot through his elbow. *Well certainly, I've not eaten in... how long? I must try to get outside...*

"Hello?" he called out weakly. His own voice sounded strange to him. He crawled on his belly toward the door using his good elbow, smearing the small puddle of blood he'd shed earlier from his wounded hand. But not even halfway there, he became dizzy. His body broke into violent chills, and his teeth began to chatter. He reached the pile of hay along the wall where he'd tossed his coat, and pulled his coat over him. He managed to get his good arm into one sleeve before lying back on the hay. He was spent. The room lurched sideways. *I must…just… rest… just for a moment…*

"God? Help me please… I need…" he croaked. His eyes fluttered. He drifted into blackness.

Chapter 8

Scotland, 1844

Éamon MacCrann sat on a box on the front stoop of his little house. He had a small diary of sums and a few coins laid out on an upturned fish crate. He was tallying up the takings he'd brought home from selling his catch. His seventeen year old son, Darrick, looked on, absorbing everything he could from his father.

"Well, son," he said. "I've seen be'er, and I've seen worse."

Éamon tipped the diary and slid a sovereign and a handful of pennies and shillings off the book into his coin pouch. Handing the diary to the boy, he stood, stretching his back.

"Check my work, lad."

The boy smiled and took up his father's pencil stub. Before he could look down, someone caught his eye—a bent figure shuffling up the road more quickly than seemed possible for his frail frame. It was his grandfather. His stomach dropped. Ré never came into the village more than a few times a year, and never looking so disheveled.

"Granda! Are you well?" Darrick called out.

Éamon jumped off the stoop and ran to meet his father.

Ré bent at the waist, his chest heaving with exertion.

"Lad," he puffed. "I'm sorry... I dinnae ken where t'begin..."

"Come inside, Dad. You look a fright," Éamon said, trying to stifle a feeling of alarm that was rising in his belly.

"No time!" Ré protested. "There's no easy way to tell you that your old dad's a failure, lad, but I dinnae have the luxury of breakin' it t'ye nice and slow. I'll just have to own up and tell you, there's a right mishanter brewin'... and it's because I let it!"

"Dad, what're you on about?" Éamon looked around to see if anyone in the road might overhear. He lowered his voice just in case. "Why've you left the Tree? Has somethin' happened to it?"

Ré fought to control his volume. "Somebody *cut it!*"

"WHAT!" Éamon shouted, before lowering his voice to a strangled whisper. "How in the name of..." He searched his father's face, but found only panic written there. "*Why* would somebody cut it?"

"He said it was for Mr. Grant!" Ré's whispers had gone up in pitch. "I think he must be a carpenter, but he didnae tell me where he was takin' it, or what he was plannin' to do with it..."

"We've got to stop him!" Éamon said, already putting his hat on. "I dinnae ken if we can undo what's been done, but we've got to find the pieces and see if we can keep it from gettin' worse."

"Aye, the air felt so strange when that lad walked by me. I could feel the disturbance. I heard a strange humming, like it used to make, but wrong somehow..."

"Dad, it always hums, you've just stopped bein' able to hear it."

"I know, lad. I know." Ré hung his head. "I'm sorry, I should've..."

"We'll have time to talk about that later." Éamon squeezed his dad's shoulder. "We should get on."

⁕

Patrick knocked at the back door of the pub. Gillian, who had just finished setting the kitchen to rights for the night, came to the door wiping her wet hands on her apron, her face pink with exertion.

"Patrick! Is Angus with you? He said he'd stop by…" she took in his expression and her brow furrowed. "Everythin' arright?"

"Gillian, where's your dad?"

"He's upstairs doin' the books, why?"

"I need him to come wi'me," Patrick blurted. "Angus is missing!"

Gillian was horror-struck. "Wha…" she began, but quickly overruled herself. "Come upstairs."

He shot up the steps two at a time with Gillian close on his heels.

"Dad! Angus is missing!" Gillian cried as they burst into his office.

"Eh?" Gordon Mayfield looked over his spectacles, pencil poised over a balance sheet. "Angus Armstrong?"

"Aye," Patrick puffed. "He went into the forest at Ecclesgrieg, lookin' to chop wood. There's been nae a sign of 'im since late mornin' and I dinnae ken if he came back to the village, or what!" He held up his finger and took three seconds to catch his breath. "Not to mention," he continued, "I heard tell there's a doo-lally gamekeeper who cannae tell a deer from a tree stump!"

Mr. Mayfield threw down his pencil and pushed back from his desk.

"I've three extra lanterns," he said, shoving his braces back up over his shoulders and mashing his feet into boots at the same time. "We'll get the reverend to ring the bell."

"I'm comin' with you!" Gillian declared.

Her father saw the tears of worry welling up in her eyes and the determined set of her jaw, and nodded. She was light on her feet, and he knew that she could easily keep pace with the men.

Between Reverend Keith, the Mayfields, and Patrick Dawson, they had been able to round up twenty men with lanterns and torches to search the forest on the estate. Even Mr. Grant took up a lantern and joined the search. They worked their way across every game trail and clearing, finding no sign.

When they reached an older, more mature part of the forest where the trees were larger and more knobbly, they found the old gamekeeper leaning against a tree near the entrance to an oak grove. Beside him stood a man in his forties, holding a lantern and a large burlap sack.

"Ah!" Grant waved. "Mr. Ré MacCrann, is it not?"

The old man raised his puffy, watery eyes to take in the party of men with their torches, then resumed staring at the ground. "Aye," he replied gruffly, "or what's left of him. This is my son, Éamon."

Grant touched his hat brim and nodded. "Mr. MacCrann, are you quite all right?" he wondered.

The gamekeeper shrugged a shoulder and sniffed.

"We're in search of a man who came into the wood earlier today," Grant continued, addressing Éamon this time. "He has dark, curly hair... He would have been carrying a rucksack. Did you happen to see him?"

"Aye, he was here," Éamon replied.

"I should have seen 'im sooner," Ré lamented.

Puzzled, Grant pressed. "Did you see him leave the forest?"

"Aye, he didnae stay long. Just took 'imself a bit of... a bit of the uhh..." Ré's fingers fluttered in the direction of the oak grove.

"A branch of a tree, is all," Éamon finished for him.

"He left afore noon." Ré shuddered and pursed his lips, holding back some strange emotion that Grant couldn't decipher.

With this new information, the search party considered amongst themselves and decided it best to check around the castle one more time. Most fanned out across the worksite, while Patrick, Gillian, and a few others opened the workshop to check the entire building more thoroughly.

Gillian peeked around the heavy door into Angus's airy workshop and lifted her lantern. As she walked forward, her eyes were drawn to something on the floor, a few feet from the workbench. Her stomach dropped. It was a smeared bloodstain.

"Angus!" she gasped.

Patrick came in behind her, his eyes darting around the room, scanning for any sign of his best friend. He strode to the bench. It looked different than before—it had been swept clean. The apron he'd seen neatly draped there earlier this evening was gone. In its place sat Angus's cap. Beside it, a glorious work of art. A frame of dazzling roses and ivy glimmered in the lantern light, while the mirror within it reflected Patrick's stunned face.

He held his lantern high over the gleaming mirror. His brain couldn't comprehend what his eyes were telling him.

"What on earth…" he murmured.

Gillian could barely peel her eyes away from the blood smear on the straw-littered floor, but she forced herself to join Patrick by the bench. The beauty of Angus's work made her catch her breath.

"Didn'he just start this?" she breathed. "How… how'd he finish it so fast?" Her fingers reached out to the delicate rose petals. She half expected them to be tacky, but the lacquer was hard.

"Not sure," said Patrick wonderingly. "I came by at seven and he was gone. I didnae see any projects goin,' besides that rocking chair over there. Just tools on the bench. The place wasnae this clean, though…" He ran his hand through his mess of sandy hair, utterly bewildered. "Maybe this mirror is somethin' from the house…" He set the lantern on the bench and carefully turned the mirror over to look at the back. Gillian peeked underneath. "Nae, there's his signature!" she gasped. "My God, what on earth is happening?"

Vancouver, WA ~ Present Day

Iris made her way down the richly paneled corridor to her first room visit. She glanced once more at the sheet that Candace had given her. *Room 105.* As she approached, she could see the door standing ajar. Inside, a gentleman with a mop of curly white hair sat in a window seat at the far end of the room, shoulders slumped, gazing out the window. She knocked gingerly. He did not turn.

"Mr. Armstrong?" she asked softly.

"Call me Angus," he said to the window.

"Hello, Angus, my name is Iris. May I come in?"

"Course. Everyone does." He finally turned to look at her. "Ask your questions, then. Do your exam, or whatever 'tis you're about."

Iris's mouth fell open slightly upon hearing him speak.

"You're Scottish!" she said with appreciation.

"I agree," he said. "What gave it away?"

Iris ignored the sarcasm and pressed, "Aberdonian, from the sounds of it?" She raised an eyebrow.

He raised an eyebrow to match hers. "Mearns… like enough. You've spent time there, then?" He leaned forward.

"I'm Scottish myself," she grinned.

"I'm sure you are." He sat back with a huff and leaned against the window pane. "And so is that social worker, and so is the nurse, and so is that mad woman in the next room, eighteen generations back on her mum's side."

Iris met his eyes with a steady gaze. She read sadness and disappointment in his face. *He doesn't believe me. Time to unleash the accent.*

"Well perhaps all those others like to *call* themselves Sco'ish because they're proud to have Sco'ish kin, but we know the feel of the North Sea wind in our faces, don't we?" she said mischievously.

His eyes narrowed. "Now why are you talkin' like that?" he snapped. "You makin' sport o'me?"

"O' course not!" Iris protested. "Listen to me talkin'! How d'ye think I knew you were from Aberdeen or thereabouts? I'm from there myself!"

"Then how come you came in here soundin' like a Canadian?" he demanded.

"Canadian, really? I was goin' for American…" Her voice softened. "I speak that way because I came to this country when I was eight. I just wanted to fit in. I got tired of people askin' me where I was from. I'm sure you know what that's like."

He conceded the point with a grunt. Then he looked her full in the face. "It's a shame to hide who you are," he said.

Iris thought she could see moisture forming in his eyes.

"But I'm glad you decided to talk normal," he went on. "You're the first familiar soundin' voice I've heard in a long time."

They lingered in silence for several seconds. Iris sat beside him on the window seat.

"When did you come to America?" she finally asked.

"About a month ago, I think." His face took on a strangely pained expression.

"What made you decide to come?" she asked conversationally, trying to keep the tone light, and perhaps draw him away from whatever dark memory was churning in his mind.

"I didnae decide. I just… came."

His tone was so solemn that Iris couldn't bring herself to ask him the questions on the checklist about hobbies, interests, highlights of his stay so far… She skipped to the last question.

"Is there anything I can do to help you today, Angus?"

He studied her, looking for sincerity.

"I wish there was some way to know... if they were arright..." he mumbled, going back to looking out the window.

"What're their names? I'll see what I can find out," she offered.

"Doubt you'll find anything," he sighed, leaning his forehead on the glass. He idly rubbed a newly healed scar on his thumb.

"Will you let me try?" she encouraged.

"My mum's name was Marjorie Armstrong. And Gillian Mayfield, she was my... she... well, she was special to me."

Iris jotted the names on her sheet.

"We lived in the village of St. Cyrus. I promise you, there'll be no mention of them. Poor people dinnae make it into history books."

"St. Cyrus? You're kidding me!"

Angus turned to face her but didn't reply.

Iris beamed. "That's where I grew up! I went to the primary school right by the little church!"

"Y'know St. Cyrus?" His wiry eyebrows lifted. "But it's such a tiny place..."

"Aye, it is, but here we both are! It's a small world sometimes," Iris grinned. "Whereabouts in the village did you live?"

"In a cottage off the main road, just down from where the new church was bein' built," Angus replied with growing interest.

"But the church isnae on the main road, it's down nearer the beach access..." Iris explained, visualizing her childhood home.

"Aye, that's the old one. The new one's on the main road. Or... it *was*."

"Not the one with the pointy clock tower?" asked Iris quizzically, making a steeple with her fingers.

"The tower was supposed to be square... I never saw it finished, though." Angus scratched his head.

"Oh, that place! That's a church hall! Or it was when I was livin' there," she answered. "What d'ye mean you never saw it finished? I thought it was built in Victorian times! Did you never look that direction?" she laughed.

Angus's face was serious. He didn't answer.

"But dinnae you miss the beach?" Iris asked, to break the tension.

Angus's expression cleared and he half smiled.

"Aye, the beach is my thinkin' place."

"Mine too!" Iris beamed. She stood. "Well, I should probably be gettin' back, but if you can think of anybody else you're wonderin' about… I thought perhaps I could check on someone for you who's… y'know… still living? Like children? Grandchildren?" Iris felt awkward. It seemed insensitive to point out to this elderly man that his mother was likely deceased.

"Dinnae have any children," he frowned. "I've not had a chance to marry yet."

Yet?

"All right. Well, like I said, let me know. And there's so much more I'd love to ask you, if y'ever fancy a chat."

"Aye, please do. This has been the first time my entire month here that I've talked to someone who sounds normal."

"Tomorrow, then? Same time?" She smiled warmly and headed for the door.

"Aye, tomorrow." He did his best to smile back, but only managed a weak effort before sadness clouded it over. "And Iris?"

She turned.

"Sorry about yellin' before. I uh… I know people round here are just tryin' to make me feel be'er. But I'm not sure that's possible. Happiness was… a long time ago."

Iris sat at one end of Candace's desk in the Activities Office and scribbled a few answers in the blanks on her checklist. On paper, it didn't look like it had been much of a visit. But Iris felt a mixture of emotion about Angus. She was dying of curiosity about where exactly he was from and why he'd come to this country, but she didn't feel right pushing him for information on their first meeting. He was a deeply bereft man, grieving for someone or something. She tapped her fingers on the desk.

"Got that form finished?" Candace asked, eyeing her tapping fingers.

"Pretty much." Iris handed it to her.

"Sweetie, you've got to ask more questions than this," Candace grimaced at the page, which was over half blank.

"I know, but he was so sad. It just didnae feel like the right time to ask some of those things. It seemed… insensitive or somethin.'"

"Now look who's having a hard time hiding her accent!" Candace was impressed. Fifteen minutes with Angus and you sound Scottish again!" She grinned. "It suits you. Well, use your best judgment, of course, but it's unlikely you'd offend him. He's getting used to all the questions people ask him every day. And he may not remember the conversation tomorrow anyway," Candace said gently.

"Oh, I think he would. He's the first resident I've met here who seems mentally together."

"He does *seem* very together," Candace conceded. "Which is why you'd be surprised to learn he's more severely affected by mental illness than most."

"Seriously? What mental illness? He doesn't sound like the others. He speaks so clearly. He never once lost his train of thought."

"No, we're pretty sure he doesn't have Alzheimer's disease or any other form of degenerative illness. The doctors believe he has a form of schizophrenia."

"What, like there's more than one of him in there?" Iris asked dubiously.

"Actually you're thinking of multiple personality disorder. Common mistake. No, he believes he's from another century. He sticks to a set of facts that are chronologically impossible, but he never changes his story. He can't remember anything between his twenties and a month ago when he was found."

"Found?"

"Yes, he's one of our five residents who are wards of the state, basically like elderly foster kids. That's why he has a social worker instead of family. Sometimes elderly people get confused and wander away from their homes. It's really dangerous because they believe they're going somewhere important, so they don't know to ask for help.

"Angus wandered onto our grounds here at Rookwood in the middle of October. He was discovered in the early morning by a delivery guy who was bringing in some stuff for the chapel renovation and called 911. Angus was in pretty bad shape, but he made a full recovery. The cops searched the missing persons database and every lead they could think of, but they could never figure out anything about him, not even his age. He knows his name, but besides that, he says a bunch of things that make no sense. He didn't seem to have a home or any identification, and since we had a bed open at the time, they sent him here to live."

"But he told me he's from St. Cyrus! The same place where I grew up! I believe him about that," Iris protested. "He seemed to know some of the landmarks. That's got to be a great lead!"

"Trust me, they've tried everything. They even asked Police Scotland to search for connections in the U.K. Nothing turned up."

"That's so sad," Iris said quietly, imagining what Angus must be feeling. "There's got to be a way to find his family."

"Well, they're hoping he'll have a lucid moment and say something that could help us figure out who he is. So far, he hasn't said anything very helpful. And lately, he hasn't said much at all."

Iris felt her heart sinking for him. "He's so lost," she whispered.

Candace put her hand on Iris's shoulder. "Yes, he is. And unless somebody comes through the front door looking for him, he's pretty much going to live out his days here with us. That's why we need to help make his world a little brighter."

Darkness held Angus in an icy grip. He was lying on freezing stone, yet felt as though he was toppling end over end down a well. Pain seared his left hand where he'd gouged it with the chisel, and his left elbow ached where he'd fallen on it. He could feel numbness spreading through his limbs.

"H-h-hello?" he rasped against the cold wind. His breath came in short gasps, and his chest constricted with the effort. He forced his eyes open and tried to take in his surroundings. He was lying on some kind of path next to boxwood hedges, soaked to the skin in cold dew. The beginnings of daylight illuminated a building some twenty yards away, nestled in among tall cedars. *Where is this? Am I still on the estate? But how is it finished already?*

He attempted to sit up, but his muscles were so spent that his arms collapsed under him. He felt as though he must have been shivering for hours on end, though he couldn't remember.

Suddenly, as though someone had transported him to a dry blanket by a roaring fire, he grew warm and felt the overwhelming urge to sleep. *I cannae sleep on the ground...* His face felt hot on one side, while the other cheek remained pressed into a slimy paving stone. A beam of early dawn light pierced his retinas. His eyelids grew heavy as he squinted against the light. *I really must get up...* He drifted.

The blackness was pierced by an unearthly wail, louder than any human or animal he'd ever heard. Through one bleary eyelid, he followed the sound to a strange covered wagon with flashing blue and red flames on its top. It seemed to be driving itself toward him without any horses. A man and a woman in matching blue work clothes ran toward him.

"Sir, can you speak?" the woman asked in a deafening voice.

"I nee heh... whaa's haaa..." Angus mumbled.

The two eased him onto his back. He could feel someone lifting his shirt and placing their hot hand on his belly. The woman had her fingers on his neck.

"Pulse is thready..." She kept her eyes on a tiny clock strapped to her wrist. "Skin pink..." she continued, "...pupils dilated."

"Looks like he was trying to take off his coat. That's not good," said the man. "Warm blankets, warm IV fluids, warm oxygen..."

Angus drifted again.

When he came to, he was in a tiny room filled with cold light, bouncing along a road at an alarming speed. He could hear the wailing again, and the same two people were still there working over him.

"Well, hi there! Are you back with us?" the man asked.

Angus tried to speak, but he was muffled by a mask over his nose and mouth.

"It's all right, you can tell us in a minute, okay sir? We're just giving you some fresh air right now and getting you warmed up. Did you fall down at the senior home? Can you shake your head to answer?"

Senior...home? Angus had moved beyond confusion into disbelief. Nothing in his situation made any sense to his mind. He had no answer. *Have I fallen? Probably...?* The entire room shuddered and bumped.

The man knocked on the wall behind him. "Take it easy!" he shouted. "We don't want him going into V-fib!"

Angus was gripped with pain and terror. He felt fear rising in him like bile. The wailing continued. *What IS this place?* A tear slipped down his cheek. He clenched his jaw and squeezed his eyes closed to shut out the sights and sounds, but he could not. He began to tremble violently, whether from the cold, or the fear, he couldn't tell.

He tore off his blankets and sat up, bewildered. All was quiet. The bedside clock read 4:30 a.m. He still shook. Deep sobs rocked his body, and hot tears poured down his cheeks. The dreams had been with him almost every night since that terrifying day. But the nightmare he'd just had wasn't even the worst one...

Chapter 9

Vancouver, WA ~ Present Day

I ris dabbed the finishing touches on her makeup and tossed her cosmetics bag in the bottom drawer.

Charlie appeared in the mirror, leaning on the doorframe behind her.

"You're up early," she commented. Her blue hair was poofed up on one side and yesterday's mascara was smudged beneath her eyes.

"Yeah, I thought I might go into work early today," Iris answered.

"Those old people take their BINGO that seriously?" Charlie yawned.

"Ha. Well, yes they do, actually. But no, I'm going to see someone. I met him yesterday."

"You've got a boyfriend after your first day?" Charlie seemed more awake now.

"Yes, Charlie." Iris rolled her eyes. "I've got an eighty-something-year-old boyfriend. We're mad for each other."

"Well how should I know who you met yesterday?"

"You know I don't date people at work," Iris reminded her. "This guy's name is Angus. You'll never believe this... he's from St. Cyrus!"

"Your hometown? You're kidding me!"

"I'm not! But he's got about a sixty- or seventy-year gap in his memory. If someone could just help him remember, he might be able to recall something important, like the names of his living relatives. Then he wouldn't have to be so alone. So I'm going to read up on him before I see him again."

"Haven't they already asked him about all that stuff?" Charlie wondered.

"Yes, but I thought talking to someone who's got so much in common with him might spark a memory. Plus, he reminds me of my granddad." Iris smiled fondly.

Iris waited behind the wheel of her parked hatchback and rubbed her hands together for warmth. She felt a little guilty for what she was about to do, but she deemed it a good enough cause to be justifiable. She was about to flirt her way into a locked building. She was at Rookwood an entire hour early, and didn't have her own key. But she'd found out that Will the chef, who was, according to Candace, "totally into her," would be arriving at work any moment to get breakfast underway.

Right on cue, she saw him trudging up the path in his black pinstriped chef pants and white t-shirt. He was carrying his chef jacket, despite the bitter frost. She bailed out of her car and hurried up the path to catch him, while trying to appear nonchalant.

"Oh! Hey Will!" she greeted him as though she was surprised to see him.

"Iris! Hey! How's it going?" Will blushed.

"It's going great," she enthused. "My first day was awesome! Thanks again for the muffins yesterday. They were heavenly." She smiled sweetly up at him.

"I-I'm uhh, glad you enjoyed them," he stammered, and dropped his keys. "Aren't you early? I thought you guys came in at eight." He bent to pick up his keys and slipped on an icy patch of sidewalk. He righted himself quickly, with as much dignity as possible, unlocked the door, and held it open for her.

Iris kept her face composed with some effort.

"Yes, a little early, but I wanted to get some stuff done," she offered vaguely, with a dazzling smile. "I'm looking forward to later today... I promised Candace I'd come down and help her approve your batch of doughnuts."

"Well, you're welcome in my kitchen any time," he said with feeling. "Y'know, like even if there's no baking to taste test. Or... even if you just want someone to talk to... like on your breaks... or... y'know, whatever." They stopped outside the kitchen door.

"Thanks, Will. I'd love to." She realized she meant it. He was exceedingly easy to talk to. She touched his arm, which felt chilly and had pronounced goosebumps. "Hey, why weren't you wearing a coat outside? Aren't you cold?"

"I'm freezing, actually. But it gets hot in the kitchen, so if I start the day with a temperature deficit, I can spare myself a couple hours of sweating. Then it's not as big a deal if I forget to drink water... sorry, you probably don't want to hear about sweat..."

"It's fine," Iris giggled. "Pretty smart idea, actually. Mmmm, do I smell coffee already?"

"Yeah, the dinner guy sets that up on a timer for us before he leaves. Want a cup?" Will pushed his way through the double doors, stopping halfway through.

"Oh, heck yes. Can I take it to go? I wish I could stay and sneak some bacon, but I've really got to get upstairs and get busy," she replied.

Will grabbed her a disposable cup, filled it, and paused. "Cream? Sugar?"

"Two of each," she replied sheepishly. He added the cream and sugar with a practiced flourish.

"My kinda girl," he said, handing her the cup. "See you later with Candy then!"

"Wouldn't miss it!" she grinned. "Thanks for the coffee!" she called over her shoulder as she made her way out of the kitchen. Will stared after her, pursing his lips in a sideways grin.

"You're very welcome," he murmured.

❧

Iris sipped her coffee as she walked toward the front desk. She wanted to pull Angus's file and read up on him. It felt like a nosy thing to do, but why else did they keep files, if not to have helpful information on hand?

The elegant crystal chandelier in the lobby was illuminated at half brightness, the canaries still slept with their heads tucked beneath their wings, and all the little round tables were empty. Becky was not yet at her desk, so Iris slipped behind the counter and scanned the bank of filing cabinets. Each was labeled with a hideous yellow card in its slot, clearly the work of Becky's son James. *What is this color?* She opened the "RESIDENTS" drawer and searched for "Armstrong." It should have been between "Archer" and "Arthur," but it wasn't. *Hmmm.* Iris thrummed her fingers on the side of the drawer. A tab near the back of the drawer, labeled "Wards," caught her eye. Behind it there were five files, the first of which was labeled "Armstrong, Angus." *Eureka.*

She looked over her shoulder and slid it out carefully. There really wasn't much in it. One page of basic stats, another two of medical records. A couple hospital forms... one admission and one release form, a week apart. A few pages from the

Social Security Administration… Washington state insurance forms… a doctor's report, notes from a psychiatric interview, forms from a court-appointed social worker, and one visit report written by Candace. A month's worth of existence, summed up in a file.

Iris quickly made copies of the interviews and the medical stuff, ignoring the rest. She borrowed a stapler, which was labeled "STOLEN FROM BECKY," and then slipped the file back into the drawer.

She felt a tiny bit burglarish as she looked around to make sure she'd left everything exactly as she'd found it. *It's not as if I'm committing a crime,* she reasoned. *All the same, I don't really know how much of this stuff an Activity Assistant is supposed to be reading. I just don't want to have to answer any questions right now.*

Papers and coffee cup in hand, she slipped out of Becky's office and headed for the sun room. She figured that would be an out-of-the-way place to read uninterrupted. As she passed the first corridor to her left, she noticed a slight movement three doors down. A head of curly white hair poked out from Room 105. Iris froze. Not seeing her, Angus emerged and turned left, headed away from her down the corridor, slowly, but with a surprisingly youthful gait. Overcome by curiosity, she followed.

He took a right at the end of the hall and continued past the dining room, through an archway that Iris hadn't noticed on her first pass through here. The brass plate over the arch read "Chapel." When she reached it, she discreetly peeked around the pillar. *I don't want to interrupt him if he's praying or something…*

The room was small, with ornate wooden benches. It was enough seating for about twenty. At the front of the room stood a small podium and a black baby grand piano. Just on the other side of it, Angus stood with his back to her, motionless in front of an ornately carved wooden framed mirror which hung on the wall. It was heart-shaped and covered in golden brown roses and ivy.

Iris was struck by it. Her brain flashed a memory to the front of her consciousness, like seeing a photo for a split second. It was of her last school trip in Scotland, when she stood with her face pressed against the grimy glass of a castle window, squinting into a once-grand parlor and admiring a dusty, dilapidated piano with a mirror hanging precariously from the wall behind it. *It's likely hanging there still. This is similar, but it can't be the same one.*

With trembling fingers, Angus reached out, as though he wanted to touch it, but was afraid it would burn him. He lowered his hand and gazed at his reflection, shaking his head.

"My hair is *white*. Why is it so white?" he muttered to his reflection. "And I'm wrinkled! What have you done to me?"

Poor guy. Does he not remember getting old? Iris slipped silently out of the archway and stole away unnoticed. It truly did feel wrong to eavesdrop on such a private moment. She pondered his strange question the rest of the way to the sun room… *"What have you done to me?" Who is he talking to?*

She settled in at one of the white wrought iron tables and began to read. She started with the doctor's report.

Angus Armstrong, DOB unknown (approx. age - 85 to 90)
Height: 5'10" Weight: 160

Pt. admitted Oct.12 presenting with moderate to severe hypothermia. Body temp 92.1°F. Symptoms included mild erythema, bradycardia, bradypnea, hypoglycemia, and dehydration. Pt. exhibited mental confusion and paradoxical undressing. Also observed, severe contusion on left elbow, likely from a fall, and infected laceration of palmar left hand, crudely self bandaged. Treated with topical and IV antibiotics and tetanus shot. Symptoms resolved with rewarming care, food, and hydration. He is otherwise in good health.

Iris had to look up most of the bigger words on her phone to understand that Angus had fallen, cut his hand somehow, and gotten so cold that he was beginning to die. *Where were you, Angus? Where did you come from?*

She picked up the psychiatrist's report. It was a summary of his first interview with Angus after they'd gotten him stable at the hospital.

Angus Armstrong Interview, by Dr. Gary Richards, Oct. 15

My initial observation of Angus is that he is extremely anxious overall. He seems startled by the smallest things, such as beeping hospital monitors, cars and planes outside the window, having his blood pressure checked, having lights turned on, etc. Even his own appearance seems to distress him. He believes himself to be in Scotland, and 24 years of age. By his accent, I would believe he does come from Scotland originally, or has had theater training.

He was found on the garden path at Rookwood Senior Home, although they have no record of his ever having lived there. I have no reason to believe from Angus that he knew where he was, or that he went to Rookwood on purpose. He was found dressed in an older style of clothing, including a work apron and overcoat. The only possessions he had with him were antiques, or excellent replicas—a mailed letter and a coin—both of which seem to have sentimental importance to him. They will of course be returned to him upon his release. One working theory is that he was working as a historical reenactor of some kind.

His memory is of great concern. For the time being, he seems to have no memories of his life after the age of 24. He does not exhibit typical signs of dementia. He is most likely schizophrenic, or in a fugue state, and requires further evaluation.

It is my professional opinion that, given his total lack of situational awareness (no money, no ID, not dressed for the weather), his heightened emotional state, and his inability to accept his surroundings, the court should declare him legally incompetent. I do not believe him to be a danger to himself or others, other than the risk of exposure if he is allowed to wander away from caregivers.

Iris read the report with a mixture of fascination and horror. *Poor Angus! Was he working at a museum or somewhere, and just lost track of reality?* She flipped to the last page in the stack, which was Candace's visit report from three days ago.

This was my second room visit with Angus. My first was of course the intake visit to welcome him and invite him to join activities. He seemed pretty stressed out when he first got here, so I was encouraged to see him coming to gardening and woodworking activities, as well as church services in the dining hall. I let him know that the chapel remodel would be finished in a couple weeks and there would be a hymn sing to dedicate it. He said he'd come.

Fast forward to that hymn sing—he kind of freaked out on me! Everyone came in after the ribbon cutting and he took a seat near the front. I had just started welcoming everyone when he stood up and started backing out of the room like he'd just seen the ghost of Jacob Marley. I called the nurse, obviously, because I had to stay and lead the hymn sing, but I did want to follow up on that. I asked him today if he was all right, if something was bothering him. He said something in the chapel gave him bad memories and he couldn't really explain it. He made no promises to join us for anything in the future, but I do hope I can get him to come back to woodworking at least. He seemed really into that.

Iris smiled a little. *Candace writes exactly how she talks.* She sipped her coffee, which had turned lukewarm. *So if Angus seems to remember nothing after age 24, but confesses to something having sparked a bad memory, that seems like something worth investigating.* She thought of Angus standing in the chapel, looking at himself in the mirror. *Was he freaked out by his own reflection?* Iris frowned. *Maybe, but why just in the chapel? He's got a mirror in his room, and he's not freaking out in there...*

"Nine o'clock, it says here!" crowed First Irene from five feet behind her.

Iris jumped mid-sip and sloshed coffee all over her stack of papers. She turned slowly. Irene was waving her calendar printout and smiling excitedly.

Iris gave her the brightest smile she could manage as coffee dripped off her chin and adrenaline coursed through her veins. "See you at nine o'clock, then!" she called back with a little wave.

Iris frantically shook out the papers, dug through her purse for a few linty tissues and dabbed the coffee away. The top page, Candace's report, was essentially ruined as the copy toner and coffee ran together in an inky puddle. She carefully picked it off the stack and shoved it into the nearest trash bin. The rest, she rolled up and tucked into her purse. Well, she'd have to take a closer look at them later, but she had a lot more to go on now. She checked her watch. 7:55. Perfect. Time to go clock in.

Angus entered the dining hall and took his usual seat next to Fred, who dozed in his wheelchair. He poured himself a cup of coffee from the carafe on the table and considered the bowl of fruit in the center. The apples were familiar, at least. But he'd been curious for a number of weeks about the long, yellow fruits. He'd been watching people peel and eat them, but he'd been reticent to try them. He couldn't begin to imagine what something like that would taste like.

His entire existence right now could be summed up this way. He watched with fascination as people stared at moving pictures inside of glowing boxes, wrote with pens that never seemed to run out of ink, and talked to themselves while they held shiny tiles up to their faces.

The strangest of all were the water closets that swallowed up your... uh, personal business, and washed themselves with the press of a handle! He'd had to get used to the water closet in his room. The nurses insisted he use it, and that there were positively no outhouses. He was finally able to press the handle without feeling the urge to run away from the loud, swirling, sucking water.

Angus avoided most of the strange things he encountered as much as he possibly could, entertaining the possibility that if he just refused to get too involved with this alien place, he might once again wake up and find it was all just a bad dream. He took an apple and bit into it.

Doris, Walter, and Betty joined Angus and Fred at the table just as plates of scrambled eggs and bacon were being served. Betty eyed her plate with suspicion and began picking bits of onion out of her eggs, tossing them behind her.

Doris, who normally sat between Fred and Walter, instead plopped into the chair beside Angus and put her hand on his knee, looking him over with her wide eyes.

"You look lonely, Sugar," she said with coy concern.

"Ehhh... I'm fine, actually," he replied awkwardly, inching away from her hand.

"Will you quit flirtin' with that guy?" Walter grumped. Doris ignored him.

"Yes, fine," she continued, "and a man so fine shouldn't be so alone. Want to meet me later for... *coffee?*"

Angus held up his full cup and smiled at her appeasingly. "Tea, then?"

Angus put his face in his palm and muttered, mostly to himself, "You're old enough to be my great granny!"

"What's that, Sugar?"

"I have to go." Angus stood abruptly, plunked down his cup, and strode from the room with his apple.

He headed for the lobby. He couldn't stand the idea of being alone in his room any more than he wanted to be around the crazy people in the dining room, so he decided to watch the canaries. He settled into one of the rich brocade armchairs and nibbled his apple.

He thought of Gillian, with her sparkling blue eyes and golden hair. *Now there's someone who could call me "Sugar,"* he thought. *Though she would ne'er embarrass a man that way.* He thought of how she'd looked when he had whispered his love in her ear. The scent of her hair. The sweet softness of her lips when he kissed her, though all too briefly. *She's got old and died by now, I suppose. Without me.* His heart felt like a lead weight in his chest.

He thought of Mum and her dimpled cheeks. The way she looked at him, as though her grand opinions of him were always being proven right. *I wonder what happened to her when I left. Where could she have gone with no rent, no money, a month left to heal? Maybe Patrick found a way to save her.*

Patrick. And his daft, freckled face. Pat always knew how to make him laugh. He made the world seem less harsh. He wondered what Pat would think of this place. *Pat would know how to fend off Doris.*

He thought of Pat's comforting squeeze on his shoulder as he stood by him in the soaking rain, while Dad's coffin was lowered into the ground. That freezing day when a piece of his heart was covered in cold earth, leaving a gaping hole. Angus had stood strong for Mum, holding her together as she cried herself to pieces at the cemetery gate.

After the burial, Pat had dogged his steps through the wind and rain, all the way to the beach—to his thinking place, where the tide of anguish poured from him and it was Pat's turn to hold him up. *He'll be gone too, of course. I wonder… who was there for him, when he was lowered into the ground?* A tear trickled down his wrinkled cheek.

Chapter 10

Vancouver, WA ~ Present Day

Iris approached the lobby, pushing a small cart loaded with cleaning supplies, newspapers, and bird food. Her mind was full of Angus. She walked mechanically, her mind replaying pictures of everything she'd just read... Angus jumping with fright at normal, everyday lights and sounds... backing out of the chapel... lying on the stones just outside, near death... She had thought that reading his file would clear up several of her questions about him, but it had only created a hundred more. She couldn't even decide what to ask him when she visited him later. Where to begin?

"You're late, Maggie!" called a gruff voice off to her right. A man with puffy, cloud-white hair beckoned her from a wheelchair in the open doorway of his room. Iris remembered the advice of Nurse Kathy yesterday: *Don't correct them, just help them around it.*

"Oh dear, am I late?" Iris answered sweetly.

"Come here, and don't take that tone with me," the man snapped.

Iris approached.

"Is that what you're wearing?"

"No, I'm going to change first," Iris went along.

"Make sure you do. And don't wear that sleazy thing you wore to the Christmas party. You'll be respectable or you'll stay home! Do you hear me?"

He must think I'm his daughter.

"Absolutely," she said, trying to keep a straight face.

The man crooked his finger at her, so she bent closer. In a flash, his hand shot out and grabbed a handful of her hair and yanked her head sideways. She heard her neck crack. In one second, Iris went from mild amusement to panicked horror.

With her hair in a vice grip, the man yanked her close enough to feel his breath on her face.

"You have too much makeup on. Everybody already knows what a floozy you are. You tryin' to get the other guys to look at you? Huh?"

"N-no," Iris whimpered. She tried to pry his hand loose, but he held his grip.

"No wife of mine is going around dressed like a whore, so get your worthless self upstairs…" he yanked again, and Iris yelped in pain, "and get decent before I have to tell everyone that you're… indisposed." He gave her hair one last yank for good measure, and then shoved her head away with his knuckles and released her, chuckling to himself.

Iris grabbed the supply cart and all but ran the rest of the way to the lobby. Her hands trembled and tears pricked her eyes. She pushed the cart up to the enormous bird cage and shakily began to pull on her rubber gloves, when she heard a man's voice behind her.

"Hello again, Iris."

Startled, she whirled around. Angus sat cross-legged only a few feet behind her, holding a half-eaten apple.

"Angus! I'm sorry I didn't see you there! The back of the chair's so tall, I just walked right past…" Her voice was higher pitched than normal. "How are you this morning?"

"You're back to soundin' like a Canadian, I see," he said with the same tone one uses when commenting on the weather. He took another bite of his apple.

"Och, I'm sorry. I'll switch back to Sco'ish faster next time I see you," she said, trying to sound lighthearted and failing.

"You shouldnae switch at all," he said glumly. "Tis a daft and confusin' thing to do."

Iris felt defensiveness rise up inside her, mingled with the fright she still felt after her encounter. She stood planted to the spot, clutching her gloves and trying to remind herself that she was surrounded by people whose minds were muddled. *It would be silly to take it personally.*

Angus took in her strange expression and raised an eyebrow. "Y'arright there? You've gone white as a sheet."

Iris slumped into the chair next to him and her face crumpled. She did everything she could to hold the tears back, but they came anyway.

Alarmed, Angus instinctively reached for her hand and patted it. "There now! What's got you so upset?"

Iris was so touched by this comforting gesture that she squeezed his hand in return. "I just had a bit of a fright on my way here, is all," she replied.

"Was it the lady in 103?" he asked with grim seriousness. "Cause she's well off 'er heid!"

Iris giggled and sniffed. "No, it was a chap who must've thought very little of his wife, and mistook me for her." She wasn't sure how much she should say, but it felt good to get it off her chest. "He yanked my hair."

Angus's hand tightened on hers and a fierce look flashed in his eyes. "That's… inexcusable! You've got to tell someone!"

"I just did." She smiled.

"I mean someone who ma'ers! That man…"

"Didnae realize what he was sayin,'" Iris interrupted. "He's not well. I'll just… keep back about five feet next time I see him."

"Nobody should treat a lady like that," Angus grumbled.

"Well I'm glad to be here with you, Angus." She squeezed his fingers again. "You've made me feel a lot be'er." She looked down at his rough, wrinkled hands. *Wow, he's got a lot of calluses for someone who doesn't work.* "Hey, how'd you get this scar?" She suspected it was the one mentioned in the doctor's report.

"Gouged it with a chisel," he replied.

"Ouch! What were you doin'?"

"Oh, just a… a woodworking project." He let go of her hand. "And what are you workin' on?"

"I'm just here to look after the canaries," she replied, at last pulling on her gloves and getting started on her task.

"Aye, poor wee things." He shook his head.

"Why poor things?" she asked as she pulled out the food trays.

"I was just sittin' here considerin' how they can ne'er be free," he mused absentmindedly. "They'd do no be'er out in the forest than I would these days."

"I suppose not," she conceded. "But as long as they get to live long, happy lives, I dinnae suppose it ma'ers where."

He grunted. "The difference bein,' of course, that they have their friends and family with 'em."

Iris gazed at the hard expression on his face, and decided to take a risk.

"Where's your family, Angus?"

"Under a mound of earth in St. Cyrus parish cemetery, I imagine," he said dryly.

"So then… why'd you leave Scotland?"

"I told you, it's not that I… left, exactly. I just… ended up here." He was frustrated.

Iris could tell he was dancing around something he didn't want to say. She tried another tack.

"D'ye remember the day you came? The day they took you to hospital?"

"Will I sound like a Jessie if I say it was the most frightening day of my life?"

"Nope. Anybody'd be afraid," Iris assured him. "All right. D'ye remember the day before that?"

"Aye, like I said, I was doin' some woodworkin.'" Angus searched her face for a moment. He started to say more, but stopped himself.

"What then?"

"You willnae believe me."

"Why not?"

"Because. It makes no sense. I cannae believe it myself, except that I have to."

Iris considered his statement while she swapped out the bird dropping coated newspapers in the bottom of the cage for fresh ones.

"Why d'ye have to believe somethin' that makes no sense?" she asked.

"Because it's what my eyes and ears tell me. What else have I got to go on? I might be just a carpenter from a tiny village, but I have my le'ers…"

"What letters?" Iris asked, puzzled by the expression.

"I mean I can read. *And* write. And do sums, too, mind you! And I'm just as sane as you. I know what the calendar says. People round here think my bum's oot the windae, but there's nae a thing wrong wi'me, besides the fact that I've somehow got ridiculously old!"

Iris chuckled. "Well I think you're a great chap. I dinnae mind you bein' old."

"Well, I do. I'm still tryin' to figure out how it happened," he grumbled.

"I'm finished here. Are we still on for a visit before lunch?" Iris asked, pulling off her gloves with a snap.

111

"Aye, makes no difference. I seem to have nowhere else to be, at present."

She squeezed his arm. "Well, good. I'm lookin' forward to it. D'ye fancy doughnuts?"

"Doughnuts?" His eyes lit up. "I had one once, at a church picnic. I love 'em!"

"I happen to know the chef here, and he just might let me sneak a few out of the kitchen for ya!"

Angus's crooked smile was youthful. This was the first time in a month he could recall looking forward to something.

Candace's eyes widened at Iris's face when she returned from the lobby.

"You alright?" she asked.

"Wha... oh," Iris remembered that her coloring of ginger hair and fair skin made it difficult to hide an episode of crying, even fifteen minutes later. "Yeah, I had a little incident on the way to the lobby."

"And?" Candace took a compact out of her desk drawer and handed it to Iris.

"And, it was no big deal. It's just the guy in 124, didn't catch his name, thought I was his wife, Maggie." Iris peeked into the compact mirror and licked her finger to smudge away the stray eyeliner.

"That's Glenn. He's definitely got a grumpy side. What happened, just meanness?"

"Well, I'm not sure it's such a big deal, since he didn't know what he was doing," Iris hedged.

"If it was enough to cause tears, I'd like to determine that for myself."

"Well, he told me I wasn't dressed right for a party, y'know, too much makeup, wrong clothes... and then he grabbed me by the hair and yanked me down. He held me there a while so he could keep threatening me, and then he let go… and laughed at me." Iris could feel hot, angry tears racing back toward the front, so she took a deep breath. "I think he might still have some of my hair in his hand!"

"Okay, wow. My gosh. Well first of all, are you okay? Any bleeding? Is your neck okay?" Candace looked at her closely.

"Yeah, I'm fine. My neck popped pretty loud, but it only hurt a little. I felt a whole lot better when he let go of my hair!"

"I'm glad you told me. When a resident begins to act physically violent, it isn't something we take lightly. We've had Glenn say some pretty nasty things to nurses, and to me, but this is the first time he's laid a hand on anyone. The nurses will need to put a note into his chart to refer him for a psych eval."

"Oh gosh, I don't want anything to happen to him on my account," Iris protested.

"Well, nothing drastic will happen, but we'll need to keep a closer eye on him from now on. You know, as a precaution. He doesn't come out of his room a whole lot, so for now I don't think he's a real danger." Candace smiled reassuringly. "But you don't have to talk to him if you don't feel safe, okay?"

Iris nodded.

"Meanwhile, if you have a chiropractor, get your neck checked out. If anything comes of that, pass the paperwork along to me. Gotta have a paper trail. And guess what?" Candace thumbed through a folder in her desk drawer, whipped out a hideous yellow sheet, and handed it to Iris. "You get to fill out an incident report!" she announced like a game show host.

"Oh goody!" Iris chuckled.

"We have forms for everything, just you wait. It's so much fun!"

"I just have to ask, once and for all… What *is* this color?" Iris asked with distaste.

"'Atomic Canary' I believe is the name of it. It's James's favorite, and he makes the copies around here."

"What would possess anyone to use so much of this color? I saw him making paper airplanes out of it yesterday."

"James is unique. He's on the autism spectrum... he has something called Asperger's Syndrome. He's super smart, super organized, and we love having him around here. But he can sometimes be a bit... awkward. Socially, I mean. And he does get fixated on certain things. I've been hoping to get him hooked on robin's egg blue. The jury's still out, though."

"That actually explains a lot. Thanks for telling me that. People around here are way more complicated than they look!" Iris smiled. "Could I borrow a pen... and your sunglasses?"

"Ah, good idea. I'm going to try that next time!" Candace handed them both to her. "I think probably everyone's more complicated than they look. We're all dealing with some kind of issue, and we all have pasts that have shaped us. Don't get me started on mine. But you wouldn't believe how far James has come in the past five years. He's so high functioning now, you'd never guess how hard Becky had it with him. I still think she could use a spa day, though. James's dad is overseas in Afghanistan."

Iris mulled over this new information. She'd pretty much dismissed the two of them as a weird kid and his grumpy, humorless mother. Now, just having a small clue about what kind of battles they faced made them both seem like warriors.

She'd been wrong about several people already, thinking that the residents here were all sweet little old people living out a cushy retirement, enjoying memories of lives fully lived. In reality, many of their lives were downright frightening. Nothing was as they remembered it. Their families rarely came to visit. They were lonely, and some, like Angus, were utterly alone. They wanted to keep some shred of dignity intact, even as their minds slipped away.

This last conversation with Angus, though… To me, he still seems like a man in his right mind. Am I wrong about him, too?

She got to the part of the form where she had to describe any physical contact that was made. Her scalp tingled in response. *That really did hurt.*

"Tell you one thing, I feel sorry for Maggie," Iris mused, as she scribbled away on the form. "I've never even met the woman, but I feel like I just got a little taste of what her life was like."

"Yeah, it's not a happy picture," Candace said grimly. "According to what I remember from his file, Glenn's wife, Margaret, went missing several years before he came to live at Rookwood. But they never found evidence of foul play."

"Do you think she ran away?" Iris wondered.

"I'm hoping that's all that happened."

"Yikes."

They sat in silence for a few moments as Iris finished the report.

"Well, on that cheerful note," Candace said, "we have twenty minutes until the sing-along. You look like you could use some doughnuts!"

"SO much yes."

"Let's get down there! Can't disappoint Willy!"

"Let me guess—you're the only one who's allowed to call him that?"

"Naturally, so don't you call him that, or else!" Candace teased.

"Oh, I won't. Doesn't mean the same thing where I come from."

Candace laugh-snorted.

The two trudged down the stairs to the kitchen, where they were hit by a wall of chocolatey doughnut fragrance. Will stood at the counter, his sleeves neatly rolled up to the elbow, a look of deep concentration on his face. He was tapping a sifter full of powdered sugar over a tray of golden doughnut rings.

Iris, who had been either distracted or focused on other objectives every other time they'd met, actually took a good look at him for the first time. He was tall, six feet at least. His sandy brown hair was cropped short around the sides and blended into a longer, perfect mess on top, complemented by neat sideburns. *You could ruffle that hair any direction and it'd still look great.* His arms and shoulders showed evidence of years at the gym, while his belly and dimpled cheeks showed slight evidence that he often ate his own delicious cooking. *Not even enough to call overweight, just sort of... a little extra padding. Oh my gosh, Iris, stop checking him out! You do not date coworkers!*

"Iris, hi!" He stopped mid-dusting to greet her with a brilliant smile. "Hey, Candy! How are you guys?"

"How am I ever, when I'm in a room full of doughnuts?" Candace replied. "And what fresh genius is this?" She pointed to a tray full of gooey brown squares.

"Oh yeah, try one!" He carefully put two on paper plates and handed them to Iris and Candace with a huge grin. "It's a new recipe I'm trying out." He cast a look at Iris. "Fudge doughnuts with custard filling."

Iris's jaw dropped. "Fudge doughnuts? You're kidding me! I haven't had a proper fudge doughnut since I was eight! How..." She looked at Will. His face had gone flaming red.

"I uh... well..." he stammered. "I just got to thinking about the pizza crunch you told me about, and I started wondering what other kinds of food inspiration come from Scotland. So I uh... I found a great recipe... and it looked like fun, so I played around with it at home last night, and then came into work and gave it a try. Anyway, I'm rambling..." He went back to dusting the plain doughnuts. "But I hope you like 'em."

"Will, you're amazing!" Iris beamed. "I have to sit down and enjoy this properly." She sat on a stool, lifted the decadent square to her mouth, and took a bite. Her eyes closed involuntarily. *Oh my word. The taste of childhood.*

The room fell silent while she chewed, in a trance of lusciousness. "Och, Lor,' there's nae a thing be'er than that…" she murmured aloud and took a second bite. "That's brah…"

Suddenly, she remembered where she was, and opened one eye to find Candace, Will, and two dishwashers staring at her with amused expressions.

Will looked fit to burst, watching her with his fist resting on his top lip, forbidding laughter from escaping his body, lest it interrupt her near-religious experience.

"It's really good," she giggled.

Will and Candace erupted into laughter.

"My kinda girl," Will said again, returning to his work.

Candace cast a long side-eye at Iris, who blushed and silently shushed her. Candace giggled.

"Willy, these really are amazing," Candace gushed after trying hers. "You're going to kill these people, but it'll be a heck of a way to go!"

"Well actually, since it's a pretty new recipe, I only did the one batch, so I'm not serving them to everybody. Just… uh, you know… staff. Or whatever. You guys can take them upstairs if you want," Will said, trying not to make eye contact.

"Oh, I'd love to take a few for Angus," Iris said eagerly. "I bet he'll remember these, if nothing else!"

"Sure, no problem. Just leave me half a dozen for James. I have a feeling I'll be seeing him pretty soon."

"It's so sweet of you to let him hang out down here with you," said Candace.

"Aw, he's a good kid." Will smiled fondly. "He has absolutely no filter, so you never have to guess what he's thinking. And lately, he's been going on so much about stamp collecting, I feel like I'm practically an expert too. I think I might be getting him interested in cooking. Imagine all that intensity applied to food."

"Wow, you're right, that would be something!" Candace agreed. "He already shows a lot of intensity about eating food, so I guess cooking it is the next logical step."

"Just don't show him any bright yellow spices, or we'll all be in for it," warned Iris.

Will nodded. "Duly noted."

On their way out the kitchen door, they saw James come trotting down the steps toward them.

"Hey, guys!" he greeted them cheerfully. "Oh my gosh, what are those?" He reached out hungrily to the plate of three fudge doughnuts Iris was carrying.

Candace slapped his hand.

"Those are for someone else, goofball," she chided. "Will saved you some."

"Yours are in here, bud!" Will called behind them, without pausing his work.

"Okay, cool! Thanks, bro!" James hollered at Will over their heads, blasting Iris's eardrums. "Iris, I have to know if you're planning on dating Will," he said, switching topics seamlessly, making no attempt at subtlety.

Iris's eyes widened. Candace stifled a snort.

"Uhhh… James, I barely know Will. I've only worked here for two days!"

"Okay, well I just wanted to know. He's my bro, and I think he's probably got a crush on you, because he's been like, obsessively Googling Scotland."

She could hear Will inhale sharply and then make a choking sound in the background.

"I'm pretty sure I probably have a crush on you too," he continued, "so I just wondered who's going to end up dating you. I don't want him to get his feelings hurt if you pick me," he said matter-of-factly.

Iris's mouth fell open. "Well… don't worry about that, okay? I don't date people I work with, so you're both safe."

"Are you sure? I just got my driver's license, so we could go fun places!"

"I'm sure," she smiled.

He tsked and shrugged. "Your loss. All the babes are gonna be wanting a piece of this right here..." He flexed a bicep.

"I know. It's very disappointing," she reassured him.

Iris and Candace made their escape up the stairs before bursting into a fit of uproarious laughter.

Chapter 11

Scotland - 1844

Gillian gazed out the window of the pub. She absent-mindedly scrubbed a table in the same place over and over, while her dad shined glasses behind the bar. The dawn breakfast crowd had trickled out. There wouldn't be much action until the fishing boats docked for the day.

"Lass, I think it's clean," Gordon Mayfield said gently.

She looked up, as if startled to find she wasn't the only one in the room.

He set down his glass and crossed the room to her. "Sweet, you've been completely distracted for a week."

"Where is he, Dad? How could he just disappear?"

"I dinnae ken, my dear. I shudder to think."

Gillian flinched at his words. Tears stung her eyes. *How could a man go into the wood and never come out? Or did he?* She hung her head.

Gordon patted her shoulder, trying to offer comfort where none could be had.

The vision of Angus's face lingered in her mind. The dark brown mop of curls that sometimes fell in front of his eyes. His serious, dark brows that showed deep sincerity and care. His chiseled jaw that developed a 5 o'clock shadow by noon. His strong shoulders, ever broadening under the weight of responsibility. His stormy blue eyes that sparkled when he smiled, saw through to the real her, and loved her with kindness and compassion.

"I love you, Gilly..." The sweet memory of his voice, now a deep baritone, once made her heart fly. Now it caused a throbbing ache in her chest.

"There, you made me say it..."

She crumpled into her father's soft shirt front and wept.

"There now," he said helplessly. "I dinnae ken what to do, Gilly. I'm so sorry."

"I have to go look for him!" she sobbed.

"Y'have," he soothed. "Every single day, you've been trampin' through the wood, and down every road. He's... he's gone, Sweet. There's nothin' we can do."

"He cannae be just... gone! He's... he's my... we'd only just..."

"Come to an understanding?"

She looked up at him through her tears.

He smiled. "I'm not completely daft, you know. That lad's loved you since you were a wee lass, that's plain. And that's an Armstrong for you. They set their course early and ne'er waver from it. I've always known he meant to marry you, if he could ever get the courage to ask."

"Well..." She sniffed. "We'd not got quite *that* far into the discussion." Gillian wiped her eyes on the corner of her apron. "But I dinnae mind tellin' you, Dad..." She looked him in the eyes. "I would've followed him anywhere. And he's not gone. Because if he is,"—she could barely choke out the words—"I'll die an old maid."

Gordon ached for his stubborn daughter, who loved hard and held fast. *Just like her mother, that one.* He had no words left, so he simply held his daughter until she cried herself out.

"I think I just need some fresh air," she said at last.

"Aye, a walk'll do you good." He chucked her under the chin. "And I know the kitchen's well in hand, as always."

"I'll be back before the fishin' boats, arright?" She kissed his cheek, snatched her shawl, and bolted out the door.

The morning air held a damp chill that smelled of the sea. The sun wasn't altogether convinced it was time to be out of bed, wrapped as it was in a thick cloud duvet. Gillian was tempted to pull her shawl around her head to fend off the breeze, but decided instead to shiver a bit. She liked the feel of her hair blowing free, and always had, despite the fact that all the other girls her age had started incarcerating their hair in proper buns, braids, and bonnets long ago. She could never bring herself to do it. No, she would not change. Especially not now.

When Angus comes home, I want him to know it's me runnin' to welcome him.

And he *would* come home. Gillian would never accept that Angus was truly gone—it felt like an act of betrayal. She knew in her soul that he was alive somewhere, and thinking of her.

She turned toward the beach path. As children, she and Angus had played away countless afternoons by the tide pools, competing with each other to see who could run farthest into the little sea cave without getting scared. (Without question, it was Angus. Gillian was afraid there might be bats in there, and he never let her live it down.) Memories of those days were precious to her, especially as she grew older and the rules of social propriety made it difficult to know just how close a friendship she was still allowed to have with Angus.

She settled herself into the sand and listened to the waves, like a vast crowd endlessly applauding. Angus still came to this beach often when he needed to think. She'd seen him several times. He had called out a friendly greeting to her as she passed by.

The last time she'd seen Angus here was different, though. He was sitting in the sand right about where she sat now, deep in thought, his back to her as he faced the sea. He'd had his arms resting on his knees as he turned his face toward the sky. He hadn't heard her approach. She drew as close as she dared, just to be near him. That's when she heard his voice, faintly carried on the wind. He was praying. She'd suddenly felt like an intruder, and slipped quietly away.

But what had sparked in her mind that day was a thought she couldn't shake: Angus was the best human being she'd ever known. If talking to God as his friend was at the core of who he was, even when nobody was watching, then she needed to know this God better. Not just the God at church—the God Angus loved.

Safe from prying eyes, she reached into the deep pocket of her apron and pulled out Angus's wool cap. It had looked so lonely sitting on the workbench the night she and Patrick had gone looking for him. Grabbing it on the way out had been a spur of the moment decision. She had thought to return it to him the next day, when the mystery of his whereabouts had been laughed off as a series of misunderstandings and he was back at the pub for tea. Except he still hadn't come.

She lifted the cap to her face and breathed in the same scent that had surrounded her when he said he loved her. A tear rolled down her cheek and into the wool.

She could sit still no longer. Replacing the cap protectively in her pocket, she meandered down the beach, unsure now why she thought that coming here would help her feel any better. She picked her way among the wet rocks that jutted out of the sand, dodging the spray from the incoming tide, until she came to the entrance of the little sea cave, which was shaped like a crooked witch's hat. It seemed so much smaller to her now. She took five steps into the cave. The deep, organic smell of sea creatures filled the air. She squinted in the dim light above her.

Hmm. Angus was right all along. No bats in here. It was perhaps only another twenty paces to the back of the cave, which wasn't big or mysterious at all. It was just her childhood memories that had made it so. She sighed. Grief rolled over her like a wave, threatening to drown her hope. And now the tide was coming in through the mouth of the cave. Small splashes absorbed into the hem of her skirts.

As she turned to leave, a sudden wave of icy water splashed across the entrance of the cave and threatened to soak her to her ankles. She yelped and tried to back away from the incoming water. Before she could complete the maneuver, the heel of her boot caught in a heavy, wet fold of her dress, causing her to lurch backward. Unable to free her foot in time to right her balance, she crashed into the wall of the cave. Sharp pain told her she'd slashed her hand open on a barnacle, but worse than that was the heavy, jarring impact of the back of her head against the jagged rocks. She fought against the blackness that threatened to envelop her as her cheek landed on the cold sand of the cave's floor. Sea water hit her face with a sharp sting as darkness overwhelmed her.

Vancouver, WA ~ Present Day

Iris and Candace were still chuckling over their conversation with James when they reached the Activity Room to set up the sing along.

"James really doesn't hold back, does he?" Iris giggled.

"He's a real straight talker," Candace agreed. "I actually love it. It's refreshing! He can say in five minutes what it takes most people days to say."

She began to shove the tables against the walls and arrange the chairs in a loose circle, leaving plenty of gaps for wheelchairs. Iris searched the supply closet for tambourines and jingle bells.

"So, Candace…" Iris called from inside the closet. "I thought the singing activities happened in the chapel."

"Oh, well some do," she called back with a grunt as she shoved a table. "The hymn sing happens there, because people expect it to. We get along much better around here if we stick to expectations. Fun singing happens in here, hence…"—another grunt—"…a second piano."

Iris could hear chair legs scraping across the floor.

"What we're doing today is more of a sensory exercise," Candace continued. "It's not religious, it's just a way to help some of our lower functioning residents maintain their coordination."

Iris popped her head out of the closet. "I don't see any tambourines."

Candace frowned. "Look in the back, on the left side, bottom shelf. Is there a bin labeled 'LUAU'?" Iris ducked back into the closet.

"Yeah!" she called back.

"The tambourines are in there. I keep forgetting to label that thing correctly."

Iris grabbed the plastic bin and a bottle of bubbles. She couldn't resist.

"So if we aren't singing hymns, what are we singing? Beyoncé songs?"

"Funny!" Candace smirked. "No, just good old songs that most of these people know. 'Bicycle Built for Two,' 'Don't Sit Under the Apple Tree with Anyone Else But Me,' 'Tea for Two,' 'Five Foot Two, Eyes of Blue,' 'When I Fall In Love,' stuff like that."

"I don't know a single one of those," Iris worried. "Not sure how much help I'll be."

"You'll catch on fast. Just sing loudly so they can hear you, which will be a trick once they all have tambourines. And if

125

anybody wants to switch to jingle bells or sticks, make sure you have their back. And don't worry, our volunteer pianist will be doing most of the leading, so just make up words if you don't know the songs. It won't make the slightest difference, I promise."

"I think I can manage that," Iris giggled. She helped Candace finish arranging chairs. "Does Angus ever come to the sing alongs?" she wondered.

"No. Like you, he doesn't know any of the songs. He doesn't seem to know much about America at all, for someone who came here in his twenties."

"I told him I'd go see him again today. Thought I'd take him some doughnuts."

"I'm all for it!" Candace agreed. "Anything to help him gain back some real memories or at least come out of his shell."

"Yeah. He just seems so sad. The two main things he's said to me is that he doesn't know what happened to his family, and he doesn't know how he got so old."

"Him and me both, about the oldness thing," Candace muttered.

"I just wish I could get some answers for him about his family."

"Well, maybe you can," she encouraged. "You're free to use the computer if you hear of anything worth doing a search on."

"Well actually, he did give me a couple of names the first time I visited him... his mother, and another person. A friend, maybe?"

"Seriously? That's new. Yeah, definitely look those up!" She looked at her watch.

"Let me guess..." said Iris. "Taxi time?"

"You got it. But today it's a little different. We'll gather the normal crowd, but first we'll go get some special guests."

Iris was intrigued as she followed Candace up the corridor to the northeast section of the building. Here there was a block of four resident rooms, and a large gym at the corner

126

of the building. Beyond the gym lay another short corridor with three rooms on each side.

"Welcome to the Physical Therapy Wing," Candace announced. "Down that far hall are the rooms for our short-term residents who only stay for a few weeks or months. They're here to do PT recovery, like after a fall or a hip replacement, that kind of thing. We have four right now. They don't often hang out with us because they're not here long enough to get attached. It's a bummer, really, because they're among the few people in this building who aren't out to lunch."

Iris smiled incredulously.

"And you know I mean that in the most loving way possible!" Candace laughed. "But here, just outside the PT wing, are the special guests I was talking about. We aren't a hundred percent sure how 'with it' they are, but we take extra special care of them so they feel as loved and connected as possible."

She knocked on the first door, which was ajar, and called out. "Hey, Dahlia!" Without waiting for an answer, she strode into the room. "Hi, Kathy!"

"Hi guys!" said Nurse Kathy, whom Iris recognized from yesterday. She was adjusting an oxygen tank on the back of a large black wheelchair. "I was just getting Dahlia ready to roll. Just gotta take her blood pressure and then she's free to go. Want to go sing some songs, Dahlia?"

Iris couldn't see Dahlia, who was facing the window, but she noticed right away that she flailed one skinny arm out to the side and patted herself on the head in a repetitive motion.

"Oh, she's into it!" Candace smiled and patted Dahlia's quiet arm. "Dahlia, this is Iris. She's new here, but she's almost as cool as I am!" Candace motioned to Iris to come over.

Iris joined them, and seeing Dahlia's face, gasped in shock. Quickly stifling her reaction, she smiled. "Hi, Dahlia! Nice to meet you. I think it's brilliant that we both have flower names!"

Dahlia blinked uncontrollably and grunted.

"Okay, girl, you go have fun now," Kathy said, gently tearing the velcro cuff from Dahlia's arm. "See you guys later."

"Thanks, Kathy," Candace replied as she wheeled Dahlia into the hallway. "Iris, will you stay here with Dahlia for a sec while I get Jim? He's just next door."

"Sure," Iris said cheerfully, but bit her lip. She wracked her brain for a conversation starter. "I just started working here…" she began lamely.

Dahlia never stopped moving. She reached one hand out over and over, grasping at something that wasn't there.

"You'll have to be patient with me because I don't know any of the songs," Iris continued. "Promise you won't laugh!" she chuckled, trying to sound lighthearted. *Oh my gosh, shut up, Iris. You don't have to fill every silence with endless chin wagging.*

"Ready?" Candace joined her, pushing Jim in a tall wheelchair. His chest and head were strapped in with padded seat belts. He had a breathing tube in his neck, and wore a terry cloth bib.

"Yep, let's roll!" said Iris, pushing Dahlia's wheelchair.

"You hear that, Jim? Iris is punny," Candace chatted casually. "You know Iris, Jim used to be a drummer in a rock band in the sixties, so he loves coming to these things."

"Is that so?" Iris joined, grateful for the ease that Candace's presence brought.

"What band was it, Jim? The Beatles?" Candace teased.

Jim made a sound that was a cross between a laugh and a grunt.

"No, I know. They were hacks. Your band was the real deal."

Another grunt.

When they reached the Activity Room, they saw that the pianist, a rather short man with dark rimmed glasses and a goofy smile, was already there organizing his music.

"Hey Jonathan, how's it going?" Candace greeted him.

"Awesome, thanks! Ready to party, as always." Jonathan stuck out his tongue in concentration as he continued to shuffle his pages on the piano.

First Irene and Lois had arrived and found seats early, as usual. Candace and Iris parked Jim and Dahlia in the circle and headed back to pick up more people.

"You seemed surprised when you met Dahlia," Candace said with a knowing smile.

"I guess I was, yeah! She's so... young! What's she doing here with all the old people?"

"Yeah, she's only forty-three. She's here because of Huntington's Disease. She's a friend of mine, actually. We worked here together fifteen years ago, when her symptoms were just starting. Our families used to hang out when our husbands were still alive."

Iris glanced up sharply at Candace. Candace's face sagged a bit as she watched a faraway memory.

"You lost... you *both* lost your husbands?"

"Yeah. Like Becky, Dahlia and I are military wives. Her guy was killed in action twelve years ago."

"Gosh, that's... awful."

"It's definitely not the phone call anybody wants to get," Candace said grimly. "It wasn't too much afterward that she had to quit nursing, because her hands shook too much, and her moods were starting to be unpredictable. She was afraid she'd make a mistake and hurt someone. Huntington's is pretty brutal."

"Is it kind of like Alzheimer's, where it sort of... eats away at your brain?" Iris asked, immediately regretting how macabre her words sounded. "Sorry, I don't know how else to say that..."

"Oh it's okay, I get what you're saying. Uhh well, there are similarities, I guess. They can both cause dementia. But Huntington's is genetic, and it hits people much younger. It makes you unable to control your body. Dahlia knew she would lose her ability to function, so when her husband died, she put a directive in place to come live here, while her kids would go to their aunt's. They kept her at home as long as they could, but she really does need full time care nowadays. She could injure herself or choke pretty easily if people don't keep an eye on her. Her kids come to visit whenever they can, but it's getting hard for them to see her like this."

"Wow. First the kids lose their dad, and now their mom is so ill. I can't imagine that," Iris said.

"Life is never easy. But we muddle through as best we can."

"K.B.O." Iris nodded.

"K.B.O.?"

"That's Winston Churchill," Iris explained. "Keep Buggering On."

"A profound philosopher, that Winston."

"I'm... really sorry about your husband, too," Iris said quietly.

"Thanks. It's been ten years, and I still miss him every day." Candace's eyes moistened.

"You just seem so... colorful and cheerful. I would have never guessed you were in pain."

"You're learning," Candace said with a rueful smile. "You can never really tell about people. But I've always been colorful and crazy. That's what Jack loved about me. I can't stop being who I am, just because my heart is broken. He wouldn't want me to. Besides," she sniffed and straightened her shoulders, "it's not moping and wearing drab colors that fixes grief, anyway. It's getting up, getting out of the house, helping others... and baked goods. Let's not forget those."

"I really am learning a lot," Iris agreed.

Candace was right about the sing along. Once the jingle bells, sticks, and tambourines were distributed, it hardly mattered what the lyrics were. Jonathan played loudly, singing out in a surprisingly operatic baritone. Iris sang as loudly as she could, the participants banged loudly, and everyone shouted more loudly between songs while their hearing aids whistled. Iris even blew bubbles for everyone during the song "I'm Forever Blowing Bubbles," while Second Irene hummed and did interpretive dance.

"You really have the touch!" Candace beamed at her, once everyone had left. They worked together to move the chairs and tables back to their rightful places.

"Really?" Iris asked doubtfully, remembering her awkwardness around Dahlia.

"Yes! My gosh, when you started blowing bubbles? I've never seen Irene get into it like that. It was several kinds of fabulous!"

"Well thanks!" Iris grinned. "Bubbles have the same effect on me."

"That, I'd like to see."

"Ha. Nah, I don't really do crazy stuff where people can see me."

"Why ever not?" Candace put one hand on her hip.

"I… I dunno…" Iris stammered. "I never thought about it. I guess maybe I don't like attention?"

"You change your accent, you hide your bubble obsession… what else are you keeping from humanity, girl?" Candace spoke with a stern, motherly tone. "It wouldn't be the end of the world if people found out you were interesting. I could use the company!"

Iris laughed. "You sound like Angus. He thinks switching accents is 'daft.'"

"He could be onto something."

"I'll try to work on it, okay?" Iris promised. "Do I have time to go see Angus right now?"

"Yep, nothing on the skedge until one o'clock. Go, visit, take your lunch break. Have fun." Candace shooed her out the door. "Get your rear end back to the office by 12:15, 'kay?"

"Can do!" Iris gave her a double thumbs-up as she walked away backwards. She realized as she retrieved the plate of fudge doughnuts from the office that, in her haste to get here early this morning, she'd forgotten her lunch in the fridge at home. She checked her phone. *Let's see, 10:15… Charlie's probably still home.*

She sent her roommate a quick text:

Forgot lunch. Eat it for me? Kthx.

No point in a perfectly good salad just sitting there getting funky all day. Charlie needs to eat more vegetables anyway.

Her phone chirped with Charlie's reply.

Are you trying to feed me vegetables again?

Iris giggled.

She considered the three fudge doughnuts on the plate for Angus. *Eh, he'll be thrilled with two.* She claimed one and took a bite, just as she heard a knock at the door behind her. She spun around with the doughnut still suspended between her teeth. Will stood in the doorway with a lopsided grin.

"Will!" she said around the doughnut. "I was just… hello! Uhh…" She put the doughnut back on the plate as color rose in her cheeks. "What's up?"

"Glad to see you still enjoying those," he chuckled. "Listen, I just, uh… wrapped up breakfast. Gotta go do prep for a bit. But in about an hour I'll have a little break before I have to start lunch service. This is probably going to sound stupid… but I noticed when you came in this morning you weren't, y'know, I mean you didn't… have… any uh, lunch-type items with you. It seems like you didn't bring any lunch. Did you? Bring any? Lunch?" His face was adorably pink.

"Uh, no actually. Wow, good eye! Nope, I made a salad, but I accidentally left it at home. I told Charlie to eat it... why?"

"Charlie? Oh, is that your..."

"No! Well, yes. I mean, no. Well, she's my roommate."

"She?"

"Charlotte. Charlie. She doesn't really look like a Charlotte. She has blue hair... why are you wanting to know about lunch again?"

"Blue hair, huh? Well, I just wanted to mention that if you need something later, just let me know. Something to eat, I mean. Lunch wise. I usually make myself lunch in the kitchen and it's pretty easy to make... y'know, two of... whatever. There's plenty."

"Thanks, Will, that sounds great. I'd really appreciate it."

"Awesome. Is there anything you don't like?"

"Celery. Literally the worst vegetable ever."

"Okay, I will never use, or mention celery in your presence." His eyes twinkled. "Well, okay, I guess I'll just... I gotta get back... See you... later, then?"

"Yes! Absolutely. I just need to visit somebody and then I'll be down."

"Oh, is it Angus? That guy you mentioned? Whose doughnut you were just eating?" He grinned mischievously.

"Ugh, you caught me! Yes, that's the guy. I still think two doughnuts is a respectable offering. What do you think?"

"I think what he doesn't know won't hurt him." He winked, and turned toward the hallway. "See you later."

"Uh-huh," Iris nodded absentmindedly.

Several seconds passed before she realized she was still staring at the empty doorway. She shook herself. *He's really nice. A nice... friend... person. That's all.*

She reached across Candace's desk and thumbed through the outbox until she found her half-completed visit questionnaire from yesterday. There at the bottom were the two names she'd jotted down. *Marjorie Armstrong and Gillian Mayfield.* She sat in Candace's chair and swiveled to face the computer.

"Alright, ladies," Iris murmured as she clicked to open a browser. "Let's see if I can find you…" She still had an active account on the Scotland's People website from when she was doing research on a college project for her history major. She pulled up the census returns. *Hmmm… I'm guessing Angus was born in the twenties or thirties, so Marjorie, you'd have been listed sometime around then…* She clicked and scrolled through several pages of census data, coming up empty each time. The census was recorded every ten years, but there was no Marjorie or Angus Armstrong living in St. Cyrus anytime between 1901 and 1951. Iris frowned. *That can't be right. If he's between 85 and 90 now, he had to be there then. Is he confused? Is he… lying?*

Taking a different approach, she clicked on "Church Registers." *Angus is religious, maybe he was christened…* This time, instead of searching by year, she searched by parish and name. There he was. Angus John Armstrong. Father: John Armstrong, master joiner/carpenter; mother: Marjorie Armstrong. Christened in St. Cyrus parish church on 23 July… 1820? Surely this was an ancestor of his… a namesake, perhaps? She knew it wasn't a typo, because she was looking at a digital scan of the registry, written in flowing script. All the other dates on the page fell in order. A few marriages, two deaths. One other baby boy was christened that summer, a Patrick Andrew Dawson. *Hmmmm.* She printed the page.

Then she clicked back to the search box and typed in "Gillian Mayfield." There were two records for a Gillian Fiona Mayfield. The first was a christening in October of 1822. There was a father, Gordon Mayfield, listed, but the mother was listed as deceased in childbirth. Her burial record was a few entries higher. The other mention of Gillian was a burial in 1844. No married name listed. She hit "Print" and tapped her fingers on the desk. "Wow, only twenty-two when she died," Iris murmured to herself. "My age."

Hmmm. Mayfield. Mayfield… why does that name sound familiar? She clicked into a fresh search bar in her browser and typed in "Mayfield St Cyrus." The first few hits had to do with real estate. *Mayfield Road! That's right! I sort of remember a Mayfield Road.* Several entries down, there was a link to a blog post about local St. Cyrus lore. She clicked. The banner photo was of her beloved beach. The article covered a few legends she'd already heard, such as the cannibal who ate the sheriff, the Eskimo's curse, and the blind piper. She scrolled to the bottom of the page, where the word "Mayfield" grabbed her attention.

She read aloud: "The sea cave is the site of another tragic death. Not only the blind piper, whose ghostly music can still be heard today, but the local pub owner's daughter who died in the cave, some say of a broken heart, whilst grieving for her lost love. Mayfield Road is named in her memory." She printed this page as well, circled the paragraph at the bottom, and tucked the papers into her back pocket. *Okay, Angus, your story checks out about a hundred years too early. What is going on with you? Did you research your ancestors and then forget who you are?*

Chapter 12

Ré MacCrann sipped his mug of oversteeped tea and considered the burlap sack in the corner of his cottage. His eyes drooped from the late night he'd spent with Éamon on the estate, combing the ground by lantern light to gather up every last leaf, twig, and scrap of bark left behind by the missing carpenter. Because they needed to wait until the strange hum coming from the Great Hawthorn had become less pronounced, Éamon suggested that they investigate the outbuilding workshop first. It was the only logical place for one of Grant's carpenters to go. Once the search party went into the woods, they were able to slip into the building unseen. It was a good thing they had.

Inside, the floor and workbench were strewn with scraps of the Great Hawthorn. A magnificent finished piece of carving also sat amidst the carnage, but they worked around it carefully, doing their best not to disturb it. Clad in long leather gloves as a precaution, they had placed the larger scraps into the burlap bag they'd brought with them. No Guardian knew for certain what would happen to a person who came into contact with the sap—although, if the missing man was any indication, caution was warranted. After sweeping the smaller chips and sawdust into a pile, Éamon had found a jar on the bench with just a thin layer of dried shellac in the bottom. He appropriated it as a vessel for the wood chips. Once the glass lid was found and screwed into place with its metal band, Ré had tucked it safely away in his overcoat pocket.

Working together, Ré and Éamon had finished sweeping the workshop in under ten minutes. Then they'd made haste into the wood, intent on keeping the search party at a distance from the Tree. By taking the most direct route, they had reached the oak grove surrounding the Great Hawthorn well before the distant lanterns glinted through the trees. There, they waited. Only when the feel of the air had returned to normal did they approach the Tree and gather the rest of the scraps from the forest floor.

What to do with all of this?

He considered burning the pieces. That would prevent anyone else from coming into contact with them. But at the same time, the very idea horrified him. Destroying any part of a Great Tree, even a part as seemingly insignificant as a twig, went against everything he'd been taught. Every bit of knowledge handed down by the Guardians before him, every tradition, was intent on preserving the Trees.

Something went wrong when this branch was cut, he mused. *Perhaps someday it'll be needed.*

Ré plunked down his mug decisively, sloshing tea onto the table. He rose shakily and shuffled to the corner of the cottage where his old steamer trunk sat. He heaved the lid open. There sat a pile of delicate, neatly folded clothes. Two dresses, one made of sturdy blue linen and trimmed with hand tatted lace. Some kerchiefs. A threadbare striped apron. Petite wool socks. Odds and ends. Ré pressed his rough, wrinkled hand into the fabric of the dresses, reveling in their softness, as the familiar scent wafted toward him and pierced his heart.

He hadn't seen these treasures in a decade. Not since... Well, she wouldn't miss them now. His eyes grew moist. There was no safer place than this trunk, and it was needed. It was time to do what he must.

He lifted the contents of the trunk carefully onto the bed in a neat pile, putting aside just one of the dresses—the one with the lace trim—in a drawer amongst his clean shirts for safekeeping. Just one memory of her. He tied the corners of his blanket around the pile to form a bundle. Then he placed the burlap sack full of branches, leaves, and twigs into the trunk, along with the jar from his pocket. He closed the lid and locked it.

Next, he sat at the table, opened his diary, and dipped his quill. For the next hour, he wrote out everything he could remember about the previous day's events. He blotted the page and sat back in his chair.

There. Perhaps one day, Éamon will find that missing man and set this to rights.

He put on his boots and hat, and gathered up his bundle of memories. It was high time that his granddaughters were given the chance to enjoy these things.

And... it was high time that Ecclesgrieg had a new gamekeeper.

Caledon, perched on the roof, looked on with approval. His heart swelled with warmth. The human had shown himself to be a true Guardian after all.

Vancouver, WA ~ Present Day

Doughnuts in hand, Iris got her accent in place and knocked at room 105.

"It's open!" called Angus's muffled voice.

She walked in to find Angus sitting cross-legged on the floor in front of a small sofa, resting his elbows on the oval coffee table and spinning a coin by repeatedly flicking it with his finger. Iris chuckled to herself. Candace had warned her that if she ever found someone on the floor, to call a nurse to help lift them. *Looks like he's just fine.*

"Hello, Angus! I brought doughnuts!"

His eyes lit up. "Bless you a thousand times," he grinned. "I missed breakfast, you see." He clambered onto the sofa, beckoning her over. The coin was still a spinning blur.

"Why no breakfast?" Iris wondered as she set the doughnuts on the coffee table, careful to leave plenty of room for the coin to travel.

"D'ye know a lady round here called Doris?"

"Ohhh…" Iris recalled Doris's flirty attentions to Walter and Fred during BINGO. "Does she fancy you today?"

"Aye, she called me 'Sugar' and asked me to meet her for coffee… whilst I was tryin' to have my coffee! She's well off 'er heid too. Practically everybody here is."

"That's rough," Iris giggled. "Luckily, she'll have forgotten you by now, so no need to worry."

The fat gold coin wobbled loudly and finally came to rest on the table. Angus took a doughnut and sank his teeth in.

"Och, there's custard in it! How fancy!" he admired as he chewed.

"Have you ne'er had a fudge doughnut? I thought everyone in Scotland had, or at least knew of 'em."

"Nae, it's a first for me, but it's ruinin' every other doughnut forever!"

"They are definitely my favorite too," said Iris. "That's a lovely coin you were spinnin' there. Is it antique?"

"Aye, it's been in my family near three hundred…" he hesitated, and seemed to be calculating what to say. "For centuries. Long time. Since it was issued, actually."

"May I?" Iris motioned.

"Aye, of course," Angus nodded, scraping icing from the top of his doughnut and licking it off his finger.

Iris picked up the coin, which felt heavy in her hand. It had to be real gold. It wasn't like a costume prop. Its edges formed an imperfect circle, and it was lightly worn from handling. There was a bust of a young girl facing left, her hair pulled back severely in a curled up-do. Around her were the words "MARIA DEI · G · SCOTOR · REGINA." *Mary, Queen of Scots?* Iris turned the coin to see a crowned coat of arms bearing a faded rearing lion, surrounded by the words "IVSTVS · FIDE · VIVIT · 1555." Iris scrunched her face, trying to recall the Latin she'd stopped learning after age eight. *The just… faith… live. The just live by faith?*

She considered the date and how Angus had just stopped himself from saying something. *Was he about to say three hundred? As in… years? But that's what, mid-1800s? Does he really think he's from another century, like Candace said?*

"It's a beautiful coin, Angus. It's amazin' to me that you've had somethin' in your family that long!"

"Aye. Great-great…" he ticked off the "greats" on his fingers, "great-great-great-great granddad Christopher tucked it away for a rainy day, and we've managed to keep it tucked e'er since. That is, until I came along," he said with a pained expression.

"What's that mean, 'till you came along'? You've still got it!" She handed it back.

"I wasnae goin' to have it much longer," he confessed, turning the coin over and over in his hand. "I put 'er in my pocket because I was headed to the pawnbroker's after work. I needed rent money, see."

"I know what that's like," Iris empathized. "Findin' work here at Rookwood is the only reason I'll make it this month. Got this job in the nick of time."

"Same happened to me!" He smiled at the coincidence. "My best mate Patrick found me some woodworkin' on the Ecclesgrieg estate where the new castle was goin' up."

"I visited that place once!" Iris beamed. "Sad to see it so broken down that they dinnae let anyone inside."

"What? Broken down?" Angus's jaw dropped. "We'd barely started on it!"

"Angus, I'm sorry, but I have to ask…" Iris began.

He held up his hand. "I know. You've figured it out—I'm off my heid like all the rest. Nothin' I say makes any sense."

"Well… it does make a *kind* of sense… in a way. But I wanted to ask if you ever… studied history. Like are you a historian? Is that what you did when you came to America?"

"Studied history?" he asked dubiously. He showed her his scarred, calloused hands. "Do these look like the hands of a learned professor to you?"

"Not really," she admitted. "But I was a history major, so…"

He looked at her quizzically.

"I mean I hope to be a historian someday. It's what I studied at university."

"You? Went to university?" He raised his wiry eyebrows. "But… you're a woman!"

"What, women cannae succeed at university?" she retorted.

"I'm sure they could," he replied. "Gillian was my equal, if not my be'er, when we were in school together. But I didnae think the universities were admittin' women, is all."

"In America, they've been doin' it since the 1840s."

"Well, I dinnae keep up much with current events."

Iris studied his face for any sign of joking. Finding none, she continued.

141

"Well anyway, as a history enthusiast, sometimes I get wrapped up in the stories of the people I study. I find myself wonderin' what it was like to *be* them… to live their lives. Look here…" She produced the pages she'd printed, and showed him the first one. "I found these names in the St. Cyrus parish register."

"There I am!" Angus cried. "And my parents. Hey look, there's Pat's name, too!"

"Well…" Iris hedged. "I thought perhaps you'd been doing some research, too. Maybe these are your ancestors? Maybe this is your namesake, and you just might've lost track of…" she trailed off.

His expression had hardened.

"Angus, I'm sorry. I'm not tryin' to frustrate you, I just want to help."

"Everybody's got a theory about what's got Angus Armstrong's heid in a jumble," he growled. "Everybody's got an explanation. He's an actor. He's a daft historian. He's a liar. He's got 'skits of friendlia.' Whatever those are. Let's give 'im a talkin' to, by a carousel of doctors! Let's give 'im pills! Well I'm not ashamed to say, I've swallowed nae a one. Those pills get flushed down the water closet when the nurse leaves, cause there's nae a thing wrong wi' my heid! You know what nobody's really got an explanation for? The truth!" He folded his arms across his chest and stared her down.

She matched the intensity of his gaze. "I *want* the truth! I've been tryin' to figure you out since we met!"

"But you're not hearin' me! Yer just like the rest of them because you start by assumin' I'm doo-lally, and go from there!"

"I've never once assumed anythin' about you, Angus! You strike me as a chap who's not the least bit confused. But you said it yourself, remember? The things you're sayin' seem impossible, even to you!"

"I know, I know…" He shook his head and buried his face in his hands. They sat in tense silence for a few moments.

Iris took a deep breath. "I'm goin' to propose we try somethin.'" She touched his shoulder.

He looked at her with a mixture of curiosity and dread.

"What d'ye say we both forget what year it's supposed to be? Let's forget the logic part of things. You just tell me what you know, no matter how daft it sounds, and let's see where we end up, arright?"

"Arright..." he began tentatively. "Well, what d'ye want to know?"

"Let's start with somethin' easy," Iris began confidently. "How old are you?"

"I'm..." he gave an exasperated grunt. "This isnae gonna work. Everythin' I say's goin' to sound daft!"

"No logic allowed, remember?" Iris said gently. "Just what you know."

"Fine then, you asked for it. I'm twenty-four years of age."

Iris did not flinch. "And what year were you born?"

"I was born in 1820."

"That makes it 1844 this year," she commented without emotion.

"Aye, last I checked."

"What's your dad's name?"

"John Armstrong."

Okay, so far he hasn't made a single mistake.

"So you live in St. Cyrus, it's 1844, and you've got a job doin' woodworking at the Ecclesgrieg estate?" Iris confirmed.

"Sounds really odd to hear somebody say it like it's in the present, but... yes."

"What do you remember about your last day in Scotland?"

"It was my second day on the job. Mr. Grant had ordered two pieces from me. One mahogany rockin' chair, and one heart shaped mirror frame, fancy as I could manage. I started the chair my first day, and whilst I was waitin' for some pieces to dry, I decided to start the frame on the second day. I couldnae find much in the lumber stacks, so I asked permission to look about the forest for some suitable green wood. I came across a tree that was such a rare beauty, I knew it'd be perfect. But it was sort of..." Angus had a pained expression. "This is gonna sound ridiculous!"

"It's arright, keep going," Iris encouraged him.

"The tree was... humming." He looked at her anxiously.

Iris's efforts to keep her face neutral were failing her.

"I told you! I sound like a lunatic!"

"What did the humming sound like?" she pressed.

"Actually..." He pointed to the light fixture above their heads. They both remained silent until Iris became aware that one of the light bulbs was buzzing slightly. "It sounded a bit like that. But also kind of like singing."

"The tree sounded like singing... and electricity?"

"Eeeelec...tricity, aye. What that's doin,' up there. But quiet. I thought the sound was inside my own ears, so I ignored it. Somethin' told me I ought to leave that tree alone, but I took a branch anyway, and took it back to the workshop. That's when things got strange."

"Stranger than a humming tree?"

"Aye, far stranger. Y'know, the older generations of our folk would say I was kidnapped by fairies or some such, for hurtin' a fairy-thorn tree. Well, I dinnae believe in fairies. But I do believe at some point I wasnae in the real world anymore."

"Where did you go?"

"Well, I was in the workshop, like I said. But I went in there just afore noon, and I became like a madman, workin' away at that mirror frame like... it was like I had no concept of time. I felt neither hungry nor tired. At one point I cut myself..." He held up his scar. "But I just kept goin.' I dinnae ken how long I was actually there. I just know that under normal circumstances, after I've worked all day, it gets dark out."

"It didnae get dark?"

"The sun was still high, though I had worked a ridiculously long time. I finished the entire project!"

Iris frowned. "Is it possible you worked all night and into another day?"

"No, because I never lost the light. I never lit a lantern."

"How long was this project of yours meant to take?"

"I was goin' to give it two to three weeks. Conservatively."

"Two to three weeks?" Iris gasped. "You got through all that work… all at once? Did you work faster than normal?"

"I worked at my regular pace," Angus answered with a puzzled expression. "You cannae rush wood curin', anyhow. It dries when it's good and ready. That's why projects take weeks, not hours. You cannae sand and shellac green wood. It's too wet. But this was arright to sand almost as soon as I'd finished carvin' it, like time was passin' all wrong. Slow for me, fast for the wood." He rubbed his forehead, as if remembering was causing him pain. "It was all just so… unreal. And it got wicked hot in the workshop, though the day was cloudy. The strangest part was how unaware of it all I was, until the end."

"What happened then?" Iris was transfixed.

"I came over all trembly. It's the most exhausted I've ever felt in my life. I fell over just tryin' to get to the door. I tried to call out for somebody, but I could barely breathe. I started shiverin.' I did manage to pull my coat on a little bit…" He pointed to a brown overcoat hanging on a hook on the back of the door. "Then I blacked out."

Iris sat frozen with her hand over her heart and her mouth hanging open. Angus reached for the second doughnut.

"And?" she breathed.

He shrugged. "I woke up just outside, well cold. I think they said I was dyin' of hype and hernia."

"Probably hypothermia," she giggled.

"Fancy word for cold, far as I can tell," Angus said, licking one finger. "But somehow, between blackin' out and wakin' up, my body'd put on about sixty years. I'm no learned professor, like I said, but even I know that a person cannae sleep for sixty years with no food. So, good sense tells me that somethin' did this to me quick. I keep comin' back to the humming tree. I dinnae ken why it brought us here…"

"Us?" Iris asked.

"Us… me and the mirror. The mirror frame came with me, see. Maybe the tree banished us somehow."

"The mirror is here? Do you mean the one hangin' in the chapel?"

"Aye, the very same. I dinnae believe in things bein' cursed, but this sure feels like a curse to me."

Iris was trying her best to wrap her mind around what he was saying.

"Are you positive it's the same mirror?" she wondered.

"Positive?" he scoffed. "I carved every petal of that frame a month ago. Dinnae you think I'd recognize my own work? Course it's the same one!"

"But how'd it get here?"

"How did either of us get here?" He shrugged.

Iris sat in bewilderment for several moments while Angus polished off his doughnut. *I'm starting to understand why the psychiatrists think he's out of touch with reality,* she mused. *This entire story is masterful, elaborate, and completely impossible.*

"What're those other pages you've got there?" he broke the silence.

"Oh, just some more stuff I looked up. It was another name you gave me. Gillian Mayfield."

Angus jumped. "Could… could I see?" he asked.

Iris was beginning to doubt whether it would be wise to continue this exercise. Angus was so far into his delusion now, that she wondered if seeing more research would make him worse. *But then again, what's the harm… this stuff happened a century and a half ago.* She handed him the pages. He scanned them eagerly, and grinned.

"There's my bonnie quine," he said warmly, and continued reading. His face fell. "Buried in… 1844?" he gasped. "Wha… But why? She's only twenty-two!" He frantically scanned the page, turning it over and back, searching for an explanation. He turned his eyes to the third page.

"Angus, no!"

Iris felt a stab of panic and tried to snatch the page from his hand, but Angus held it away from her and continued scanning. His eyes fell to the paragraph about the pub owner's daughter who died a tragic death while grieving for her lost love. He froze. Iris's stomach dropped.

Angus's breath started to come in heaving sobs. He crumpled the paper in his hand and pressed both fists to his forehead.

"Oh, Angus, I'm so sorry… It was so stupid of me to show you that…" She reached for his shoulder. He stiffened and shook off her touch.

"Please…" he sobbed. "Please go. Leave me."

"Angus…"

"Please, Iris!" He tossed the crumpled paper to the floor and turned his back.

She gathered the pages she wished she'd never brought, and slipped quietly from the room. When she was safely outside, the door shut behind her, she chided herself. *That was the thickest, most insensitive thing you've ever done, Iris Jacobs!* She felt a chill as the most anguished sobs she'd ever heard arose from the other side of the door.

Chapter 13

Vancouver, WA ~ Present Day

Iris slumped to the floor in the corridor. Her face was hot with shame as she listened to Angus weep inconsolably. She mashed the printed pages into a fat rectangle and stuffed them into her pocket. Never had she so badly wished for a time machine, so she could erase the last ten minutes. She knew she couldn't stand vigil outside his door the rest of the day, but it felt wrong to abandon him when he was so distraught… especially because it was her fault. *He was letting me in. He was starting to open up to me. And all I did was try to prove him wrong. He'll never trust me again.* The corners of her eyes began to tingle with incoming tears.

"Iris?" said a soft voice above her.

She jerked her head up. It was Nurse Kathy.

"Hi, Kathy!" She stood quickly.

Kathy listened for a moment, and frowned. "What's wrong with Angus? Is he hurt?"

"He's... uh... r-really upset," Iris stuttered, searching her mind for an explanation that would make sense to Kathy.

"Yeah, I can hear that! And why were you sitting there..." Kathy searched her face with a piercing gaze, "...also clearly upset?"

"Um..." Iris hung her head.

"Never mind. It's okay. I'll just check on him. It's time for his medication." She breezed past Iris and knocked on the door, letting herself in at the same time.

Iris stood rooted to the spot.

"Angus? How ya doin,' guy?" she heard Kathy say. "You need some help?" Angus, whose cries had settled into muffled whimpers, replied just loudly enough to make out: "I killed her."

Iris covered her mouth with both hands in shock.

"No, hon, you didn't kill anybody," Kathy soothed. "You're here in your room, and everything's okay."

"Y'dinnae understand," Angus whimpered. "She would have lived... I should've been there!"

Iris bolted. She had heard enough. The weight of the damage she'd done felt like a crushing boulder on her chest. She flew down the stone steps toward the break room, intent on the purse and car keys in her locker. She would use her lunch hour to drive, clear her head. Maybe hit the Coffee Villa drive through. She came to a halt in the doorway of the break room, and froze. *Will.* The tall chef was just putting his smartphone back into his locker. He slammed it shut, gave the padlock dial a twirl, and turned.

"Oh, hey, Iris! Ready for lunch?" His cheeks became slightly pinker, and then concern spread across his face. "You okay?" *Curse this complexion.*

"Yeah! Yeah, I'm good," Iris lied with a forced smile. "It's just been... an interesting day so far."

Will crossed the room toward her and seated himself on the nearest table with his feet on one of the plastic chairs.

"Listen, I'm not great with small talk," he began gently. "But I've been told I'm a pretty decent listener… if you ever need someone to talk to." His brown eyes were earnest.

Iris considered telling him everything, but then she'd have to admit her foolish idea of talking a poor schizophrenic man out of his delusional world with mere facts. Will could see that she was battling with herself.

"How about an omelette?" he suggested.

The idea of a good meal made her mouth water involuntarily. She was definitely feeling a sugar crash from the doughnuts, and her coffee escape plan suddenly seemed like a headache waiting to happen. She nodded, trying not to cry again.

"C'mon," he said, taking her elbow and ushering her into the kitchen.

She took a stool near the counter as he drizzled olive oil into a pan and set it over the flames. He cracked eggs into a bowl and whipped them mercilessly.

"Where is everybody?" Iris asked, glancing around the kitchen.

"Prep's done, so they're on break until lunch service starts."

"All except you," she said guiltily. "You're still here working on your lunch break."

"No I'm not," he grinned. "I'm having lunch with a friend."

Iris watched in amazement as he deftly chopped onion, mushrooms, fresh rosemary, and bits of bacon and tossed them sizzling into the pan faster than she could have cut one mushroom.

"Wow, you're so fast!" she marveled.

"Let's hope so!" he chuckled. "Head chefs get no respect if they don't have the chops."

"I see what you did there," she half smiled. Being around Will was starting to lift the weight from her chest.

"Are you a cheese person?" Will asked with one eyebrow raised.

"Only if I'm awake," she replied.

"My kinda girl. We have… let's see…" He opened the fridge. "Swiss, blech. Too stringy. Sharp cheddar? Muenster? Oh, and havarti."

"I agree with you about the Swiss, but the rest sound great, so I'll just have what you're having."

"Combination it is!" He grabbed several blocks covered in cling wrap. Iris's stomach growled.

"Thanks for cooking, Will. Seriously. I didn't realize how hungry I was."

"My honor. Omelettes are easy, anyway. I can make them in my sleep."

"How do you know?" She eyed him suspiciously.

He let out a belly laugh, caught off guard by the mental picture.

She giggled with him. *He has a good laugh.* She was starting to love how easy it was to be around Will. He offered a listening ear without nosy questions. He made her lunch because he saw she had none. And despite his frequent blushing, he hadn't made any passes at her.

In almost no time, a steaming plate of cheesy omelette perfection sat in front of her, garnished with chopped chives and sliced tomatoes. His plate looked almost as beautiful, but hers looked as if he'd put extra effort into the presentation. He plucked two forks and knives from a rack of dishes that had just emerged from the dishwasher.

"Your weaponry, m'lady…" He handed her the silverware with a flourish.

"I thank you, kind sir." She nodded her head regally.

"Start in, I'm just going to grab us some waters," he said as he grabbed two glasses from the same dish rack.

"Oh wow," she beamed as she tasted the first bite. "It's no wonder Candace and James are always down here! Will, you're an amazing chef!"

"Aw, thanks," he said. "It's no big deal, it's just an omelette."
But he smiled with satisfaction as he filled the glasses.

Iris took a few more bites. The memory of Angus's horrified face and the sound of his cries began to crush her once more. She took the plunge.

"What it is, basically… I've totally messed up my chances of Angus ever trusting me again," she blurted.

"Wow, I feed her, and she talks!" Will smiled. "Why would Angus never trust you again?"

"Because he believes he's a man who actually was born in Scotland in 1820, so I looked that person up and showed him there's no way it could be him. Instead of helping convince him, it made him worse. And because I should have known be'er. Because he's an old man with bigger problems than someone like me can solve in one conversation. And because I'm a total eejit."

Will tried to concentrate on eating his omelette and listening, but his eyes kept widening as Iris's accent turned more Scottish.

"The icin' on the cake, however," she continued, her voice rising in pitch, "is that I looked up a name he told me was a 'special' person to 'im, and bein' the stupid numpty I am, didnae put two an' two together till it was too late, and let 'im read all about how this poor girl died searchin' for her lost boyfriend! Him! Course! That's what he believes, at any rate. Now he's convinced he's directly responsible for her death, even though it was in 1844! And now he's cryin' and it's all my fault!" Iris paused to catch her breath.

Will's eyes were wider than ever, at seeing this side of Iris.

"Hmm," he mused after a beat. "Well, I don't know a lot about mental illness… but it seems to me that if he's really delusional, then this mood he's in will go away as he forgets about all that stuff."

"No such luck," Iris moaned. "He doesnae forget things, he just thinks he's in the wrong century. There really *was* an

Angus Armstrong back then. His story's spot on! Nothin' in the records contradicts him, except that he's still alive. But he cannae be the *same* Angus Armstrong, obviously. It's just not possible!" She took a sip of her water.

"Maybe he's done a lot of research on this person," Will offered.

"That's what I thought, too. But I just don't see how," Iris said, frowning. Her accent was beginning to fade back to a 50/50 mixture. "He doesn't use computers. He doesn't even like light switches! I suppose he could have seen the original parish records while he was back in Scotland. But if he had, then he'd have seen the same thing I did—that this girl died in 1844. But he honestly didn't know. Will, you should've seen his face. He was truly... *shocked.* You can't fake emotion like that. It's like he felt close to this girl somehow... like he knew her!"

"There's something to it, then," he stated confidently. "You shouldn't give up."

"Excuse me?" Iris blinked. "What do you mean there's something to it?"

"I mean that people are deeply complicated. If his story checks out, and his emotions are real, then there's got to be something more to it. There has to be a logical explanation. If you keep looking, you'll find it."

"You make it sound so simple," she said glumly.

His smile was sympathetic. "Simple isn't the same as easy."

After thanking Will for lunch, Iris trudged back upstairs, deep in thought. *I hurt Angus horribly, and it was because I was trying to prove a point. I'll never make that mistake again. But maybe Will's right. Maybe there's something I'm missing.*

She resolved to make it up to Angus. She would uncover the truth and help him find his family, one way or another.

One thing was becoming increasingly clear—Angus had a connection to that mirror hanging in the chapel. Whether it was something real or imagined, or some combination of the two, his reaction to it was undeniable. The first time Angus saw it hanging there, he had backed away in shock. Iris recalled the time she saw him talking to it. *"What have you done to me?"* And now he was claiming to have carved the frame with his own hands and then been… what, banished here with it? By a humming tree? *Not bloomin' likely.* She shook her head. Will was right. If she kept looking…

It's simple, she reasoned. *I just have to figure out where that mirror actually came from. That might lead me to the person who last saw Angus.*

She checked her phone. She still had fifteen minutes until Candace wanted her back in the office. She headed for the lobby. A few tables were occupied with residents playing board games and shouting pleasantly at one another. The canaries chirped and fluttered as she walked by their cage. Becky was away from her desk, but James was sitting in his mother's chair, eating a fudge doughnut.

"Hi Iris!" he shouted so loudly across the lobby that it made a couple of the chess players jump. He waved his long fingers at her. He reminded her of a Great Dane puppy who hadn't yet grown into his paws. She waved back and approached.

"How was your date with Will?" he asked with perfect nonchalance.

Iris coughed. "What date with Will?"

"Lunch in the kitchen, obviously. Why do you think I'm eating up here? He kicked me out! In the nicest way, but still…"

"He makes great omelettes," Iris sighed. She could see that there was no way James would stop analyzing her friendship with Will, so she gave up trying to dissuade him. "Listen, James, I need your help."

He perked up. "Well I'm the right person to ask, since I know just about everything," he beamed.

"So I've heard!" She grinned. "What can you tell me about that mirror hanging in the chapel?"

"That girly lookin' flower one that looks like a heart?" James wrinkled his nose.

"That's the one."

"It's old. Like, super old. A hundred or something."

"Has it been here at Rookwood a long time?"

"Nah, it's new."

Iris suppressed a smile. *It's old, it's new. That clears it up.*

James continued, "The owners just bought it. They're like, obsessed with antiques because they look good around here with all the antique people." He chuckled at his own wit.

Iris looked around awkwardly, but it seemed that nobody had overheard.

"Where'd it come from?" she asked.

"Someplace in Europe. A real castle! Hang on, I can check the files. My mom keeps all the receipts in a folder…" He stuffed the last bite of doughnut in his mouth, wiped his hands on the front of his shirt, and yanked open a file drawer. "It was like a month ago, so I'll check October…" he muttered to himself. He thumbed through the pink and yellow carbon copies in a folder, getting bits of sticky icing on a few of them, until he found the one he was looking for. "Ah. 'Kay. Here's the packing slip. It says here… the original seller was from… Ehhhh… Eckle… Ecklies-Greg. Whatever. Somewhere in Scotland. Here." He handed her the receipt.

Iris felt a chill. *Ecclesgrieg Estate Architectural Salvage,* she read silently. *Posted from St. Cyrus, Aberdeen, Scotland. Delivered 12 October. Item description: Victorian era mirror, floral frame."* The words swam in front of her eyes as goosebumps rose on her arms. She handed the page back.

155

"What's the big deal with that mirror anyway?" he wondered.

"Oh nothing, I was just thinking of getting one for my room," she said absently, her mind reeling. "Thanks, James."

Iris sat in one of the brocade arm chairs, tapping the arm rest. Something was niggling her. *October 12th. Why is that date familiar?* Her mind flashed back to the pages she'd copied from Angus's file. *Wasn't the doctor's report from October 12th? The day he went to the hospital?* She sat up abruptly. *Candace had said something earlier. What was it... Angus was discovered in the early morning by a delivery guy who was bringing in some stuff for the chapel... The delivery guy!*

She jumped up and ran back to the desk where James had bit into another doughnut.

"James, could I see that page one more time?"

He lifted his elbow off of a yellow sheet on the desk. "Didn't even put it away yet." Iris grabbed it. Fingers trembling, she pulled her phone from her back jeans pocket and snapped a picture of the delivery company's contact information and the driver's name.

Iris stepped outside the front doors. The gray November sky was puffy and cold, threatening snow. The nipping breeze pierced right through her sweater, but she didn't care. She dialed the number from the packing slip.

"Speedy Northwest Courier Service, can I help you?" a lady answered.

"Hi, I have a question about a delivery from a month ago. Is there any way I could speak to the driver who brought the package?"

There was a pause. "What is this regarding, if you don't mind?"

"Oh it's not a complaint," Iris assured her. "I just wondered if the driver saw something while he was here."

"Okay, which driver? I'll see if he's around."

Iris lowered her phone, pinch zoomed into the upper corner of the photo she'd snapped. "Uh, Mike."

"Sure, I'll see if I can grab him before he leaves again. Hang on a sec." The line switched to elevator music.

"This is Mike!" said a loud voice.

Iris jumped. "Hi Mike, my name's Iris. I have an odd question, so bear with me…"

"Sure…"

"I work over at Rookwood Senior Home, and your name is on the delivery slip for an antique mirror that was delivered a little over a month ago."

"Uh-huh?"

"Could I ask if you remember anything unusual happening during that delivery?"

"Well yeah, that was the place where I found that guy on the front walk," Mike replied. "Didn't see nothin' when I brought the crate in, but when I came back outside, this poor old guy was passed out on the path, so I called 911."

"Thanks, Mike. That really helps," Iris said.

"Yeah. You don't really forget something like that. Anything else I can help with?"

"Nope, that does it."

"M'kay, have a good one!" The line clicked.

So Angus and the mirror really did arrive at Rookwood at exactly the same time…

Iris came back inside and headed toward the chapel. This would be the final test. She would look at the mirror for herself. She would find the manufacturer's logo on the back, probably Google it, and her mind would be satisfied that it was mass produced in a factory somewhere. Everything else had to be a coincidence.

She paused at the entrance to the chapel. It was deserted and solemn. A reddish, golden light shone through the stained glass window onto the grand piano at the front, and the mirror on the wall behind it reflected its beauty. Iris walked slowly up to the mirror. The roses on the frame were so realistic that they seemed to be showing off. They shimmered intensely in the sunlight, as though they had drunk liquid gold through their stems before being preserved in smooth shellac.

She ran her fingers delicately over the petals and ivy vines. Every detail was exact. *This had to be done by machine.* She grasped the sides of the mirror and lifted it away from the wall. It wasn't heavy, but she was still afraid of dropping it, so she lowered it to the floor and turned it over. She saw no manufacturer's imprint or logo. Just a circular brown stain, and a bold signature scratched in pencil:

Angus Armstrong
1844

"Blimey," she murmured. "Angus, you're not crazy… you're… a time traveler!"

Chapter 14

Vancouver, WA - Present Day

Iris was thunderstruck. For the rest of the day, her mind kept returning to Angus. Every interaction they'd had began to take on new meaning. Every comment he'd made, every detail of his story… it all made sense. That is, if she was willing to believe in time travel. And if she did decide to believe, whom could she tell? How much could she say about this without losing all her credibility? She was starting to understand Angus's frustration. Short of giving him her public support and receiving her own "skits of friendlia" diagnosis, what could she even do to help him?

She'd set out to reunite him with his family, but he was right—they were truly gone. He was completely alone, cut off in the prime of his life from everyone and everything he knew, with no way back. At least until today, he'd had the luxury of hoping that the woman he loved had lived a long life and found a way to move on without him. Now, even that was gone. *Brilliant job, Iris.*

"Iris, would you wipe the tables in the Activity Room real quick before you go?" She gave a start as Candace interrupted her thoughts.

"Uh yes! Yep, I'll go do it right now," she blurted.

"You okay?"

"Yes, I just… I guess I'm just distracted. Lots going on." Candace raised an eyebrow.

"This wouldn't have anything to do with Angus having a meltdown earlier, would it?" she asked.

"Oh… you heard about that?"

"Of course. I hear about most things. I ran into Kathy in the hallway and she looked pretty concerned. Didn't you visit him earlier today?"

Iris felt a painful stab in her gut, and hung her head. "Yes."

"Any idea what got him so unbalanced? Was he saying anything that seemed like his symptoms had gotten worse? Kathy was thinking they might need to adjust his meds."

"I think…" Iris hesitated as she fought tears. "I think it might be my fault."

"How so?"

"Well, you know how I was planning to research those names he gave me?"

"Yeah…"

"It turns out that… he thinks one of them was his girl-friend, and..." She took a deep breath. "He wasn't aware of the circumstances of her death. Until now."

Candace's mouth fell open. "Oh, Iris…"

"I thought he would have known! It's public record! And it was so long ago, I didn't see how he could possibly know some-one who's been gone since 1844. I didn't think he would get this upset over it!" Iris rubbed her forehead. "I feel so awful."

"Well, I understand why you thought that, but people with schizophrenia sometimes have unpredictable reactions to things. I realize you didn't know any better, but we can't afford to be careless with Angus. He doesn't process facts the same way we do, especially when it comes to events he feels are connected to his own life."

"Believe me, I haven't been able to stop thinking about how much I wish I could take it back." Her cheeks burned.

"What's done is done," Candace said gently, and gave her arm a gentle squeeze. "But I'm going to have to recommend that you not visit Angus again. At least not until he's stable again."

Iris looked up sharply. "Wait, but... for how long? I really need to apologize to him!"

Candace gave her arm another squeeze and fixed a motherly gaze on her. She paused a long moment, considering her next words. "I don't know how long. Sometimes, caring for someone means putting what's good for them ahead of what you need. Apologizing might ease your conscience, but it also might cause him more pain."

"I never meant to cause him pain," Iris said quietly.

"I know. And I think Angus will come around. Just give him time."

Time is the last thing on his side, Iris thought.

Charlie came home from work smelling of hair products and carrying half of a cold Hawaiian pizza in a smashed box. She tossed her keys on the counter directly below the key hooks that Iris had hung their first day in the apartment.

"Iris! I have pizza—WHOA, what happened to you?"

Iris was curled up at the end of the sofa with a blanket wrapped around her. Her eyes were puffy and red from crying.

"I'm fine," she moaned. Her face scrunched. She sniffed hard.

"Sure you are." Charlie tossed the pizza box next to her keys without taking her eyes off her roommate. She crossed to the coffee table and sat on a stack of junk mail. "What happened?"

Iris looked as if she were about to speak, then pursed her lips. She shook her head. Finally, she spoke. "I kind of… got in trouble with my boss at work today. Also, Angus hates me."

"Angus… is that the old guy who reminds you of your grandpa?"

Iris nodded.

"How'd you get into trouble your very first week?"

"I upset Angus. He was…" Iris stared vacantly at her lap, replaying the sound of Angus's sobs in her mind. "He was *really* upset. I mean, what kind of person tries to talk a sweet old man out of his own history?"

"Uhhh… you do, I'm guessing?"

"Yep."

"And why's that? Does he think he's Professor Plum or something?"

Normally, that would have made Iris chuckle. "Actually, I would have preferred that," she sighed. "Then I'd know he was living in his own version of reality like almost every other person at Rookwood. This is far worse."

"What, is he Mafia?"

Iris shook her head. "Charlie, you're my best friend. We've known each other since our first day in fourth grade. You know I'm not insane, right?"

"As much as you've been able to fool everyone, yes."

"Charlie, be serious."

"I'll try." She smiled wryly. "Seriously, Iris. Talk to me. What's got your undies in a wad? I promise I'll believe you, no matter what it is."

Iris took a deep breath as she weighed her next words. "I think Angus might be… I mean, I'm pretty sure he's… this is going to sound so *nutty*…"

"Just spit it out."

"I think Angus is a time traveler."

Charlie's eyebrows shot up. She suppressed a cough.

"I told you it sounded nutty."

"Well... yeah." Charlie cocked her head to one side and studied Iris's face. "But if you're pulling my leg, it would be a first. What makes you think he's a time traveler?"

"Basically, nothing else explains him. The way he talks, the way he acts. Everything he says about himself matches the records of a real person who was born in 1820."

"And you're sure he's not delusional?" Charlie crossed her arms.

"I thought he was... at first. That's why he's so upset. I tried to explain to him that what he's saying is impossible. But that's exactly the problem—he already knows how impossible it sounds." Iris rubbed her forehead. "It doesn't dissuade him, it just takes away his hope."

"What hope?"

"Of being with his family. Getting home... seeing 1844 again."

"Okay, wait," Charlie put up a hand. "I'm sorry. I mean, I believe you... I think. But I'm struggling to keep up, here. How did you get from *delusional* to *probable* on the whole 'time travel' issue? I mean, you were a history major, for cryin' out loud. You'd be the last person on earth to believe that people can just go skipping around from one time period to another, like some trippy episode of Doctor Who."

"I know! Believe me, I've been having this argument with myself all day. But nothing else explains him! He talks about St. Cyrus as though he's only seen it the way it *used* to look. He knows the layout of the town as well as I do. But there's an old church hall there that was built in Victorian times, and he said he never saw it finished. Same with the castle on the estate! That only adds up if he left when he says he did."

"Seriously?"

"Yes. I looked those buildings up as soon as I got home. They were both under construction in 1844. Not to mention, he looks like he's crowding ninety years old. People that age have lived through the Great Depression, two world wars, the space race, the dawn of the computer age. But until today, I don't think he'd even *used* the word 'electricity' before! And then... there's the evidence."

"There's actual evidence?" Charlie moved from the coffee table to the sofa, kicked off her clogs, and sat forward with great interest.

"Yeah. Angus's last woodworking project," Iris replied. "It's the frame of a mirror that hangs in the chapel at Rookwood. And when I say 'frame,' I really mean it's a work of art. The roses he carved on it look so real! I didn't believe him at first, but I looked at the back of it myself. It has his signature right on it, along with the year, 1844. He said he made it for his boss only about a month ago, out of wood that he cut from a really weird tree. He said that the tree was making a... a humming sound."

"A humming tree?" Charlie asked skeptically.

"I thought it was strange, too. I can't really explain that, and neither can Angus. But he described how time started passing all wrong after he cut this tree. I don't know much about woodworking, but I know for a fact that this mirror frame couldn't have been made by hand in just one day. Angus figured it should have taken two weeks minimum with drying time, but he did the entire thing in one shot, before it even got dark enough to light a lantern. As if... time had stopped. When it was finished, he lost consciousness. He woke up here somehow, in an aged body."

"Wait, he made this thing back in Scotland? How did it get here?"

"Somebody bought it. I guess the mirror must have hung in the castle back in St. Cyrus for well over 150 years. Charlie, I think I actually saw it once, on a school trip when I was eight." Goosebumps rose on Iris's arms. She recalled the image of the forlorn parlor she saw through the dingy castle window. *If it wasn't Angus's mirror hanging there, it was one very much like it.*

164

"The owners of Rookwood seem to have a taste for Victorian antiquities from Europe. The mirror was shipped overseas from Scotland and delivered right around a month ago, on the same day Angus was found on the front steps. And it's from the same castle where Angus used to work! I saw the paperwork myself!"

Charlie's mouth was hanging open. She blinked a few times, stood, and retrieved the pizza box. She set it between them on the sofa, opened it, and without a word she selected a piece and munched away thoughtfully.

Iris took a slice and bit into it. Her thoughts swirled with carved roses, ham, castles, pineapple, and humming trees.

"Okay," Charlie mused. "That explains how the mirror got here. It's logical. Back in the day, he makes the thing. It's art, it's kept in a safe spot. Time passes. It gets sold, shipped, bla bla bla… bam, it's in America now. But that does *not* explain how a Scottish dude gets transported across the ocean during a freakishly long nap, and isn't dead of old age. Actually, I'm very confused about that part."

"You and me both. Angus wondered if he was… banished somehow, like he was cursed by the tree for harming it."

"A magical humming tree that curses people?"

"Well it sounds ridiculous when you say it like that!" Iris protested.

"I hate to burst your bubble, but it sounds pretty ridiculous no matter *how* you say it! If this guy Angus actually traveled here from the past, from a different continent—basically traveled across time and space—then there's got to be a more scientific explanation than a tree curse."

"Then… you think it's actually possible he's telling the truth?"

Charlie gazed at her thoughtfully, considering the question as she chewed her pizza. "I mean, scientists keep coming out with new discoveries all the time," she said with her mouth full. "Remember physics class, senior year? Mr. Reynolds loved to geek out about how the gravity of black holes can bend light and change the flow of time."

"How do you remember all the way back to high school physics?"

"What? I loved that class! The universe is awesome." Charlie took another piece of pizza. "I would've become a particle physicist and moved to Switzerland if there wasn't so much math involved." She picked off a chunk of pineapple and popped it into her mouth.

"You are a constant surprise."

"Yes, I know." She blew her blue bangs out of her eyes. "So maybe... who knows, there might be some kind of black hole equivalent here on earth—like miniature black potholes or something—and maybe Angus fell into one?"

Iris cracked a smile for the first time since lunch with Will. "How does *that* sound more plausible than a magical humming tree that curses people?"

"It does to me! At least black holes exist!" Charlie sniffed. "And give me credit—I may have just invented the best excuse EVER for missing work. 'Sorry I didn't come in yesterday, boss. I fell into a black pothole on my way in, and was transported a whole day into the future!'"

It felt so relieving to laugh with Charlie, and to know that someone believed her about all of this. Angus deserved to know that she believed him, too. She would have to find a way to see him. Charlie had also given her an idea. Who better to ask about time travel than a science geek like Mr. Reynolds?

"Well, I stink. I'm going to hit the shower," Charlie said. "You can have the last piece of pizza."

"Thanks. I might save it, though. My carrot sticks are calling me. Want me to grab you a few? You need to eat more vegetables."

"I'll make some popcorn later," Charlie called as she disappeared into her room. "That's a vegetable, right?"

Iris shook her head and chuckled. She pulled her laptop from the computer bag on the floor next to her and tapped in her password. The ancient machine debated long and hard about whether there were any signals in the universe worth picking up. Finally, it decided to sample enough sporadic bits of wifi for Iris to pull up her old school's website, locate Mr. Reynold's email address, and fire off a quick "hey, remember me?" with a request for an appointment at his earliest convenience.

His reply arrived an hour later:

Hi Iris,

    Heck yes, I remember you—the girl who loved scientist stories! And yes, I still love talking about black holes. Actually, I'm a bigger nerd than before... I've almost finished my Ph.D. in particle physics. I'm always delighted to talk science, especially with my wildly successful former students. Come on down tomorrow afternoon around 3:45. I should be free then. Same classroom as five years ago, except this time you'll be looking for a guy with gray hair. I'll let the office know you're coming, just make sure you sign in. See you soon.

                           Jason Reynolds

Hm. Strange to think of her old teacher as a "Jason." Her brain had always thought of his first name as "Mister."

She was grateful he hadn't suggested an early morning meeting. Tomorrow was her day off, and sleeping in was at the top of her priority list.

Mr. Reynolds was erasing the blackboard when Iris walked in. He was dressed in his typical jeans, dark gray blazer, and high tops. He had a pencil tucked behind his ear. His hair, though still cut and combed into a perfect low fade, had definitely gone gray.

"Hi, Mr. Reynolds!" Iris waved.

"Well hello again!" He turned and smiled, looking over his horn-rimmed glasses, which had slid down his nose. His t-shirt depicted two cartoon atoms. The one on the left said, *Are you SURE your electron is missing?* The other said, *I'm positive!!*

Iris smiled, remembering how he'd been kind enough to wear that shirt as a clue on test day when she'd been in his class.

"Thank you for seeing me," she greeted him warmly.

"Iris Jacobs. It's been a while!" He dusted the chalk from his hands on the front of his jeans and shook her hand. He gestured to an aging brown chair next to his desk. "What's on your mind?"

"Kind of a philosophical question, I guess. I was talking to my best friend yesterday—you probably remember her—Charlotte Stuart?"

"Ohhhhh, Front Row Charlie! Sure! Gosh, you two were like Frick and Frack. She still sporting that buzz cut?"

Iris laughed. "Nah, it's only short on one side nowadays. But it's blue!"

Mr. Reynolds nodded approvingly.

"Anyway, we were actually discussing a funny subject... time travel." Iris searched his face for any sign of incredulity, but his expression was earnest. She continued, "Charlie reminded me how much you used to love talking about black holes, gravity, all that stuff. And I guess I just wanted to ask you straight out... Do you think time travel is actually possible?"

"Sure," he replied without hesitation. "I mean, we've traveled ten seconds into the future since you asked me that."

"You know what I mean!" She'd forgotten how mischievous Mr. Reynolds could be. It was the perfect defense mechanism for interacting with high schoolers all day.

He chuckled. "Well, yes. Time travel the way you're talking about is totally impractical—but possible—theoretically. Remember what I taught you guys about relativity?"

"It's... been a while." She gave a sheepish little shrug.

"Well, if I was to boil it down for you…" He scratched his stubbled chin. "Einstein was the first famous guy who realized that time doesn't always flow at the same rate. It's relative to where you are, and how fast you're going through space."

"That's kind of ringing a bell," Iris mused. "Although I've never read much about the concept."

"Well, there wasn't a lot about it in the textbook." Mr. Reynolds' eyes twinkled. "High school physics class is mostly about playing with magnets and talking about energy changing from one form to another. But I like to go off-script."

"That, I remember." Iris smiled back. "But I don't get how time can be relative. It seems like such a steady, reliable thing."

"I know, it's a real mind bender, isn't it? But the only real constant is the speed of light. Time is actually flexible. It only seems constant because the average person doesn't spend much time traveling in space or going at the speed of light. The only changes we might experience in the flow of time are so tiny, we don't notice them."

"So… then how is time travel even possible?"

"Well, the math works out. Someone experiencing much higher gravity or velocity would experience time passing more slowly, relative to other people. We've actually observed this happening in small ways. Scientists have seen time flow at different rates depending on how close they are to the earth. Time flows slightly faster at higher altitudes. Clocks on satellites are a little faster than the ones on earth, so their computers have to correct for it. Even your head is experiencing time ever-so-slightly faster than your feet. At least when you're standing." He smiled with great satisfaction at this idea.

"I must remember to lie down more!"

"Indeed. Clearly, so should I!" He grinned, smoothing his gray hair. "But, going any place where you'd experience relativity so profoundly that you'd actually 'time travel'"—he made little air quotes with his fingers—"would take tremendous energy, and it would require technology we just don't have yet."

"Oh…" Iris's shoulders slumped. "So essentially it wouldn't be possible to travel, say, a hundred years into the future, then?"

"Probably not in our lifetimes. Going a few seconds ahead, maybe. But that far into the future relative to everybody else? Nah. Too many problems getting that kind of mass moving at a high enough velocity."

"Okay," Iris sighed. "And that's for sure the only way to time travel… going really fast?"

"Well I guess you could always park yourself near the event horizon of a black hole and make use of the crazy gravity," he mused with a quirky grin. "You wouldn't live to tell the tale, though. Oh! Well, I guess you could also figure out how to remain stationary and make spacetime warp around you."

Iris straightened. "Could that work?"

He looked at her over his glasses. "Are you trying to build a time machine in your basement or something?"

"N-no, I'm just…"

"It's okay, I'm just teasing!" he laughed. "It's actually an interesting subject. A Mexican scientist named Alcubierre did a paper on that in the nineties. Since going the speed of light is impossible, he thought of a way around that. He figured if you could create a bubble and then manipulate spacetime around it, you could propel a spacecraft through time. Again, the math checks out with Einstein's theories, but how in the heck would you build something like that? Plus, you'd have to have the technology to generate enough negative energy to keep the bubble stable enough not to collapse and have the gravity crush you to death. It's hardly feasible."

"Hmm…" Iris's brain began to churn. If it was theoretically possible to time travel while essentially remaining stationary, Angus's story was starting to seem more possible. *Maybe the tree that Angus talked about had some kind of gravitational field. Maybe it created some kind of "bubble" around him, and when he got out, the world had aged over a century. But how did he cross continents if he was stationary?*

"So," Iris continued her thinking out loud, "if time travel to the future is possible, in theory, what about time travel to the past?"

"Well, that gets tricky." He shook his head. "You have to remember that time and space aren't exactly separate things. They pretty much go together. The problem is, space has no particular direction, but time does. Time is always headed toward the future. Trying to go against that is like trying to reverse entropy... there are ways to do that on a micro scale, but I'm not sure you could do it with people."

He picked up his coffee cup, swirled the last inch of cold liquid, and chugged it before continuing.

"The only theoretical way around that is a wormhole—y'know, a shortcut between two parts of space? But you run into the same problem as you do with warp bubbles. You can't keep a wormhole open long enough to pass through it without it smashing you like a bug. You'd have to stabilize it with a bunch of negative energy—antigravity, basically. Nobody really knows where to get negative energy outside of a vacuum, especially in any meaningful amount. And that's provided that you could even locate a wormhole in the first place."

"How would you know a wormhole if you saw one?" Iris wondered.

"I'm not sure you would. I mean we don't even really *see* black holes. We just know they're there because of how everything around them behaves. It'd probably be the same with wormholes."

"So if everything around a certain area was behaving differently, that'd be a good place to look, right?"

"I guess. It could be any number of things, though, like radiation or a geomagnetic anomaly. Plus, a lot of scientists believe that if wormholes even exist, they'd be microscopic and only last a few nanoseconds before collapsing. Others—the really imaginative ones—think they could someday be widened and stabilized. But since nobody's ever seen one…"

"What if they looked like something else?"

"Hmmm…" He stared at her for a long moment. "Well since we got off into the realm of science fiction a while back, I'll bite. I guess if a wormhole was big enough to see with the naked eye and it had matter around it to indicate where it was, it could blend in or seem to be part of that matter… But again, that's provided you had all the right conditions in place. It's astronomically improbable."

"But not impossible?" Iris squinted.

He let out a hearty laugh. "No, Iris. I guess it's not impossible."

"Thanks, Mr. Reynolds." Iris jumped up and shook his hand.

"Hey, any time. It's been stimulating. Glad to see you still like science. Oh, and… good luck with… whatever it is you're doing."

"Thanks. I'll need it."

Chapter 15

"*A*ngus!" *Gillian called from over the dune. "Where are you?"*
Angus couldn't answer just yet. He needed to stay quiet. The warm breeze ruffled his dark curls over his brow and swooshed across the tufts of beach grass where he crouched, his hand poised over a stripy brown lizard. The lizard had a very serious expression, its stubby snout pointed into the wind. With a deft movement, Angus snatched the lizard from its perch, being careful not to grab it by the tail.

"Hallooo, I'm over here!" he called back to Gillian with a wave. "Look what I found!"

Gillian turned back in his direction and started toward him. She was barefoot, having rolled up the cuffs of her pantalets and kicked off her shoes somewhere she'd have to remember sooner or later. Her blond curls were wild in the breeze, and her ivory calf-length linen dress swayed like a bell as she picked her way across the clumps of grass. A collection of mussels, limpets, and cockle shells clinked around inside her apron as she held its corners in one hand.

"*What is it?*" *She eyed him curiously.*

Angus beamed and held up the unfortunate lizard for her to see. The sudden change in altitude had caused the creature to renew its protests. Its tiny elbows flailed across Angus's thumb, and below his hand, its slender tail had begun to whip in a circle.

Gillian shrieked. Her seashells clattered to the ground as she sprang back. "*Angus! You... Ugh!*" *She struggled for words whenever she was flustered.*

His eyes widened. "*Sorry, Gilly...*" *This had not gone how he'd imagined it. He stooped and released the struggling lizard.* "*I thought you'd like 'im!*"

"*Like 'im? He's a snake with legs!*" *she fumed, her late summer freckles glowing from more than just the sun.* "*And you startled me!*" *An angry tear threatened to escape the corner of her eye. She frowned and batted it away with the back of her hand.*

"*Aw, dinnae be vexed, Gilly. He's harmless. And he's long gone, anyway, see?*" *He held up both his sandy hands in apology.*

She huffed. "*I'll forgive you when I'm done bein' vexed.*"

Angus searched her face for a moment, and then relaxed. Already, her frown had eased. He bent down and gathered her sea treasures into his wool cap.

"*What d'ye reckon?*" *he said.* "*Should we head back? Mrs. Keith said at church today that's she's startin' that school, and Dad says I ought to go tomorrow.*"

Her eyes lit up. "*My dad's makin' me go, too! If you're there, that means I'll nae be the eldest in the class!*"

He grinned down at her as they started down the beach. He'd hit a growth spurt this summer and suddenly found himself a head taller than her.

"*You're only twelve,*" *he commented.* "*Now me, on the other hand...*" *He leaned down and plucked a sprig of delicate blue harebells.* "*I'm ancient.*"

Her laughter was like music.

"*Hmm, fourteen years of age...*" *She nodded with mock solemnity.* "*Soon to expire. Y'best make out a will.*"

"Aye. Not long now." His smile was warm.

Angus held out his cap, still full of seashells. Gillian lifted her apron, forming a cradle. They stopped walking for a moment while he tipped the shells gently back into her possession, careful not to crack any. He beat the sand out of his cap and placed it back over his curls at a jaunty angle.

He bowed at the waist and presented the wildflower to her with a flourish. "Shall I walk you there tomorrow, then?"

She blushed, brought up short by the gallantry of his gesture. Was it mostly in jest?

"N-nae..." she hedged. "I'll meet you there."

Unable to comprehend her expression, He looked into her face one more time, hoping to understand her better. But her blue eyes sparkled with an intense look he'd never seen before.

She curtsied with aristocratic flair and accepted the harebells, her hand brushing his ever so slightly. Her face went from pink to red.

"See you tomorrow!" She turned on her heel and ran.

"Gilly! W—"

Angus jerked awake.

"Wait for me," he whispered into the dark.

Iris blinked in the dim of early morning. Her choice of alarm tone had sounded so mild and friendly last night when she'd set it. Now it was like an annoying kid yelling, "Nyah, nyah-nyah nyah-nyah!" She fumbled for her phone and missed, knocking it into the crack between her bed and nightstand while it continued taunting her.

"Gahhhhhh..." She slid from her warm bed onto her knees, snatched the phone, and silenced it, resisting the urge to throw it. Sleeping in yesterday had made today's wakeup that much more annoying. She rested her forehead against the mattress and nearly fell back asleep on the floor, right where she sat.

Then she remembered that today, she had to see Angus. She would do whatever it took to see him… to tell him everything she'd found out. She was the only person in this world who believed him. He needed to know that someone did.

Getting ready took on a new urgency. She'd decided to show up an hour early again, hoping that Angus would be awake. The last time she'd been there at that hour, not only was he already up, she'd seen him tiptoe into the chapel and have a perplexing discussion with a mirror. Now she understood how that very mirror was the pivot upon which his existence had radically shifted. Somehow, the wood in that frame was connected to what had happened. *Wood from a humming tree. I wonder if that tree is still standing back in Scotland.*

Another thought popped into her mind as she did her hair. This whole plan was going to hinge on getting Will to let her into the building again. *Would he mind? Is he going to start feeling like I'm using him?* Her hand froze mid-air over her head, still clutching her hairbrush. *Is he even working today?*

Her chagrin deepened as it dawned on her how little she really knew about Will. As she replayed their interactions in her mind, she realized that most (all?) of them had been about her. He'd taken the time to ask about her, listen to her problems, notice when she didn't have a lunch, and make her favorite doughnuts. What had she done for him? What did she even know about him besides the fact that he was adorably kind to her, had a passion for cooking, and seemed to like multiple kinds of cheese?

You're off to a brilliant start, Iris. Even if you have no interest in dating Will, which… you don't… what kind of friend are you? He deserves better.

She considered bringing him a treat, or… what, a coffee maybe? She knew he was a coffee person, but she hadn't hung around long enough to find out how he liked it. She gave herself a withering look in the mirror and shoved her brush into the drawer.

Charlie's alarm went off in the other room, followed by a moan and a small crash. Iris suppressed a giggle. Charlie was clearly having a similar morning to hers. Iris checked her watch. Here was one friend she *did* know something about, and she had five minutes to do something unselfish.

She located Charlie's favorite insulated cup in the kitchen, washed it, and filled it with Charlie's favorite coconut cold brew—fixed just the way she liked it. She scribbled a quick note on the sticky pad by the front door:

Thanks for the pizza and chat.

You're the best. ♡ Iris

After affixing the note to Charlie's cup and leaving it the bathroom—knowing it was the first place she'd go—Iris grabbed her things and slipped quietly into the dim morning light.

As she turned to lock the door behind her, a half formed thought floated into her mind.

Is that a lame idea? she wondered. *Doesn't matter, I'll risk it.*

She slipped back into the apartment to snatch a gallon sized plastic bag full of tiny dried leaves, flowers, and stems from the kitchen drawer. She stuffed it into her purse before she could change her mind, and dashed to work.

Iris decided to be upfront this time. No flirting.

When Will pulled up in his black pickup, Iris got out of her hatchback and waited while he switched off his Van Halen

CD, cut the engine, and gathered his chef jacket and keys. He caught sight of her through the windshield and a huge grin deepened his dimples. She waved.

"Good morning!" he greeted her. "To what do I owe the pleasure? More work to do?"

"Yeah, I'm hoping to see Angus. I've really gotta make it up to him," Iris confessed.

"Good for you. It's important not to let stuff fester."

They began the trek up the path to the employee entrance.

"Very true. I just hope he agrees with you. Oh, by the way, I brought you something," Iris said, producing the bag of herbs from her purse.

Will examined it, and then his eyes lit up with recognition. "Is this thyme?"

"Aye, it's wild thyme." Iris brought out the accent. "My granny gathers it for cookin' and brings me bunches of it when she visits from Scotland. I dinnae ken how to cook with it, and a girl only needs so much thyme for her sock drawer."

Will laughed. "I'm going to put this to good use! How cool is that? Wild herbs from Scotland!"

"Well, I can see how much you like experimenting, so I thought, why not? Granny says it's pretty mild stuff, so don't be shy with it."

"Hmm... You've got my wheels turning now. Also, I see once again you're without a lunch. Are you doing this on purpose so I'll cook for you?" He gave her a sly grin as he unlocked the door and held it open for her.

Iris's mouth fell open as she remembered her poor abandoned turkey, havarti, and tomato sandwich back home in the fridge.

"It must be subconscious," she said. "I really *am* trying to bring a lunch every day, but deep down, I must not want to!"

"In that case, you are officially invited to dine with me in the kitchen."

"Thank you, Will... but only if you have the time."

He held up the bag. "I definitely have thyme."

"Ha. Thanks for letting me in," Iris said. "I really do appreciate it."

"Eh, it's nothin.' Go make his day."

Angus stared out the window. His blue eyes were bloodshot. Sleep had been eluding him more and more. He couldn't decide whether he preferred the good dreams or the nightmares. At least when he awoke from the nightmares, the real world offered some relief. But dreams like that last one—where everything he'd ever wanted, everything he cared about, was right within reach—made this world a waking nightmare in comparison.

He had donned the soft cotton shirt and ill-fitting blue trousers given to him by the social worker (she called them "jeans") and wandered to the lobby. Watching the canaries used to lift his mood, but today it reminded him of Iris, the practical Scottish lass who thought he was a daftie. Sitting alone in his room was out of the question today. It felt like being in a tomb. But being out in the corridors carried the risk of having to endure soul-sucking chatter from people who barely knew him and cared even less.

He settled into the same brocade armchair he'd always chosen, next to the massive bird cage. He felt sick. Adjusting to this place and wading through his confusion had taken time. It wasn't until lately that he'd begun to grasp just how hopeless his situation was... how far from home he was. *Home.* Longing enveloped him like a quagmire, threatening to suffocate him.

"God, you could chime in any time," he choked. He clenched his fists, fighting for control. *What am I supposed to do now? I tangled with something mysterious, and... what? I'm just meant to be lost? Like wreckage?*

"Hello, Angus."

Angus jumped. Iris stood beside him, holding two lidded paper cups. Her red hair framed her blushing face. She looked contrite.

His face hardened. He turned his back to her. "I've got nae a thing to say to you," he mumbled. "I'm done."

"I dinnae blame you," she sighed. "I've not been a very good friend to you, Angus. I'm sorry."

He turned to face her.

"Tea?" She held out one of the cups. It had a little string protruding from under the lid. "My mum says the best way to make up with someone is to talk it out over cups of tea."

"You really think *tea* is goin' to fix my problems? Like I said, I'm done talkin.' To you, to everyone."

Iris set the cup on the round table next to him and sat in the adjoining chair. She studied him with her sharp green eyes.

"Arright, you're done talkin.' That's fine. Then just listen. I made a right mess of things when I told you about Gillian."

Hearing Gillian's name mentioned out loud sent a stab of pain through his chest.

"She means everythin' to you, and I should have seen that. Talkin' about her the way I did was... well, I wish I could erase that whole conversation. I also didnae believe what you said about yourself," she continued. "But I want you to know somethin'... I do now. I believe you were born in 1820, I believe you're somehow still only twenty-four, and I believe you got here under mysterious circumstances."

"Why believe *me*?" he asked dryly. "I'm just a daft old man."

"Because it's what my eyes and ears tell me."

"Hmph." Angus recalled his own words now being repeated to him by this girl. He eyed her, wondering what she was playing at. However, she seemed completely sincere.

right. Someone who believed him, talked like him, and even
knew how to find tea in this godforsaken place? She was no
Patrick, but she cared. He could see that. He took another
sip of tea.

"I suppose while we're exchangin' apologies, I ought to say
sorry, too. I've been crabbit as a hedgehog of late."

"You've had your reasons."

"Makes no difference. I... I ought to keep hold of my
manners, at least. I assume that's still somethin' people do,
nowadays?"

"Some more than others." Iris smiled again.

181

"Well it's time I came to my senses, I suppose. I've no call raisin' my voice to a lady. My mum raised me be'er than that. And of course I forgive ye. God didnae forgive all my failin's just so I could turn round and stick it to somebody else."

"Well thank God for that." Iris raised her cup. "To friendship?"

"To friendship. Slàinte!"

They sipped.

"Tea is magic," Iris giggled. "My mum said so."

"Aye, my mum swears by it, too."

"Oh by the way," Iris remembered, "I'm not technically allowed to talk to you. My boss is afraid of me upsettin' you again."

"This friendship is arready off to a winnin' start."

"If you just… I dunno, request to see me, and tell them you're not upset with me any more, then they might allow it. Otherwise I'll have to keep comin' to work an hour early."

"If there's tea, I'll let you!"

"If you let me sleep, I'll show you how to make yer own tea!"

"Arright…" Angus conceded with a sigh. "I'll say nice things about you." He smiled around the brim of his cup as he took another sip.

Chapter 16

Scotland, 1844

P atrick opened the worn cedar chest at the foot of his bed and dug through its contents until he found what he sought at the bottom: a black armband. He debated. Gillian wasn't family, but…

He stroked the black fabric and wondered what people would say. Angus would know. He knew how to read people. While Patrick was good with the stories and laughs, Angus always seemed to understand how people felt.

"I'm no good at this, mate," Patrick whispered. "What do I do?"

Tears swam in Patrick's eyes. Ten days ago, his best friend had disappeared without a trace. No body. No funeral. Only questions.

And then just two days ago, the love of Angus's life had perished. The vivacious spark that was Gillian Mayfield, known and loved by the whole village, was gone. No warning. Only questions. The one mercy? Angus wasn't here to see it. He'd have worn the black armband. Probably for good.

Patrick made up his mind. He slid the armband into place over his sleeve, realizing it was a bit more snug than it had been for his parents' funeral. He would wear it on Angus's behalf. Besides, Gillian was the closest thing he would've had to a sister-in-law.

There was a line of mourners out the door of the pub, winding down the street. Everyone in the village had turned up to pay their respects. Patrick bypassed the line and made for the door, his two sisters following close behind. Perhaps Gordon Mayfield needed a hand... or a friendly face. After all, Gillian was the only family he'd had left.

When Angus had disappeared ten days back, Patrick had put every waking moment into searching for him, for an entire week. Since that had put him a week's wages short, he and his sisters had needed help and support. Without being asked, the Mayfields had offered them both food and friendship. He didn't know how they would have survived the past week without them.

He scanned the room for Gordon's balding head and walrus mustache. He was at his usual post, drying glasses as if this were just another day at the pub. However, a linen cloth covered the mirror over the bar. Gordon's eyes were puffy, and his brow was knit with a look of despair. He was avoiding eye contact with the mourners, deliberately keeping himself away from the corner of the pub where Gillian lay. Six chairs had been shoved together, two at each end and two behind, to provide a platform for her simple pine coffin, which was heaped with wildflowers.

"Some way I can help, sir?" Patrick offered.

Gordon jumped. "Och, lad," he spoke without stopping his work. "I didnae see you there. Hello, ladies." He nodded to Patrick's sisters.

"Sir, would you not prefer to stand by Gillian now?"

Gordon paused a full ten seconds before answering, his hands limp and his eyelids heavy.

"Aye, that I would," he finally replied. "But I've such washin' up to do since the wake, short though it's had to be, God rest her. Down to a quarter supply of whisky—every lad in town loved her and came yesterday to say so."

He began to polish the glass in his hand with renewed vigor.

"Had the kisting this morning with the church ladies. Though half of yesterday, I was up to Inverbervie to find the wee lass a coffin… "

A pained expression crossed his features as though he instantly regretted reminding Patrick that St. Cyrus no longer had a carpenter. A solitary tear streaked into his mustache. His voice was gruff as he continued.

"Layin' her to rest this afternoon at three, o'course. Have to remember to pay the reverend four pounds for the hire of the mort cloth. That still leaves me the feast to do, although I dinnae ken how many might turn up for that. Everyone, likely. I've had nae a moment to rest, to think… to see what I've got in… to go out to market for fish. She always…" His shoulders began to shake as deep sobs erupted from him. "I've had nae a moment to tell her goodbye."

Patrick maneuvered quickly behind the counter and put his hand on Gordon's shoulder. He motioned to his sisters, taking the towel from Gordon's hand and tossing it over the bar to Ailsa, the elder sister. A look of fiery determination came into her eyes as she and Patrick exchanged looks, and she nodded.

"Perhaps y'ought to just nip upstairs and take a breather," Patrick suggested, while giving the large man's arm a firm tug that was more than a suggestion.

"Aye, a few minutes might be good," he agreed. "I must look a fright."

"My sisters and I have things in hand until you come back down, arright?"

"God bless you, lad," he mumbled, and trudged up the stairs.

Within thirty seconds, the three Dawsons had divided the tasks. Ailsa had tossed Gordon's towel back to Patrick, who continued clearing up the mess behind the bar. He tried to do this with as little clinking as possible. Mourners from the village continued to file past the bier, each gently brushing Gillian's brow with their fingertips, leaving a flower, whispering their sadness to her.

Patrick kept his eyes on his task. He would have to pay his respects soon, though he keenly wished he could just content himself remembering his friend as she had looked last week. Gordon had kept the wake mercifully short. Patrick was grateful for that. There had been no one to send for, thus no reason to prolong it. Having the pub closed down was a strain, not just on Gordon and his finances, but on the whole village. Patrick wasn't sure how much more the poor man could take.

In the kitchen, Ailsa had tied on one of Gordon's aprons and busied herself rummaging in the larder for whatever ingredients would make the most helpings for the least expense. This was a particular talent of hers. She could see that he was nearly out of bread and sausages, but well supplied with oats, barley, tatties, onions, parsnips, cabbage, smoked haddies, neeps… All the makings of a thick, warming fish soup and a load of bannocks. Nothing fancy, but perfect for heavy hearts. She found a knife and set to work.

Bridget, the younger, had availed herself of the remaining apron she found hanging on a hook, hoping that doing so wasn't disrespectful of the dead. She stoked up the fire in the stove and began hunting down Gordon Mayfield's best serving dishes. There were few, since he and Gillian had never served large family meals, only pub fare one plate at a time. She did manage to locate some delicate, seldom used tea towels with which to line a few bread baskets, and a sterling soup ladle with a lovely shell on the tip of the handle, likely a wedding gift. Once the dishes were sorted, Bridget joined her sister chopping vegetables and flaking fish.

Patrick watched the last of the mourners file out, leaving just a huddle of men outside waiting to bear Gillian's coffin to the kirkyard. It had been nearly an hour by his guess, though the motionless clocks couldn't corroborate, since Gordon had gone upstairs. It was time.

He climbed the creaky stairs gently, hoping not to startle him. The bedroom door was open, so Patrick peeked in. Gordon had freshened up, donned a clean shirt and tie, made a pass at shaving and combing his remaining hair, and subsequently fallen asleep in his magnificent arm chair. Patrick recognized the chair as one of John Armstrong's creations— little wonder that Gordon had been comfortable enough to conk out.

"Sir?"

Gordon snorted awake. "Eh?"

"The mourners have gone."

"Aye, lad. Thankee, I just..." He gripped the arm rests. "Let's get on with it, then."

Gordon descended the stairs heavily and approached the coffin with a vacant stare. He stood still for several moments, as if not comprehending the sight before him.

"What to say, lass?" he whispered. He touched a strand of her hair and caressed it between his fingers. "Time's got us backward. You were nae supposed to beat yer ol' dad to heaven."

He leaned down and kissed her forehead. Then he produced a small pair of scissors from his waistcoat pocket and snipped a lock of her blonde curls, tucking it inside his pocket watch.

"God help me," he said, with one last look at his daughter. "God help me without you here." He turned and joined the huddle outside.

Patrick approached the bier and stopped short. This was not Gillian. It couldn't be. Gillian was wild and beautiful, vivacious and full of color. This figure before him, marbled with gray pallor, her hair parted and tucked neatly aside with a ribbon, looked nothing like her. Yet it *was* her. And it was a waste. It wasn't "meant to be," it wasn't "her time." It was all wrong, and nothing else. Patrick felt a strange mixture of rage and horror welling up within him. He longed to have Angus standing with him and felt such relief at the same time that he wasn't.

"She'd slap whoe'er did that to her hair," Bridget commented.

She and Ailsa had only just emerged from the kitchen to pay their respects, slipping in beside their brother unnoticed.

Patrick let out a laugh, which sounded strange and hoarse, but released tension nonetheless.

"Bridget, dinnae speak ill of the dead," Ailsa chided her.

"Nae, it's meant as a compliment!" Bridget returned. "Besides, it's true."

She stepped toward the coffin and held up a folded wool cap. "I found this in your apron pocket, Gillian. I thought you might like to have it." She tucked Angus's cap neatly into the folds of Gillian's winding cloth. Then, she gently loosed Gillian's hair from the fussy ribbon. She plucked several of the showiest wildflower blooms from around the foot of the coffin and expertly set them in a splendid crown around her head.

"There," Bridget sighed with satisfaction. "At least she looks more like herself."

"Much be'er," Ailsa agreed.

Patrick took a bold step toward the coffin and touched Gillian's cool forehead.

"Fare you well, dear friend," he murmured. "I dinnae ken if you see Angus up there in heaven. If you do, smack 'im for me and tell him I'm in a right fix without him. But maybe you were right... maybe he's still round here someplace. If he is, I'll find him. I promise you that. I'll never give up, Gillian."

He turned quickly to the door before his sisters could see the tears streaming down his stubbled face.

"I'll second that." Marjorie Armstrong stood in the doorway, leaning heavily on a cane. Her voice was clear and strong, though her eyes were red. "Not about slappin' him, necessarily, but about not givin' up."

Marjorie reached for Patrick and enveloped him in an embrace that made him miss his own mother.

"I should have come round to fetch you," he mumbled next to her hair.

"Nonsense." She held him at arm's length and patted his cheek. "I'm slow, but I'm not a cripple. I'm feelin' be'er all the time."

Marjorie hobbled to the coffin and gazed upon Gillian with a tender smile. "How many a day did you come back from the beach with Angus with yer hair done just like that? Lass, I really thought we'd be family on this side of heaven. What God has up his sleeve, I'll never know. I've stopped tryin' to work it out."

She sniffed and reached into her pocket.

"This was under Angus's pillow. I know he meant to give it to you, but y'know how he is. Has to work up the courage to speak his heart. It says... well, I'm sure you know." She tucked the scrap of paper under Gillian's hand. "God bless ye, lass, for fillin' my Angus's world with beauty."

The four final mourners stepped outside, where Patrick joined Gordon in the huddle. The men gently closed the coffin, laid the heavy black velvet cloth over it, hefted it onto their shoulders, and carried it feet first out of the pub. Ailsa and

Bridget upended the chairs it had rested on, then resumed their work in the kitchen.

The procession to the kirkyard was solemn, but at the same time, occasional bursts of laughter rang out as the men traded stories of the times Gillian had told a good joke or put one of them in their place. Eight men at a time bore the coffin, some trading out to give another a turn. But Patrick and Gordon remained quietly at the front.

Though the people of St. Cyrus talked, feasted, and danced away the waning day, their devastation was palpable. All knew in their hearts that the village would never be the same again.

Caledon watched the dark clad line of villagers trickle out through the cemetery gate. From his vantage point hundreds of feet above, he could watch the strange proceedings while keeping an eye on the tree Guardian. Something about the death of this young woman unsettled him.

Almost in answer to his turbulent thoughts, a messenger appeared at his side, creating a small crackling shockwave in the ether.

"A dispatch from the Three," the messenger said.

"Report."

"The time disturbance of ten days ago is still rippling. A plan is in place. Brennus has been relocated to sentry duty over the Jacobs family."

"Jacobs… the fisherman Jacobs?"

"Yes. His descendants must be watched closely."

"Noted. Thank you."

The messenger disappeared with another small crackle in the air.

"Hmmm." Caledon crossed his arms and gazed down at the procession on its way back into the pub. Sure enough, there was Brennus, his comrade, hovering close to one villager, a young bachelor. "This should be interesting."

Vancouver, WA - Present Day

"My heart hurts when I think about her."

"Of course. You loved her. And she loved you."

"Aye, she really did. I wish I'd said somethin' to her sooner."

Iris joined Angus on the window seat of his cozy room and smiled at him tenderly. "But the point is, you *did* tell her."

"Aye." Angus closed his eyes and leaned back against the glass, savoring the thought. "She looked so beautiful that mornin.'" A sudden shadow fell across his features. He opened his eyes and looked at Iris. "Y'know, I was the only woodworker left in the village…"

"Yes?"

"I…" He frowned. "I would've had to… build her coffin."

"Oh, Angus…"

"I wonder if I could've. 'Twas hard enough to build my dad's."

He put his forehead against the rain splattered window and gazed out at the drippy clouds.

"Sometimes it feels like I cannae catch my breath."

She knew there were no words for this moment. They sat in companionable silence for several moments.

At last, he shook himself, sniffed loudly, and blinked back his tears. "I've got to stop this, or the nurses will send you away again."

After a week of persistent requests, he'd finally convinced the nurses that he could handle visits with Iris. He'd had to stop talking about home and start pretending to be convinced that he was born this century. Not much else to be done when the truth of your life is considered a symptom.

But it had been worth it. He finally had someone to talk to. A real friend. Today, Iris had come with biscuits—cookies, rather—and a surprise.

"So these are sugar cookies?"

"Yep. If you ask for a biscuit in America, you're likely to get something much closer to a scone, but not as good."

"Hm. Wee bit confusing." Angus took one and munched thoughtfully. "Good, though. A bit like shortbread." His hand trembled slightly from the effort of pushing away his dark thoughts. He focused on Iris instead. "So what's the surprise?"

"Well, I got to thinking," Iris began. "We're not so different, you and I. We come from the same village. I'm an only child... so are you. We both want to follow in our dads' footsteps. You're a brilliant craftsman like your dad. Me, I want to be a history professor like my dad. He's obsessed with antiques, and that's what got me started. It turns out, you and I both have antique coins. I wanted to show you the pride of my collection. It was a gift from my dad."

She reached into her back pocket and pulled out a small clear plastic case and handed it to Angus.

"It's a sovereign." He seemed unimpressed as he turned it in his hand.

"Aye, it's a sovereign! But see? It's an 1817 with George and the dragon! I know it's not that old to you, but from where I'm sittin', it's over two hundred years old. I could get more than five hundred pounds for that."

Angus's eyes widened. "Five *hundred* pounds?"

Iris nodded.

"Blimey. What could you buy with five hundred pounds?"

"Oh, not even a month's rent. But still..."

Angus's eyes widened even more. "Rent is more than *five hundred* a month? How does anybody live indoors anymore?"

Iris laughed. "Well, wages are far higher, too. I dinnae think things are so different these days, we're just working with bigger numbers."

Angus shook his head in disbelief.

"I've got a total of three of these George sovereigns in my collection," Iris continued. "This one's in the best condition. Top of my wish list, though, is a Victoria sovereign minted in 1841—one of the rarest ones to find. I'll probably never afford it. She can be worth ten times old George here. More, if people get into a bidding war."

"Rare, eh?" Angus mused. "I had one back home. Too bad that one didnae go in my pocket as well."

"Aye, you really must plan be'er next time you travel to another century."

"I'll work on that."

"Y'know…" Iris picked through words in her head, trying to find the right way to broach this topic. "I chatted to one of my old professors last week about… your journey here. I didnae mention you specifically, more of a 'what if' kind of thing. He not only agrees that traveling forward through time is possible, but in theory, it may also be possible to go backward."

Angus froze. "Backward? But how?"

"Not sure. I mean, he said a lot of things about how difficult and improbable it is, but he said the same thing about goin' forward, too…"

"I dinnae ken how I even came here."

"We know it has something to do with that humming tree, right?"

"Likely. But that tree is a little far away, yeah? If it's even still standin.'"

"Well, perhaps I'll go back to Scotland and check it out sometime."

"I'd go with you right now, but I doubt they'd let me out of here. And even if I did get out, I'm not sure how I'd do on a long sea voyage. I never really fancied boats."

Iris giggled. She'd have to fill Angus in about aeroplanes.

"Angus, I'm not tryin' to raise your hopes, but what if there really *was* some way to put things back the way they were?"

"I understand what you're tryin' to do. Honest. But if a body puts on sixty years every trip, I'd never survive a second journey. Gettin' here nearly killed me. And that's even if there was some way to know where you're pointed when you mess with that tree. I think your old professor is right. It's highly improbable."

"But here you are. You've already done the improbable! Who's to say you cannae do it again?"

Angus gazed at her for a long moment. "I cannae even tell you how much I wish that were true."

"I'm not giving up. The day we met, I wanted to help you find your family. It's still what I want." She squeezed his hand. "Well, I ought to get on," she sighed. "It's about time to decorate for the birthday party."

"Whose birthday is it?"

"Everyone's."

He shook his head. "This place is bedlam."

He handed Iris's coin back to her. "Thank you for showin' me this. I can see why you treasure it. I hope someday you have wee ones to pass it along to."

Iris blushed slightly. "Not sure I'm prepared to think about that for at least another decade."

"How come? I think you'd be a brilliant mum. You have a good heart. And you're clever."

Iris smiled. "Thank you, Angus. I'll think about it. And if I ever meet the right guy, I'll name the first one after you." She pushed away the face that came instantly to her mind.

He grinned. "Well, let's hope the first one's a boy, then."

Chapter 17

Will was waiting for her when Iris descended the stone steps to the kitchen. A deep, savory aroma filled the corridor and beckoned her even before she reached the double doors. She peeked her head into the kitchen and breathed deeply.

"I can't figure out where I am," she exhaled after a long draw through her nostrils. "It smells exactly like my granny's kitchen on Christmas day!"

"Well, Christmas isn't for another two weeks," Will assured her with a grin, wiping his hands on a towel. "And I am most definitely not your granny."

"That's for sure. She's way prettier that you. But seriously, what am I smelling? What's in the pot?"

"A special no-recipe Scotch broth, full of all sorts of things."

"Ooooh. I'm in." Iris took a stool.

Will picked up an industrial sized soup ladle and began to dish the thick stew into bowls.

195

"Let's see… there's mutton, herbs, barley, split peas, lentils, carrots, turnips, cabbage, leeks, rutabagas—which I found out are called 'neeps.' So naturally, I *will* be calling them that forever, because 'neeps' is a cool word. Here, try…" He dipped a small spoon into the pot and held it out for her.

She allowed him to spoon the bite into her mouth. The flavor and texture were familiar, yet better than she could remember having eaten before.

"Oh my gosh… the meat is… perfect! How did you do that? It's so flavorful…" Iris chewed, searching through flavor memories. "Different."

"Yeah. No offense to your ancestors, but it goes against my nature to chuck raw meat into boiling water. Mutton deserves to be treated better, y'know? It wants to be rubbed with garlic and salt, seared, roasted properly. *Then* you add it in at the end, with some of the pan drippings. If you're nice to your meat, it will be nice to your soup."

She nodded. "Seems like this mutton feels appreciated."

Will grinned. "I also don't like the name 'Scotch broth,'" he went on, "because it's not broth. It needed a more creative name, so I'm calling it 'Thyme Travel Stew.'"

Iris's jaw dropped. "What did you say?"

"Thyme Travel… it's a—"

"Why are you talking about time travel? Did someone say something…"

Will cocked his head quizzically. "Iris, what are you talking about? It's just a play on words. Y'know, because the *thyme* you gave me this morning had to *travel* a long way to get into the pot? *Thyme travel?* Plus the concept of the soup is centuries old… "

"Ohhh…"

"Well *I* thought it was clever. Maybe I'll get a second opinion from Candace on the name." He handed her a bowl.

"No, it was. It's clever. I'm sorry. I'm just in a really weird headspace lately."

"Well, have some of this. It's the best soup I ever made. I should know."

Iris dug in. Two bites in, she was back in Granny's kitchen. She closed her eyes and savored the memory of the little cottage where she watched Granny at the stove, humming and stirring, talking to the pots, telling them to "just boil arready!" while sassily swishing her ginger-turned-silver hair up into a knot on top of her head. Then Granddad would shuffle in and give Granny a playful pat on the rump, admonishing those pots that they'd better listen to Her Majesty, Queen of the Kitchen and All She Surveys.

The corners of Iris's mouth lifted at the warmth of her thoughts. When she opened her eyes, Will was sitting across from her, eating his soup, but watching her with slight amusement. He'd placed a plate of golden brown rolls between them. She picked one up and took a small bite, having another moment of instant recognition.

"You didn't."

"I did." His smile was almost smug with satisfaction.

"Aberdeen butteries?"

"Aye."

"Is this a conspiracy to bring back my Sco'ish accent or somethin'?"

"Why, is it working?"

"Maybe."

Will nodded. "Good. You should be proud of who you are, not trying to hide it."

"That's funny. Angus says the same thing."

"Well, he's right." Will was quiet as he took a few more bites. "I like who you are."

"Thanks, Will." She smiled.

"No, I'm serious. I… I really do. I was thinking, maybe… if you want to, sometime, you and I could, y'know, go get coffee. Or maybe… go out. For noodles."

"Noodles?"

"Well, I was trying to think of something I don't like to make myself. I don't actually like most restaurant food… at least, not the kind I can afford. Except there's this little place I know about where they make fresh pasta that's way better than mine, and with the right sauce, it's really… am I babbling?"

"Kind of."

"You get what I'm saying, though, right?"

"You like fresh pasta?"

"I want to spend time with you, Iris."

Iris's spoon halted, suspended halfway between her bowl and her mouth. Several drips escaped before she let the spoon down with a sigh.

"Okay, here's the deal with that," she began. "I'm trying this thing lately, at the suggestion of both Candace and Angus, and now you, to just be more open with people. To be less… I dunno, closed up. Relationship wise. Give and take. Y'know?"

Will nodded.

"So… here goes. Basically, I think the world of you. Every time we've hung out, you've impressed me. You're a great guy. And I've been trying to get to know you better… I can see you'd be a great friend to have. I want that."

"Why do I get the feeling there's a 'but' coming?" He smiled sadly.

"Well… because there is."

"I get it. I'm a nice guy, but you just don't think of me *that* way."

Iris gazed at him, weighing her words. "Actually, I *do* think of you that way." Color rose in her cheeks.

Brilliant, Iris. This is why we don't usually say this stuff out loud!

"Wait, seriously?"

"Ha!" Iris let out an awkward laugh and laid the back of her fingers against her warming cheek. "I can't believe I just said that. Um, yeah. Really. Pretty much since day one. But I'm trying not to go there. After my last job, I decided it's better not to date coworkers. The last one got a little... complicated."

"'Complicated' sounds like another way of saying 'terrible.'"

"It was. And since I seem to be going for broke with the honesty today, I'll tell you why. My last job was serving at a restaurant, and the guy who complicated my life was a chef."

"Oh dear."

"Yeah. Oh dear. He was charming... at first. He kept asking me out, so I finally agreed. We went on two dates, and then his personality changed. He started getting angry whenever I spoke to male coworkers. He was always wanting to know what we were talking about. He started making crude jokes about me, and spreading rather, uh, *detailed* rumors about us sleeping together, even though we never did. And when I told him I never wanted to see him again, he shoved me against a wall and said he could make me a lot less pretty, and make it look like an accident."

Will was stunned. Without realizing it, he had curled both hands into tight fists in his lap. His teeth were clenched.

"Well anyway, I had proof he did that because the security cams caught it. He ended up getting fired, and I had to get a restraining order."

Will took a deep breath to steady his voice. "Does this guy know where you live?"

"No, thank goodness. Like I said, we only went on two dates. I always met him places. He never drove me home. But he does know my car."

Will's eyes narrowed. The intensity of his expression startled her.

"I'm sorry, Will. I don't know why I told you all that. I guess... I just want to avoid all possibility of something like that happening to me again. It's not you, I promise."

"I don't even know what to say."

"I wish I'd met you first." Her smiled was pained.

"I wish you had, too. Because I would never—"

"I know. But that guy really shook me up. Y'know? I just... need some time."

Will sighed with resignation, but his concerned expression remained. "You've got it... friend."

Iris put her hand over his and squeezed. "I like the sound of that. For now, okay?"

"Hey, take all the time you need. I'll be here." He squeezed back, lingering a moment before releasing her hand. "But can we still get noodles? I feel silly going by myself, and I am *not* taking James there again. That kid can eat his weight in linguine."

Iris burst out laughing, imagining James on a mountain of pasta. "Yes, for goodness' sake. Friends get noodles. Let's get noodles." She popped the last morsel of her buttery roll into her mouth with a dazzling smile.

"Here..." he said, fishing through his pockets until he found an old receipt. He pulled a pen from a pocket on the sleeve of his chef jacket and scratched something on the back of the receipt. He handed it to her. "That's my cell. If you ever need anything, call me. Whether it's to make you some chicken soup, change a tire, or beat somebody up, feel free. Okay? Any time. You don't have to give me your number unless you want to, but I'd feel better knowing you have mine."

"Will, I..." Iris held the receipt in her hand for several moments like a treasure. She pulled her phone from her back pocket and typed in Will's number. She sent off a quick text message.

Will's phone chirped.

Thank you! 😊

"You're welcome." He grinned.

"And I feel better knowing you have my number now, too," Iris said seriously. "In case you run into a noodle emergency."

He laughed. "It's bound to happen."

"Wow, did we just have the DTR already?" she asked, trying to sound casual.

"DTR?"

"Yeah, that inevitable conversation where you have to Define The Relationship… DTR. You've never heard of that?"

"Nope. But you're the first person I've ever had to define anything with, so that might explain it."

"You… what? You've never dated anyone? Or had a friendship turn serious? Nothing like that?"

"Nope."

"Was that on purpose?"

"Just never met anybody I liked enough to ask. Until now."

Iris smiled, feeling a little sheepish. She had no ready reply for that.

Iris bounced back up the steps, feeling lighter than she had in weeks. *This being real about who I am is actually rather fun. Maybe I'll bring back the accent after all.*

As she neared the Activities Office, she heard a commotion at the far end of the corridor. Nurse Kathy was standing outside the open door of a resident's room. A cold metal gurney emerged from the doorway with a paramedic at either end. Iris squinted. As they turned the gurney and began wheeling it in her direction, she saw a shock of white, curly hair. *Angus.*

"Angus!" Iris broke into a sprint. She met the gurney just as they turned toward the lobby. She could see a waiting ambulance outside the grand stained glass window. "What's going on?"

Nurse Kathy caught her elbow and tugged her gently aside.

"Let's stay calm, okay? Angus needs us to do that. He's had a little heart attack."

Iris felt her stomach drop.

"They're just taking him for observation to make sure—"

"A heart attack?" Iris blurted. "How could he have a heart attack? He's only—" She stopped herself before saying "twenty-four" out loud. "He's been so much better lately," she finished lamely.

"Well, he was having some chest pain and shortness of breath after lunch," Kathy explained. "He collapsed."

Before they reached the huge double doors, Angus tried to speak, but he was muffled by the oxygen mask over his mouth.

"What's that, sir?" A paramedic lifted the mask away from his face.

"Iris," he gasped. "That's my friend…" He pointed. "I want…"

"He's asking for Iris?" the paramedic called to Kathy. "Is that person available?"

"She's right here," Kathy called back. She turned to Iris. "You can ride along if you want. Might help him stay calm. I'll let Candace know, okay?"

Without a word, Iris dashed to Angus's side. Tears welled up in her eyes as she fought panic. They loaded him into the ambulance and she climbed in next to him, taking his scarred, wrinkled hand in hers.

"I'm here, Angus."

"My heart hurts again."

"I know. Dinnae worry. We'll get you be'er."

He squeezed her fingers.

Angus's social worker signed the last of his medical forms with a flourish and handed the clipboard back to the receptionist. She scanned the chairs in the waiting area until her eyes rested on Iris. Her sensible shoes clicked smartly across the tile floor as she approached.

"Are you the Rookwood rep?"

"I… I work there. Not sure I'd call myself a 'rep.'"

"Hm." The forty-something woman pursed her lips. "Well I'm late for a hearing. Mr. Armstrong's paperwork should be in order. Get in touch if there's anything else." She handed Iris her business card.

"Thanks."

Iris watched her click-clack down the hallway.

"That social worker's nice enough, but it always seems to me like there are a hundred other places she has to be."

Iris turned with a start to find Candace standing next to her chair, gazing down the corridor where the social worker disappeared behind a set of glass double doors.

"Sad that she's so overworked." Candace plopped into the chair next to Iris and patted her knee. "Sorry if I startled you. I'm pretty good at sneaking up on people in these shoes." She tapped her heels together like Dorothy in *The Wizard of Oz*. Today's Converse were a subtle glittery pink.

"It's fine. Too quiet in here anyway."

"How's our guy?"

"Scared. He really doesn't like hospitals."

"I can't think of many people who do."

"Yeah. I guess it's good that he hasn't had to spend much time in one until now."

"What's the latest?"

"Well, they were concerned about the chest pain and shortness of breath, so they're doing tests on his heart," Iris replied. "They'll call me when he's done."

"You never clocked out, y'know." Candace nudged Iris's shoulder with her own.

"Oh, I'm so sorry, Candace! I completely spaced it. I—"

"Relax. We'll work on your timesheet later. It's a little unorthodox for an activity assistant to be here with a resident, but Angus doesn't have family, and he definitely needs a friend. We'll just call this the longest room visit ever."

"Thanks. I really want to be here for him, but I can come back if you need me…"

"We'll be fine. I have emergency protocols in place."

"Emergency protocols?"

"James is calling BINGO." Candace winked. "If anybody can give Third Irene a run for her money, it's James. But I should get back. Just wanted to make sure you were okay."

"I'm as okay as I can be under the circumstances."

"Angus is lucky to have you, Iris. Oh, by the way… normally, the doctors aren't allowed to tell you anything because of privacy laws, but I asked the social worker to add you to the approved list. Thought you should stay looped in, since you're the closest thing he has to a relative."

"Thank you, Candace. That really means a lot. And thank you for letting me be here for him."

Candace patted her knee one more time and left, just as a tall nurse in scrubs appeared in the doorway of the corridor where they'd taken Angus.

"For Mr. Armstrong?" he announced.

Iris popped up. "How's he doing?"

"Come on back, you can see him now. What's your name?"

"Iris."

"Hey, Iris. Okay, your friend's being admitted, but he's stable. I'll let the doctor tell you more about his condition."

Iris followed the nurse into Angus's room. He sat propped up in bed, wires protruding from the neck of his hospital gown, an IV line taped to his wrist, and a far off expression on his face as he gazed out the large window. A doctor wearing green scrubs under a white lab coat turned and greeted her when she walked in.

"Hi there! Angus, it looks like you have a visitor," she said.

"Doctor Walters, this is Iris," the nurse introduced her.

"Hi, Iris. Thank you, Jamal."

Jamal tapped his brow in a little salute, smiled at Iris, and closed the door behind him with a quiet click.

Iris sat in the chair next to Angus, trying to comprehend his expression.

"Well now," Dr. Walters began, "I thought I'd wait and explain what's going on to Angus until he had a support person here. That way he doesn't have to try to repeat it." She smiled.

"Is he going to be okay?" Iris asked.

"Definitely," she replied. "In fact, he didn't even have a heart attack. We got his labs back, and they're negative for any of those elevated enzymes you'd see with that kind of cardiac event. We took some pictures of his heart. His angiogram was clear—no blockages of any kind. Actually, he has the heart of a twenty-five year old. He must get lots of exercise!"

"Twenty-four," Angus muttered under his breath. Iris suppressed a smile.

Not hearing him, Dr. Walters continued. "What we *did* find was a slightly abnormal shape to his left ventricle. For whatever reason, sometimes the body responds to emotional trauma with a surge of stress hormones that temporarily disrupts the pumping motion of the heart on one side, which makes the other parts of the heart have to work harder. Then we see this sort of ballooning shape in the left ventricle. That's what was causing the chest pain he was feeling. It's called 'takotsubo cardiomyopathy' in medical speak. But it's better known as broken heart syndrome."

"Broken heart?" Iris felt a stab of dread. She looked over at Angus, but he didn't seem to be listening. He kept staring out the window. "But you said he's going to be okay."

"He is." Dr. Walters nodded. "This condition isn't permanent. He just needs to rest. I can prescribe a mild diuretic to take some of the load off the heart. If he doesn't improve, an ACE inhibitor might help, but I'm going to wait on that for the time being. Like I said, his heart appears very healthy otherwise. I want to keep him here a few days for observation, maybe up to a couple weeks, depending on how quickly he improves. We'll be listening to his heart and lungs the next few days, just to make sure he doesn't develop any complications. But it looks like he'll make a full recovery."

Iris sighed with relief. "Thank you, doctor."

"Just try to help him stay calm." She turned to Angus and raised her voice slightly. "I'll be back later to check on you, okay? And your nurse right now is Angela. Just hit that button if you need anything."

Angus didn't turn to look at her, but nodded absently as she left the room.

"Angus?" Iris took his hand.

At last, he faced her. "Why'd they bring me here again?" He sounded more exhausted than she'd ever heard him. "People talk at me like I'm deaf. I've been stabbed, prodded, pushed about on a trolley, dressed like a wee babe, and labeled." He held up his wrist with the hospital bracelet. He sighed and shook his head. "I had such hope of dyin' when the pain started. Why'd they not just let me die on the floor? I'd be so much be'er off."

"Angus! Why would you say such a thing?"

His blue eyes were piercing. "I'd be with Gillian again." His voice broke, so he went back to staring out the window. "I fancy bein' out amongst the trees there. Makes it feel less like I'm in here. That one," he pointed, "is a cedar. Best thing to make a nice steamer trunk... maybe a cupboard. Keeps moths out."

"Angus, dinnae give up." Iris fought for composure. "You believe in God, right?"

He was still for several seconds, and turned to her with tears in his eyes.

"Don't you?" she asked again.

"Aye. Though He's been awfully quiet of late."

"Well, what would He want you to do now?"

"What *can* I do?" Angus demanded with a sudden surge of anger. "What's a tree supposed to *do* when it's hit by lightning and falls into the sea? It becomes driftwood. It goes where it

goes. It lands where it lands. It ne'er sees the forest again…
like it ne'er even existed in the first place. So what does Angus
Armstrong *do* now? Is there any choice involved?" He sighed,
his voice resigned. "Does it even matter?"

"It always matters," she replied, tilting her chin up. "Listen.
I've decided I'm going back home for Christmas. I've not seen
my granny and granddad since graduation. They invite me
every year."

"I'm happy for you." He tried, and failed, to muster some
enthusiasm. "It'll be rather difficult though."

"How so?"

"Christmas is two weeks hence. You should've left ages
back."

Iris suppressed another smile. *How to explain this…*

"Angus, I'm going to fly there."

His wiry brows furrowed. "Is this the part of our friendship
where I say, 'thanks for believin' me about the humming tree,
so I guess I believe you can fly'?"

Iris's laugh felt like it came from her toes.

"It's not me that does the flyin.' It's an aeroplane. Not
only have people figured out how to replace steam engines
with gasoline powered ones, they've figured out how to put
them on wagons, ships, and great metal tubes with wings.
They've even figured out how to build great big rockets and
travel to the moon and back! So flyin' across the ocean isnae
goin' to be difficult."

"Blimey. People have gone to the moon?" He rubbed his
stubbled chin.

"Aye, the moon," she giggled.

"What for?"

"To say we did, I suppose."

"So you're flyin' home, then? In a rocket?"

It felt *so* good to laugh. "No, in an aeroplane. A metal tube
with wings. It'll go so fast that I'll get there in a day. And the
reason I decided to go was… to get you some answers, Angus."

"Answers?"

"Aye. I'm goin' to find your tree." Her eyes twinkled.

He sat bolt upright in bed and grabbed her hand. He searched her face for a moment, and then spoke with determination. "Take me with you."

Her eyebrows shot up. "Take you *with* me? Angus, I—"

"I have to get out of here," he said. "I dinnae belong—I'm like a canary in a cage!"

"Angus, I cannae do that!"

"I know everyone I know is gone, but at least I'd be home. If you just—"

"I'd get in so much trouble!" She lowered her voice to a whisper. "Your legal guardian is the state. If I took you away, they'd come after me for kidnapping."

"I'll tell 'em I went willingly."

"I'm afraid they'll see it differently. They think you cannae make those kinds of decisions on your own."

"Oh, right. Because I'm off my heid," he huffed, and slumped back against the pillows.

"I dinnae ken what to say," she said lamely. "I want so much to help you…"

"Iris, I *need* to get back. My life, as I knew it, is over. What's left for me? I just want to die and be buried there… with my family. I want to go home."

Iris squeezed his hand and met his gaze. A fiery resolve settled over her spirit.

"Then I'll find a way to get you there."

Chapter 18

I ris listened to the official-sounding voice on the other end of the phone. She rubbed her forehead in frustration as she paced her bedroom floor.

"But he just needs to travel one way. It's unlikely he'd ever leave the country again," she said.

She listened to the reply.

"Okay, but he's never *had* a UK passport."

A question.

"Because he didn't need one when he came here. It was a… work thing."

Another reply.

"He was born in Scotland! Of course he's a British subject!"

Another question.

"His birth records? They're… uh… lost."

A long explanation.

"So let me get this straight. He can't get emergency travel documents without reporting a missing passport, he can't get a new passport without a birth certificate, and he can't get a birth certificate without a photo ID… like a *passport*? Is that what you're telling me? So basically he's a prisoner in the United States?"

A snarky reply.

"He doesn't *have* any of that! That's what I'm saying. He's *old*. Nobody's going to sign a birth affidavit, because nobody who attended his birth is still alive! What's he supposed to do?"

Iris plopped onto her stomach on the bed. She crossed her eyes and made a series of funny faces while the immigration official droned on.

"Fine. Thank you for your time." She pressed the red button on the phone's screen before the person had finished speaking.

"Wow," Charlie said. She'd invited herself in and sat on the floor in the open doorway, eating a blueberry yogurt. "Scottish temper getting the better of your European manners?"

"Oh my gosh, Charlie, these people are unbelievable!" Iris buried her face in a pillow and growled.

"I couldn't help but overhear," Charlie confessed. "I took the liberty of Googling some ideas."

"Okay…"

"Well, there's the obvious, but slightly less official route, of course—swipe somebody else's passport and try your luck."

"Ha. That's kind of a felony. Besides, I already thought of that. Apparently, passport fraud isn't exactly considered a 'little white lie' in the eyes of the federal government. They hold it right up there with terrorism nowadays. And they use facial recognition scanners now. Even if I found someone who looks enough like Angus, close enough probably wouldn't be close enough. It'd be a quarter million dollar fine and a decade in jail, for each of us."

"Yikes."

"Yeah. And to be honest, I can't believe I even seriously considered doing that. I'm not exactly the criminal type."

"Okay, so maybe not the felony route. What if you got him a U.S. passport?"

"He's not a U.S. citizen, though."

"Well, on paper, he's nobody. So he could be a citizen of anywhere, theoretically."

"You haven't heard his accent. It's thicker than mine."

"Well… tell him not to talk." She licked her spoon. "I didn't read too much about it, but it looks like there's a way to get a U.S. passport without a birth certificate."

"What? Okay, I'll look that up. Thanks, Charlie. You're a lifesaver."

"I know, I'm amazing. I can Google things."

"You know what I mean," Iris giggled.

"Just remember this feeling when you go looking for your turkey sandwich later." Charlie winked.

After sucking down the largest mocha on Coffee Villa's menu and researching everything the internet had to offer about unusual passport requests, Iris had a plan. More like a rough set of goals. She would sneak into Angus's file again, make a copy of every official-looking paper she could find with his name on it, and try to get him a Letter of No Record from the state of Washington. Basically, it was an official document saying there *were* no official documents about a person. With that in hand, she might be able to get him an expedited passport. Maybe. As long as she could dig up some way to make it look like he'd been in the U.S. before age five. Somehow. Although, once she'd done that, exactly how she'd get him to an appointment at a passport agency was a kink she was still working out.

And this is supposedly easier than getting him a UK passport? I must be insane.

Will didn't even question why she was at work early any more. Though she still had only a vague idea how he liked his coffee, she'd taken a risk and ordered him a cup of her favorite: a double shot orange mocha. He might like it... or more likely, he'd think she was as weird as Charlie did. But either way, he'd learn something new about her.

"Hmm. I really like this," Will said after several sips. "It's kind of... like something out of a box of those chocolate truffles with different cream fillings."

"Are you just saying that so I don't feel like a weirdo?" Iris asked suspiciously.

"I would never do that, because I actually prefer weirdos. Look at the company I keep."

"I could pretend to be offended."

"I'd probably see right through it." He nudged her with his shoulder. "Anyway, professionally speaking, I'd call this kind of flavor profiling a sign of genius." He took another sip. "Yep. I might have to keep you around, in case I ever need inspiration."

"Then by all means, keep me around." Iris smiled with satisfaction. "Well, I'd better get up there before Becky comes in." She took two steps toward the stairs and turned. "Am I crazy for doing this? I mean... I met Angus a month ago. Does it make sense that I keep getting this involved in his life?"

"I think it does," Will replied. "It always makes sense to help someone who needs help. And he's your friend. Friends get involved."

"How involved? Hypothetically, I mean."

"I'm not sure I understand the question."

"I mean, how far would *you* be willing to go to help a friend? Would you ever, I dunno, say like... do something... illegal?"

Will frowned. "Are we still talking about Angus?"

"Yeah..."

He gazed at her for a long moment. "What's this about, Iris?"

She weighed her answer. *Will's a very "do-the-right-thing" kind of guy... how flexible is he about what the "right" thing is?*

"Well... right now it's mostly... kind of a paperwork thing," she hedged. "I'm not really officially allowed to, but I'm trying to figure out how hard it would be to get him... a passport."

"A passport? Interesting. Is he even fit to travel? You told me he's in the hospital."

"He is. But they think he'll make a full recovery. He just really wants to get home to Scotland, but nobody takes him seriously. He's going to be a ward of the state for the rest of his life... he might as well be a prisoner here. Officially, he's a problem that's already been solved. Transferring him somewhere internationally is a red tape headache that nobody would ever bother with. But it could mean everything to him."

"Yeah, I can see how you're bending the rules a little bit there, but I'd probably do the same thing."

If he only knew... Iris pursed her lips.

"Thanks, Will."

꧁

The lobby was dim and quiet. It still seemed like nighttime with the sunrise still half an hour away, and only the faintest traces of gray blue peeking through the stained glass windows.

Iris knew exactly which file drawer she was headed for this time. She snatched Angus's folder without hesitating and sank to the floor, spreading it open on her lap. She shuffled through the most recent pages on top, fighting the little voice in her head...

Normal, sane people don't do things like this.

She was looking for anything that could vouch for Angus's identity—maybe something stamped by the Social Security Administration, or... *Hello, what's this?* Iris held up a single sheet from the DOH Center for Health Statistics. It hadn't been in the folder last time she'd snooped. It bore the state seal and a notary's imprint. Her mouth fell open.

"Oh my gosh," she murmured. *A Letter of No Record! He already has one? They must've searched for his birth records officially and gotten this as part of the paper trail! This is going to save me so much trouble...* She read down the page.

"Good grief, they searched birth records from 1925 through 1940?" she muttered under her breath. "They really have no idea how old you are, Angus." The letter designated Angus's birth date as July 18, 1930. *Well, they got July 18th right, but why 1930? Random guess? Nice round number?*

Hands trembling, she scanned a color copy of the letter and carefully filed it, then slid the original into a manila folder and tucked it into her shoulder bag.

I'll have to put it back as soon as I can. No harm done.

She checked to make sure that everything looked undisturbed, and turned to leave, when a niggling thought occurred to her. *Iris, you are so paranoid. This is a senior home, not the CIA. Still... it couldn't hurt to be thorough.*

She glanced around her, tiptoed back toward the printer, and poked through the menus on the touch screen until she found "jobs." Sure enough. The top one, date and time stamped from two minutes ago, was still stored on the memory card. She deleted it and put the machine back in sleep mode.

Angus sat cross legged in his hospital bed, gazing out the window once again. He still had an IV cannula taped to his arm, but it was no longer hooked up to a bag. He had graduated from the breezy, backless gown to a white t-shirt and a pair of flannel pajama pants. He had given up picking through his plate of lunch, since over half of it was unrecognizable to him. Its cold remains lay on the tray table next to three used tea bags and what was supposed to be his dessert.

"Dinnae you want your Jello?" Iris asked from the doorway.

He turned. "Would *you*?" He poked the edge of the plastic dish with his finger, setting the red cube in motion. "What's that even supposed to be? It doesnae look like food."

"I guess it's an acquired taste. What else did they bring you?"

"Tea. They bring me all the tea I want—it's brilliant! But this…" He stabbed with his fork. "Some kind of meat. Couldnae tell what unfortunate creature it used to be. And mash… looks like. Hard to tell by the taste. I recognized the carrots, though. They were decent."

"Sounds about right for hospital food. I thought that might happen, so I brought you some of Will's cookies!" She sat in the plastic chair beside his bed and handed him a small paper bag.

"Aye, cookies, not biscuits. I remember," Angus said, eagerly opening the bag.

"Will whipped these up after breakfast this morning. Ever had a chocolate chip cookie before?"

Angus's eyebrows went up. "But chocolate's a drink." He held up a cookie and examined it, turning it over in his hand. "How'd they turn it into chips?"

Iris shook her head. "A lot's happened since your time. Some might even contend that the invention of eating chocolate was more important to mankind than going to the moon."

Angus took a bite. "I'll agree with you about that. It's far more useful." He held out the bag to her.

"Thanks!" Iris grinned and accepted one, and began nibbling the edge. "Wait…" The cookie had a surprising flavor—vaguely familiar. She squinted at it, and saw tiny flecks of what she was tasting: orange zest. *Chocolate orange cookies. Will, you sneaky genius.*

"Angus, can you taste the orange peel in there?" she giggled.

"I had an orange once!" he replied. "Not sure I'd remember the… oh wait…" He took another bite. "Aye, I can taste it a wee bit. What sort of idea is that, putting oranges and chocolate together?"

"I think it might be mine!" Iris beamed.

"Not bad!"

After a few moments, Iris grew serious. She peeked at the doorway to make sure no one was within earshot. "Angus…" she said just above a whisper. "You still wanna get out of here?"

His eyes widened. "Aye…"

"I might've figured somethin' out." She leaned in. "There's half a chance I can get you a passport."

"What's a passport?" he whispered.

"The government makes you carry a little booklet with your photograph in it to prove who y'are, and they stamp it when you go from one country to another."

"That sounds difficult to get."

"You would not believe how difficult." Iris shook her head. "Especially for someone like you, with no birth records! It usually takes a long time to get one, too. But we can get it sooner if I take you in person. If I were to get your tickets… y'know, pay your passage, to prove you need to travel soon, I'm hopin' we could get the papers rushed through."

"But I thought you said," he whispered, checking the doorway, "that if I left here with you, they'd think I was kidnapped."

"Dinnae worry about that. I… I'm goin' to work somethin' out. The first step will be getting to Seattle. It's a big city not far from here. That's where we'd have to get your passport, and where the airport is."

"Air… port? You mean I'd have to… fly in an aer…aero—"

"Aeroplane, yes. We dinnae have any other options."

"Blimey…"

"Anyway, my friend Charlie's parents have a little vacation cabin near there. We can stay there until I figure all this out."

He shook his head. "Wait, I thought you said you were barely makin' rent, like me. When did you suddenly come into the kind of money that buys two passages across the ocean?"

"Well, my granny and granddad are paying for my ticket. For our Christmas visit, y'know. But… I'm trying to put some money together for yours. I'll borrow if I have to."

"Iris, I cannae let you do that," he said at full voice.

"Dinnae you want to get home?" she replied, just as loudly.

"I do, but…" He lowered to a hushed whisper. "What kind of friend lets someone else end up in debt, maybe even in jail…"

"That's *my* decision." She took his wrinkled hand in hers. "It's not your fault that modern governments have no contingency plan for lost time travelers."

"You really believe that's what I am?"

"With all my heart. You bent the laws of physics gettin' here. We're just going to have to bend a few more laws to get you back on the right continent."

"At least let me help. Take my old coin. Maybe you can get somethin' for it," he suggested.

"The one that's been in your family since the sixteenth century? There's no way I'm doin' that."

"I was gonna pawn it anyway, so you might as well—"

"There's no time, Angus. It's so old now, I'd have to have it authenticated and take it to a proper auction. It's be'er off in your pocket."

He crossed his arms. "I'm so helpless here," he huffed. "I'm just a have-nothin', do-nothin' old beggar."

"There's nothin' wrong with lettin' people help you!"

"You sound like my mum. I'm sure you're right, but it seems like that's all I ever do any more," he muttered. Suddenly, his eyes lit up. "Wait, do people buy old stamps?"

"Stamps?"

"Aye, stamps. For the post? Seems like, at least from what you said about your King George sovereigns, that people are willing to pay a lot for old things. I've a le'er from my aunt… I was meant to deliver it home to my mum… it's got a nice stamp on it with Her Majesty's face. Just a penny stamp, but… I dinnae ken, it might be worth a little something."

"That's a brilliant idea! I can find out. Where is it?"

"Still in my coat pocket, hangin' on the back of my door."

"Thanks, Angus. That might really help."

Angus smiled with satisfaction.

Iris took a deep breath and looked him straight in the face, her eyes bright. "You absolutely sure you're up for this? Might get a little crazy."

"Listen, crazy started way before I met you. How much worse can it get? Besides, I cannae stay here. I'll get home, or die tryin.'"

He began to feel the slightest tinge of an old familiar feeling creeping back into his soul: hope. "And are *you* absolutely sure *you're* up for it? I cannae believe you'd do all this for me."

Iris smiled at the new light in his eyes. "Sometimes, doing the right thing looks different in real life than it does on paper. We're not so different, you and me. If I were the one in your shoes, well… like you said—I'd get home, or die tryin.'"

"They're gonna catch us!"

Iris turned with a start, almost dropping the box of baking supplies she was carrying to the Activity Room. Walter, who was peeking from the doorway of a room that wasn't his, waved Iris over.

"Who's going to catch us, Walter?"

"The Feds! They've been all over me since that tax thing in '82!" He picked up his shiny black cane with orange flames on it and poked it in the direction Iris was already headed. "You be the lookout. I'll cut 'em off at the pass."

"Walter, I've got a better idea," she whispered conspiratorially. "Why don't you come bake cupcakes with us? They'd never suspect you of doing that."

"Cupcakes, eh? Genius. Throw 'em off the scent."

"Exactly. I'm headed there now…"

"Okay. But if they find me, I'm using you as a human shield!"

"Fair enough. But they'll never find you, Walter," Iris assured him. "I mean c'mon, cupcakes? They'll never see it coming."

Walter hooked his arm in hers and shuffled along beside her. "Keep this up, rookie. I'll send your name up the chain for a promotion."

Iris giggled.

As they rounded the corner into the Activity Room, First Irene waved her calendar. "Three o'clock, it says here!" she crowed.

"Exactly right!" Iris replied cheerfully, laying out boxes of cake mix and cans of frosting.

"I think she's a mole," Walter whispered, eyeing Irene. "She's everywhere!"

"You could be right," Iris whispered back. "I'll keep an eye on her."

Walter tapped the side of his nose and gave her a wink.

Candace breezed through the door behind them, pushing elegant Gladys in her wheelchair. Today, Gladys was wearing a ruffled lavender blouse with pearl buttons on the cuffs and collar. Iris could tell by her perfectly coiffed silver hair that the beautician had just completed her weekly wash and set.

"We've saved an apron just for you!" Candace was saying to her as they entered.

"Well, I'm not dressed for it, but if you need help..." Gladys said.

"We love it when you help us," Candace assured her.

"Hi, Gladys!" Iris greeted her. "Would you like to line the cupcake tins with these little cupcake papers?" Iris knew she'd prefer a less sticky job.

"Oh, sure!" Looking relieved, she reached for the liners, which Iris had already separated and restacked to make it easier for her shaking fingers to do the job.

Candace turned to Iris. "This group is probably more than big enough. I'm going to have to miss this time, though. Paperwork to do."

"No worries, I'm an old pro at this now," Iris replied.

"Yes, you are! I don't know how I ever got by without you!" Candace flashed her a grin and turned for the door. "I'll log the attendance, though, ok?"

"Thanks, Candace." Iris reached over and turned on a CD of classic hits from the forties and fifties.

"Bye! Goodbye!" Betty waved, doing a little boogie to the music. "Come again!"

"Bye, Betty!" Candace called over her shoulder.

"Wake me up when it's time to taste 'em," Fred muttered, settling his chin on his chest for a nap.

"Typical," snorted Third Irene, who was dumping cake mix into a bowl.

"Typically adorable," cooed Doris, who sat with a whisk in her hand, but had yet to do any stirring.

Iris stifled her laughter and did her best to walk the group of twelve participants through two hours of mixing, baking, frosting, and decorating. While they waited for the cupcakes to cool, she had them decorate little toothpick signs with their names on them to help identify whose cupcake was whose.

She looked around her at the now-familiar faces and realized that she was beginning to understand what Candace had meant before. These were truly lovely people. She didn't see dementia any more when she spent time with them. She just saw quirky personalities in need of connection and friendship. Each of them still had desires, preferences, things that mattered to them. She knew not to let First Irene near the frosting, or to seat Third Irene near Gladys unless she wanted to clean up a food fight. She even remembered to stand behind Betty, ready to catch the unfrosted cupcakes when Betty began to "sort" them and throw out the "defective" ones.

She suddenly realized something else—these people were her friends.

What might it mean if she and Angus couldn't pull off an escape? Jail time, maybe. The end of any possibility of a career, likely. And, near the top of the list… not being welcome back at Rookwood. Never seeing these faces again. Could she risk all of that for one man's freedom?

After putting away supplies and wiping tables, Iris switched off the music and headed for the door. *Hmmm. Second Irene loves that CD, but I didn't see her today. I'll have to stop by her room and say hi.* Iris checked her watch. There was just enough time to see her before clocking out. She made her way to Irene's room, but stopped short just inside the doorway.

Everything looked different. Instead of the usual chintz curtains and ruffled throw pillows, there were sparse white window blinds and a plain sofa. In place of the knick knacks and art projects that normally littered the desk, there stood a solitary cardboard box. The flowered quilt and shams were gone, and the bed was made up with a tightly tucked white sheet. Instead of a pillow, there lay six crimson roses. Iris felt her stomach drop.

"Wh—"

"She went peacefully in her sleep last night," said a voice behind her.

Iris turned to see Becky the receptionist standing there, holding a second cardboard box.

"I'm so sorry," Iris half whispered, as unsure of what to feel as what to say next.

"You were really good to her," Becky said quietly. "I could see that she liked you." She entered the room and began collecting picture frames from the walls, dusting them, and placing them in the box. "But she's with Dad now. I'm sure she's much happier."

Dad?

"Irene was your... mother?" Iris gasped. "I had no idea."

"Well..." Becky sniffed. "Neither did she, by the end." She didn't turn from her task, but Iris could see large tears welling up in her eyes. "I started saying goodbye to her years ago, so..." She dabbed her cheek with the back of her hand and let out a frustrated sigh. "I thought this part would be easier."

"I'm going to miss her," Iris said earnestly. "It's going to be so different around here without her."

"Yeah..." Becky continued to dust and box her mother's possessions.

Iris remembered holding Irene's petite hand as they sang loudly together down the hallway. *I'm forever blowing bubbles...*

"Don't say anything to James, okay?" Becky interrupted her thoughts. "I'll tell him tonight when we get home."

"I promise. And Becky?"

"Hm?"

"I really am so sorry for your loss. She was one of my favorite people here."

Becky nodded. "Mine too."

Iris turned from the room and fled into the hallway with her emotions. It didn't feel right somehow, bursting into tears over someone she'd only known just over a month. Especially in front of Irene's own daughter, who had been through the harrowing ordeal of watching her mother's mind disappear day by day.

Becky's the one who deserves to cry. What right do I have? Except that she was sweet and wonderful. And I'll never see her again.

Iris's nose tickled and her eyes blurred. She clocked out, grabbed her purse out of her locker, and headed for the door, not even trying to stop the tears that came.

There is no way I'm waiting around until they put roses on Angus's bed.

Chapter 19

"Iris!" James panted as he jogged up to her in the parking lot.

"Hey, James!"

"Whoa, your face looks weird," he puffed. "Are you crying?"

Iris decided to be honest. "Yep." She unlocked her car and tossed her purse onto the seat.

"Does it have anything to do with me?"

"Not at all."

"Cool. Well I researched that stamp you gave me..."

"What'd you find out?"

"First of all, how cool is it... oh, here's your thing back..." He handed her Angus's envelope. "How cool is it that you know I'm into stamps!"

"Will told me a while ago that it's an interest of yours."

"More like an obsession! We should totally go out for dinner and a movie and then talk about stamps."

"James, remember how I said that I don't date coworkers?"

"Oh okay, that's still a thing? Just making sure. I didn't know if this was one of those times where being persistent would help." He shrugged his lean shoulders. "It's really hard to read people."

"I promise, I will always say exactly what I mean."

"Hey, me too! Well we can talk about it right here, I guess. So basically that stamp is worth some money. Are you selling it?"

"I might be… how much money are we talking?"

"Well, there's kinda some fun things going on with that. First of all, it's in great condition, like, super nice. Where's this thing been?"

"Somewhere safe."

"Yeah, okay. Makes sense. Now, see the edges of the stamp?" He reached out and tapped the corner of the envelope in Iris's hand. "It's cut with scissors, so it's pre-1853. That's when they started perforating the edges. And it's cut straight, which is good. The sloppy ones aren't worth as much."

"Well, that much I knew. It was from around 1844, actually."

"Oh okay. Really? That's good then. That means it was probably from plate 42, 43, maybe 44… Plates are the thingies they print off of."

"James, how do you keep so many random facts in your head like that?"

"Oh, well I'm not sure. I'm not really trying to. I thought this was such a cool stamp that I've been reading up on penny reds all day. Couldn't really stop!" He laughed, and his voice cracked. "I only have to read something once, and it's like, in my head forever. Maybe there's space in my brain for it because I don't hang onto stuff like manners. Sometimes it's a curse. Do you have any gum?"

Iris blinked. She could never get used to the sharp turns in conversations with James. "Uh… yes." She turned and fished a pack of gum out of her purse on the seat, lifted one stick so it was easier to grab, and held it out to him.

He took the entire pack and tucked it into his shirt pocket. "I'm saving that for five minutes from now," he said, "because I *do* remember you're not supposed to talk with your mouth full, and I don't know if gum is in that category, but it probably is.

"Anyways, if your stamp is from those plates, that's pretty cool because they were the last ones to be cancelled with this thingy…" he tapped again. "It's called a Maltese Cross. The cancels started using mostly numbers and names of towns and stuff around 1844. And this design is super wacky, not really like most of the ones out there. It's got way more lines on it, see? I looked it up and it's from a place called Stonehaven, in Scotland. It was only used in that one post office. Pretty cool, huh?"

"Yeah, I—"

"Also, the cancellation, it's supposed to be in black ink. Because the stamp is red. But somebody messed up, because this one's bluey purply. I have no idea why. That might be good, though. When people mess up it usually means it's valuable later. Like those upside down airplanes. The other cool thing is the letters. See the little letters in the corners? The plates were lettered starting with 'AA' and going to 'TL.' This one's 'I' and 'J'—your initials! Fun, right? Some people like that. The sheets came with two hundred and forty stamps in twenty rows…"

"James?"

"Hm?"

"What does all this mean?"

"Dude, are you serious? I've been telling you."

"Just pretend I'm really dumb."

"You should take it… to a stamp guy… and sell it," he said slowly. "Much… cash."

Iris playfully whacked his arm with the back of her hand. "What stamp guy?"

With a lopsided grin, James held up a bright yellow sticky note with an address scrawled on it. "I knew you'd ask that."

Iris snatched it. "You're the best."

"That's very true," he replied, pulling a stick of gum from his pocket and mashing it into his mouth. "Do I get a commission?"

"Don't push it." Iris grinned and got into her car. "Thanks, James."

Next stop: A stamp guy.

Somewhere over the Atlantic ~ Present Day

"Caledon, I got your message. Is there a new assignment?"

"Brennus," Caledon greeted him with a nod of his head. "Not so much a new assignment as a new development. You've guarded the Jacobs family well these past generations. The time disturbance is healing, but many elements of the Perfect Will are missing, or out of place. My charges, the Guardians of the Hawthorn, have been greatly distressed ever since that dreadful day, it's been their fervent wish to see the disturbance resolved. I'm doing all in my power to help them, but you and I will have to work in tandem to make that happen."

"I don't understand. What has the Jacobs family to do with the disturbance?" Brennus wondered. "They were never affected by it."

"It doesn't appear so, on the surface… though every person within a certain distance is always affected when a human life is taken before its time, in ways that are difficult to measure. But the pieces of the plan are moving again. Did you never wonder about the Lost Carpenter?"

"I did, but I assumed he was with the Three."

"Strangely, no. He lives on… in the flesh! Aimsir, his guardian, wasn't reassigned as we supposed, but watches over him even now."

"You mean—"

"Yes, it's the same man. One of your charges has befriended him!" Caledon shook his head in wonder.

"No wonder they had to be moved across the ocean!" Brennus laughed. "The pieces of the puzzle come together at last!"

"Have your sentries guard the rest of the family while you focus on the daughter. She will soon require great favor. You will then rendezvous with Aimsir and the two of you will ensure the travelers safe passage."

"So be it," Brennus agreed. "It's fascinating to see how the Three draw the strands together. This assignment got off to such a strange start."

"What, guarding the fisherman before his family even began?"

"No, even weeks before that…" Brennus chuckled at the memory. "My assignment was to go to a tiny post office and hide an inkpad and a rubber stamp. For some reason, the Master wanted them canceling postage with the outdated ones for a couple hours. I'm still waiting to understand His reason."

"How great is He!" Caledon exclaimed with triumph. "Such attention to detail!"

Vancouver, WA

"This is very odd," said the pudgy man behind the counter. He wore magnifying lenses over his spectacles, giving his eyes a wild appearance as he scrutinized the envelope in his gloved hand.

"What's odd?" Iris asked, trying to hide her apprehension.

"This entire thing, to be honest," the man replied, glancing at her over his glasses before returning to his examination. "Nothing special about this stamp, really. It's your basic penny red. Millions floating around out there. I have a hundred of 'em myself."

Iris's face fell. *I guess James was wrong.*

"But this specimen…" he continued. "Well frankly, it's superb. I've only ever seen covers in this condition when they were kept tucked away inside a thick book, away from all light and oxygen. There's a tiny bit of dirt on the corner, but otherwise…" He turned the envelope over and over in his hand. "Unopened… interesting. Makes one curious, doesn't it?" He gave Iris a mischievous grin.

"Very curious," she said patiently, hoping that any moment he would provide some solid information.

"Someone took great pride in the details here," he went on. "Notice how the stamp is cut perfectly on all sides and applied both parallel and equidistant from the edges of the envelope."

"Is that good?"

"Aesthetic appeal is *always* good," he replied over his glasses, as though not comprehending how anyone could even ask such a question. "Most curious of all is the cancellation—"

"Yes, I was told by a… an expert… that it's a Maltese Cross from a town called Stonehaven?"

"Your expert is correct. It's most distinctive! There are relatively few quality examples of it in existence any more. But two additional things give it even greater distinction—"

Three things, actually… whispered Brennus, who sat cross-legged on the glass countertop, concealed in shadow, between Iris and the stamp dealer.

"Oh, actually three things!" the man corrected himself. "Look here—not only is the Stonehaven Maltese cross quite unique, this one is lightly applied in a violet ink peculiar to that region. It's quite rare to see. Additionally, there are no recorded instances of this cancellation being in use after early 1841. But I suppose there's always the odd clerical error where someone's having an off day and grabs the wrong one."

Brennus laughed with satisfaction. The stamp dealer's bulldog barked suspiciously from behind the counter.

"George Washington, hush!" the dealer scolded the animal affectionately. He turned back to Iris. "Goof-ups like that are golden moments in philately! Know what I mean?" His over magnified eyes widened even more.

"Definitely!" Iris nodded vigorously, trying to remember what philately was. "Did you say there was a third thing?"

"Yes indeed!" The dealer held the envelope up in front of Iris's face with awe. "Her Majesty has been socked on the nose."

"Socked… on the nose?"

"It's beautiful, isn't it? Such a rarity to find the cancellation struck so squarely in the center of the stamp. It makes many a collector quite giddy."

"So… any idea of its value?" Iris steered him back to the point.

"I'd be hesitant to give you a solid figure without collaborating with several trusted colleagues," he hedged.

"Ballpark?"

"Well, I did forward the images that James emailed me yesterday to a colleague at Stanley Gibbons. He's an expert in Victorian line engraved stamps. He seemed quite eager to see this specimen for himself. He could give you a more thorough appraisal and help you put this item in a proper auction."

"I'm afraid I don't have that kind of time," Iris admitted. She hated revealing her disadvantage, but didn't see a better option.

"As long as the provenance is genuine…" The dealer raised one eyebrow at Iris.

Oh relax, it's genuine, Brennus whispered to him.

"And I see nothing to indicate otherwise..." The dealer smiled. "I'd be comfortable offering fifteen."

"Fifteen?" Iris frowned. "That's it?"

"Well, my dear, keep in mind that this is without an appraisal. I'd need to have it appraised and certified, plus pay auction costs, as well as recoup my investment. I'm sure you could get more if you were willing to take more time—"

"It's okay," Iris sighed. "Fifteen is better than nothing."

He smiled with satisfaction. "It will be the pride of someone's collection, I assure you. I'll be right back with your check."

Iris drummed her fingers on the glass countertop. "Well, George Washington? What d'you think?" she asked the bulldog, who had a prominent underbite, and was drooling a bit. "Am I silly for driving all the way over here?"

George Washington perked up his ears and let out a tiny "bph."

"Yeah, me too."

Five minutes later, the dealer emerged with his glasses pushed up on top of his head, making his gray hair stick out in funny directions. He handed Iris a check.

"There you are, my dear," he said. "Fifteen thousand dollars."

"Fif—" Iris coughed. "Fifteen *thousand*?"

Brennus let out a hearty guffaw. George Washington barked again.

The dealer, who had begun sliding the little envelope into a plastic cover, dropped his shoulders with a look of chagrin. "Have you changed your mind?"

"No! Nope, this is great. We said fifteen, didn't we? We did. Okay…" She absentmindedly stuffed the check into her purse.

"You're quite sure? Because like I said, you'd likely see more at auction…"

"I'm fine. This is fine! It's perfect. Thank you."

"It's been a genuine pleasure," the dealer said. They shook hands. "Send my greetings to James."

"I will." Iris smiled shakily and scooted out the door before the dealer suspected her of having a nervous breakdown.

"Iris, are you insane?" Charlie cried, her scissors now motionless halfway across the roll of blue snowman wrapping paper. "*You're* going to take him? I thought you were just trying to see if he could even *get* a passport! Now you're talking about abducting someone from a hospital?"

Iris dug through the bag of used Christmas bows and tossed a coordinating silver one across the table.

"Charlie, they think he's mental. They're going to keep him locked up. He'll never see his home again unless someone takes drastic measures!"

"So now you're now his self-appointed drastic measure taker... er?"

"I don't see anybody else volunteering!"

"Yes. That's because nobody else wants to go to jail."

"It's not that I *want* to go to jail, Charlie. It's just that... some things are worth going to jail for. This is one of them. Besides, I'm taking precautions."

"Precautions, right. Because you've had *so much* experience kidnapping people..." Charlie finished cutting the paper and began wrapping it around a little box of Legos.

"Is that for your nephew?"

"Yes, it's for my nephew, and don't change the subject!" Charlie snapped.

"I'm being careful, okay?" Iris assured her, handing her a tape dispenser. "Our flight isn't for another three days, but I told my boss I was leaving this morning. She thinks I'm already there. They won't suspect me if I'm supposedly already out of the country. When Angus goes missing, they'll just assume he's wandered off on his own. They already think he's in the habit of doing that."

"One tiny problem… don't they watch him around the clock at the hospital?"

"They're releasing him tonight. I told him what to do."

"Okay… But won't he be missed at the senior home?" Charlie stuck out her tongue in concentration as she folded the corners of the wrapping paper and taped them down. "I mean, they do a head count once in a while, don't they?"

"Well… they'll eventually wonder where he is. But I'll have some time before that happens."

"How so? Gonna create a diversion like they do in the movies? Set off a smoke bomb in the bathroom or something?"

"What! I'm not a criminal, Charlie!" Iris handed her the sheet of foil gift tags. "Actually, it's better. The social worker thinks that someone from Rookwood is picking Angus up in the van. But I predict that somehow, the van driver at Rookwood will get the notion that the social worker is driving him back. Paperwork can get so mixed up sometimes." She grinned.

"Yeah, especially with you around." Charlie rolled her eyes. "Does Will know what you're doing?"

"No, why would I—"

"Because I thought the two of you were getting all buddy-buddy."

"I didn't think it would be a good idea to involve Will. I don't want him having to lie for me. And to be honest, I'm not sure if he's even capable of lying."

"Ohhhh, I see. So Will gets to remain blissfully ignorant of your felonies, but you'll let *me* lie for you?" She slapped a large reindeer gift tag in place and searched the table for a pen.

Iris pulled the pen from its hiding place under a scrap of wrapping paper and slid it across the table. "Actually…" she pursed her lips and squinted her face into a sheepish little smile. "I was hoping you'd be my accomplice."

"For real?" Charlie grew serious. She frowned at Iris for several moments. "If you're really going through with this, I guess I'd better help make sure you don't get caught." She yanked the cap off the pen with her teeth and spoke around it. "What do you need?"

"I just need to borrow the key to your parents' vacation cabin in Seattle."

"Okay…"

"And…"

Charlie took the pen cap out of her teeth. "Oh, goody. There's more?"

"Would you cut his hair? It's so curly and white, you can spot him from a mile away. I was hoping you could make him a little less obvious."

"Sure."

"Really?" Iris grabbed Charlie's hands across the table and gave them a squeeze.

"Yes, really. On one condition…"

"Anything!"

"Get your chef boyfriend to make me some doughnuts. I'm going to need sustenance." She scribbled her nephew's name on the tag.

"Done. And he's not my boyfriend."

"Whatever you say."

"Mr. Armstrong, your IV is out, and you're good to go!" the nurse said a little too loudly as she patted a bandage into place on Angus's arm.

"Thanks."

"You've been such a good patient. Just take good care of yourself and come back and see us if you're having any more trouble, okay?"

"Yep." Angus tried out the unfamiliar word to see how it sounded. *Hmm. Not bad.* He'd heard a lot of Americans using it instead of "aye."

"Your discharge instructions are right here," she went on, "but I'll make sure the next nurse coming on shift goes over them with your caretaker before you leave, okay?"

"Yep."

"Do you need anything else? Maybe an apple juice?"

"I'm just fine."

"Okay, well just sit tight. Someone will let you know when your ride gets here."

Angus smiled and nodded reassuringly to the nurse as she left the room, closing the door behind her. He checked the clock. 6:55 p.m. *Perfect. It's now or never.*

He dove for the large, glittery "Get Well Soon" gift bag that Iris had left for him. Inside it, hidden beneath a stuffed bear the size of a human baby, were a black rucksack and a set of blue scrubs—pants, shirt, and cap—that Iris had bought at a thrift shop. He donned them as fast as he could, stuffing his jeans, t-shirt, and discharge papers into the rucksack. He put the strange white shoes back on—"sneakers" as the social worker called them. *How apt.*

Once he had tucked his white mop of curls into the cap as best he could, he checked the mirror. *Close enough.* He stuck the bear back into the gift bag and propped it back up in the same place it had been sitting all day. He slung the rucksack over his shoulder and reached for the doorknob. He froze.

That wretched label!

He scanned the room for something to cut the bracelet off. Finding nothing, he set to work on it with his teeth. After a minute, he was able to create enough of a fault in the band to yank it free and stuff it in his pocket. He picked the edge of the bandage on his arm and ripped it off in one jerk. He tucked it into his pocket with the bracelet.

He opened the door a few inches. He could see a huddle of nursing staff at the far end of the corridor, crowded around a whiteboard. He slipped from the room, closing the door behind him, and walked off in the opposite direction, assuming as casual a gait as he could manage.

He followed the route he'd memorized from the drawing Iris had made for him. The halls seemed to stretch on forever. He passed only two people. Although his heart was in his throat, he resisted the urge to bolt. One person gave him a polite nod, and the other barely noticed him.

At last, he reached the stairwell that was supposed to lead him to an underground "parking garage," whatever that was, where he was to wait for Iris. As soon as he emerged into the noxious smelling basement full of motorized carriages, he was shocked at how brightly lit it was. Finding Iris might not be as difficult as he'd imagined.

Just as he began to look around him in earnest, a small green carriage pulled up beside him with Iris's smiling face framed in the window. She was wearing a stocking cap and tartan scarf. The glass window pane in front of her face slid down and disappeared into the door with a strange whirring sound.

"Go around and hop in!" she said.

Angus obeyed, trying to take everything in, but without slowing down. Iris reached across him, pulled a strap across his body, and buckled it.

"What's 'bout to happen that you gotta strap me down?" Angus asked, eyes wide.

Iris laughed. "Nothin' out of the ordinary. That's the idea," she replied. "There's a law that you have to wear a seatbelt in a movin' car in case of... well, you just have to."

Angus nodded. "I thought you said the car would be white."

"Yeah, last minute change. Charlie thought I should take her car just in case someone starts lookin' for mine, so we parked mine at the airport."

"Where we headed?"

"My place real quick, then Seattle."

"Your place?"

"Yeah, Charlie's going to make your hair look a little different so it's harder to spot you in a crowd."

"This Charlie sounds like a wonderful friend to have," Angus said.

"I dinnae ken what I'd do without her," Iris agreed.

It was a twenty minute drive to Iris and Charlie's. Iris kept up a running commentary on modern amenities such as fast food, shopping malls, freeways, and telephones, in order to distract him from the fact that they were traveling at seventy miles an hour down a wet road at night. Although his eyes were wide and he stared out the windows constantly, Angus managed to hold up his end of the conversation without giving in to the panic he felt creeping up on him.

This is her world, he reasoned. *She knows what to do. I can trust her. God, I've already put myself into her hands. Please, help us. She's risking everything.*

Chapter 20

"There you go, mister!" Charlie spun Angus around to face the bathroom mirror. He was perched on Iris's office chair and covered in one of Charlie's old practice capes from beauty school.

His mouth fell open. "I've never had my hair this short— not since I was a wee babe!" He turned his head side to side.

"You don't look a day over eighty!" Charlie beamed.

"Not a curl in sight. The silvery gray is a nice touch, too," Iris added. "If they're looking for a chap with white hair, they're not going to find one."

"It's brilliant!" Angus flashed Charlie a sheepish grin. "I have to confess, I was a little worried when first I saw you. Wasnae sure what color hair I'd end up with. Green, maybe..."

"Ha!" Charlie swept the cape from Angus's shoulders. "Not sure you could pull it off," she answered with a wink.

"Thank you again, for everything," he said.

"Just get home safe, and it'll all be worth it," Charlie replied.

"I have something else for you, Angus," Iris said. She went to the hall closet and pulled out a paper grocery bag. "I couldnae take much from your room because it would look like you'd planned ahead, but here…" She handed him the bag.

He peeked inside, and a huge grin spread across his face. "My coat! Och, bless ye." He pulled the brown coat from the bag and laid it reverently across his lap. "I was sorely vexed to leave it behind. It was my dad's."

Iris smiled with satisfaction. "Best of all," she said, "you've still got ol' Mary."

Angus's eyes widened. "That's right! She was in my…" He reached into the pocket and pulled out the coin. He closed his hand tightly around it and nodded, eyes misty. "Thank ye so kindly, Iris. This…"

"It's okay, Angus. I couldnae let you leave that behind."

"It's just that… this means she's still in the family. There's finally one thing I've not failed at."

"You think comin' here made you a failure? It was an accident!"

"Was it?" He hung his head. "Maybe it's punishment. I had a strange feelin' about that tree, and I ignored it. I was trying to impress my new boss. And on top of that, I was about to pawn away my family's legacy."

"But—"

"I left Gillian. She'd never have gotten hurt if I'd been there. I left my mum with unpaid rent, unable to work—"

"You think that's what they cared about, in the end? Any of that?" Iris protested. "I'm sure they grieved you with all their hearts, but it wasnae your missing wages they longed for, Angus. It was *you*. Any woman would be lucky to have a son or husband as devoted and hardworking as you."

A tear spilled onto Angus's cheek.

"To love people so well as you do," she went on, laying her hand on his shoulder, "that means you're a success."

Angus nodded, another tear escaping. He wiped his nose. "I never used to cry this much back home," he said with a hoarse laugh.

"No shame in it," Charlie said. "It's anti-aging."

"Well, then!" Angus chuckled. "Perhaps I should do it more often."

The oven timer dinged.

"Ooooh, pizza!" Charlie skipped into the kitchen and pulled two pizzas from the oven. "Angus, do you like pineapple?"

"Pine… apple? You've got strange pine trees here, then, because I—"

Charlie and Iris burst into laughter.

"What?" Angus emerged from the bathroom and into the tiny kitchen to see what Charlie was talking about.

"It's a tropical fruit with a funny name," Iris explained. "It's got nothing to do with pine trees."

Charlie presented Angus with a paper plate, loaded with Hawaiian pizza. "So… this is pizza…" Charlie fished for words. "It's kind of a flat bread with stuff on top. There's tomatoes cooked into a sauce, cheese, ham, and pineapple. Then you cook it in the oven."

"Blimey," he said, lifting a slice of pizza and examining it. "Tropical fruit, eh? It must have been dearly expensive to get that here. Thank ye for sharin' this with me." He took a bite. "I dinnae ken how you had time to cook all that, but it's delicious!"

Charlie and Iris shared a look.

"Well, nowadays, you can buy them already made," Iris told him. "But I'm glad you like it! It's our favorite."

"Pizza," Angus mused, taking another bite. "Strange word."

"Um, Iris?" Charlie said, holding her phone up. "We may have a problem."

"Oh no… what?"

"Guess who Washington State Patrol just put out a Silver Alert for? It's on the news."

"That's just great…" Iris muttered as she switched on the television and found the local news channel.

The news anchor was mid-sentence.

"…*is where Armstrong was last seen. He's believed to be between eighty-five and ninety years old, and suffering from dementia. Police are asking citizens to call if they see this man.*" A drawing that looked only a little bit like Angus popped up on the screen. "*He was wearing blue jeans, a white t-shirt, and white sneakers. He's five foot ten and has curly white hair.*"

Iris turned the TV off. The three sat in silence for a moment.

"The good news is, according to this article, they think he's on foot," Charlie went on, scrolling on her phone. "The bad news is, they think he might try to head for a train station."

Iris met Angus's eyes and her shoulders slumped. "If they're watching train stations, then I guess we're not getting to Seattle that way."

"Just take my car," Charlie volunteered.

"Charlie, you need wheels. How're you supposed to get to work?"

"Leave me your keys and claim ticket, and I'll go get your car out of long term parking. If anybody asks, I'll say you gave me permission to use it while you were away… and… how bout… mine's in the shop?"

"Wow, you thought up that lie pretty quick! You're a natural!" Iris grinned.

Charlie fluffed her hair. "I know. It's scary."

"Sounds like we should get going, Angus," Iris said. "Bring your pizza. If we make good time, we can get some decent sleep before your appointment at the passport place in the morning."

Angus donned his coat and slung his rucksack over his shoulder.

"Key swap!" Charlie said, holding up her car keys by their fluffy purple keychain. "The cabin key is on there, too. It's the big one."

Iris pawed through her purse and handed each item to Charlie as she located it. "Parking ticket… blue lot, bus shelter C. Here, have some moolah…" she handed Charlie a hundred dollar bill. "That will pay for the Uber to the airport, parking, gas, coffee, more pizza, being extra awesome…"

"Sweet." Charlie pocketed the cash. "The job's paying well, I see."

"So are stamps."

"Stamps?"

"Long story. And here's the key to Daphne." Iris held up her keychain.

"It's so weird that you named your car."

"You don't know her. If you did, you'd understand."

"Well, I will be very good to Daphne while you're gone," Charlie promised.

Iris pulled her into a hug. "I don't know what I'd ever do without you. Thanks for everything."

Charlie hugged her tightly. "Just don't get caught."

The journey to Seattle was dark, cold, and covered in a downpour so insistent that it was difficult to see more than ten yards ahead, even with the wipers at full speed.

After polishing off his third slice of pizza, Angus climbed into the back seat, stretched out as much as possible, and fell asleep, using his coat as a pillow. Iris was grateful. He had looked so exhausted standing there in the parking garage when she had pulled up beside him. She needed him as fresh as possible in the morning so they could figure out what to say during his appointment at the passport agency. Iris had a feeling that spinning a web of lies wouldn't sit well with Angus, even if it meant his freedom.

"God… you there?" Iris whispered. *"Angus believes in you. I guess maybe I do too, since I'm talking to you… please help. We've gotten this far, just… please, make this work out somehow."*

Above them, two figures sat serenely on the roof of the car, the frigid December rain passing through without touching them.

Brennus glanced at his new partner. "Aimsir, you felt that, right?"

Aimsir nodded, an adventurous gleam in his eye.

Brennus grinned. "Heads up," he murmured. "Yours is waking up and mine's falling asleep."

Aimsir whispered rest and peace into the mind of the sleeping passenger, while Brennus reminded the driver what was at stake.

Twice during the journey, Brennus dashed ahead—once to shoo a deer back into the woods, and the other to pick up a screw before the tire rolled over it. He shielded the front of the car from the worst of the rain with his cloak, improving visibility by half. Aimsir guided the tires across several deep puddles. Three times, he had to press against neighboring vehicles with his foot to keep them at a safe distance.

"I was told that Interstate 5 would keep us pretty busy," Aimsir commented.

"It's a war zone!" Brennus agreed.

Iris had been to the cabin during the summer on three other occasions, but always with someone else driving, and always in daylight. Just when she was beginning to wonder whether she'd made a wrong turn, she spotted the hand etched sign that Charlie had made in woodshop. It said "Stuart" with an arrow pointing down a narrow lane into a stand of trees.

It was nearing midnight when Angus finally put his head on the pillow. Neither he nor Iris had had the energy to locate linens and make up the beds properly, so they pulled two sleeping bags from the hall closet and tossed them onto the beds.

Angus had been in good spirits when Iris woke him to come in from the car, but he lay down on his sleeping bag with some difficulty.

"Angus, y'arright?" she asked, concerned by his pained expression.

"Aye… y'know, just tired. Hard to tell night from day in a hospital, what with people buzzin' about at all hours. Not sure I ever got a full night's sleep in there."

"Arright… you sure? Looked like you had some pain, there."

"Just…" he sighed and closed his eyes. "Just my chest hurts a little… I'll be fine."

Iris felt a stab of panic. *What if he should still be in the hospital?*

She took off her fitness watch and strapped it to Angus's wrist.

"What's this, then?" he murmured, not opening his eyes.

"It's my watch. It tells me what your heart rate is, in case I wanna know. Just go to sleep. Everything's fine. I'll wake you when it's time to go."

Angus was already half asleep and didn't reply.

At one o'clock in the morning, Iris's phone rang. She had just fallen asleep, and the sound shot through her brain like an electric jolt. She snatched the phone from the bedside table, hoping it wasn't Charlie calling to report some kind of disaster that would abort the mission. She peered at the screen with one eye. Not recognizing the number, she tried to press "Ignore" but accidently picked up the call instead.

"Iris?" a voice said on the other end.

Iris groaned into her pillow, but then tried to sound as awake as possible.

"Yes, hello?"

"It's Candace! I didn't wake you, did I?"

"Hm? Of course not! No, I was just—"

"I stayed up extra late to call you because of the eight hour time difference," Candace explained.

Iris's brain churned, trying to make sense of the words.

"I know it's 9 a.m. there," Candace continued, "but you probably have jet lag, you poor thing."

"Yes. Jet lag," Iris replied, finally comprehending why Candace would call her at this hour. *I'm supposed to be in Scotland.* "So what's up? Is everything okay?"

"I'm afraid not." Candace sounded distressed. "I don't know how to tell you this, but Angus didn't make it home from the hospital. He… he seems to have wandered off."

"What? Oh no, that's awful," Iris replied, trying to sound sincere.

"I know. Nobody saw him leave. The nurses were right in the middle of a shift change. They checked the CCTV cameras, but couldn't see him. He's just… nowhere! We're all very concerned because of how cold it is outside."

"Don't they have any leads?" Iris fished.

"Not really. I just wondered if maybe… did you ever give him your phone number, or a way to contact you?"

"No… I don't think Angus knows how to use a telephone."

"Oh… hm, maybe not. I guess it was a long shot, but I was hoping he'd tried to get a hold of you. The first twenty-four hours are critical. If we don't find him soon…"

"Yeah. He must be so scared."

"Well, I hope not. I hope he's indoors, wherever he is. I'm so sorry to disturb you during your holiday," Candace sighed. "I was hoping I wouldn't have to involve you at all, that we'd just find him walking somewhere and get him back safely. But I thought maybe you'd know more than we do, since you'd been spending so much time with him lately. Any idea where he'd go? Did he ever talk about wanting to be somewhere specific?"

Iris squeezed her eyes shut, hating every second of this conversation, deceiving a person she'd come to think of as more friend than boss.

"I just know he felt very trapped," she hedged. "He was lonely. He missed his family… and he would do anything to feel free again." She sighed. "I'm sorry I can't give you anything more concrete."

"Iris?" Angus called from the other bedroom.

"Wow, I almost thought I heard him just now!" Candace exclaimed.

"Oh no, that's just my granddad," Iris fibbed. "I should go see what he wants."

"I understand," Candace replied. "Well, you have a great visit with your grandparents, and I'll text you when we find him, okay?"

"Thanks, Candace. I hope he's okay."

Iris clicked off the line before any more could be said, and ran into Angus's room.

"Angus! You okay?" She flipped the light on.

Angus was sitting up in bed. His face was pallid, and he held his hand over his heaving chest. "I had a bad dream," he breathed. "Gillian was… she needed me, and I—" He gasped. "It hurts."

She checked the watch on his wrist. The pulse reading said 152.

"Angus, your heart is working too hard." She tried to keep her voice from rising with panic. "I need to get you to a hospital."

"Absolutely *not*," he huffed, grabbing her hand. "You take me there, and I'll be locked up again, and so will you."

"Angus, I cannae let you die!"

"Nae, see… you *can*. That's what it's come to. Arright? Promise me. I'm never goin' back there. I go home… or die tryin,' remember?"

"That was a hyperbole!" she cried.

"A what?"

"Colorful language…"

"Not to me," he stated simply.

She met his gaze for a long moment. The hardness in his blue eyes startled her.

"Angus, I should take you to a doctor…"

"But you'll not do that."

"I might!"

"Nae…"

Iris huffed through her nostrils. "Angus, you stubborn…"

"Ox?"

"Sure! Let's go with that."

"I've heard it before." He smiled.

"No doubt…" Iris lifted his wrist and checked the watch again after a minute. It read 125. "Fine. You *scared* me, arright? No more dreamin'! You in pain, still?"

"Aye, though it's gettin' a wee bit be'er," he replied.

She rose and went into the kitchen, rummaging in the cupboards until she found a first aid kit with a small bottle of aspirin. She fetched a glass of water and returned.

"Swallow these," she instructed.

He obeyed.

"Eight o'clock comes early. We'd best try to sleep as much as we can."

"So you say *all* of your birth documents were destroyed?"

"Yep," Angus replied, trying to sound American, as Iris had coached him all morning. She'd said that his best bet was to stick to one-word answers. He smiled winningly at the graying brunette behind the desk, who looked at him critically.

She tapped her beige acrylic nails on the desktop.

"Well, this Letter of No Record should suffice in place of an official birth certificate," the woman said, looking over the seals on the document. "However, I'm going to need as much data as you can provide, and copies of any early childhood records you may have."

Iris opened her shoulder bag, produced a manila folder, and handed it to the agent. She had spent days searching the internet for a way to make it look like Angus had official school records or even a church baptism certificate from some obscure little rural town in Washington state between 1930 and 1935. She'd thought she could edit his name in digitally, or even luck out and find an Armstrong listed somewhere and just claim it to be Angus. She kept coming up empty.

In desperation, she'd resorted to the truth. She had brought the scans she'd found of Angus's actual birth and baptism records from the church registry at St. Cyrus. Not even close to being American, but they had his full name on them. They had the words "Parish Registry" at the top, and they had the correct dates on them... as long as you zoomed in closely enough to crop off the year.

The woman flipped the folder open and glanced over the papers, taking in very few details before closing the folder again. She sleepily typed a couple things into the computer. Without looking up, she continued her questions.

"In what town were you born?"

"Aberdeen," Angus replied truthfully.

"Grays Harbor County," she muttered and clicked away on her keyboard.

Angus looked at Iris, about to say something, but Iris shook her head. Angus closed his mouth.

Iris squirmed. *Was all this struggle going to pay off? Were they cutting it too close?*

The agent continued to type. Several minutes passed. The clock on the office wall ticked like a bomb.

"Well, Mr. Armstrong, everything appears to be in order," the agent concluded at last. "I see from your travel itinerary that you're booked to leave the country tomorrow evening. That should be no problem."

Iris could feel her heart in her throat. Angus sat wide eyed, one knee bouncing.

"Normally," the agent continued, "it would be two to three days' processing time without a life or death situation, but it'll actually work out better today if I just put this on through and you can pick it up before the holiday. Can you be back around 5 p.m.?"

"Yep!" Angus couldn't contain his huge grin.

"We so appreciate your willingness to expedite this," Iris added.

"Merry Christmas," the woman replied, looking bored. "You can pay your fees and get your photo taken just outside this door. Remember, no eyeglasses. And please do not smile."

"Thank you," Iris said, pulling Angus up and out the door.

They kept it together throughout the rest of the process until they clambered back into Charlie's car, looked at each other, and burst into laughter.

"How on earth did that go so well?" Iris beamed.

"I dinnae ken, but my prayers were answered!"

"To get a passport?"

"To get one without having to lie," Angus explained.

"Granted, we had to let her assume a few things…"

"Aye…"

"But soon, we'll be on a plane!" Iris sighed happily.

Brennus whooped with delight. "That was genius, the way you held your hand in front of that agent's face so she noticed just the right details."

"Thank you," Aimsir smiled. "I've helped a lot of people across borders. You pick up a few things after centuries of practice. And having the coffee cart *mysteriously* run out of coffee right when she got there? Brilliant idea, Brennus."

"I can't take credit. A sentry tipped me off. He told me that this one grossly underestimates herself. She hardly cares about anything until she's had at least two espresso shots. In her state of mind, she might've approved just about anything."

"I'm going to take you to Lowell's for some fish and chips," Iris announced. "I didnae realize until now how hungry I was! How does that sound?"

"Sounds brilliant!" Angus agreed. "Such a strange morning—the last thing on my mind was food."

"Same here, but now I could eat a cow."

"Another hy… hyperbole?"

Iris winked.

They made their way to Pike Place Market and parked, then began winding their way through the crowds. Someone stepped on Angus's foot.

"This reminds me of that time I went to Glasgow," Angus muttered.

"Sorry, we're almost there… Oh, look! You'll love this, Angus, watch… the guys over there actually throw the fish to each other!"

Angus watched for several moments. "I'm not sure what I'm supposed to be impressed by."

"They're throwing the fish! Look, they never miss! It's brilliant!"

"It just looks like another day at the docks back home."

"So you're impressed by pizza, but not by fish flying through the air?"

He shrugged.
"Oi. Fine. Let's go."

Iris and Angus rolled up to the cabin around seven o'clock, long after dark, feeling exhausted and accomplished. After their brunch of fish and chips, they'd spent the day shopping around the University District for some practical clothes and supplies for Angus. He'd left the hospital with one change of clothes, a backpack, and a disguise—hardly suitable for a trip to Scotland.

They'd managed to pull together a set of toiletries and a limited, but decent wardrobe for him, including a new wool cap, much like his old one. He was pleased to discover that the style was still in fashion.

But Angus had been suffering from sticker shock all day long. Iris had to keep reminding him not only about inflation, but about the fact that he actually *had* money. She had lost count of the times she'd had to say, "Yes, but this is how much they cost now," and "You can afford it."

After picking up Angus's shiny new passport, they'd topped off the day with a sumptuous meal at MacLeod's, where Iris dove into a shepherd's pie and Angus reveled in a plate of bangers and mash.

"This is the best day I can remember havin' in a very long time," Angus sighed happily, plopping onto the sofa and putting his feet on the ottoman in the cabin's tiny living room. "My heart hasnae hurt all day."

"I'm so glad," Iris said, sitting cross legged in the armchair beside him. "I was afraid the pace we were keepin' was going to wear you out!"

"Just the opposite. I've got more energy than I've had in weeks!"

"Or is that the Seattle coffee you had earlier?"

"Ha. Maybe partly. Nae, it's just… d'you know what it is? Two months, I've been… essentially helpless. At the mercy of people who were tryin' their best, but treatin' me like a lunatic about to expire any day. Nothin' to do. Nae a soul in their right mind to chat to, exceptin' yourself, of course. But thanks to you, I'm findin' my feet a little bit."

Iris smiled at him.

"It's amazing to think," he went on, "that I'm actually headed someplace familiar! And, no small thing…" he patted his thighs, "…it's been such a relief to choose my own clothes! I'll nae take that for granted again—ownin' a decent cap, and trousers that fit."

"That *is* no small thing," Iris agreed. "And it's been my honor to help, Angus. I've truly never met anyone like you. Nor will again, likely."

"You mean I'm the first time traveler you've met?" He rubbed his chin. "Strange."

"Yeah! Weird, right?" she giggled. "You're truly a great friend, and always will be. I'll visit you in the village whenever I can."

He grew somber. "It'll look completely different now, I imagine. Full of strangers. I'll have to find a cottage… a wage…" His eyebrows knit together with concern.

"We'll figure it out," she assured him. "You're a talented woodworker. That's worth a lot. We'll figure out a way to get you proper citizenship papers and transfer the stamp money into your name once we get there, okay? It'll be fine, you'll see. Meanwhile, we fly tomorrow evening. We'll rest all we can durin' the day, because there'll be no sleep again until we hit Sco'ish soil."

Angus's stomach did flips. "Sco'ish soil…" The corners of his mouth lifted.

Chapter 21

Seattle-Tacoma International Airport was a dizzying bustle of people and suitcases. Angus and Iris were both traveling light, using only their backpacks. She'd taught him how to arrange his clothes in long stacks and then roll them into sausages in order to fit everything in. He was grateful she had, as he watched the harried travelers around him lugging heavy wheeled suitcases behind them.

Once they were through security, Iris checked her watch. "We've got time to get a bite, if you're hungry," she said.

"Do they have pizza here?" Angus wondered.

"Of course," she replied, "but maybe you should expand your horizons a little."

"I feel like that's all I ever do, with you around!" he chuckled.

"Our gate's that way..." she pointed to the left. "But I'll show you my favorite place to eat here. C'mon." She tugged his elbow and they banked right, toward the central terminal.

After providing Angus with several lengthy explanations while standing in line, Iris managed to order them two enormous steak and cheese burritos with guacamole and rice. He agreed with her that avoiding beans before a transatlantic flight was a sensible idea.

They found a table near the colossal sixty foot high wall of windows. Angus was indeed hungry, and the burrito smelled exotic and savory, yet he could barely peel his eyes away from the sight of the airliners taking off and landing on the distant runways.

"How do they do it?" he murmured in wonder.

"How do the planes fly?"

"No... how do they keep these windows so clean?" Angus turned to her and winked.

Iris laughed in surprise. "Angus, you're funny!"

"I'm not that funny," he said with a modest smile. "I was just imagining what my mate Patrick would say right now, if he could see this place."

"I like this Patrick! He sounds like a great influence."

"So are you," he said, "considering I'm about to eat a food pillow the size of my heid... what'd you call it?"

"A burrito!" she giggled.

He peeled back the foil and sniffed it. "And it's from what country?"

"Mostly Mexico, with a bit of American influence."

He hefted it in his hand. "I may not have to eat again for a week."

"Aye, that's the American bit."

The pair sat idly at gate A13, waiting to hear the boarding call for Aer Lingus flight 142 to Dublin. They'd both saved over half their burritos, and could still detect the faint aroma of salsa in their backpacks.

Angus gazed at the immense blue mural on the window, depicting mythic astrological beings in a surreal dream sequence.

"What's that supposed to mean?" he wondered.

"Well, it's art. So it probably means whatever *you* think it means."

"I think it's nonsense."

"Then it's nonsense."

"But it's massive. Why go to all the trouble to paint a massive wall of nonsense?"

"Because… it's pretty?"

"But it's not pretty, it's… *embarrassing*," he whispered.

"Why?" Iris whispered back.

"That married couple… in *bed*… *together!*"

Iris nodded gravely. "You're right, that's quite inappropriate," she agreed, stifling a giggle.

"Aye. I'd much rather see the sky."

The gate agent began calling their flight. They queued up, showed their boarding passes, and trudged down the jetway. Angus's stomach did the same flips as before when he first realized he was going home.

"We're in row 21, Angus. Seats A and C."

His shoulders slumped. "We're nae beside each other?"

"Aye, we are. A and C are next to each other."

"Where's B?"

"There is no B."

"Wh—y'know what? I'm nae goin' to ask," he said, shaking his head as they made their way down the appropriate aisle of the plane and found their seats.

"Another seatbelt," Angus commented. "But this one's half sized. Does that mean we'll be goin' slower than in a motor carriage?"

"Actually, we'll be goin' a whole lot faster! This seatbelt is just to protect you from bumps in the air."

"The air has… bumps?"

"Aye," Iris nodded encouragingly. "Like waves in the ocean."

"Ah." Angus looked with trepidation out the window at the enormous wing. "But it's so heavy! Hundreds of people, lifted up on great metal wings with no feathers. How does it even get off the ground?"

"*Powerful* engines." Iris grinned.

"Is it his first time flying?" asked the plump lady across the aisle from Iris.

"First time pretty much anywhere," Iris replied with an awkward smile.

As the plane pushed back from the gate, the video screens on all of the seat backs suddenly lit up with cheerful music and graphics.

Angus jumped. "Blimey, what's that?"

"It's just the safety video. They play it every flight," Iris explained.

He gazed at his screen, transfixed. "Look at the funny little people! Are they puppets?"

"It's an animation. Just listen," Iris shushed him as sweetly as she could.

Angus did his best to focus on what the video was saying, even though a good portion of it used vocabulary he'd never heard in his life. He practiced buckling and unbuckling his seat belt along with the animated man on the video. When they got to the part about assuming a crash position, Angus practiced that, too. With his head between his knees, he asked Iris in a muffled voice, "What's this for again? I didnae hear when we're supposed to do this part!"

She tapped his shoulder. He sat back up.

"That's plenty," she giggled. "It's just… to limber you up for a long sit."

"How long of a sit?"

"Nine and a half hours."

"Good grief! I'll be doin' that several times, then."

Someone in front of them snickered.

The video continued, *"Each exit is fitted with an escape slide, which can also function as either a raft or a flotation device, in the event of landing on water…"*

Angus's eyes widened.

"Please take some time now to note the position of the exits in your area."

He craned his neck in every direction.

"There's a life jacket in a package under your seat. To use this, you should take the jacket from its package and put it over your head…"

He elbowed Iris. "Should we put on the yellow jackets?"

"No, that's just if we land in water. I've never had that happen."

When the video got to the part about oxygen masks, his jaw dropped.

"Y'mean there's nae enough air to breathe where we're goin'?" he whispered loudly to Iris. "Are we goin' into outer space?"

Someone behind them giggled.

"The air inside the plane will feel normal." She patted his arm. "The oxygen masks are only for emergencies. I've flown loads of times and never even touched one."

He shifted nervously in his seat. "I'll lay a guinea there's still more people on the steamship crossings than on aeroplanes. Who'd want all this worry?"

"Dinnae worry." She smiled reassuringly. "Aeroplanes are really safe, okay?"

He nodded, chewing his thumbnail.

The plane had reached the end of the runway.

"Here we go! Ready?" Iris wiggled her eyebrows.

"Ready for what?"

The engines roared to life. Angus clutched his armrests and plastered his back to the seat as they barrelled down the asphalt. A strange sensation bubbled up inside him, which began like a giggle. By the time the nose of the plane lifted off the runway and they lurched into the air, Angus was belly laughing in a fit of full-on hysteria.

"I love it!" he whooped. "This is AMAZING!!"

Iris couldn't help laughing, nor could everyone else within three rows.

"I'll lay a guinea there's nought but cargo on the steamship crossings anymore!" Angus shouted with glee. "Who'd want to miss this?"

"Angus," Iris whispered, her face growing pinker. "You needn't shout…"

"Aye, sorry…" He pressed his forehead against the window, then shouted again, "This cannae be real! Look! Everythin's a tiny anthill down there!"

Iris smiled at her fellow passengers, giving them an apologetic shrug, and turned to Angus. "We'll go higher yet!" she whispered.

He looked at her sharply. "How high?"

"Six or seven miles above the ground," she beamed.

He shook his head in wonder and looked out again. "We just flew right through a cloud!" he cried. "I didnae feel a thing!"

Iris simply smiled, remembering her first flight. She, too, had wondered whether flying through a cloud would slow the plane down, like flying through thick cotton candy.

"My ears feel strange," he muttered, working his jaw up and down.

"That's just the changing air pressure." She offered him a stick of gum. "Might help to chew on this. Dinnae swallow it, though."

Angus accepted the gum, still peering through the window. "There's nought but wee lights below. Like the world's disappeared."

She smiled. "Ears doing be'er?"

He smacked his gum a few times and nodded.

"Well, it's too dark to see anythin' else now," he said, leaning back in his seat with a contented sigh. "'Tis an amazin' world you live in."

"You live in it, too, Angus."

"Aye... I guess I do."

"I bought us some passes, so we can go straight to the FastTRACK lane for passport control since we didnae check any baggage," Iris said when they'd disembarked from their short hop to Edinburgh on a turboprop. Angus followed her, having little idea what she'd just said, but grateful that she knew where to go.

The past twelve hours had been surreal. He and Iris had made the best of the journey—he, filling her in on the finer points of relief carving and how to select the best wood for different types of applications, while she listened patiently and with great interest. She then provided him a rundown on the differences between the psychological and sociological viewpoints of societies throughout history, followed by a detailed tutorial on how to blow the largest possible bubbles with chewing gum. They compared notes on living in St. Cyrus during their respective lifetimes, swapped childhood beach stories, and finished their burritos. This had necessitated a three hour nap.

During landing, Angus had managed to keep his thrill to a slightly more manageable volume, especially when he realized that his fellow passengers were giving him an amused side-eye, hoping for more entertainment. Still, he couldn't help giggling the entire time, culminating in a burst of "HA! WOW!!" when the pilot engaged the engines' reverse thrust. It just couldn't be helped.

After a short layover in Dublin, followed by an equally short flight in a regional prop plane, which Angus found both fascinating and terrifying, they were here.

Scottish soil. Blimey... Angus thought. *How'd we cover so much distance overnight? I suppose nowadays, people can live just about anywhere they want to. And I've never wanted to live any farther than a few miles from where I started. How did I get here, God? Am I ever goin' to feel at home?*

"Angus?" Iris interrupted his thoughts.

"Hm?"

"You need to sign your landing card... right here. I've already filled in the rest."

He signed. "What's this for, then?"

"More papers for the government to shuffle about, that's all."

He grunted.

"This way..." Iris nodded toward a queue. "We're non-EU."

"What's 'EU' and why are we not it?" he asked.

"European Union," she giggled, "and we're non-EU because..." she wiggled her passport, "we're Americans now!"

"Right. I keep forgetting."

A Border Force officer waved them over and shuffled through their documents.

"And what's the purpose of your visit to the UK, miss?" he addressed Iris.

"Christmas vacation," she answered truthfully, leaving out the bit about smuggling a time traveler. She offered her passport to be stamped.

"And you, sir?"

Angus squared his shoulders and readied the American accent he'd been practicing. "Just wanted to see the worrrld..."

He tried to spread out his "r" as Iris had coached him, but it came out like a long tap and sounding rather Scottish.

The officer gazed at him critically.

"Grandpa's been working on his Scottish accent!" Iris interjected brightly in a pronounced California accent. "He's getting pretty good, isn't he?"

"Mmm. Hunky dory. Never heard anything like it." He stamped Angus's passport after only a quick glance.

"Awesome, Gramps! You'll have to keep practicing!" Iris beamed.

"Yep," Angus nodded.

The officer rolled his eyes and muttered, "Aye, that'll help." Then he added more audibly, "Enjoy your stay."

They sidled off as quickly as possible, calling a quick "Merry Christmas!" over their shoulders, and made for the exit, barely stifling their pent-up giggles.

"Gosh, it's always *so weird* to drive on the left side!" Iris exclaimed as someone honked at her and she drifted back to the correct side of the road. They had rented the least expensive little car they could find at the airport, and made their way up the winding M90 out of Edinburgh. Iris was finally settling into the two hour drive toward St. Cyrus. Once she'd sat in the right seat for a while and the traffic had thinned out, she and Angus both felt less jumpy.

"If it's so strange, why not take the train?" Angus wondered, still clutching the edge of his seat.

"I guess I like the challenge." Iris grinned. "Plus, I like having my own wheels whilst I'm here. Lets me get out to see the sights, meet up with old friends." She pulled her extra large latte from the cup holder and took a sip. "I mean, I moved away when I was eight. I still know people here, but I feel like more of a tourist than a native most of the time."

Angus nodded. "I know how you feel."

"Granny and Granddad are expectin' you, though! I told them all about you—well, the semi-official version, anyway—bein' from the village and then emigrating to the U.S. when you were twenty-four. That's relatively true, right?"

"Give or take."

"Told them I met you at work—also true—and that you'd decided to visit the old place at Christmas and see about making a permanent move back. They offered you the guest room!"

"What? I dinnae want to impose…"

"Actually, they insisted. Especially since we *somehow, coincidentally* ended up taking the same flights here." She laughed.

"Funny. You fibbed to yer own granny?"

"You'd rather I told her you're a twenty-four year old from the past, trapped in the body of an old man?"

He sighed. "I guess not… I just hate deceivin' people. Especially when they're bein' kind to me. I just figured I'd find a place at an inn, or—"

"You'll be off to a fine start, refusin' my granny's hospitality," Iris warned. "She's fierce when it comes to lookin' after people."

Angus crossed his arms.

"She's makin' her flaky pastry meat pies for tea…"

"Ohhh arright! You win!" He threw up his hands in surrender. "Good grief, how can I refuse a room with a lovely family and a plate of home cooked food?"

"Exactly. I knew you'd come to your senses. Besides, you're kind of stuck with me for a while, until I can figure out how to get your money transferred to you."

"So… did *I* actually hire this motor carriage?" he asked mischievously.

"Nae, that was me. But you bought your own plane tickets… and these coffees!" Iris held up her cup and winked.

"What a gentleman I am!" he chuckled, lifting his luke-warm coffee from the cupholder and taking a swig.

"Aye, that y'are. And you'll have to start rememberin' to call them *cars*, y'know." She elbowed Angus playfully. "Nobody says *motor carriage* anymore."

"But it makes sense! You take a carriage, unhook the horses, put on a motor… bang, it's a motor carriage. What's a carrrr? Sounds like a stranded bit of a train."

"You're *in* one! That's what a 'carrrr' is, y'numpty."

"I'll say it, but I dinnae have to like it." He glanced at the map navigation on Iris's phone screen. "Is that right? Will we really be there in twenty minutes?"

"Aye, pretty close. Nervous?"

"I just want them to like me, I guess. It'll be the first time anyone besides you has treated me like a normal person since… the day I got lost."

"Angus, they'll love you! You're a wonderful man! Never doubt that, just because others couldnae see it for a while. Honestly, I cannae wait for you to meet my granddad… I know you'll really like him."

"What's his name again? I dinnae suppose I'll call him 'Granddad.'"

"He's called Liam, and my granny is Cora."

"Liam and Cora Jacobs," Angus rehearsed.

"Actually," Iris said, "I've kinda been wantin' to tell you somethin' about Granddad for a while now, but I've decided to keep it a surprise. It'll be a lot more fun to let him explain it to you."

"What in the world are y'on about?"

Iris giggled. "Oh it's fun! Dinnae worry! It's just another… kind of coincidence. Although, I still think the two of us meeting must've been the biggest one of all."

"Oh, it was nae a coincidence," Angus stated matter-of-factly. "It was the grace of God."

"Think so?"

"I know so. I was thick headed enough not to heed the warnin' in my heart when I met that tree, and so I was lost. I see that now. But nae a thing nor person *ever* gets lost from the eyes of God. He led you to find me."

"You really believe that? It just seems so... *random* to me."

"There is no *possible* way that's so. Not when you know God like I do."

"I must not. I've prayed maybe a couple times, but I dinnae ken what good's ever come of it."

"Nae but *good* ever comes of prayin.'" He looked at her earnestly, his blue eyes penetrating. "How many people like me would you say are out there... who've gotten stranded the way I did?"

"I dinnae ken... very few, likely. You might even be the only one." She squirmed in her seat. "It must be a pretty rare event."

"Aye, and here you are, at the center of it. How can you find it a coincidence that you were there, not a month later, to meet me... yet you come from the same tiny village as I do? God might as well be holding up a massive sign that says, 'I SEE YOU, IRIS JACOBS.'"

Iris giggled.

It was his turn to elbow her. "It's just plain good sense, that's all." He smiled.

⁂

"Och, there she is, our bonny lass! Gies a bosie!" Cora Jacobs squealed as Iris ran up the drive into her granny's tight embrace. "You *are* sight for sore eyes!" She held Iris at arm's length. "You've gotten prettier, that's certain."

"Granny, I have not. I've gotten more freckles, is all."

"You *have* gotten prettier, and no more arguments!" Granny patted her cheek. "Your hair is different, too. You're all grown up!"

"Arright, my hair is different. You win." Iris hugged her again and squealed. "Gosh, it's so good to see you! And Granddad!" She pulled him into a hug.

He patted her on the back. "Good to have you here with us at last. Have you decided to sound Sco'ish after all, then?" His eyes twinkled with admiration as he looked at his granddaughter.

"Aye, and it feels wonderful," she beamed.

She turned to Angus, who had been waiting patiently beside the car.

"This is my friend Angus," she said, pulling him toward the huddle with a gentle tug on the arm.

He lifted his cap to Cora. "Tis a pleasure to make your acquaintance, ma'am. Sir..." He turned to Liam and shook hands.

"Well Angus, we're honored to have you as our guest," Cora reached out and squeezed his hand. "Gosh, a gent who tips his hat! I feel like the Queen of England!"

"Every lady in this family is a queen," Liam said in her ear, giving her a little hug around the shoulders. "Especially you."

Angus smiled at the interaction, thinking of his parents as he'd seen them together, not half a year ago to his mind.

"You two must be exhausted, up all night on a plane and eight hours lost!" Cora said. "Y'might as well be time travelers!"

Iris and Angus shared a look.

"Come on in and get settled," Cora went on. "I've got tea almost ready. D'ye like meat pies, Angus?"

"I've ne'er met a pie I didnae like!" Angus replied.

Angus settled into the guest room, unrolling the clothing sausages from his backpack and finding, to his surprise, that they were relatively free of wrinkles. Whether it was the packing genius of Iris, or these new-fangled fabrics, he couldn't tell. He laid the trousers across the bed and the shirts over the wooden rocker in the corner of the cozy room. He couldn't help but inspect the joints and finish of the chair, admiring the handiwork. It was both sturdy and elegant, built to last, and fine enough to bring beauty anywhere you put it.

Once the four had settled around the table and Liam had said grace, they dug into Cora's gorgeous meat pies, mushy peas, and buttered tatties. Angus said little, enjoying the food so intensely he thought he might die happily right at the table. After several minutes of letting the women catch up, Liam spoke.

"So Angus, what is it that you do? Are you retired?"

"Well, I… I was—"

"Angus is a carpenter, Granddad! A master craftsman," Iris said proudly. "I've seen one of his pieces. It's to die for."

"Is that so?" Liam's eyebrows rose with approval. "In that case, I'll have to show you my shop out back."

"Oh, so you're a—"

Iris looked fit to burst. "Granddad's a master carpenter himself, Angus!" She grinned.

"That's brilliant!" Angus smiled at them both. "Is that your work upstairs, then, Liam?"

"The rockin' chair? Och, aye, that's an oldie. Did that in my twenties for Cora to rock the wee ones. Iris herself has had a turn or two in that chair as well."

"It's a masterpiece," Angus said sincerely. "I was admirin' the craftsmanship just a bit ago." He stirred a sugar cube into his tea.

"Well thank ye!" Liam was pleased. "We've done those chairs for generations. I come from a long line of carpenters in this village, all the way back to old Ewan the fisherman."

"Ewan the *fisherman*?" Angus asked, mid sip. "There's got to be a story there," he chuckled.

"Aye, bit of a tragedy, that. The story goes that a pair of carpenters, a father and son, lived in the village when old Ewan was comin' of age in the mid 1840s. He had a flair for carpentry, Ewan did, but there was no call for it, so he followed his father into the fishin' trade. Then, the elder carpenter died of sickness one winter. His son perished under mysterious circumstances the following spring. By the end of the year, the village was feelin' the stress of not havin' a tradesman in residence. Ewan saw both the need and the opportunity, so he found himself an apprenticeship. He returned to the village soon after, and became the first in a long line of Jacobs men, and even some women, who were talented woodworkers. Nowadays, some of us are contractors, some are artists, some are craftsmen. I prefer the smalltime stuff, myself. I've never had a desire to erect buildings, but I love the feel of a rockin' chair comin' together—y'arright, Angus?"

Angus had become so enraptured in Liam's story, he hadn't realized that his eyes had grown misty.

"Aye, of course... it's... just a sad story, is all. A father and son, gone within months of each other."

"Och, aye. 'Twas a brutal time to be alive, back then."

Angus nodded and busied himself with his supper, unsure how to respond to such a statement. He'd never considered his world to be brutal. It had been full of beauty... simplicity. Peace. The North Sea sparkled just as brightly, the cuckoos sang just as cheerfully, in his day. He missed his community, his little church that felt like family, his mother's voice. And Gillian. The girl who kept her own sunshine with her, making even the dreich days of winter seem trivial. A world full of noise and fast paced distraction... a world without *her* in it? *That* was brutal.

"Angus, you must be tired," Cora said tenderly. "It's alright if you'd like to head up the wooden hill. We'll have plenty of time to get acquainted tomorrow."

Angus shook himself and returned her smile. "Aye, I must look dazed! It's been a long one, for sure. Thank you again so kindly for your hospitality."

"Of course, dear. Make sure to let me know if there's anythin' you need."

Angus excused himself and trudged up the stairs, feeling more old and tired with every step. He kicked off his shoes, tossed his pile of trousers onto the chair, and fell into bed fully dressed.

And just like that, the village moved on without me and Dad. God, how do I find a place in a world that doesnae miss me anymore?

He drifted into a fitful sleep and dreamt of Gillian all night long. In one dream, he was carrying her across the threshold of a beautiful cottage. In another, he was building her a coffin.

God, please. I cannae take much more...

Aimsir stood by, speaking over him in a faraway language that was like a song.

Chapter 22

Iris awoke to the sound of kitchen clatter. Her eyes felt glued shut. She tried to boot up her brain and compute an explanation for all the racket, but came up with a blinking cursor. She flopped onto her belly and threw one of her pillows across the room.

"Charlie, what the heck?" she moaned.

Light footsteps approached. The bedroom door creaked open several inches.

"So sorry, Poppet," Granny whispered. "Had a wee disagreement with gravity…"

Iris opened one eye. "Oh! Granny…" she croaked. "Forgot where I was. What time is it?"

"Nearly half ten," she whispered back. "But take your time, dear. The kettle's still warm, and I've left scones on the table for you and Angus. Granddad's out back in the workshop. I've got to run and get the messages. Just a few last minute Christmas things, y'know."

Iris sat up. "I could come with you…"

Cora took in Iris's bleary eyes and bed head with amused affection.

"No dear, just have a relaxing mornin,' arright? Have your tea. Go for a lovely walk. We'll decorate the tree this afternoon."

Iris nodded, and Cora slipped back into the hallway.

"Granny?" Iris called.

"Aye, dear?" Cora turned to look at her through the half open door.

"It's so good to see you."

Cora's grin revealed deep dimples on her wrinkling cheeks. She was an elegant woman who, in all other regards, defied her age. Though she was sixty-seven, she looked fifty, and acted thirty. It was only when she smiled that her face held the evidence of thousands of smiles over many decades.

I hope I'm that pretty when I'm a granny.

Iris yawned and set her feet on the floor, part of her wondering whether Angus was awake, and a greater part of her wondering what kind of scones there were. She dressed in her most comfortable warm jeans and slouchy green sweater that had been a Christmas gift from Granny and Granddad last year—not handmade, of course. Iris was grateful she'd never been one of those children subjected to itchy hand knitted reindeer sweaters. Granny's only claims to homemaking fame were her cooking and baking. For gift giving, she stuck to her strengths: ordering online.

When Iris reached the bottom of the stairs, she found Angus just inside the back door, kicking off a pair of Granddad's soggy black wellies on the mat. He was wearing one of his new tartan flannels and tan trousers, along with his old coat. His cheeks were pink.

"Look who's awake!" he called to her with a little wave.

"Sorry, I always sleep like the dead after that plane ride," she admitted.

"Aye, no wonder. How did I escape? I'm surprised I feel so normal." He hung his coat on the row of hooks by the door and wandered into the kitchen in his socks, rubbing the back of his neck where the prickly hairs were starting to grow back from Charlie's haircut.

"Where've you been?" she asked.

"Down the beach first. Then Liam showed me his workshop."

"I bet that felt nice." Iris smiled affectionately, holding up the plate of cranberry white chocolate scones.

"Aye, twas dreich, but not rainin,' at least." He took a scone and bit into it. "Best part of all was just bein' free to walk out that door if I wanted to! Never realized what that kind of freedom meant, till it was gone."

"I cannae even imagine." Iris shook her head, pondering what it must have felt like to be shut inside for months. "How was the beach?" She pulled two sachets of earl grey out of a box on the counter and plopped them into the cups Granny had left out.

"The bluffs have changed shape a wee bit, but… same old beach. I recognized several of the buildin's I walked past in the village, but it's amazin' how many new ones there are!" He took another bite, then frowned at his scone. "What's this, then?" He picked out a morsel and held it up.

"White chocolate," Iris explained.

"That's rubbish. How can it be chocolate when it hasnae chocolate in it?"

Iris was brought up short. "Huh. Actually, I've no idea."

"Still…" He shoved the morsel back into the scone and took another bite. "Nae a thing wrong with that."

Iris giggled. "I imagine the village does look pretty different to you. Thankfully, it's still a wee place, so it might not be so bad, gettin' to know people round here." She poured hot water from the copper kettle into the bright yellow cups. "Y'know two of the sweetest people in the village arready!"

"True," he agreed. "They're lovely people. I really appreciate you bringin' me here."

Iris handed him a cup. "How could I not? You belong here."

"Aye, in this village, to be sure. But bein' with your family, that's beyond…"

"Och, relax. It's an honor to help out." She sat at the little kitchen table. "Besides, I like havin' you around!"

"What for? I'm nae good for much."

"What! Of course y'are. You're one of the most interestin' people I've ever met. A historian's dream! I can learn so much from you."

Angus sat down and sipped his tea. He was quiet for several moments.

"So…" He began the sentence, then shook his head, then began again. "That's what this is about? You've been helpin' me so you could study me? Like a school project?"

Iris set her cup down. "What?"

"Nae, it's fine. I guess it makes sense."

"What in the *world* are you haverin' on about, Angus?"

"I *am* pretty fascinatin,' I suppose. Like a circus freak… but educational."

"Are you *serious*?" Iris's face went pink. "We're friends!"

"Are we? I've been tryin' to work out why that is exactly, ever since we agreed it."

"What's that even supposed to mean?" Iris could feel tears prickling in her eyes, but she fought them.

Angus gazed at her for a long moment before he finally spoke, more gently this time. "I just dinnae understand what's in it for you. This whole thing makes no sense to me—why you'd risk your job, your freedom… It cannae be pity. That's not enough of a reason."

"I see, I see…" Iris nodded, eyes fiery. "So you've worked out that I must be keepin' you around for, what, some kind of… academic exercise?"

"What other reason could there be?"

Iris pushed back from the table and stood. "You can be really *thick* sometimes, Angus! Y'know that?"

"Well explain it to me, then! Because *this...*" he pointed to himself, "is a pretty sorry choice of friend for someone like you."

"Someone like me?" She put a hand on her hip. "I see, and what kind of person am I?"

"Young. Beautiful. You could have any friend y'like. D'ye really need an old man, with nae a thing goin' for 'im, hangin' about? Slowin' you down?"

"Angus!" Iris threw up her hands in exasperation. "You're... not... OLD! For cryin' out loud, you're only two years older than I am! But you're actin' like an infant at the moment! Why should it ma'er to me *what* you've got goin' for you? It's never ma'ered before!"

"Because *now...* y'have a choice, arright? You *had* to check up on me at work. It was your job. You dinnae have to any more." He suddenly looked very old and very tired.

Iris sat back down. She folded her arms and studied him.

"Well, maybe I want to. Ever think of that?"

"But why? I'm nae good to anyone. Not anymore."

"So I should only be friends with people I can get something from?"

"No, I dinnae mean that..."

"Sounds exactly like what you mean!" She shook her head. "So it's fine if *you're* kind to people, but if they're kind to you, there must be some hidden motive? Or maybe the kindness is genuine, but racks up some kind of cosmic debt that you have to repay somehow?"

He shrugged one shoulder and stared at the tabletop. "Why not? I'm such a burden. My load should be on my own back, not other people's."

Her eyes narrowed. "Interesting idea. Where'd you learn that? At church?"

"What?" He looked up at her and frowned.

"Well you're such a religious man and all. That's quite the foundational belief you have goin' there… 'Thou shalt not be a burden.' I only went to church till I was eight, but I dinnae recall any stories about Jesus tellin' people to quit needing help. Is that what *you* would've told the crowds?"

"Of course not!"

"So… your principle only applies to yourself, then."

Angus let out a frustrated sigh through his nose, but didn't answer. Iris could almost see the wheels turning in his head.

Her voice softened. "I cannae figure out why you'd be so nice to other people, but so mean to yourself, Angus. Y'think you only deserve kindness and compassion when you're pulling your own weight? As though God only loves you when you're useful? You're not livestock! I thought He supposedly loved you just how you are. I do remember that bit."

"Aye… He does."

"Well then, maybe you should let Him. Have you ever considered that you might have control issues?"

He raised an eyebrow.

She went on, "As in, you have a hard time accepting kindness from others because it means you're not the one in control of the situation?"

"Never heard it put quite like that before." He crossed his arms. "I just dinnae like to put people out."

"Well maybe 'put out' isnae what people feel. Maybe they feel joy!"

Suddenly, Angus thought of his mother, her sweet face beaming as she reached her hands out to help her neighbors. *Joy.*

"Maybe," Iris went on, "just bein' around you and having your friendship is enough. Remember friendship? That thing where you like somebody and spend time together because you *want* to? Because you *can*?"

"Aye, I remember. Fine friend I was, too. Left them all behind. Especially—"

"Patrick, right?"

Angus looked up sharply. "Aye..."

"Did *he* put up with your crap?"

Angus did a double take. "My what?"

"Your *crap*. What you're doin' right now. Talkin' absolute rubbish about yourself?"

"It's not rubbish!"

"Oh, it's not? You just called yourself a circus freak! What happened to you bein' a rare event, never lost from the sight of God? What happened to our meeting bein' because of grace, and not some random coincidence?"

"Aye, but—"

"So now... according you, God had us meet each other... against all odds...*just* so I could have an interesting project to work on? Or maybe He *had* a plan for you a month ago, but it got lost on His desk?"

"I suppose not. I..." Angus shook his head.

"You cannae have it both ways, Angus. Either you believe what you said about God, or you don't."

"I guess I do."

"And either you believe what I said, or you don't."

He looked at her with watery eyes.

"How did Patrick feel about you?" she asked gently. "Did he love you?"

"Like a brother."

"Then why's it so hard to believe that I love you, too?" She put her hand over his. "Friendship. That's what's in it for me, okay? And you're right. Nobody's payin' me to check up on you. But you're not on your own."

He melted. His shoulders shook. Iris held onto his hand. She didn't shush him, soothe him, or try to talk him out of it. She just took it in, and allowed a few of her own tears to escape. She could barely comprehend his pain. Even he was only beginning to.

He quieted, and then let out an awkward laugh. "More anti-aging tears... Charlie would be proud."

"Hey, you cry a lot less than I would if I were in your position," she said. "You've lost your home, your friends, your lady, your parents... losin' even one of those would be enough to make anyone cry."

"I really try not to, it's just..." He dabbed his nose with his sleeve. "Sometimes I get so weary of hurtin' inside, my face just sort of explodes."

"It's okay. Obviously you're still processing all of the trauma..."

"Doin' what to the what?"

"Processing..." she fished for words. "Everything that's happened to you has wounded you. It's going to take time to figure out how to heal, to move forward. There's fear, there's pain. There's people bein' nice to you, even though you dinnae think they should." She smiled gently. "But... no need take it out on me, arright?"

"Sorry about that. I really am."

"I know."

"You're a great friend, Iris."

"I know." She winked. "So are you."

They finished their tea and decided it would be best to follow Granny's suggestion of a walk outside for some fresh air, damp though it was. They donned their coats and borrowed wellies, and headed out under the threatening sky. They'd only crunched down the gravel driveway about twenty steps when Iris had an inspiration.

"I know what we should do!"

"Please, no more shoppin'," Angus moaned, thinking of their day in Seattle.

"No, nae even close to what I was thinkin'!" She stopped in her tracks and faced him, eyes bright. "Angus… we should find that tree!"

His stomach leaped. He'd actually had that exact thought this morning, but a stab of dread had turned him eastward toward the beach instead.

"The tree's likely nae even there any more," he hedged.

"Why not?"

"I dinnae ken, maybe it fell down…"

"Well then it would still be there."

"I dinnae think it's wise," he worried. "What if one of us gets too close and disappears to… China or someplace?"

"China?" Iris looked doubtful.

"We know nothin' about this tree!"

Iris considered his objection, but something Mr. Reynolds had said during their conversation was niggling her… *If a wormhole is big enough to see with the naked eye, it might be visible because of how everything else around it behaves. What if we could actually find something like that near the tree?*

"Dinnae y'want to learn somethin,' then?"

"I've learned enough, thanks."

She cocked her head. "You were fine until you cut into it, right?"

"Aye…"

"Well, let's not bring an ax, then."

He pursed his lips doubtfully, but didn't refuse.

"We'll take the motor carriage if you like," Iris coaxed. "In case it rains?"

He huffed in resignation. "Fine, I'll show you where it is, but no touchin' it."

"Deal."

Darrick MacCrann sat at his desk with a steaming mug of his favorite tea—Edinburgh blend with a splash of milk. He scanned the bank of monitors. All looked quiet. He rotated each of the security cameras back and forth ninety degrees to verify that they were fully functional. He turned up the gain on the vibration sensors and listened for a few seconds, then turned it back down. The overnight readings on the waveform monitor looked steady.

Darrick had repeated the same process every single morning for the past twenty years. He considered himself blessed, however. The job gave him plenty of time to write his books, and technology had made it possible to keep a better eye on things than his predecessors ever could, even with their hourly walk-arounds.

He turned up the speakers to listen to the forest sounds for a bit. He could make out the distinctive trilling of a flock of waxwings somewhere nearby. Leaning back in his chair, he laced his fingers behind his head and propped his stocking feet on the desk.

Katie, his wife, crept up behind him with a mischievous twinkle in her eye and quietly reached out to poke him in the armpits.

"Y'realize I can see you, crazy woman," he said without turning.

"Fine, spoil my fun," she whispered in his ear, wrapping her arms around his shoulders.

He tilted his head to kiss her cheek. She took that as an invitation to sit on his lap—which it was.

"I love this cuddly beard of yours," she sighed, running her fingers down his jaw. "I've waited ages for you to grow it. Didnae realize how ginger it would be."

"Aye, like Dad's." He kissed her nose. "And it's goin' gray."

"I think it makes you look distinguished!"

"*Ex*tinguished, maybe." Darrick grinned at her. "The boys must be out," he commented. "Hav'nae heard anyone whinging at us to get a room."

Katie giggled. "Aye, they're Christmas shopping. The day Callum got his driving license, I swear I could hear angels rejoicing." She reached for her husband's cup to steal a sip of his tea. He caught her wrist and kissed her hand.

"I'd take a bullet for you. Y'know that, m'wee bonny gingersnap. But get your own cuppa." He picked up his mug and sipped it with a flourish, just inches from her nose.

"Charming." She slid off his lap, kissed the top of his head, where wispy brown curls were turning to silver, and meandered to the cottage's tiny kitchen.

He followed her with his gaze, and she walked like she knew it. He chuckled.

Darrick turned back to the desk and reached over to turn the speakers back down, when he heard another faint sound over the piping song of the waxwings.

Voices?

Something tripped one of his proximity sensors, causing his phone to ping, and then his watch to vibrate a half second later. He searched the monitors with an intense gaze, his sharp blue eyes taking in every detail with a practiced sweep.

Aye, voices.

Just as he began to make out their words, a man and a woman came into view on one of the security cams.

"It's just through there."

"Blimey, these trees are so old!"

"Aye, they were old last time I was here! Arright, so... head through the oaks to the great big hawthorn there in the middle. See the berries?"

Darrick's eyes widened in alarm.

"What in the world..." he muttered. "How do they know exactly which one it is?" He zoomed the camera in on them. It was an old man and a younger lady. The lady spoke again.

"Is it this one, Angus?" She pointed.

"No..." Darrick shook his head. "No no no no no..." He dashed to the door, jamming his feet into his boots.

Katie popped her head out of the kitchen. "'No' what? What's goin' on, sweets?"

"People!" Darrick yanked his jacket on over his cardigan as he replied. He jabbed his finger toward the monitors.

Katie's jaw dropped. "Well, this is unheard of!"

Darrick grabbed his wool cap and scurried out the door, heading for the oak grove at a jog. He could be there in thirty seconds.

The magnificent hawthorn was just as immense and sprawling as Angus remembered it, although instead of tiny white flower buds, it was ablaze with crimson berries. Without leaves to soften its thorny appearance, the old tree had bristled into a fierce defensive stance.

Angus stood still, trying to quell his inner turmoil. He was chilled to his core, not as much from the biting temperature as the desire to get as far from this place as possible. Iris hooked her arm in his and stood quietly beside him, spellbound.

"I hear it," she whispered.

The hum from inside the tree was so faint that even a light breeze would obscure it, but being close enough to touch it, they could just make it out.

"Where'd you cut into it?" she asked softly, as if in a library rather than a forest.

Angus pointed, and the two stepped gingerly around bits of underbrush, ducked under a low hanging limb, and stopped.

"There."

"I see it," she nodded.

The stub of limb had healed over, and in its place had grown two thinner branches which curved upward toward the sky. They were fully as long as the old branch, and their bark had developed ridges and fissures to match the rest of the tree.

Iris squinted and studied the branches from every angle, but saw nothing unusual.

"I dinnae see the point of bein' out here any longer, Iris." Angus shivered. "It's nae as if the tree's goin' to speak to us."

"Aye, maybe you're right," she conceded. "I guess I thought there might be a… a portal or something…" She turned toward Angus. "Oh!" she gasped.

Angus whirled around to see what had startled her.

Not three feet behind him stood a man with piercing blue eyes. His approach had been so silent that neither of them had noticed him. He wore a green tweed hunting jacket, wellies, and a wool cap, but carried no gun. His posture registered as casual, but his expression was vigilant, almost suspicious.

"Can I help you?" he asked.

"Sorry, are we trespassing?" Iris asked politely.

"A bit," he replied, crossing his arms.

"Are you the gamekeeper?" Angus asked.

The man looked mystified. "Sure, let's go with that," he answered finally. "Is there somethin' in particular you're lookin' for?"

Angus and Iris looked at each other, unsure how much to reveal to this stranger. They hadn't agreed on a cover story in advance. They'd never considered the possibility of being seen out here. Finally, Angus spoke.

"I lived in the village a long time ago, and I was just showing my… *granddaughter* here… this beautiful tree."

"Why *this* tree?" The man didn't blink.

"I uhhh… I thought she'd like it?"

The man turned to Iris. "D'you like it?"

"What do you mean?" she asked.

"Happy you came out to see a thorny old tree in the middle of the wood on a freezing, nasty day… instead of cozying up at home by the telly?" His eyes narrowed.

Iris couldn't come up with a reply.

"Somethin' particularly interesting about it?" he pressed. "You've been lookin' it over for quite a while…"

Iris shifted her feet.

"Here now!" Angus jutted out his chin. "No need to harass the lady. We'll get off yer land. I cut a bit of this tree a while back, and I just wanted to see I hadnae done it permanent harm. Looks like it's gettin' on fine, so we'll be off. Let's go, Iris."

The man held up his hand. "You did *what*?"

"Cut it. I had the owner's permission beforehand…"

"That's impossible. I would've seen you."

Angus cleared his throat. "I meant… a *really long* while back."

"Where did you—"

Angus pointed to the healed stump below the newly grown limbs.

"But that's…"

The three of them stood motionless for several moments.

The gamekeeper studied Angus with a mixture of awe and dread. He took several steps forward, until he was inches away, and continued to study. He locked eyes with Angus.

"You're Angus Armstrong." It was more a statement than a question.

Angus's heart skipped a beat.

"No need to answer," the gamekeeper went on. "I can see it." He pushed Angus's shoulder with two fingers, causing him to sway slightly. "Quite solid. Interesting…"

Iris shook her head, dazed. "How did you know his name?" she demanded. "Who are you?"

The man finally looked away from Angus. An exhilarated smile spread across his face.

"I'm Darrick MacCrann, Guardian of the Hawthorn." he replied. "And you…" He let out an exuberant laugh. "You're the Lost Carpenter!"

Chapter 23

"Brennus! Aimsir! It's good to see you both again."

"And you, Caledon," Aimsir replied.

"America was such a rewarding assignment!" Brennus grinned. "Short—only fourteen years—but interesting."

"You've both done well," Caledon said. "You've brought the travelers together and seen them to their homeland safely."

"Will they be safe here, at last?" asked Brennus.

"I only know that we've been ordered to increase our watch," Caledon replied.

"*Increase?*" Aimsir was surprised.

Caledon nodded. "Crucial decisions are yet to be made, and a time of great testing is still to come."

"Meaning?" Brennus wondered.

Caledon's eyes sparkled. "I think the Master is going to authorize a repair."

Brennus and Aimsir exchanged looks. Broad grins spread across their faces. They drew their swords.

Angus was speechless. His mind could barely register the idea that there was another human being alive who knew his name. Not only knew his name, but understood who he was. He blinked several times, but could only stare at the man in response.

Darrick laughed again, a jolly sound that echoed through the bleak winter forest. "Gosh, that's fun! I've never introduced myself that way before! Strictly confidential, y'see."

"Why? What's a... Guardian of the Hawthorn?" Iris asked.

"That's goin' to require a seat by the fire and a pot of tea or two. C'mon. My cottage isnae far." Darrick beckoned with a tilt of his head, turned on his heel, and began tromping back through the wood.

Angus and Iris exchanged astonished looks and followed.

Angus finally found his voice. "D'you live in the little stone cottage?"

"Aye, Woodstone Cottage. Now then, I didnae catch your name," Darrick said to Iris, turning to look at her as they walked along.

"Iris... Jacobs," she replied, attempting to match his brisk stride.

"Jacobs... as in Jacobs Construction?"

"Aye, that's my great uncle's company."

"So are you really this chap's granddaughter, or was that just an almost-clever lie to throw me off track?"

Iris rolled her eyes and smiled. "I wouldnae count lyin' as one of Angus's talents," she confessed. "I'm just a friend."

"Pleased to meet you." Darrick stopped to shake Iris's hand, then looked at Angus again, turning his head side to side in wonder. "Blimey, I just cannae believe it's really *you*! Angus Armstrong, of all people. Standin' right here in front of me!"

Angus could offer nothing more than an awkward smile and a little shrug.

They continued walking. Before long, they found the little footpath to the clearing where a modest but charming stone cottage stood. Tendrils of smoke wisped lazily from the chimney.

"The old place has changed a bit," Darrick said as they followed the garden path to the rounded wooden door. "It has electricity now, and a second story. It's is the oldest continuously inhabited building in Scotland."

"Really?" Iris said skeptically. "Historic buildings are an interest of mine, but I've never heard of it."

"I doubt you would've," Darrick replied with a wink, opening the door for them. "My family's lived here for about… oh… " He pursed his lips and closed one eye. "Over four thousand years. Roughly. The records get a little muddy before 2000 B.C., but we dinnae go splashin' that about. Draws too much attention."

Iris's mouth hung open.

"Come on in!" Darrick chuckled. "Katie my dear, we have guests!"

As they laid off their coats and wet boots, a petite lady in jeans and a red flannel shirt came bouncing down the stairs. Her hair was dark, the color of coffee, save for a single streak of silver in front, and swept into a carefree bun on top of her head. She was no taller than five feet, and had the face of a teenager, but with laugh lines.

"Welcome!" she greeted them with genuine delight. "What fun! We never have guests, save for family!"

"These are *not* just any guests…" He put his arm around her shoulders. "Katie, this is Iris Jacobs and… Angus Armstrong."

Katie reached out to shake Iris's hand. She froze when she heard Angus's name. Her eyes darted from Angus to her husband and back again, a question in her expression.

"Yes. *That* Angus Armstrong," he finished her thought.

"Blimey…" she gasped, shaking his hand. "The Lost Carpenter!"

Darrick chuckled. "Aye, that's what I said!"

She sprang to life. "Have a seat and I'll pop the kettle on. D'you like tablet? I've just done a batch..." She disappeared into the kitchen before they could answer.

Darrick shook his head fondly. "Do try it. She puts whisky in. Shall we sit?" He gestured to the modern leather sofa and matching chairs next to the ancient stone fireplace, which was adorned with pine boughs, tartan ribbon, and popcorn strings.

Darrick tossed a gnarled log into the fire while Iris curled up on one end of the sofa and tucked her feet beneath her. Angus took the seat beside her, leaving the two armchairs for Katie and Darrick.

Katie returned with a tray of tea, tablet, and shortbread in under two minutes. Once mugs had been passed around, Darrick leaned forward, elbows on knees, and spoke.

"Iris, you asked what a Guardian is. I owe you an answer. But please bear in mind, both of you..." he looked at Angus and back to her, "that what I'm about to reveal is privileged information. The only people on earth who know about the Guardians are other Guardians and their families." He trained his gaze on Angus. "I'm only allowed to speak to *you* of these matters because the Council passed a resolution over a century ago, granting special permission to any Guardian in my family who might encounter you."

"Me, specifically?" Angus marveled.

"Aye, you specifically—Angus Armstrong, the Lost Carpenter. We had no idea when you might pop up, you see. Provision was also made for one companion, if you had one. So Iris, you may stay. But you must never reveal to another soul what you learn from me today."

Iris frowned. "What happens if I accidentally mention it to—"

"You'll forget," Darrick interrupted her.

"I have an excellent memory."

"Nae, you *will* forget. All of it. I dinnae understand exactly how it happens, but it does. I've seen it. Twenty years ago, a friend of mine used rather poor judgment and told a girl he was dating about the Guardians and the secrets of the Trees."

"Och, was that Shannon?" Katie asked, stirring her tea.

"Aye, poor Shannon," Darrick replied. "They broke up a few months later. When she tried to tell one of her friends about the trees, she couldnae think of what to say. After that, she forgot his name... and that they'd even dated."

"People thought she'd gone round the bend," Katie said, with a hint of amusement.

"Are you threatening to wipe my brain or something?" Iris was incredulous.

"Oh, not us—it happens on its own. And it's not a threat, it's just a fact," Katie said with a casual shrug. "The only people who can retain the secrets are the Guardians, and those whom the Guardians confide in directly. Take it any further, and it's gone. On the positive side, it's rather a convenient way out, if you'd rather *not* remember. Darrick offered me that chance after we were engaged, just in case it was all too much for me. But here I am!" She smiled and patted his leg.

"So basically," Darrick said, reaching for a hunk of short-bread to dunk in his tea, "if you want to retain anythin' I say, then keep it under yer hat."

Iris and Angus both nodded gravely.

"Anyway, there are Great Trees in every part of the world, not just here. The Great Hawthorn is one of thousands. My family has been livin' here since people first inhabited this part of the world, and we guard the Hawthorn. Even our surname comes from a word that means 'tree.' It's our role to see that no harm comes to the tree."

"Y'mean... the tree I cut a hunk off of?" Angus's smile was sheepish.

"Aye..." Darrick shook his head. "That day was quite the debacle for the MacCrann name, I can tell you."

"I didnae see a soul that day," Angus said sincerely. "Not till it was too late. If I had, believe me, I never would've—"

"I know. Nobody blames you. And I've heard the tale many times, as first told by poor old Ré, whom y'startled in the wood that day in 1844. He's the one who should've warned you off, like I was tryin' to do earlier. He never forgave himself."

Angus pondered that idea, feeling a bit gloomy for the old man.

Iris was bewildered. "Could we back up a bit? I still dinnae understand the deal with these trees," she said. "Obviously, they're unique. I mean, they *hum*. And, we've seen what happens when you mess with one. But *how* does that happen? What are they actually for?"

Darrick's expression was pensive as he swirled the tea in his cup. "Excellent questions... But we've come to the bit that's a little tougher to explain." He considered for several moments, then set his cup back on the tray, and straightened in his chair. "Y'believe in God, of course?" he asked.

"Aye," Angus confirmed without hesitation.

A moment later, Iris nodded.

"Well, the Great Trees have been around since the second day," he began.

Katie smiled and curled up in her chair, her brown eyes alight. "I love it when he tells this!" she whispered to Iris.

Darrick shifted into a formal speaking style, reciting the oral tradition taught to him as a boy.

"When the Master created the infinite universe," he began, "He put into it creatures who were too fragile to withstand infinity. They needed their existence marked out by the movement of celestial bodies, by the changing of seasons, by the passage of days and years. He created the finite fabric of Time, and wove his creation into it.

"Far above us, where days and months are sufficient to mark the passage of Time, it is the stars and planets which anchor this fabric in place. On earth, the fabric is bound into moments… therefore, the anchors must be more closely spaced. The Great Trees are the anchors and conduits of time on earth."

"Time trees?" Angus interrupted, his expression full of awe.

"If you like." Darrick nodded. "Basically, yes. They form an overlapping network of energy that reaches high into the atmosphere, like an invisible woven fabric. Einstein called it 'spacetime.'"

Angus frowned. "Who's Einstein?"

"A really clever man," Darrick said simply.

"But how can trees form an invisible net made of energy?" Angus wondered. "They're just wood."

"Ah ha," Darrick held up one finger. "Because they're not actual trees!" He grinned. "They only *wear* trees as camouflage. The soul of the tree is the time energy that flows through it. Scientists call this 'dark energy' because they're nowhere close to understandin' it properly. But it's no more a tree than you are a body."

"So by appearing to be regular plants, the trees are hidden in plain sight," Iris said.

"Aye." Darrick nodded. "Hidden and protected."

"Oh, do the last bit," Katie encouraged him.

He continued his oration where he'd left off.

"The trees were once guarded by Messengers of The Three. Mankind had become corrupt, yet a single man could live almost a millennium. Men had too long to ponder the source of Time, and too much temptation to interfere with it. Thus, they were never told of the Great Trees.

"But after the time of floods, when the lifespan of mankind was barely a century, the care of the Great Trees was passed to them. Messengers of The Three now watch over the human Guardians. Each Guardian must protect his tree with utmost secrecy, and teach his son to do the same, down through the generations," he finished.

The room was quiet for several moments.

"Fascinating," Iris murmured. "What if a Guardian has no son?"

"Every Guardian always has a son. Plenty of daugh'ers, too, of course. But always at least one son. It's never been otherwise."

"So the same family always protects the same tree… *forever?*"

"Exactly."

"What if they want to move?"

"A Guardian would never consider that possibility until his son has taken over."

Iris sipped her tea, wondering. *Is this real? There's a secret subculture of families around the globe protecting the fabric of reality while the rest of us buzz about in blissful ignorance?*

"Okay…" She tapped her cup with her fingernail. "What about when people move in and start building up cities around a tree? Or if the land changes hands?"

"Some Guardians become rangers or environmentalists," Darrick answered without skipping a beat. "The Guardians were the first to invent parks and nature reserves. Another trick we like to use is buildin' a graveyard around a Great Tree."

"That's a bit creepy!" Iris wrinkled her nose.

"Well, nobody bothers the trees!" Darrick chuckled. "Others simply buy the land on which their tree grows and live near it. My family were some of the earliest settlers here… Picts. We've always lived near our tree. When this land passed to the aristocracy in the fourteenth century, we saw to it that we were kept on as gamekeepers."

"Actually, there may have been some supernatural intervention involved there," Katie interjected. "It was a pretty unusual arrangement they had with the noblemen."

"Aye… to this day, nobody's quite sure how my ancestors got them to agree to such generous terms," Darrick agreed. "But when the estate fell into poverty after the last war, we had to switch tactics. Instead of being paid employees, we had to find outside work and pay rent to stay on the land. Yet stay we did, and the tree remained untouched. That is, except for the day *you* came to the wood."

"Aye. Another winnin' day for Angus Armstrong," Angus said in disgust.

"Dinnae be too hard on yourself. How were you to know? I tell you what, though, you're a legend."

"A legend?" Angus pursed his lips doubtfully.

"Aye. You're known by Guardians the world over! I've heard the story many times. Ré, whom you met, is my fifth great-grandfather. He was Guardian then, a widower livin' alone in this cottage. Though his hearing was failing, he still felt capable of doin' his duty. But he was wrong on that count—he heard neither you nor your ax!"

Angus shuddered.

"My great-great-great-grandfather Darrick, my namesake, was a boy of seventeen on that day. He and his father, Éamon, who had yet to inherit the Guardianship, were still livin' in the village as fishermen. But old Darrick later told his children in vivid detail of watchin' his Grandfather Ré come rushing up to their cottage in a panic, tears streamin' down his face, cryin' that he had failed… that a young man, he knew not whom, had taken a piece of the tree."

"Aye, I believe I saw Ré in the wood," Angus confirmed. "He seemed afraid."

"Och, he was terrified! No one could guess what consequences would be unleashed by the interruption in time—lives never lived, children never born… Actually, we may never fully know the consequences."

Unbidden, images of Gillian invaded Angus's mind, making his chest ache. He pushed them away.

"So why don't the Guardians just figure out how to make the trees do what they want? Go back and fix it when things like this happen?" Iris wondered.

"Because it's forbidden, and far too complex anyway. Guardians dinnae understand the trees well enough to access

291

their power without causin' unintended damage. We're only meant to guard the trees, not manipulate them for our own purposes."

Iris sighed. "So there's nothin' you can do for Angus?"

Darrick looked at Angus with compassion. "Honestly, after all this time, I'm not sure. Perhaps we can figure out some answers. Guardians hand down everythin' they learn from livin' near a Great Tree and watchin' it grow. We keep meticulous diaries. So I do know some of the signs which occur around a time disturbance.

"After you disappeared, Ré, his son Éamon, and even young Darrick watched the tree carefully. Right away, they heard a more pronounced hum comin' from the tree. They waited to approach until it died down, because they were unsure of its effects.

"They could also feel a heaviness in the atmosphere around the cut, trailin' off in the direction you left the forest, Angus. With a more modern understanding of physics, later Guardians came to speculate that this was a pocket of increased gravity from super dense particles and antimatter leaking from the tree…"

Angus shook his head, lost, but Iris was starting to catch on.

"Angus, I think he's sayin' that you ripped a hole in the time fabric."

"Exactly. My grandfather was a physics buff, too. He theorized that the trees hold a balance of both dense matter and antimatter in their branches. When they sustain damage, the leaking matter rips a hole in spacetime, much like a black hole. It should collapse in on itself immediately, and crush whatever's in it, but the antimatter cancels it out and holds the breach open temporarily."

Darrick smiled encouragingly at Angus, who was clearly still perplexed. "Basically, the tree protected you from bein' pulverized."

"Ah." Angus nodded and drank his tea, head spinning.

"As my ancestors watched the cut seal off," Darrick continued, "they noticed the heaviness in the atmosphere diminishing. In place of the one branch, two grew back. The fabric was supported once again, so things seemed pretty normal after that. Those branches were growin' at a steady pace ever since. It's only in the last couple of months that they've stopped."

"But why two branches? Why not just one?" Iris asked.

"I have my own theory about that," Katie answered. "Two branches, two options. One for what *should* have happened. One for what happened instead."

Iris nodded. "Yeah, like an alternate timeline or something?"

"Exactly," Katie agreed.

"It's entirely possible." Darrick shrugged. "It's as good a theory as any. The only other unusual thing that happened was that night, when a search party came to the wood looking for a missing man. He was never found. At least not until today."

"But why would they send men into the woods, when I was back in the workshop already?" Angus wondered. "I was in there the whole time."

"Did you see anyone on your way back?"

"Plenty of people."

"Did they see *you*?"

Angus stopped short.

"I… I'm not sure. I didnae speak to anyone… I was so focused on the work, I hardly noticed."

"What happened when you got to the workshop? How long were you there?"

"I dinnae ken, that was the odd part. Maybe I really was away with the fairies, because I became like a man possessed. I got absorbed in my work, as always, but it's usually my stomach that brings me back to the present, or realizin' it's dark out. Those things never happened."

Darrick stroked his beard. "The sun stood still, am I right?" he asked.

Angus nodded, eyes wide.

Darrick slapped his knee. "I *knew* it! A time pocket! Somehow, you'd already fallen into the breach, and the wood was leakin' so much gravity around you that time was barely passing at all, compared to the rest of the world."

Iris's eyes widened in recognition. "Relativity?"

Darrick nodded at her, then turned back to Angus. "What happened then?"

"Not sure how long I worked, but it was like time had no meanin'! I know I did two weeks' work that day. I'd carve a piece, lay it to dry, carve another. When I'd finished the second, the first was already dry. I just kept goin' without thinkin' what it all meant. When the mirror frame was finished, it was the first time I felt I'd got something exactly right. The wood was so… perfect. I could say it was the best thing my hands ever made, and I wouldnae be exaggeratin.'"

"I believe that. The diaries record a carving of exquisite beauty left behind by the Lost Carpenter. My ancestors were impressed!"

Angus smiled faintly.

"What happened after you'd finished the mirror frame?" Darrick asked.

"I felt heavy. Everything was heavy—my tools, my arms. I was tired… hot… overwhelmed. I was startin' to think I should call for help, but I couldnae make much sound. I fell… only made it part way to the door. Then I blacked out."

"Hm. It would seem that the longer you worked that wood, the greater your exposure to the gravity leak. Frankly, I'm astonished you survived it. Even Guardians dinnae touch the trees without gloves. I'm sure you were in a right miserable state."

"Aye… I truly hope I never experience anything like it again."

"But how did Angus end up in America? Why *this* year?" Iris asked.

"That *is* a puzzle," Darrick agreed. "Why indeed?" He poured himself more tea, and took a chunk of tablet. He took his time, mulling it over in his mind as he worked through several bites. Just as the silence had reached a length bordering on awkward, Darrick glanced up sharply at Angus.

"You made a mirror frame out of the hawthorn wood *itself?*"

"Aye…"

"Why?"

"My boss ordered it as a gift for his wife. Hawthorn wood is perfect for somethin' like that."

"And you made it while you were in the breach…" Darrick frowned, his eyes darting across the carpet, following his train of thought. Finally, he looked up.

"Did you shellac it?"

"Aye. Turned out lovely," Angus said.

"Well, that's how they missed it."

"Who missed what?" Iris asked.

Katie touched Darrick's knee. "Y'have to fill them in, dear. They cannae read your thoughts."

"Sorry!" Darrick shook his head, his frown replaced by a lopsided grin. "According to the diaries, Ré and his son Éamon went back into the forest and the workshop, and gathered up every scrap of the Great Hawthorn you left behind. They wanted to protect others from the leak, as well as safeguard the wood, in case it was ever needed."

Iris was puzzled. "How could you possibly tell which wood was which?"

"Guardians are especially sensitive to the sound of the Trees," Darrick said. "We can tell when a piece of wood comes from a Great Tree because of how it vibrates. Ré and Éamon picked up everything and saved it, or so they thought. Apparently, the biggest pieces were sittin' right in front of them and got left behind, because the shellac sealed off the wood and masked the vibration."

"What would've happened if they'd had all of it?" asked Iris.

"They probably could've fixed it," Darrick said sadly. "Éamon made a fascinating discovery several years later, when one summer, lightning struck the Great Hawthorn. He wrote in great detail about how lightning sheared off a long strip of bark and several small limbs. He ran to check on the tree, and got there in time to watch the tree pull all the pieces back in, like a magnet. Over the next couple days, the tree repaired itself. The cracks glowed and hummed. When it finished, it was like the damage had never happened!"

"Pretty ingenious," Katie grinned. "Cannae have time bein' rewritten every time the wind blows too hard."

"Aye, thank goodness!" Darrick agreed. "So Éamon and his son had the idea to bring out the Lost Carpenter's scraps of wood and lay them near the tree, to see what would happen. But with such a huge chunk missing, the wood just sat there. They had no other ideas, so according to the journal, they put the scraps back in storage and called it a day."

Angus was horrified. "So what you're sayin' is, the best thing I ever made is the very thing that kept me lost?"

"I'm afraid so," said Darrick sympathetically. "In fact, as soon as you severed the branch and worked it into a new shape, you changed its destiny completely. Since you and the wood became linked within that little time pocket, its path became yours as well, for as long as you stood in the breach. What would have happened to the mirror led it in a certain direction, and you were drawn there with it."

Angus put his face in his hands and let out a dejected moan. Iris patted his shoulder.

"Where is the mirror now?" Darrick asked.

"It's hangin' in a chapel, in Washington state," Iris said, crestfallen.

"And is that where you woke up?" Darrick asked.

"Aye, right nearby," Angus sighed. "So that's how I got all the way over there?"

"Seems so. The mirror would've hung in the castle, and passed to Mrs. Grant's heirs. I happen to know there's a Grant still in charge of the estate, and to keep up some cash flow, he occasionally sells items of architectural interest to buyers lookin' to own a piece of history. He's sold mantelpieces, gates, doors, mirrors…"

"I saw the invoice," Iris spoke up. "It *was* from here. It was delivered the same day Angus was found. But I dinnae understand… it could have been there any number of years, and will probably stay there for many more to come," she protested. "Why did Angus end up in *this* year?"

"Short answer… because that's exactly how long it took the tree to heal. As I said, the branches stopped growin' about two months ago. When did Angus show up?"

"About two months ago," Angus groaned.

"Well, then." Darrick sipped his tea. "We seem to have identified the exact moment the tree finished replacing the branch. Very interesting."

Katie shot him a disapproving look.

"What?" He looked stunned. "I'm sorry if I seem unfeeling, but you must understand… as a Guardian, I've never actually seen this much evidence of a time disturbance before. You're the first person I've met who was flung that far forward!"

"This has happened to *other* people?" Angus asked in shock.

"Aye, in rare instances, round other trees. It was a matter of minutes or hours, though—not over a century, as it was in your case! But as I said before, the Guardians have been watchin' this tree since Éamon's time, and it was only just this year that the severed branch has been fully replaced. It's taken the tree this long to heal and regrow. That could account for why the separate timeline has stopped… the fabric is once again supported, and the snag is repaired."

"I only half understand what you're sayin,' but it looks to me like nae a *thing's* repaired!" Angus's eyes flashed. "I'm in the wrong century, y'might've noticed. Everyone I know and love is long dead. What about *my* path, *my* destiny? Where did it go? What happened to the life I should have had? Did it just… disappear? Does my existence not ma'er, in the end?"

"Of course it ma'ers." Darrick locked eyes with Angus and spoke earnestly. "It did then, and it does now. I think deep down, you still believe that, Angus. Every man's destiny is precious in the eyes of God. But without knowin' the effect your presence would've had, there's no way for us to see how your absence changed things. That part is a mystery to the Guardians, I'm afraid. It's impossible to see all ends. I can only see the mirror's path because of where it is now. I cannae see that about you, because you really should *not* be here. It's impossible. What year were you born?"

"I was born in 1820."

"Exactly my point. If your life had progressed naturally through time to this point, you'd be in a graveyard somewhere, not here talkin' to me."

Iris gasped at his insensitivity.

"So why *are* you here? Why're you still alive?" Darrick squinted.

"I dinnae feel alive, I feel half dead. And I look it."

"Actually, you look quite young for your age. How do we get a man around two centuries old lookin' as if he's in his eighties?" Darrick continued, musing mostly to himself.

"Young for my age? I'm twenty-four! At least… I was two months ago."

"Yes, quite the mystery. I keep wonderin' about the tree sap. You were exposed to plenty of it. Course, I say *sap*, but that's a misnomer. Some of the Guardians are scientists, and they still cannae identify what kind of substance it actually is, despite years of research. But my question is, did you ingest any?"

"You're askin' if I… *ate* some of the tree?" Angus asked, befuddled. "Even carpenters dinnae love wood *that* much."

Katie snort-laughed.

"Silly question, I guess. It's just that, one autumn, I saw a young coney nibblin' at the tree's bark, and then it disappeared. Half a minute later, it reappeared, quite elderly, still chewing. I think the internal exposure must have aged it dramatically. If somethin' similar happened to you, it might account for why you dinnae look your age... so to speak."

"Well," Angus shrugged, "I can honestly say I've never nibbled on a tree."

Katie and Iris giggled.

"I only ate breakfast that day, and a..." Angus stopped short, mouth open.

"What?"

"A tattie..." He looked at his palm. "There was sap on my hand. Plus, I cut myself with a chisel. Maybe..."

"Aye. Maybe." Darrick nodded. "Like I said, your situation is so strange, it's hard to know much for certain."

The four sat in silence, lost in thought. Occasionally, someone would sip on remnants of cold tea. After a while, a chunk of burned log fell into the ashes of the fireplace, scattering coals and sparks.

"What if..." Iris broke the silence. "Hm..."

"What if what?" Angus asked.

"What if it's not too late? To fix the tree?"

Darrick looked doubtful. "Iris, I'm not sure..."

"What if y'had all the pieces?" she pressed. "Would the tree pull itself back together, like you said?"

"It might've when the cut was fresh, but the wood's regrown now. There's no gap to repair anymore. The changes are permanent."

"But what if they're *not*? Maybe one would replace the other!"

"Maybe it would, or maybe it would destroy *both*." Darrick stroked his beard and stared into the dying fire. "What you're suggesting..." He shook his head. "It's so risky, having two conflicting versions of the same time period together at once. It's never been tried."

Katie leaned forward. "Actually, that could work."

"I've no idea what would happen," Darrick admitted. "Maybe nothing. Or it might be like a bomb goin' off. It could create a hole from which you'd never emerge. It might kill you. Or… it might fix everything."

Angus's head jerked up. "You think there's a chance?"

Darrick's expression was pained. "There's just no way to know. The last thing I'd ever want to do is give you false hope, Angus. And anyway, we dinnae have all the pieces. The mirror's long gone."

"It's not gone! We know exactly where it is!" Iris declared. "If I can get it here, will you help us?"

Darrick's eyebrows shot up. He looked at Angus. "Is this what you want?"

Angus set his jaw. "Absolutely. How much longer can I last here, as an old man? If there's even the slightest chance of gettin' home, I'm takin' it!"

Darrick studied Angus for a long moment. His voice was stern. "You could die."

Angus gazed back, resolute. "I know."

"And if I let you go through with this, you must act alone. We cannae risk anyone else being lost like you were."

Angus nodded. "I understand."

Darrick shook his head. "I cannae believe I'm agreein' to this." He turned to Iris. "How will you get the rest of the wood here?"

Her eyes sparkled with determination. "Just leave that to me."

Chapter 24

Iris's brain was buzzing with ideas on the short drive back to her grandparents' house. She'd wanted to start figuring out a plan immediately, but there were more pressing issues. They'd spent over two hours talking with Darrick and Katie, past when Granny likely expected them back. Not to mention, she and Angus were both famished after having consumed nothing more than what amounted to sugar and caffeine all morning.

She checked her watch. *Half twelve. Too soon to call anybody in the States. Might as well help Granny with lunch and decorate the tree. Still...*

She set an alarm for 2:55 p.m.

"Should we have gone Christmas shopping?" Angus wondered aloud.

"I did everythin' online before I got here," Iris answered.

"Online?"

"All my gifts will be arrivin' in the post," she explained.

"Oh. I was just wonderin,' because tomorrow's Christmas Eve," Angus said. "We never celebrated Christmas in my family—we were more for a party at Hogmanay. Was I supposed to get somethin' for Liam and Cora?"

"Of course not! Dinnae trouble yourself. They're not big into Christmas, either. The main reason Granny does the tree is to humor my American upbringing. She makes it nice because she knows it's what I'm used to. But really, we dinnae make a big deal out of it. We only exchange one gift on Christmas. We save the rest for Hogmanay, too."

"Arright, if you're sure. I hope they didnae get me anything."

"Granny did, but that's just who she is."

"I'd feel terrible acceptin' anything if I dinnae have a gift for her…"

"See what I mean?" Iris huffed.

"What?" His eyes widened.

"Stop tryin' to balance the cosmic scales all the time! Just accept some kindness, will you? Repay her by *enjoyin'* it. Quit complicatin' things."

"Arright, arright! Blimey, you're opinionated!"

"I just despise awkwardness in all its forms. I want you to relax and enjoy yourself for a change."

Angus crossed his arms. "Y'sound like Patrick."

"High praise, I take it?"

"Very."

"Here's an idea," she said. "Rave about Granny's cooking. That's a great gift!"

They pulled into the driveway just in time to see Cora getting out of her car with several parcels and a few shopping bags. She waved. Angus jumped out of the car and rushed over to help carry things into the house.

"Och, thank ye, Angus! Such a gentleman!" Cora gushed. "Y'ought to give lessons to some of these youths in their twenties round here. They could stand to learn a few things!"

Angus cast Iris a loaded look.

"Aye, these youths in their twenties," Iris agreed, stifling a giggle. She took a few of the parcels from Granny. "Now which prezzies are these? Yours or mine?"

"Well, they're all addressed to me and Liam, but I dinnae recognize the return addresses on some of them. We'll have to open them all up to see what they are, and exchange backwards so we can wrap them, and then pretend to be surprised when we exchange again! Aren't we clever?" she chuckled.

"I'll address my gifts to myself next time!" Iris laughed.

❧

After a lovely lunch of mutton pies, Liam reached for the fruit bowl in the center of the table.

"I always like to top off with a bit of fruit," he explained. "It's good for my constitution."

"I'm sure we're all very happy for your constitution, my dear," Cora chuckled.

"Angus, y'ought to join me," Liam said, shoving the fruit bowl toward him. "We're not gettin' any younger, my friend!"

Angus smiled. "Aye, that's a fact!"

He looked over the fruit—apples, oranges, pears, and bananas. Feeling suddenly inspired, he grabbed a banana. As soon as he did, he half regretted it because he had no idea how to get into it. *How were they doing it back at Rookwood again?*

Iris could sense his hesitation.

"Angus, wanna split?" She held out her hand. "I could use the potassium." She winked.

Relieved, he handed the banana over. He watched carefully as she peeled it halfway, took off the top, and handed it back. He managed the rest of it quite handily, and soon realized he should never have waited so long to try bananas.

"Och, these are glorious!" he cried. "It's like pudding, but..." he chewed. "...but not." He took another bite. "Mm. Lovely."

Liam raised an eyebrow.

"He's not had a banana… in a while," Iris explained.

"Well, we should all appreciate the little things more," Cora agreed.

Iris's watch alarm buzzed on her wrist.

"Granny, is it arright if I join you for decoratin' in a while?" Iris asked, gathering the plates from the table into a stack. "I wanted to make a phone call."

"Aye, dear. I'll just show Angus all the photos I have of you as a wee babe."

"Oh Granny, spare him the torture. I'm sure he—"

"Angus," Liam interrupted. "I could use a hand in the workshop. Care to join me?"

Angus looked relieved for the second time and heartily agreed.

"Well then! I shall put on some Bublé and wrap gifts!" Cora said happily.

The two men headed out the back door, already in enthusiastic conversation about planers. Iris saw the look of satisfaction on Cora's face and realized that this was the exact result she'd intended.

"Subtle, Granny," Iris giggled. "Very subtle."

"Well, Angus seems shy," she replied with a fond smile. "And Liam can be such an oyster sometimes. They'll have a grand time together. Especially now that they think it was their idea."

"Not just a pretty face," Iris marveled at her grandmother.

"Och," she waved her off. "It's nothin.' Go make your phone calls, Poppet. I really do have wrappin' to do."

Iris planted a kiss on her cheek, put the stack of plates in the sink, and headed upstairs. Soon, the velvety smooth sounds of "Have Yourself a Merry Little Christmas" floated through the house.

Iris pulled out her phone and sat on the bed, wondering what to do. Angus needed that mirror back. The solution had seemed so clear when she was sitting across from Darrick and

Katie, able to speak openly for once about Angus's strange journey. But now…

She shifted her phone from one hand to the other, back and forth, debating. He'd be getting to work right about now… best time to call.

But what am I going to say? 'Hey Will, would you mind stealing a priceless antique and FedExing it to me, no questions asked?' This isn't going to be so simple.

Iris put her head in her hand and let out a little growl.

Why did I think that would actually work? I can't ask that of him. I'll just have to do it myself.

She opened a browser and searched for round trip airfare back to Seattle.

If I go right after Christmas, I can be back before Hogmanay— Granny will be a little bit disappointed, but I'll just tell her I've gone on a little side trip with some old mates. She might buy it.

Her eyes widened at the ticket prices.

Last minute international flights during the holidays. Cannae get much worse.

If she left the morning of the twenty-sixth and did a marathon trip with a short night of sleep, she'd have a one hour window to steal the mirror and get back on the road to Seattle for her return flight. Assuming she wasn't caught. The soonest she could be back was the twenty-eighth, late in the afternoon. Angus could hang on that long. His heart seemed to be doing just fine now.

She debated. *What if I do this, and it doesn't work? If Angus really is stuck here, he's going to need all the rest of his money, and more. I'll just have to buy the tickets myself and pay them off sometime in the next decade.*

She entered her payment information. Her finger hovered over the *Pay Now* button. She took a deep breath.

The phone rang. It startled her enough that she dropped it on the floor. When she retrieved it, the screen showed a Washington phone number she didn't recognize.

"Hello?"

"Iris? It's Candace."

"Oh hi! How are you?"

Candace hesitated. "Not sure yet. I was hoping maybe you could help me out with something."

"Sure, whatever I can do."

"The police were here yesterday… about Angus."

"Did they find him?" Iris tried to sound casual but concerned.

Candace was quiet. "I think you know they didn't."

Iris's heart leaped into her esophagus. "Wh-what do you mean?"

"Well, it's interesting. They went through his file… y'know, routine part of the investigation. And it just so happens that one of the documents in there, a rather important one at that, is a *copy*."

Iris squeezed her eyes shut. She felt sick.

"Now why would we have a very nice-looking color copy of such an important document?" Candace went on. "Where's the original? That's what the cops wanted to know. So far, they have several theories, ranging from insurance fraud to identity theft, or worse. Now, anybody who handled Angus's file is under investigation. That'd be Becky, the social worker, the administrator… oh yes, and *me*. Depending on how it goes, any one of us could lose our jobs."

Iris's hands trembled. "Candace, I—"

"Wait, it gets better!" Candace interrupted, her voice rising in pitch. "I came in early this morning to do a little digging of my own. I pulled up security footage from Becky's office, and guess who's on it, making copies of files during her off hours… on more than one occasion?"

Iris's jaw dropped. *There's a security cam in there?*

"I—uh…" She'd suddenly lost her ability to recall any useful words.

"You have the document, don't you?"

The line was quiet for several moments.

"Yes," she finally whispered.

"Oh, Iris! What in the world are you thinking? You can't possibly have a use for something like that unless..." She let out a deep breath. "Do you know where Angus is?"

Iris's mind floundered for an explanation, a lie, a story, *anything*.

"He's... safe," she hedged.

"How can you possibly know *that*?" Candace snapped. "He just got out of the hospital!"

"His heart is fine..." Iris fumbled. "He's—"

"You're not qualified to handle the safety of someone with a heart condition!" Candace protested. "And you're especially not equipped to assess the mental state of a person with dementia! Do you understand how much danger you've put him in?"

Iris had never heard her so upset.

"Are you even in Scotland right now, or did you lie about that too?"

"Yes, I'm in Scotland." Her voice quaked.

"So let me guess, you lied about *when* you were leaving so you could bust him out of the hospital... then what? Stash him someplace?"

"What! NO!" Iris grew defensive. "I would never do that to him!"

"Iris? Where... is... Angus?"

Iris's head spun. *This can't be happening.* Words wouldn't come.

"Oh my gosh," Candace said with sudden realization. "He's with you, isn't he? Iris... Tell me he isn't with you."

Still, no words would come. Only tears. Iris tried to hold back the sound of her sobs, but the fear and heartbreak rising up within her left her no choice.

Candace let out another deep breath. "I'm trying my best to stay calm here, kiddo, but you have *got* to tell me what's going on."

"Angus isn't crazy!" Iris finally spoke through choked sobs. "He just wanted to get home!"

"Home? Home, as in Scotland? He doesn't have a passport!"

"He does now. That's... why I needed the—"

"Okay. I don't know how you pulled it off. I don't want to know. The less I know, the better, actually. Because you're in a world of hurt now. Do you understand how bad this is?"

Iris shuddered with crying. "But he's so happy here!"

"That's great, but do you realize what you've done? Passport fraud, international kidnapping... this is FBI stuff!"

"Please don't tell anyone!" Iris begged her.

"That's your solution? Don't tell anyone? Then what? It never happened? Unfortunately, I don't have that luxury. Because of my position, it's mandatory that I report this. If I don't, I lose my job. I might anyway, considering this happened in my department. You really stuck my butt on the line."

"I'm so sorry, Candace," Iris whispered. "I didn't know what else to do."

Candace let out a sorrowful sigh. "I was hoping there was some other explanation for all this. I've never been so wrong about trusting someone before."

A fresh flood of tears hit Iris. Her head bowed under the weight of emotion.

"I'm so sorry, to do this Iris, but... you're fired. I hope this was worth it. My next call is going to be to the police. I don't have a choice. The only thing I can do for you now is offer a bit of friendly advice—stay put and cooperate. Okay?"

The line clicked.

Iris was stunned. She stared at her phone until the screen went black. A wave of panic hit as she realized the sudden impossibility of her situation. If Candace was calling the police, how much longer would it be before they referred the case to someone here? How long would it take them to find her grandparents' address and send someone from the police station in Montrose to pick her and Angus up?

What will they do with him?

She made a snap decision. Flying back to get the mirror was no longer on the table. She was left with only one option if she wanted even the slightest hope of getting Angus home.

She woke her phone up and scrolled through her contacts until she found *Will Donovan.* She pressed the call button without hesitating. She didn't even bother rehearsing what to say. It no longer mattered what he thought of her.

She got up from the bed, tucked the phone against her shoulder, and began stuffing her clothes into her backpack. Will's voicemail picked up.

"No no no…" she muttered, dialing him back. He answered on the fourth ring.

"Hey, Iris!" He sounded a bit flustered.

"Hey Will, how's it going?"

"You just caught me! I'd just shut my locker when I heard the phone ringing in there, so I ran back. What's up?"

"Will, I really hate to do this, but I have to ask you for the hugest favor."

"What's going on? Are you okay? You sound upset."

"I *am* upset." Her face crumpled. "And I can't really explain why." She sniffed.

"Okay…" He sat on one of the break room tables and put his feet on a plastic chair.

"It's kind of an emergency, and it's going to sound completely insane. Do you think you could do something for me, and just trust me that it's the right thing to do, even if it seems a little… off the wall?"

He was quiet for a moment. "I guess that depends. It's nothing illegal, is it?" he chuckled.

Iris hesitated.

"Wait, *is* it something illegal?"

"It's kind of a life and death situation."

"You're kind of scaring me."

"I'm sorry. I'm not trying to scare you, but I really need to know if you'll help me or not." She used her arm to sweep a few makeup items and a pair of earrings off the top of the dresser into her open backpack.

He considered for several seconds. "What do you need?"

"I need you to go to the chapel right now."

"What? My shift started fifteen minutes ago. I have to—"

"Will… please. It'll be quick, I promise. Just don't let Candace see you."

"It's 7:15. Candace doesn't come in till eight."

"She's there."

"How do you—"

"She's there early, okay? Just… *please…*" Iris was beginning to sound panicked.

Will frowned and took a deep breath. "All right, hang on."

Iris almost wept with relief.

Will poked his head out of the break room. Seeing no one in the hallway, he took the stone steps two at a time and made a left.

"The chapel's just beyond the dining room, right?" he whispered into the phone. "I hardly ever come up here."

"Yes. Through the arch."

While Will was walking, Iris ran through different scenarios in her head, trying to come up with one that would put Will at the least amount of risk. She yanked the zippers on her backpack closed. Then she crossed the hall and began packing Angus's things.

"Okay, I'm here," he puffed. "What am I doing?"

She took a deep breath and plunged ahead. "See the mirror on the wall behind the piano?"

"Yeah… kind of a flowery wooden frame?"

"That's the one. I need you to break it."

"Break… the mirror?" He stood in front of it, perplexed.

"Yes."

"Aren't you in Scotland?"

"Yeah?"

"How does my breaking a mirror *here* help you clear over *there*?"

"I told you it would sound insane."

"Is this some kind of Scottish superstition thing?"

"Of course not!" she huffed.

"Of course not..." he muttered, rubbing the back of his head. "Because *that* would be absurd..."

She sighed. "I can't explain. But if you do this, you might just save someone's life. You'll have to trust me. Are you in?"

Iris stood still. All was quiet on the other end of the phone. Then suddenly, she heard the sound of shattering glass. She smiled. *I think I might love him.*

He came back on the phone. "That... is the most... idiotic thing... I've ever done!" he huffed as he jogged back through the dining room toward the stairs.

"Act casual!" Iris warned him.

He slowed to a walk. As he reached the stone steps, he met Candace on her way up from the kitchen, holding a cup of steaming coffee. He tried very hard to look nonchalant.

"Okay, Mom!" he said loudly into the phone. "Talk to you later!" He slid the phone into his pocket without hanging up. "Hi, Candy! You're up early!"

Iris froze, listening intently. Her heart thumped.

"Hey, Will," she greeted him in a somber tone. "Yeah, just had to do some... stuff. What are you doing up here? I thought you'd be in the kitchen."

"Oh, I just... Hey, it sounds like I should make you some brownies later."

"Normally I'd be all over that, but I'm not sure even your brownies would help me today. Thanks, though." She meandered down the corridor toward her office.

Will finally reached the safety of the break room.

311

"Okay, *what* was that all about?" he demanded. "Candace looks like her dog just died, and I just threw a hymn book at a gorgeous antique!"

"I'm sorry, Will. It had to be done. I need the mirror here..."

"If you need the mirror, then why did you just tell me to break it?"

"Because I didn't want anyone to see you taking it. This way, the janitor will take it down. The maintenance shed backs up to the employee lot. All you have to do is sneak out there on your lunch break and put it in your truck."

Will was dumbfounded. "Iris, are you serious? I'm helping you steal this thing?"

"I'm so sorry, Will. If there was any other way—"

"If I get caught, I could lose my job!"

"You knew that before you threw a book at it, but you did it anyway."

"True..."

Will's thoughts tumbled. *I must be out of my mind. What kind of girl is she, anyway? I don't even have a parking ticket, and in five minutes, she's convinced me to commit a felony.* He squeezed his eyes shut and rubbed his forehead.

"So..." he said, "assuming I'm successful at pulling off my first grand larceny, what am I supposed to do with this thing?"

"I need you to rush ship it to me. It's going to be insanely expensive, and I'm really sorry about that, too. I'll pay you back, I promise."

"Where am I sending it?"

"I'll text you an address really soon. From a different phone."

He sighed. "This all sounds completely dodgy and a little nuts. Actually, I have no idea why I'm going along with it."

"You've trusted me so far. Please, don't let it be for nothing. I promise, if you knew everything, you'd know you were doing the right thing."

He was quiet for a moment.

"All right. I trust you."

Iris breathed out her relief. "Thank you. And Will?"

"Yeah?"

"This means everything to me. I'll never forget it."

"I just hope you know what you're doing."

"I hope so, too."

Iris stayed upstairs another fifteen minutes, making sure she'd packed everything. It also gave her time to give her blotchy face and red, puffy eyes a chance to return to normal before she had to face Granny. She held a cool washcloth over her face, trying to come up with a better story than going on a side trip with old schoolmates. That idea was absurd. She realized that now. An introvert like her, dropping everything in the middle of a family holiday to spend time with people she'd barely spoken to in the last ten years? Granny would see right through it. Thankfully, she'd finally hit on an idea that was far more believable, because in a way, it was the truth.

She felt a pang of guilt for having to deceive her own grandparents, but she was so far into this thing now that there was nothing for it.

Suddenly, a sickening thought came to her—the looks on Granny and Granddad's faces when the police came knocking, wanting to know where their granddaughter was. *Their granddaughter, the suspected kidnapper.* It was bad enough that her parents were going to be questioned back in the States. Probably in the next few hours, in fact. She might be able to get them to understand once she'd had a chance to explain. As long as she left the Guardians out of it.

But to disappear with Angus like a fugitive, and then have Granny and Granddad hear the worst from the police... the idea broke her heart. Especially because of what they'd say about Angus. That he was mentally ill… lost… incompetent… a victim. Iris couldn't stand it. She had to take a deep breath to stop herself from crying all over again.

What if Granny and Granddad aren't home when the police come?

Iris made another snap decision. With several more clicks on her phone, she'd maxed out both of her credit cards. *Worth every penny.* She prepared her story, and headed downstairs to put the wheels in motion. The first step was to talk to Angus alone. She could hear Granny singing along to "Feliz Navidad" in the bedroom as she sidled past and slipped out the back door.

She poked her head into the workshop. Angus and Liam were both wearing work aprons, and Liam was watching, enraptured, as Angus chiseled flowers into a block of wood.

"Iris!" Liam called to her. "Blimey, you've got to see this. Angus is quite the artist!"

"I told you, right? His work is magnificent!" she agreed. Trying to stay in character, she tried not to smile too brightly, even though this sight warmed her. "Angus, I'm sorry to pull you away, but could I speak with you outside?"

Angus took in her expression for a second, and concern rose on his face. He untied his apron and stepped toward her.

"Excuse me, Liam." He smiled pleasantly. Once outside, his smile faded as he faced her. "What's goin' on?"

"Angus, I'm so sorry, but we have to go. You're not safe here."

"What? Why?"

"My boss figured out what I did."

Angus's eyes widened in shock.

"She knows you're here with me, and she's goin' to turn me in." The words tumbled out of her, her voice tinged with fear. "I dinnae ken how long we have until someone comes to pick us both up!"

"We've got to pack..." Angus started for the back door.

"Everythin's arready in the car."

He stopped and turned. "What do we say to them? Liam and Cora? They're such gracious people, but... just to flee without explanation..."

"I have an idea, but I dinnae think you're goin' to like it. I have to tell Granny something, but it's goin' to be a hard sell unless you help me. Can you stick with me on this?"

Angus nodded, looking shaken.

They went inside. The music had stopped.

"Granny?" Iris knocked softly.

"Oh! Wait one second!" Iris could hear Granny shuffling around. She emerged a few seconds later. "Had to tuck a few things away from pryin' eyes..." She scanned the room behind them. "Is Liam still out in the shop?"

"Aye, he's tryin' his hand at carvin' roses," Angus said.

"Och, that's lovely, Angus. I'm so glad you're here," she said, patting his arm.

"Actually, Granny, that's what we wanted to talk to you about. I've just been on the phone, and it turns out that plans have changed."

Granny's brow knit with concern. "Is everythin' arright?"

"Well, not really. Angus has to leave earlier than expected because there was an accident."

Cora looked aghast. "Really? My goodness, what's happened?"

Angus was startled, and trying not to look it.

"Someone fell—one of Angus's really good friends—and hit her head. It's serious. Angus wants to go to her right away."

Iris looked at Angus for confirmation, hoping he would go along with it so they could get going, but a strange look had come over his face—a mixture of bitterness and disbelief. He shook his head, too overcome with rage to speak.

"That's awful! I'm so sorry, Angus. Clearly, you're quite upset, poor thing," Cora soothed.

He didn't seem to hear her.

She went on, "Well, there's no question—you must go and see to your friend right away! We'll be prayin' for a full recovery, of course. Is there anything y'need?"

"Oh, it's arright, Granny. We'll be fine. I'll drive him and make sure he's okay. Sorry to miss the festivities here… After that call, I felt bad about how things would go here without us, so I got you a surprise!"

"What d'you mean, a surprise?" Granny raised an eyebrow suspiciously.

"Well I know how much you like a festival, and it's been years since you went to one. So I'm sendin' you and Granddad to the winter festival in Aberdeen! Check your email, it's all in there. I got you tickets to a lovely show that's on at the Tivoli, and I booked two nights at a hotel right near the theater. Plus, you love the Christmas village. They're doin' an ice rink this year, and a carousel…"

"Och, Poppet, you didnae have to do all that!" Granny hugged her.

"But I wanted to," Iris squeezed her and gave her a peck on the cheek. "And it's just a quick little drive up there—not even an hour. Just throw a bag together, check into your lovely hotel, and you'll be eating wee little pancakes and petting reindeer by suppertime!"

"By suppertime? You mean *tonight*?" Cora's jaw dropped.

"Sure, why not?" Iris beamed, trying to make her awkward smile read as lighthearted spontaneity. "And then we'll all be back by Hogmanay for presents!"

Cora patted Iris's cheek. "You do beat all. I love how you forget that old people like us dinnae blow with the wind like the youths! Still…" She got a faraway look. "I do love a festival. And if we *did* go tonight, that would mean I dinnae have to cook. Nothin' wrong with that!"

"That's the spirit!" Iris encouraged her.

"Well, you two had be'er get on," she said, shuffling them toward the door. "And I'll tell Liam we're about to embark on a little holiday of our own!"

They exchanged a few more hugs and Iris received the normal admonishments about safe driving and putting on one's scarf if the wind picks up. They pulled out of the driveway five minutes later.

"Love you, Granny!" Iris waved out the window. "Tell Granddad too! See you in a few days!"

Iris headed north toward Woodstone Cottage. "I cannae believe how well that went!" she began.

"You've got a lot of brass," Angus spat.

Iris felt a chill. "Angus, I—"

"I know I ought to be grateful for everything you're doin' for me, and I am. But that was…" He shook his head, unable to find a suitable ending for his sentence.

Her cheeks burned with shame. She tapped the steering wheel. "I know it's no excuse, Angus… but I was runnin' out of time and out of ideas. It was the only thing I could think of that would get us out of there quickly. We cannae be there when the police come… my grandparents either."

"You used her," he said through clenched teeth. "The person I care most about in the world, on the worst day in her life, and you used her as fodder for an excuse to get out of a Christmas party!"

"No, Angus," she shot back. "Not just a Christmas party. How about both of us bein' locked up? I needed an excuse Granny'd believe, because she's like a human lie detector! Arright? I couldnae make up an excuse about me, because she knows everyone I know! Even if she bought it, she would've tried to persuade you to stay. So what could I say about you? Your mother's got a broken leg? Also true, but by the looks of you, that'd make her about a hundred and ten years old!"

"I just…" He leaned his elbow against the door and gazed gloomily into the darkening sky. "You're right, I guess. It *was* all true. She did fall, and I do wish I could be with her. I just didnae expect to hear it come out of your mouth like that."

"I'm so sorry, Angus. I should've thought harder… come up with something be'er than that."

"Y'did what you had to."

"I'll never do it again. I promise."

He looked at her, eyes questioning.

"You have my word," she said earnestly. "She's off limits. Unless you want to talk about her. I'm happy to listen."

"That's another way you're like Patrick," Angus said gruffly. "Cannae stay mad at him either."

"So I'm forgiven?"

He crossed his arms and looked at her, his frown beginning to ease. "O'course you're forgiven. Gotta keep you close by, in case I need someone to break the law again."

Chapter 25

I ris knocked on the door of Woodstone Cottage. She and Angus shivered in the deepening twilight as the biting wind lashed at their backs. Callum MacCrann opened the door. At seventeen, he was the image of his father, with piercing blue eyes and wispy brown curls, but he had his mother's cheerful smile.

"C'mon out of this nasty cold!" he greeted them, holding the door wide. "Dad! They're here!" he called out. Then he grinned broadly at them. "I'm Callum, the Guardian Heir. You must be Iris?" He shook her hand, then turned to Angus with reverential awe. "Are you really Angus Armstrong?"

"Aye, that's the rumor," Angus said, doffing his cap to shake hands with the boy.

"I cannae believe my luck!" Callum said, giving Angus an enthusiastic handshake before helping Iris out of her coat.

"I cannae believe my luck either, sometimes," Angus replied, rolling his eyes.

"Back so soon?" Darrick appeared behind Callum, holding a mug of tea.

"Things got a little... complicated," Iris began.

"Complicated how?"

"Well..." She struggled for words. "Getting Angus here from the States was not the easiest thing. I didnae exactly... have the *legal* right to bring him here."

Darrick frowned. "And why's that?"

"Because nobody understood who he really was, so he was institutionalized. He was declared legally incompetent and made a ward of the state. I had to... work around the law a little bit."

"So he's what, a fugitive?"

"Technically, *she's* the fugitive," Angus replied cheerfully. "I'm the victim of a kidnapping."

Iris whacked his arm. "I thought I got out clean, but a couple of hours ago, they figured out that I was involved," she explained. "Staying at my grandparents' house seemed like a bad idea."

Darrick's expression grew alarmed. "Did you drive here?"

"Aye, we parked out at the road..."

"Keys." Darrick held out his hand, fluttering his fingers urgently.

Iris handed them over, unsure what was happening.

"Callum, go move their car. It's a..." He looked at Iris.

"A white Kia," she finished.

"Park it across from the post office, laddy. Leave the the keys in it. Jog back so you stay warm."

"No worries, I got it," Callum said, grabbing the keys from his father and his coat from the hooks near the door. He was gone in less than a minute.

"What just happened?" Iris wondered.

"Oh, is this your first time as a fugitive?" Darrick chuckled. "Guardians spend their lives learning how to point attention elsewhere. Having the police sniffing around an abandoned car is the kind of thing we prefer to have happen closer to town… say, near several bus stops? Get me?"

"Ohhh…" Iris nodded. "Sorry, Darrick. I didnae think about how my car would bring the police around here."

"Nae bother," he replied with a sly grin. "They'll just think you skipped town on the bus line. Callum will make it look good. Come on in! Hungry?"

"Just some tea would be wonderful," Iris sighed, relieved to have a respite from the tension of looking over her shoulder.

"Angus, how about it?"

"I hope there's still some shortbread," he smiled.

When Callum returned twenty minutes later, Darrick, Katie, and their freckle faced ten year old son Brody were deep in conversation with Iris and Angus around the fireplace.

"How'd it go, lad?" Darrick asked him.

"Smooth as custard," he replied, hanging up his coat. "Left the keys in the glove compartment."

"Anyone see you?"

"Of course not."

"Leave any prints?"

"Good grief, Dad, I'm not an amateur!" Callum said with mock offense, then grinned. "I also tossed in some snack wrappers and a map of Dublin, just to make it fun."

"That's my boy!" Darrick laughed.

"Aye, it's just lovely that our darling son is a budding talent at subterfuge," Katie said dryly.

"Last I checked, it's not a crime to leave a map in a car," Brody spoke up.

"Hush, you." Katie chucked him under the chin with a wink.

"Angus was just about to tell us about his daring escape from hospital!" Brody said to his brother.

"I was hoping not to miss anythin' interesting!" Callum said brightly, taking a seat on the floor by Brody.

For the next hour and a half, the two travelers regaled the family with the story of how they met, right up to the part where Iris was getting fired. They were all so engrossed in the telling that when Iris's phone chirped, they all jumped.

"So sorry…" Iris pulled her phone from her pocket and checked the screen. It was a text from Will:

Got it. Where to?

"Oh my gosh! I cannae believe I forgot! Hey, Darrick? A friend of mine is shipping the mirror, but we cannae use my grandparents' address. Where should I have him send it?"

"Oh, no worries. Here…" He pulled out his phone. "What's his number?"

Iris showed him her screen.

He made several keystrokes, and then stuck his phone back in his pocket.

"There. Your friend cannae reply, but I sent him an untraceable message with the address of my uncle Rowan's auto repair shop in the village. Rowan gets parcels every day, so one extra will go unnoticed. He knows that anything labeled 'D.M.' after his name comes to me. He'll be in touch."

"Thanks, Darrick… for all your help," Iris said.

"All in a day's work," he replied with a little shrug. "Are you sure this friend of yours can be trusted? I told him to delete the text I just sent. That would make some people want to do the opposite."

"We can trust him."

"Arright, if you're sure. It's all very cloak and dagger, so I hope he's got the stomach for it."

Iris smiled, imagining Will chucking a hymn book through the air. She nodded. "He seems like the type to follow through once he's made his mind up."

"Well then! Looks like we're doing this thing!" Darrick was buoyant. "In that case, there's somethin' the two of you should see."

Darrick led them through the kitchen and into a small study. The ceiling was low, held by ancient timbers and stone. Two of the walls were lined with floor to ceiling bookshelves. Tall, dusty volumes with hand sewn spines occupied over three fourths of the space. A handsome mahogany desk sat against the far wall beneath a bank of monitors. The twelve small screens to the right showed different live feeds from night vision cameras. To the left sat two sizeable speakers, upon which sat two larger computer monitors. One monitor showed nothing but waveform readings, and the other showed several small colored dots plotted on a blue grid.

"Blimey," Angus breathed in amazement.

Iris took it all in, and turned to Darrick. "No wonder you were onto us in about a minute! You can see everythin' from here!"

He laughed. "Aye, it sure makes the job easier. I usually only see animals, so you can imagine my excitement at the prospect of chasin' people!"

"What is all this?" Angus asked.

"Perimeter motion sensors, so I can tell if anythin's incoming," Darrick pointed to the blue grid. "Those dots blink and the computer sends me a text if they get tripped. It's a right pain during hail storms." He pointed to the waveform monitor next. "Vibration sensors attached to the tree, so I can hear any changes in the tree's condition. I can amplify the vibration and listen to it through that speaker there. The other one picks up the surrounding forest sounds. And over here," he waved toward the camera monitors, "I can see the tree from every angle."

"Och! Look there!" Angus pointed at one little screen, where a deer appeared in black and white, crossing in front of the camera. It paused to listen for a moment, its eyes glowing white, then moved on.

"Other than yourselves, that deer's about the most exciting thing I've seen with those cameras," Darrick laughed. "Still, it's important work, and I love doin' it."

Iris was overcome with curiosity, so she risked a personal question.

"You said earlier that after the war, your family had to find outside work and pay rent to stay here. Is that still the case?"

"Aye, it is. It's an interesting arrangement, though—we sign fifty year leases and have free reign to improve the property any way we like. I dinnae think a landlord has even stepped foot out here since my grandfather was Guardian."

"What outside work do you do, then?" she probed.

A sly grin spread across Darrick's face. He pointed to a bookshelf directly behind him. It was loaded with an assortment of newer fiction books with colorful, dramatic covers. Iris recognized several of the titles, and had even read three of them. A sudden realization dawned on her.

"*You're* D.M. Hawthorne?" she shrieked.

Darrick threw his head back and laughed merrily. "That depends! Are you a fan?"

"Oh my gosh, I *love* your books!"

"Okay then, I'll admit it!" he said.

Iris pulled one of his books from the shelf and opened the back cover to see his author photo. "I didnae recognize you with that beard!"

"Aye, it's never been photographed! First time I've ever let it get like this," he said, rubbing his chin. "Not sure if I'll keep it. Katie likes it, though."

"Wow…" Iris shook her head. "I cannae believe I'm actually talking to D.M. Hawthorne!"

"Eh, I'm just Darrick. Same chap you were talkin' to before I got famous a second ago," he chuckled as his face turned slightly pink.

"So that's a pen name! Makes a lot of sense now… it's brilliant!" Iris giggled.

"I thought so," he winked. "But enough about my silly side job. What I really wanted to show you is under here…"

He rolled back the green and gold Persian rug to reveal a trap door in the floor. He grabbed the brass ring near the edge and heaved it open. Below lay a set of stone steps descending into cool darkness. He grabbed a small flashlight from the top desk drawer and headed down, motioning them to follow.

The short flight of ten steps opened into a large storage room with earthen walls and stone shelves.

"This house was pretty remote, initially," Darrick explained, "so my ancestors went all in for great cold storage."

Canning jars of all descriptions lined several of the shelves, along with winter squashes and a few boxes of fresh red and green apples. On the far side of the room stood a shelf with several more dusty volumes on the upper half, and an old steamer trunk shoved below.

"There's somethin' here that belongs to you, Angus," Darrick said, pointing his flashlight at the trunk. "Go ahead."

Angus's expression was befuddled, but he stepped forward. He knelt in front of the trunk and cautiously opened the lid. Inside, he found a burlap sack and a jar filled with wood chips and sawdust.

He lifted the jar and squinted at the crusted shellac in the bottom. "Is this my jar?"

He opened the sack. "You're jokin,'" he murmured. "This cannae be…"

"The same branch? Aye, what's left of it," Darrick confirmed. "It's all there."

With trembling fingers, Angus reached out his hand and brushed a piece of furrowed bark. Instantly, he both heard and felt a faint humming vibration, like a distant harmonica playing a single low note. He snatched his hand away, looking up at Darrick in disbelief.

"It's… still alive?"

"Very much so." Darrick gave a solemn nod. "And it's kept down here for that very reason. Ré stored this trunk in the cottage, but he was hard of hearin,' you'll recall. When Éamon took over, the sound was drivin' him batty, so he moved it down here."

"I cannae hear anything," Iris said. "I could hear the tree, but not this."

"I'm not surprised," Darrick commented. "It's a really faint sound to most people. I think my sensitivity must be genetic, and Angus's must be from exposure."

"I cannae believe you saved all this," Angus murmured.

"Great Trees are a precious resource," Darrick said. "And when it's time, I'm hoping that every bit of this finds its purpose once again."

Angus slept soundly on the sofa by the fireplace, while Iris had taken a cot in Darrick's study. She'd fallen asleep watching little moths and bats flicker across the monitors. Her first conscious thought the next morning was that she smelled bacon and coffee, and that she was too comfy to move.

Then she remembered it was Christmas Eve. Although it was no big deal to Granny and Granddad. They'd planned to have a quiet day, take a walk down the beach, make treats, and watch telly together. She hoped they were having a grand time in Aberdeen.

But if Iris were back in the States, she'd be loading up her car to spend the night at her parents' house, where they'd be throwing a massive Christmas party tonight for everyone they knew. Mum would be playing carols at the piano while Dad sang in his booming baritone and played his guitar. Iris would be the official decorator, seeing that the tree was trimmed perfectly and the nibbles were arranged in neat rows on the trays. Then she'd put on her green velvet dress and greet people as they came through the door, as she'd done every year since she was ten.

I wonder if I'll ever go to another Christmas Eve party… or if I'll even get to be free after this. I wonder if the police are listening to Mum and Dad's phone, hoping I'll call. What must they think of me right now?

She had worked so hard to make her parents proud. She'd graduated with honors and tried to be a devoted daughter and hard worker. She had caught her dad's sense of wonder at the stories of the past. Her dream was to be a history professor like he was—to write fascinating stories about the way that time changes the world.

I wonder if that's over now. God, what did I just do? I thought that if I held to my ideals and stuck up for someone who needed help, that everything would work out. But instead, I think I may have just ruined my life. I've lost my job, I'm hiding from the police, and I can't even call my own family. I'm kind of freaking out, here. Please… if you really see me, like Angus says you do, you've got to show me what to do. Because even if we do get him home, I may never see the light of day again.

A tear trickled onto her pillow.

"Iris?" Katie whispered.

"I'm awake," Iris mumbled.

"I brought you some coffee…" Katie tiptoed in. "And a mince pie."

Iris sat up. "Thank you, Katie. Listen, I'm sorry about all the trouble I'm putting you guys through… invading your house right during Christmas and everything."

"Please," Katie scoffed. "Are you kidding? The MacCrann men have never been such a happy lot. Angus Armstrong: The Man, The Legend… under our roof? Father Christmas has come early!"

Iris sipped the coffee. "I just hope bringin' him here is going to be worth it."

"Sounds like it arready is. It's down to you he's made it this far. You were the first to believe, Iris. You helped him, even when no one else would. And if this experiment works, and he does make it back home, you'll be the one who restored countless lives to what they should have been. It will have untold impact on generations of Angus's family and everyone they'll meet. Never forget that."

Iris absorbed Katie's words, thirsty for courage. She swallowed back the lump in her throat.

"Angus says we met because of God," Iris said softly. "D'ye think that's possible?"

"Absolutely. I can see it quite clearly."

Iris stared into her cup. "Seems like God wants me in jail, then."

Katie smiled faintly. "Oh… not sure I'd put it quite that way. It's arright to be tested, Iris. Doin' what's right can be tough, and we have to be willin' to face the consequences. Puttin' yourself at great personal risk on behalf of someone else is a very… *Jesus* thing to do. I think God approves of that. Why not trust Him with the outcome?"

Angus and Iris spent Christmas Eve chatting with the MacCranns and making themselves as useful as possible. They were both trying to focus on anything else besides what was happening in the world outside the cottage—everyone Iris loved and respected thinking she'd turned to a life of crime while police combed two countries for them. Nor did they want to think about what was coming—facing the tree that nearly killed Angus the last time he'd messed with it. Worst of all was the possibility that they might have come all this way, only to fail. The perfect antidote to their anxiety was enjoying the fellowship of this family and getting as involved as they could in the household tasks.

Once everything was done for the evening, Darrick disappeared into his study to write some letters. The women were laughing in the kitchen, so Angus tried watching a bit of telly with Callum and Brody. When *A Christmas Carol* starring Alastair Sim came on, Angus was enthusiastic.

"It's Mr. Dickens' new one! I read it last year! Mrs. Keith let me borrow it... och, it's brilliant."

The boys looked at Angus in amazement.

"So they've made it into a play, then?" Angus asked.

"Uh, basically," Callum replied.

"Why's it all gray?"

"It's a really old movie. It was filmed before they invented color TV," Brody answered.

"Was that before or after people walked on the moon?" Angus wondered, starting on his second mince pie.

The boys looked at each other.

"Before," Callum replied.

"Interesting..." Angus muttered, eyes glued to the screen.

Angus lasted until the Ghost of Christmas Yet to Come took over the screen with his menacing presence. Then he suddenly decided to get up and chat with the ladies in the kitchen.

"Too scary for you, Angus?" Iris asked him as he walked in.

"Course not! I just… needed a little stretch, is all…"

Iris smiled at him suspiciously.

"I did! You dinnae have to believe me…"

Katie and Iris giggled.

Darrick appeared in the doorway. "Well, ladies and gents, I just heard from Rowan. It looks like your package is on its way."

Angus could feel his heart skip a beat.

"He was notified of an international shipment due in the mornin'," Darrick went on, "so we'd be'er call it a night. Big day ahead."

The family said their goodnights and headed up the stairs.

Angus and Iris took turns in the bathroom and then wished each other sweet dreams. Iris went into the study and shut the door.

Five minutes later, just as Angus was settling into the blankets on the plush leather sofa, Iris crept back into the living room and sat beside him on the floor. He looked at her face in the dying firelight. She was thinking hard again. Finally, she spoke.

"I wanted to give you somethin.' A Christmas present, I guess." She handed him a little wooden box.

He sat up. "I—I dinnae ken what to say," he said, looking over the plain little box.

"The present's inside, ya numpty. Open it."

"Ohhh…" He lifted the lid.

Inside were three gold sovereigns, emblazoned with the head of George III on one side, and a depiction of George mounted in battle against a slithering dragon on the other side.

"Iris, these are from your collection! You're givin' me all three of them?"

"Aye, I brought them with me from home because I knew I wanted you to have them."

Angus turned the box over and tipped the coins into his hand. "I still dinnae ken what to say."

"It's a symbol of hope, Angus. Imagine... what if this works? What if we really can put things right? You'll arrive home, with old Mary still in your pocket, and still needin' rent. There was no time to get you your money from the stamp, and it's probably too dangerous to try it now. Everythin' else in my collection was minted after 1844, but you could spend these!"

Angus closed his hand around the coins. "Thank you, Iris. This means a whole lot."

"You're very welcome. And... if things dinnae go the way we want them to tomorrow, then at least you'll have somethin' to remember me by... no matter where I end up."

His face looked stricken as he considered what might be in her future, but she reached out and covered his hand with hers.

"Angus, I think you were right. God must be in this, somehow. We're both going to be okay. So no matter what happens, I want you to know that you've changed my life for the be'er."

"I have no idea where I'd be without you," he said earnestly. "You've changed my life, too. For example, I've nae a thing to give you in return just now, and I refuse to feel bad about it!" He grinned proudly.

She giggled. "See you tomorrow."

"Happy Christmas."

"Happy Christmas, Angus."

Angus, Katie, and Iris sat around the kitchen table, staring. They'd been having the strangest Christmas breakfast of their lives—not because the food wasn't delectable, but because none of them could think about anything besides the Great Tree looming in the wood. They had little appetite, and could think of nothing to say except "please pass the marmalade."

Darrick and the boys had stuffed their faces in about three minutes and then rushed into the cold, dark morning to fetch Will's shipment from the village.

When the front door opened, Angus almost dropped his cup. Darrick carried the large box into the living room. Without a word, everyone gathered as he set it on the coffee table. Will had marked the package as "custom critical" and paid an exorbitant fee just to shave half a day off its journey. Iris felt a rush of gratitude. When she'd said "rush," Will had given her the literal extreme. If he were standing right here, she would have thrown her arms around him and cried. She probably owed him over a thousand dollars now, but she didn't care.

Darrick pulled a pen knife from his trouser pocket and sliced through the labels and tape, then straightened and took a step back. "It's all yours, Angus."

With intense focus, Angus pulled back the box flaps and unwound the packing material. The golden roses and ivy gleamed in the firelight, surrounding Angus's shattered reflection.

"Well…" he muttered. "We meet again, you gorgeous misery."

"Wow," Callum whispered.

"You *made* that?" Brody murmured.

"Aye." Angus lifted his wrinkled face. His eyes settled on Callum. "Ne'er forget how important your legacy is, lad. You are so… *needed*."

Callum nodded solemnly.

Darrick laid his hand on Callum's shoulder and nodded, giving him a little squeeze.

"Angus, I have a few things to go over with you," Darrick said. "Iris, you can listen if you like."

The three of them went into Darrick's study, where he pulled a parchment envelope from his desk and handed it to Angus. It was addressed to Ré MacCrann.

Angus looked at him quizzically.

Darrick laughed. "Like I said, Guardians always share their knowledge with one another... although this might be the first time in history it's been attempted backwards. If our experiment works, this message will ensure that the Guardians dinnae have to wait over a century for a full explanation."

Angus nodded. "I'll make sure he gets it."

"That brings me to the next bit," Darrick went on, with a look of growing concern. "I'm not entirely sure what's going to happen once we start this. There are elements of this process I dinnae fully understand—things I cannae predict. For instance, if it works, then this future will be undone. You may not be able to remember any of it... meeting Iris, coming here, everything that's happened."

"But how's that possible?" Angus protested. "It *happened!*"

"Not if you undo it."

"Does that mean that you'll forget all of this, too?" Iris wondered.

"Actually, no. I dinnae think so. I did some readin' up on that last night in the central database. A Toltec Guardian, in what is now Mexico, did some writings on this subject in the twelfth century. According to him, Guardians are gifted with a special ability to retain time fluctuations. If Angus pulls this off, and if I've understood the writings correctly, then I'll remember this week two different ways, like it happened twice."

"So... will I forget Angus?" Iris asked quietly.

Darrick looked at her for a long moment and shook his head. "I'm just not sure."

They stood quietly, grieving the possibilities.

Angus broke the silence. "Anythin' else I should know?"

"Well, I'm not positive what another intense exposure to the Great Hawthorn will do to you," Darrick replied. "It's possible that since we're attempting a repair, we'll see a sort of reverse entropy, like when the tree undid its own damage. But it's also possible that your body may not follow."

Iris gasped. Fear pierced her heart. "What do you mean... not follow?"

Darrick was somber. "He may remain stuck here, and die from exposure. Or he may arrive in the past as... just a body, long dead."

Angus took a deep breath. "I've no fear of dyin'," he said. "I never wanted my life to be short, but I'll be with God sooner or later. Sooner is arright, too."

"Well..." Darrick sighed. "I guess that's it, then. You should get dressed, Angus."

Angus frowned. "I *am* dressed."

"Not for 1844, you're not." Darrick looked him over. "If we're successful, we cannae have you showin' up in the Victorian era wearing polyester. That shirt is too modern. The trousers will do... wait, is that a zipper? Never mind, they'll have to go. And let's see... what size are your feet? About a ten?"

"I... think so?"

"Be right back." Darrick disappeared up the stairs. He returned five minutes later with a rugged pair of antique work boots, dark brown woolen work trousers, a simple tan waistcoat, and a coarse linen shirt with three cloth buttons at the collar. "This is what happens when the same family occupies a house for centuries," he explained with satisfaction. "We're always good for a costume."

Angus emerged from the bathroom several minutes later, feeling very much at home in his new old clothes. "The trousers might fall down," he said, hitching up his waistband, "but otherwise everythin' fits pretty nice."

"Callum, do you still have those braces you wore to prom?"

"Aye, I'll grab 'em!" He dashed up to his room.

"We might even be hoarders," Darrick chuckled.

Callum returned, and once the braces were buttoned into place and a few adjustments made, Angus looked like a man from another century once again.

"I know my coat is arright, but can I keep my cap? I'm rather fond of it."

"Aye, it's just fine," Darrick assured him. "We should get on. Callum, fetch the trunk up from the cellar. I'll carry the mirror."

"Can I come too, Dad?" Brody asked.

"No, son. It's too dangerous. I'm not sure what's goin' to happen out there. I need you here to look after your mum, just in case. Arright?"

Brody looked disappointed, but Katie ruffled his hair.

"We'll watch from the study, arright? You'll see plenty."

Angus donned his wool cap and his father's coat—in one pocket, four antique coins; in the other, a letter to a Guardian long dead. "I'm ready."

The four stood in front of the Great Hawthorn. Wilting blood-red berries littered the massive, craggy branches and forest floor. The bewitched fascination Angus had first felt for this tree was replaced by an eerie dread. It was not unlike the difference in feelings he'd have had about a lion, depending on which side of the fence he was on.

They stepped hesitantly around the tree, ducking low branches, and came to a halt next to the healed cut. Callum set the steamer trunk on the ground.

"Good luck, Angus," he said, and backed a stone's throw away.

"This is as far as we go," Darrick said. He set the cardboard box containing the mirror on the ground next to the trunk. "I wish I could do more, but I'm not even sure what a safe distance is from something like this. I cannae risk leavin' my family behind."

"I understand," Angus said, offering Darrick a warm handshake. "Thank you for everything."

"Come away soon," Darrick warned Iris, then went to join Callum.

Angus turned to Iris. Her eyes brimmed with tears.

"I hope I remember you, Iris," he said earnestly. "You're my best friend."

Her tears broke free, and for the first time, Iris disregarded Angus's nineteenth century sensibilities and threw her arms around him. "You're mine, too," she whispered. She released him quickly, and with one last squeeze of his hand, let him go.

"God, bless her," he whispered as she walked away. "I can never repay her kindness, so I'm askin' You to do it for me."

Chapter 26

Angus turned and knelt by the steamer trunk. He had no idea how to proceed, but he imagined it would be best to remove as many hindrances as possible, allowing the pieces of wood to move freely.

What a strange idea.

He began by turning the mirror frame on its face to pop the pine backing out and release the remaining fragments of broken glass. Next, he opened the trunk and lifted the burlap sack from it. He pulled out every scrap of bark, leaves, twigs, and branches, and set them on top of the sack directly below the place where he'd cut the tree.

The faint humming vibration had returned in earnest. He soon realized that each piece of wood was vibrating at its own distinct frequency. The more Angus touched the pieces, the more clearly he could hear them.

Other than the sound, nothing out of the ordinary was happening. He looked over at the others. Iris stood motionless, watchful. But Darrick and Callum were covering their ears. Clearly, *something* was happening…

Angus squinted. *What is Darrick doing? Pointing. What's he pointing at? Now he's miming something… kind of looks like he's opening a…*

"The jar!" Angus gasped. He'd forgotten it in the bottom of the steamer trunk! He snatched it and struggled to unscrew the metal band, but years of storage had petrified it. He tried using his thumbs to push the glass cap into the jar, but the rubber gasket held fast against the band with maddening stubbornness.

In desperation, he looked around him until he spotted a jagged stone jutting out of the ground just below the branches. He drew back his arm and heaved the jar at the stone. It shattered with a sickening thud, scattering wood chips and sawdust, along with shards of dingy glass, across the forest floor. The bewildering clamor that followed was like a sustained chorus of crickets, tea kettles, and piccolos—some so high in pitch that they were barely audible.

Angus stood still for a moment, wondering what was supposed to happen next. The pieces of wood he'd laid across the ground were growing louder. He knelt and touched the mirror frame… it was beginning to vibrate. The shellac he'd so carefully applied began to crackle and fall away, revealing the raw wood beneath.

He stood once again, so he could be eye level with the two branches that had grown from the cut. He studied them intently. Though the air was still, they began to tremble. After several more moments, his eyes widened in surprise as the branches began to shiver and emit a low tone. Crimson berries and dried leaves began to drop among the wood chips and broken glass.

The air began to crackle with an electric sensation. Startled, Angus took a step back. Several of the wood scraps floated up from the ground, rising toward the branches that stood in their place. Within half a minute, Angus was standing in a cloud of debris that was humming at every imaginable frequency.

As each fragment of wood came within a few inches of the Great Tree, it was repelled by an invisible force which sped its travel upward, where it arced through the air and fell back toward the ground, only to be caught up once again and drawn toward the tree. On and on, the cloud of debris churned upward through the center and back down, accelerating by small increments at every pass, growing ever louder.

"Oh, no…" Derek moaned. "This is *not* good…"

"What's happening?" Iris demanded. "Is this not supposed to happen?"

"No! No no no no…" he shook his head back and forth, looking more horrified the longer he watched. "The older pieces are tryin' to reattach, but the new growth is repelling them! It looks exactly like a magnetic field!"

"So what does that mean?" Iris's voice rose with panic.

"The debris is *not* goin' to reattach! It's goin' to keep looping and accelerating until the cloud becomes like a circular saw and rips the tree apart!" Darrick shouted over the din.

"Dad, what do we do?" Callum yelled, his hands still over his ears.

"Lad, go get my ax!" Darrick yelled back.

Callum bolted in the direction of the cottage. He tore through the trees and slammed back the door of the wood-shed. He seized the ax with two hands and sprinted back as fast as he could.

Darrick grabbed the ax and strode toward Angus, who stood transfixed near the churning cluster. The hairs on his arms stood on end in the static charged air.

"Angus!" Darrick called. "Y'have to cut off the newer branches! They're stoppin' the old ones from reattaching!"

Angus's face went pale. "I cannae cut this tree!" he shouted back. "That's how I got into this fix in the first place!"

339

"It's the only way! I have to stay back! You're the only one who can do this—otherwise this mess will destroy the entire tree!" He held out the ax.

Angus's face was a mask of horror. Behind him, the exquisite mirror frame floated upward and snapped in two as it was repelled backward from the tree. It tumbled through the air, weightless and picking up speed, at the mercy of the energy field. The entire section of the Great Hawthorn which supported the branches was now shuddering at the disturbance.

"Please, Angus! It'll be havoc if we dinnae fix this—it'll rip Time apart!"

Angus narrowed his eyes and set his jaw. He grabbed the ax and gave Darrick a sharp nod. Darrick retreated and stood protectively in front of Iris and Callum as Angus strode toward the tree, shielding his face from the tumbling mass of wood chips and bark. He found the exact spot where he'd chopped last time and aimed his ax.

Beside him, concealed in shadow, Aimsir shielded Angus with his cloak, preventing several large chunks of debris from hitting him. Caledon placed the tip of his sword at the base of the branches to guide the path of the ax.

Angus swung. The blade made perfect contact. A blast of sound emitted from the tree that set Angus back on his heel, but he righted himself for another swing. After five more chops, the first branch fell to the ground.

Dark energy oozed from tree and the severed branch, spreading across the forest floor and drifting into the energy field. Angus breathed hard. Drops of sweat began to form on his forehead. He shook himself, fighting nausea, and raised the ax. He took two more swings. They landed perfectly, but made less impact, as Angus's arms grew weaker.

The low moan from the tree assaulted his ears as he swung again. The cloud of debris continued to pick up speed. Bits of wood were now whizzing past him as he took one more chop. His vision grew blurry as he squinted, trying to gauge how much further he had to go. His arms felt like rubber. He set the ax blade down near his foot to rest a few seconds, when suddenly, the world tilted at a crazy angle. Dizziness hit him like a wall, knocking him sideways. He went down on one knee.

"Angus!" Iris cried. "Darrick, what's happening to him?"

"It's the gravity leak… it's a huge exposure—"

Iris lurched forward. Darrick caught her by the wrist and pulled her back. "You have to stay back, Iris! He's caught in it now!"

Angus struggled to stand, using the ax handle for support, but slipped back to his knees.

"But he might be dying!" she sobbed.

"He might be!" Darrick's voice was stern. "He knew the risks!"

"God, help him!" she whispered through sobs. "What can I do?"

Angus heaved himself off the ground at last, panting with exertion, and hefted the ax onto his shoulder. He took one more swing, which made barely a dent, then fell to the ground with a crash.

Without even a conscious thought, Iris broke free of Darrick's hold and sprinted toward Angus.

"Iris! NO!" Darrick shouted, but she could think only of making sure Angus was okay.

The air was thick around him. When she got within several feet, she felt like she was slogging through mud. She ducked to avoid flying bits of wood and threw herself down beside him.

"Angus!" She shook him, tears streaking her face. She lowered her head to listen to his heart. *Still beating, but slowly.* "Angus, wake up!"

"Iris…" he muttered weakly. "You're gonna get hurt…"

"Angus, get up!" she urged him. "Y'have to finish!"

"It's so heavy… I just need to rest a second…"

Aimsir stayed by Angus on the ground, massaging his heart, coaxing it to beat.

The Great Hawthorn began to shudder and creak. The energy field had expanded, forcing other branches to bend to the point of snapping.

Iris grabbed the ax from Angus's limp hands and stood. She'd never used an ax before, except to split kindling. She lifted it above her shoulder and aimed.

Brennus batted a few more flying pieces of debris out of the way with the flat of his sword, then sheathed the weapon and put each of his hands over Iris's to add some strength to her swing. Caledon used his sword to guide her blade. With three more chops, the second branch began to topple with snaps and moans. Iris was already winded, breathing hard. She rested the ax on the ground, her arms burning from swinging the blade at several times its normal weight.

One more chop. You can do it. Almost done.

The ax felt even heavier than before. As she lifted it for the last time, she misjudged the weight and accidentally dragged the blade against her leg. She gasped at the searing pain as a river of blood flowed from a deep cut near her shin. A pool of red spread across her pant leg.

Iris steadied herself and swung the ax a final time. The second branch dropped. She let the ax down with a thump and collapsed a few feet from Angus.

She drifted into blackness.

Darrick and Callum watched as Iris fell, their faces horror stricken.

"Dad! What should we do?" Callum cried.

Darrick shook his head, bewildered and angry. "Nothin,'" he said. "We do nothin.' She left us no choice."

"Should we try to—"

"It's forbidden. Y'arready know that, lad."

The mass of whizzing scraps gradually slowed to a stop. The cacophonous hum quieted by half as the fragments of shattered tree hung in the air. Gradually, almost imperceptibly, the pieces rearranged themselves, nestling precisely into their former places and drawing tightly together until a single branch materialized. The chaotic frequencies emitting from the different segments settled into one harmonious vibration.

As the base of the branch reattached itself to the Great Hawthorn, a bolt of current shot into every vein of the newly assembled portion. A wave of energy rippled into the air around the tree, easing the thickness of the atmosphere.

Darrick and Callum took several cautious steps forward. The branch still hummed and vibrated more loudly than the rest of the tree, its seams and fissures glowing with strange light as they slowly knit together.

"They're gone!" Callum said in alarm.

Darrick looked around. Sure enough, Angus and Iris were nowhere to be seen. Scattered beneath the Great Tree lay the ax, shattered jar, flattened burlap sack, empty steamer trunk, and cardboard box covered in shipping labels. Beside the box lay a heart shaped panel of pine, blood stained, with Angus's signature on it.

"I wonder where they are..." Callum said.

"Not a hundred percent sure, lad," Darrick replied, carefully retrieving his ax and inspecting the blade. It bore traces of Iris's blood mixed with inky sap. "We'd best not touch those," he cautioned, eyeing the two fallen branches as they sizzled and popped on the ground. Wisps of caustic smoke drifted from the cuts.

"What about *that*?" Callum asked, pointing to the glowing, vibrating branch.

"We watch."

Iris awoke to the sound of song thrushes tweeting above her. Squinting at the dappled sunlight stabbing through her eyelids, she felt around her, trying to determine what she was lying on. Leaves crunched beneath her palms.

I'm outside... under a tree? She sat up and blinked. *Under a tree in a forest.*

Sizzling pain coursed up her right leg, followed by a throbbing to match her heartbeat. Her pant leg was plastered to her skin with dried blood. The knees of her jeans were streaked with mud and berry stains.

There are no berries anywhere...

She looked above her at the huge hawthorn tree. It was just beginning to show the first white buds of spring. Her leg complained while her brain refused to make sense of where she was. She reached out and tried to pull the fabric free from her wounded leg, but it was stuck fast.

Wait, what happened to my hand?

She examined both of her hands, front and back. They were wrinkled, covered in brown spots. The usually golden blonde hair on her arms was white. She grabbed the ponytail at the nape of her neck and pulled the hair forward over her shoulder. It was tangled, full of dried leaves, and... silvery white. She gasped.

Iris heard a deep intake of breath and a moan. She turned. An old man lay on the ground a few feet behind her, regaining consciousness.

Angus.

Memories began flooding back... the noise... the fear... the ax... her friend lying on the ground, his heart barely beating.

"Angus!" She scooted over to him and shook his shoulder.

He moaned again and opened one eye. Confusion registered on his withered face. He rubbed his eyes and then opened them both. He frowned and sat up.

"I'm sorry, I'm..." He looked at her with hesitation. "I think I might be lost. Have you seen a lady round nearby, early twenties... ginger hair? Goes by Iris?"

Her mouth fell open. She stared at him, searching his face for any sign that he might be joking.

"*I'm* Iris!"

His frown deepened. "But you're not... I mean..." He looked her up and down, taking in her disheveled appearance.

"Angus, I dinnae ken what's happened to me, but I'm Iris. I promise!"

"How do I know?"

"Check your coat pocket. Mary, Queen of Scots should be in there keepin' company with the three Georges I gave you last night on Christmas Eve!"

His eyes widened. He pulled the four coins from his pocket, looked them over, and stuffed them back in.

"Iris! What's happened? You look so... *old!*"

"Do I?" She touched her hands to both cheeks. "*How* old?"

Angus cocked his head. "Perhaps... eighty?"

Iris gasped.

"The tree must've got you... same way it did me."

"Does this mean... Angus, d'you think it worked? Are you back home?"

He froze, a look of fear and yearning on his face. "I'm almost afraid to find out!" He bowed his head and squeezed his eyes shut. "I've prayed for so long..."

"I know this isnae the same place we left," she coaxed. "Look... it's spring!"

He peered all around him. A patch of bluebells nodded as the light breeze rustled the tender greenery above their heads. A cuckoo called from a nearby pine.

"Aye, 'tis spring, sure enough… but which one?" His eyes were drawn to a pale shape about ten feet away, nestled in amongst the dried leaves and ferns on the forest floor. He rose shakily to his feet and walked over to it. He nudged it with his foot.

"What is it?" she called.

As he picked it up, his hands recognized the sturdy sailcloth.

"It's my rucksack!" he shouted. With fumbling fingers, he worked the buckle and opened the drawstring. He pulled out a small ax, and turned it over fondly in his hand. He reached back in. "Ha! It's still warm!" Face beaming, he pulled out a roasted potato wrapped in a handkerchief.

"Angus, you *are* home! You did it!" Iris exclaimed.

Angus walked back over and plopped onto the ground beside her, suddenly crestfallen. "Maybe I am… but look at me. I still look like an old man." Fear crossed his features. He rolled the potato distractedly between his palms. "Nobody's goin' to recognize me. It'll be just as tough as before."

Iris squeezed his arm. "Maybe it'll be alright. We'll figure somethin' out, okay?" She tried to stand, but sucked a breath through her teeth at the sharp pain she'd just caused herself by moving too quickly. "Ugh… I think I cut myself on Darrick's ax."

Angus's face filled with concern. "That looks bad, Iris. It could be infected. We should see to it. Maybe the Guardian's at his cottage. Come on, I'll help you." He slung his rucksack onto his back and lifted her easily from the ground, draping her arm over his shoulder.

"Angus, wait…"

He stopped. "What?"

"How'd you do that?"

"Do what?"

"You just lifted me up like it was nothing!"

"So?" He searched her face, trying to grasp her meaning.

"Angus, your face!"

He lowered her back to a seated position on the ground and knelt beside her. "What're you sayin'?"

She gazed at him, filled with astonishment. Before her eyes, the lines, furrows, and brown spots of age melted away, replaced by youthful, sun-kissed skin dotted by several freckles. His scruffy, close beard faded from grizzled gray to black against his chiseled jaw. The deep blue of his eyes, now framed by full, dark brows, took on even more intensity. Curls the color of dark chocolate protruded from underneath his wool cap. Astounded, she reached up and pulled his cap off.

"Iris, what're you doin'? We've got to get on…"

"Angus…" Her eyes sparkled. "Y'really *are* twenty-four!"

"Aye, am are! I've said that all along!"

"Well it's pretty easy to believe, now!"

He took a deep breath, then fixed her with an intense gaze.

"Tell me *exactly* what y'see," he said.

"Your hair is dark brown!" she replied earnestly. "Y'look… *young*, Angus!"

"White hair's gone?"

"Nae a one left!"

"Wrinkles?"

"Welllll…" she squinted at him. "Laugh lines, but only twenty-four years' worth."

"*Really?*" He stood, spread his arms, and threw back his head in exuberant laughter.

Iris grinned at him, awestruck by his transformation. Now that he wasn't bent with age, he was easily a full six feet in height, with strong, broad shoulders. How was this the same Angus? Yet it was. This handsome face, merry with laughter, was the same old Angus she'd shared chocolate orange cookies with in the hospital… who shouted like a little boy on aeroplanes. The same Angus who had told her to "quit talkin' like a Canadian" and be proud of who she was.

"Blimey," he shook his head, still grinning. "The way Darrick talked about the tree sap, I figured the change was permanent! How am I back to lookin' the right age?"

"Well, you saw yer tattie," Iris answered. "Y'never ate it, so the sap from your hands never got into your body."

"True…" He looked at his hands. "My scar! It's gone!"

"What scar?"

"Remember?" He held up his left thumb. "I gouged it with the chisel while I was sculptin' the roses. But if we're back to the part where I never cut the tree in the first place, then I never carved it either! So I guess I never cut myself."

Iris was having a realization.

"You… cut yourself," she murmured.

"Not anymore!"

"No, I mean… Angus, you cut yourself with a tool covered in *sap*. That's one way you could have gotten it into your blood—through a cut! Maybe that's what aged you. I cut myself with the ax, and look at me! It's the only thing that makes sense."

"You must be right…" he pondered. "And my aging was undone because the cut was undone. How can we undo yours?"

Iris shook her head. "I'm not sure we can. I might be stuck like this." Her brows furrowed. "What will I do here, Angus? I'm hurt. I've nothin' to wear. I cannae cook, I dinnae ken how to do *anything* without modern inventions! I have no skills besides waitin' tables and writin' research papers…" Her voice grew desperate. "And now I look older than my granny! I'll be useless here!"

"Shhhh…" he put one finger over her wrinkled lips. "You're in my world now, dear friend. This is where Angus and Marjorie Armstrong live. We take care of our own. Nothin' bad is goin' to happen to you here. I'll not let it."

He lifted her easily in his arms and carried her toward Woodstone Cottage.

Ré MacCrann knelt in his garden, turning over clumps of soil and breaking them into bits with a trowel. He picked over the ground, tossing away stones and pulling up tiny seedlings of lambsquarters.

Before he could hear him, he saw a young man picking his way through the undergrowth with confident strides, carrying a frail old woman who was... *wearing trousers?* Plainly, this was no passerby stumbling across his clearing by chance. This man was making a beeline straight for the cottage, as though he knew precisely where he was going.

Ré stood and brushed his hands on his trousers, watching the young man approach. The man veered toward the wood pile near the front door, where Ré had been splitting firewood earlier that morning. One small log still remained on the stump he used as a chopping block, with his hatchet sunk into it. The man reached out with his foot and tapped the log with his boot, deftly knocking it out of the way, then lowered the old woman so she could sit on the stump.

Ré hobbled over to the pair, his arthritic knees complaining. He regarded the silvery haired woman with curiosity, not just because of her unusual attire, but because of the sizeable blood stain on her trouser leg.

"Ré MacCrann?" the young man addressed him. "Guardian of the Hawthorn?"

Ré's stomach leaped. He must have blanched visibly, because the dark haired man reached out a hand reassuringly.

"I'm sorry if I've startled you. Dinnae worry, I'm a friend," he spoke calmly, "but I cannae spend much time on niceties right now. I'm Angus Armstrong. This is my friend, Iris. We need your help."

Ré squared his shoulders. "Of course. You're both quite welcome... please come inside. We'll see to that leg, madam."

"Thank you," Iris replied. Relief flooded her. The pain in her leg had grown so intense that she could barely keep a straight face.

Angus helped Iris hobble through the rounded door after Ré—the same door they'd left just this morning following Darrick.

The interior of the cottage was entirely different, however. The furniture was simpler, more rustic. There were no dividing walls between sitting room, bedroom, and kitchen. A wooden bed sat next to a bureau in the far corner, where they knew Darrick's study would someday be. A steamer trunk sat on the floor near the foot of the bed. Most noticeably, there were no stairs. The cottage still had only one story.

"I've not had anyone address me by my title since I can remember," Ré said, moving several books off of a dusty settee and motioning them to sit. "Since you seem to know who I am, is it safe to assume you're a Guardian as well? Or perhaps a Guardian Heir?"

"Actually, no. But I've got a le'er for you…" Angus began.

"Eh? What's be'er for you?" Ré scratched his chin.

"No! A *let-ter* for you!" Angus projected, pulling Darrick's envelope from his coat pocket.

"Ah!" Ré took it and looked it over with fascination, but set it aside.

"First, that leg," he said. "Give us two ticks." He disappeared outside, returning moments later with a long strip of freshly cut sphagnum moss. He bustled about, rummaging in cupboards and drawers, finally returning with an assortment of tools and a basin of clean water. He knelt beside Iris. "We cannae stand on propriety, I'm afraid. I'll have to expose the leg, if that's arright?"

"Of course." Iris nodded. *He's afraid I'll be embarrassed… if only he knew I wore shorts all summer.*

Ré carefully cut her pant leg up the side and around the top, just below the knee. He dipped a cup into the basin and used it to trickle a stream of cool water under the denim, rehydrating the dried blood and coaxing the stuck fabric off the skin. Finally, it fell free, revealing a four inch gash next to the shin bone. Iris felt instantly better. The pain was still nagging, but not as intense. Ré cleansed the wound delicately and applied a strip of moss directly to the cut, then wound it with a strip of linen.

"Moss?" Iris wondered.

"Moths are be'er for headaches!"

"No… *moss!*" she said louder.

"Aye, moss is great for keepin' infection away," he nodded. "I'll make you some ginger and rose hip tea for the pain. Just rest yourself, my dear." He lifted her ankle and shoved a little footstool under her calf.

"We really appreciate this," Angus said.

"It's my pleasure," Ré replied. "I never have company, save for family!"

"Aye, we've heard that about Guardians," he chuckled.

"Really? What other Guardians have you met?"

"Darrick MacCrann…" Angus began.

"Och, my grandson!"

Angus paused, then plunged ahead. "No… well, actually, the Darrick I'm talkin' about is your great-great-great-great-great grandson."

Ré was gobsmacked. "Wh—I dinnae understand…"

"Best if you read the le'er."

Iris sipped her tea while Ré read through Darrick's letter a third time.

"This is remarkable," he breathed. "A le'er from someone who'll not be born for generations!" He shook his head in wonder, then looked up at Angus. "So… you actually whacked off part of a Great Tree and survived it, laddy?"

"Aye, barely." Angus smiled ruefully.

Ré was dismayed. "I should've been there to save you the trouble."

"Well, it's done now," Angus said. "The tree's repaired, so it never happened. Although, according to Darrick, at some point you'll remember it happening, as well as not happening, at the same time."

"Blimey, I'll look forward to that," Ré said sarcastically. "At least I'll understand why I disagree with myself, and not be forced to assume I'm off my heid!"

The three shared a good natured laugh.

"What's not in the le'er," Iris said, "only because Darrick was not yet aware, is what it took to get the tree to repair itself."

"Scare itself?"

"No, *repair* itself!" Angus shouted.

"Aye," Ré nodded. "This le'er mentions that the tree will be hit by lightning sometime in the next few years, and my son Éamon will see the repair process firsthand! The pieces just… stick back together?"

"Exactly," Angus confirmed, "but that's goin' to be all original wood that heals itself after the lightnin' strike. We were trying to recreate an original branch where another had arready grown back. Nearly killed ourselves!"

Ré gasped. "What happened?"

"The old and new were repellin' each other," Angus replied. "Pieces were flyin' through the air, hummin' and screechin' fit to wake the dead. Had to take an ax to the new growth so the older bits would have a place to settle."

"You've *got* to be jokin.'" Ré's eyes goggled. "You took an ax to the Great Tree a *second* time?"

"It was that, or watch the whole thing be ripped apart!" Iris declared.

Ré shook his head. "That kind of cut would take tremendous precision! You could never do it with an ax! Not without leaving holes in the—wait… did you see anyone else there?"

"Nae, it was just Iris and me," Angus answered, frowning.

"I'll wager it was not."

Iris looked quizzical. "What're you on about?"

"Did Darrick fail to mention that we Guardians have guardians of our own?"

Angus sat back on the settee, searching his memory. "Y'know, he did mention somethin' about that…"

Ré put his hands on his knees, leaned forward, and recited: "But after the time of floods, when the lifespan of mankind was barely a century, the care of the Great Trees was passed to them. Messengers of The Three now watch over the human Guardians…"

"That's exactly what Darrick said!" Angus smiled.

"Aye, that's the oral tradition of the Guardians. Every one of us knows it by heart in his own tongue. Glad to hear it's still as robust as ever."

"You're sayin' there were other… *beings* there? Helpin' us?" Iris gasped.

"Had to be," Ré said simply. "What you're talkin' about is basically surgery, and you did it with an *ax*… while all manner of bedlam carried on about yer heids. Chances of that goin' well are extremely remote… without a little help." He winked.

Iris was dumbfounded.

Ré chuckled. "I see 'em sometimes, y'know."

"See… the beings?"

"Sure! Somethin' strange about that?" Ré smiled with satisfaction, as if that were the end of the matter.

He grasped the armrests of his chair and pushed himself to a stand. "Well, madam, it appears you're in need of suitable attire. Cannae have you goin' about in them alien clothes from the future and only three quarters of a pair of trousers, can we?"

Iris giggled. "I'd be grateful."

"Well I've not much but men's clothes round here, but I've a couple things of my dear Eidith's."

"I'd be honored, if she'd be arright with it…"

"It's unlikely she'd object, since she passed on ten year ago." Ré smiled faintly, a far off look in his eye. He shuffled to the steamer trunk and lifted the lid. With great reverence, he laid out several items on the bed.

"I'll leave you to change. Angus, let's get on with some wood splittin.'"

Iris took her time sorting through the strange garments, finally understanding what to put where after a few wrong tries. She looked at herself in the mirror above the bureau and gasped.

Who is that?

She might as well be looking at a painting of somebody else. The Georgian style chemise gown was soft and flowing, made of sturdy blue linen, with a high-waisted tan belt and a modest trim of handmade lace at the high collar. It was at least ten years out of fashion by now, but that suited, considering her elderly appearance.

She realized that her hair was still a mess, so she pulled the twigs and leaves out of her ponytail, smoothed it into a braid, and wound it into a bun. She hid her elastic band beneath the silvery white strands as best she could.

Eidith had had slightly smaller feet than her own, but the simple brown buttoned walking boots were comfortable enough. She made for the door, but gasped in pain, realizing she would need to slow down until her cut had a chance to knit together properly. She started again, more slowly this time, with a pronounced limp.

She made her way out the front door, feeling refreshed despite her pain. Ré looked at her with delight.

"You do that dress proud, madam. Eidith would have loved to see it out in the sun again. It was her favorite." His eyes lit up as a thought came to him. "Wait here!" he said, and puttered back into the cottage.

Angus and Iris looked at each other questioningly.

"Here…" Ré puffed as he returned with a small leather satchel. "It's Eidith's other dress and a few of her things. You might need 'em. No tellin' how long you'll be here."

"Thank you for all your kindness," Iris said, slinging the thick strap over her shoulder.

"It's been extraordinary," he replied. "I'm sorry you seem to be out of your time for the moment, but y'never know what'll happen. Things could still change."

"You mean I might get back?" Iris's eyes widened.

"Tough to say," he replied. "But in your day, the Great Tree could still be healing. As for what side of the gap you land on when it finishes… time will tell."

Chapter 27

Scotland ~ 1844

Angus led Iris through the wood on her injured leg as best he could, holding branches out of her way and picking out a trail with as few obstacles as he could manage. Five minutes into the walk, he took her satchel from her and slung it across his shoulders with his rucksack. Ten minutes in, she had to stop. He helped her sit on a fallen log near an oak tree.

He looked at her, concern on his face. "I dinnae ken how we're goin' to get anywhere before dark, at this rate. But your leg will never heal if you dinnae let it rest."

"I'd give anything for some ibuprofen," Iris grunted. "Wait, has aspirin been invented yet?"

"Ass-what?"

"Never mind. Probably not."

Angus opened his rucksack and pulled out the potato. "Hungry?"

"Not really."

"Neither was I, when I first traveled by Tree." He untied the handkerchief and bit a hunk off the potato. Then he reached back into the sack. "What I wanted was... aha!" He pulled out his little ax, and approached the big oak behind Iris. "Let's see..." He crunched through the undergrowth until he located a few fallen branches on the ground. He picked up the largest one and held it in his hand for several moments, feeling it... waiting. He held it up to his ear.

"What on earth are you doin,' Angus?"

"I want to make you a walkin' stick, but..." He was still another several seconds, listening. "Just makin' sure this really *is* oak. After last time..." He shook his head.

"Aye, the last two months would be enough to make anybody paranoid!" Iris giggled.

He threw her a knowing look, with a twinkle in his eye, and turned back. "This will do just fine," he said. He chopped off the excess wood, peeled the bark away, and then presented her with a rough, but functional, walking stick.

"Thank you!" she said. "I might be able to go a bit faster with this."

"You'll do nothin' of the sort," he chided. "That's for later. For now, just carry it. We'll save that leg as much as we can."

He swept her into his arms and strode through the forest, carrying her at double the speed she could walk.

"I'm tryin' to remember exactly how this day was supposed to go," he said, ducking a branch. "I came out here lookin' for a piece of hardwood to carve, I know that much. But I've no idea how long ago I said that. Could've been a couple hours, or half the day by now."

"And instead of a chunk of tree, you're bringin' back a little old lady," Iris finished.

"Oi! I'm older than you!" he teased.

"So what's the best way to do this?" Iris wondered. "I want your life to be as normal as possible from now on."

"Dare to dream, I guess," he said with a little roll of his eyes. "Well, my first instinct is to take you straight home," he said, hitching her weight back up in his arms without breaking stride. "But parading you across the estate grounds is goin' to raise a lot of questions with all the men at work there. If I tell 'em you're my granny or somethin,' they'll understand why we're together, but they'll wonder why you were wanderin' in the woods alone. If I say you're a stranger, my boss might offer to take you in for the night. He's a generous man, see."

"But I want to stay with *you*, Angus," Iris protested. All at once, she had a fresh appreciation for how lonely and vulnerable Angus had felt for the last two months. Being in the care of total strangers, and having no real answers to give people about her situation, suddenly seemed intolerable. How had he lived like that for so long, and not been driven to total despair?

"I know. Ye'll stay with me, I promise," he assured her. "I told you I'd not let anythin' happen to you. But if I insist on takin' you home with me in the middle of a work day, I could lose the entire day's wage, maybe even my position."

Iris stuck out her chin. "I cannae let that happen. Can you hide me somewhere? The workshop, maybe?"

"Sure you'll be arright?"

"Of course. I think I just need some water…"

"Well, that's easily gotten." Angus smiled at her encouragingly as they emerged from the forest of Woodstone Hill. He was tempted to cut through the fields to make better time, but the freshly turned soil made that option less appealing when carrying another human being, so he kept to the lanes.

"Look, Iris! There's the sea! Och, I love home," he said with great emotion.

She gazed at the distant strip of blue ocean beyond the fields, trying to imagine her beloved village as it stood right now. *Not quite home for me.*

They entered the forested edge of the main estate grounds within five minutes. Angus was finally starting to break a sweat.

"Are you sure you're arright, carryin' me all this way?" Iris asked.

"Aye, you dinnae weigh much," he replied. "But I'll be honest, I'm a wee bit out of condition from sittin' round on my bum doin' nothin'!" His grin was contagious.

"Good grief… If this is out of condition, what's normal for you? Caber toss?"

Angus gave a hearty laugh.

"Okay, if you're sure. Heart doin' okay? I mean, you *were* just in the hospital last week…"

"Nae a flutter since we got back," he said. "I think it likes bein' here."

"Good." She patted his chest with a little smile.

They could soon make out the distant sound of tools clanking and workmen shouting. Making sure they weren't seen, Angus made a final dash to the rear of the whitewashed outbuilding and set Iris on her feet.

"Wait here."

She leaned on her walking stick.

Angus straightened, and assuming a casual gait, walked around the front of the building and slid the large door aside. The scent of hay and wood greeted him, as well as the beautiful sight of a workbench filled with his own tools. His mahogany rocking chair project, only a day underway, sat waiting. He nearly cried.

"There you are!" said a voice behind him. "Where you been, mate?"

Angus froze. *Patrick?* He spun.

There stood lanky Patrick Dawson, half a roasted potato in his hand, smudges of brick dust and chalky mortar on his face and shirt front.

"PAT!" Angus threw his arms around Patrick and hugged the breath out of him, knocking his potato to the ground.

"Oof!" Patrick made a guttural sound at the impact.

Angus released him, suddenly realizing how out of place this gesture looked, but only half caring.

"I know I'm irresistible, mate, but crikey!" Patrick looked around to see if any of the other men had witnessed the awkward exchange.

"What can I say? It's good to see you!" Angus grinned.

"And you're *wud!*" Patrick grinned back. He brushed his shirt and retrieved his potato from the dirt. "I think you've finally cracked." He pulled out his pen knife and cut the sandy portion off the potato, chucked it into a nearby bush, and resumed eating. "Comin' out for lunch?"

"Aye, I'm starvin'! Just a second, I left somethin' back here…"

While Patrick waited, Angus dashed behind the building where Iris still stood.

"I just saw Pat!" he whispered excitedly.

"I heard!" she giggled. "Angus, I'm so happy for you."

"Listen, I'm going to walk over with him and grab some food for both of us, arright? I'll leave the door open a bit. As soon as we're clear, can you get yourself inside?"

"Aye, nae bother," she whispered back, with a little shiver.

His eyes flickered with concern. "Y'arright?"

"Yep. Go on," she shooed him.

❧

Angus returned fifteen minutes later with a handkerchief full of food cart fare—two sausages, another potato, two baps, and an apple. He also carried two enameled tin mugs, one full of cool water, and the other full of coffee.

"I took everythin' I could," he called out, laying everything on the workbench. "One worker's portion might be a little thin for both of us…" He looked around him. "Iris?"

"Here," she called weakly from the back corner of the room.

Angus walked over and found her seated on a bale of hay, out of sight behind a stack of lumber. She was resting her head against the back wall, eyes closed. Her face was pale and drawn, with a tinge of blue, and had grown more wrinkled.

"Iris! What's happened?"

She drew in a slow, shaky breath through her nostrils, and opened one eye. "S-s-somehow, I dinnae think this mode of travel's going to c-catch on," she answered. "D-did you feel like you were dyin,' Angus? That's the only w-way I can describe this. I'm so… tired."

Angus placed his hand on her forehead. It was cold. A pang of dread shot through him.

"You're too cold, Iris. I remember this happenin' to me!"

"Actually, I f-feel a little w-warm…"

"Well, you're *not*." He whipped his coat off and pulled it around her.

"No, Angus, I dinnae want it. I'm h-hot," she protested feebly, trying to shove it off.

"Keep it on, or I'm tyin' you up!" he growled. "This is the same thing I had, hypo somethin.'"

"H-hypo-th-th-thermia?" she shuddered.

"I must've been keepin' you warm on the walk here. Just hold on." He ran back to the workbench and returned with the mug of warm coffee. He held it to her lips and she sipped.

"It f-feels too hot." She trembled. "M-maybe I should just rest."

"It's not too hot, I promise. I checked it. I know you just want to sleep, but you have to get warm first, arright? You'll be good as new in a couple hours."

"Hardly new," she croaked.

"Still sassy," he remarked with a little smile.

Iris closed her eyes and drifted. She could hear Angus's voice far away like it was under water, but couldn't figure out how to reply. She felt herself being lifted, then fell into unconsciousness.

Pain woke her. There was a stabbing in her right leg, but also a jarring sensation on her back. And the noise! As she regained consciousness, she realized that the noise was her teeth chattering, and that Angus was rubbing her back to create warming friction. She could feel heat soaking into her skin, and realized that she was sitting sideways on Angus's lap, resting her left shoulder against his chest. He had moved her to a patch of sunlight that shone onto the floor through a high window.

She moaned.

"There y'are," he whispered soothingly. "Thank God. I've been prayin.'" He pulled his coat tighter around her. "I had a fancy hospital on wheels to get me through this," he lamented. "All you have is me."

"Th-th-this is f-f-f-fine," she assured him through chattering teeth. Her muscles shuddered violently, but the warmth of his body felt like a life giving fire. She burrowed in closer.

"It's almost over," he comforted her. "You're comin' out of it. Endure just a little longer for me, arright? Stay awake."

Iris nodded, but it was difficult to tell it apart from the uncontrollable shivering. She stayed awake as long as she could. At last, her body began to relax. She closed her eyes and allowed herself to drift into delicious sleep.

Angus held her for another hour, feeling her cheek, checking the pulse in her wrist, listening to her breathing. He let her sleep, satisfied that she was out of danger, but unwilling to take away the extra body heat just yet.

The stillness of the workshop gave him space to think. His mind wandered to Gillian, as it did in almost every quiet moment. Gilly was the one person whose face had lingered as a constant presence in his mind. But every dream, every memory had been stained with heartache. Hope had left him, replaced with the sickening certainty that he'd never lay eyes on her again.

But now… His stomach did tiny flips. Was it really only this morning that he had declared his love for her? It had been mere hours, but seemed like decades, since he'd felt the softness of her lips. *She's two miles away. Two miles! Is she thinking of me now?* He smiled.

Unless… A chill ran through him. *When did she fall?* From what he'd read in Iris's time, he knew only the year. *This year. But when? What if it's today?* He closed his eyes and took a deep breath. *Get it together, Angus,* he scolded himself. *She's at the pub, like always. She's fine. She must be.*

First things first. What am I going to tell mum? Tomorrow's Friday, and I'll have the rent, thanks to Iris. But how am I going to explain how I came by three more pounds… and an old woman? Iris needs a lot of lookin' after. Mum will be completely willing, but is she well enough? How do I even get Iris home?

Iris stirred in his arms and let out an unsteady sigh. She was like a frail little bird now. Since they'd met, he'd known her to be such a strong, capable, independent person. She could drive motor carriages, find her way through bustling cities, and figure out the answer to just about anything in the world. Now she was withered with age, clinging to life.

He felt something akin to what he imagined fellow soldiers must feel after months of fighting side by side. It was more than camaraderie—it was kinship. Iris was family. They'd laughed and cried together, fought, made up, had more transparent conversation, and seen more extraordinary things than some friends did in a lifetime. She'd been loyal to him when it made no sense to be. And getting him home might have just cost her everything.

He pulled her closer. It wouldn't cost her her life. He wouldn't let it. He'd see her safe, no matter what.

"God, be near her now," he whispered.

A few minutes later, Iris awoke. He felt the change in her breathing.

"Welcome back," he murmured against her silvery head.

"Hi." She smiled up at him. "Was somebody else in here?"

"Just us."

"Oh... I just thought... hm. Must've been a dream."

"What was it?"

"I thought I saw a man in a green cloak... He had such a friendly face. He was *blowing* on me. I felt so warm."

Behind them, Brennus smiled.

Before long, Iris felt well enough to sit up and have a meal. Angus was flooded with relief to see her smiling again, acting like herself.

"It does my heart wonders to see you turned around so quick," he said. "Like a direct answer to my prayers. Took me a lot longer to feel this good after!"

"Aye, it's grand to feel warm again," Iris sighed and tore off a piece of bread. "I'm sure it helps that I wasnae face-down on freezing pavement in the middle of October, like you were."

"Good point."

"So what should we do now, Angus? I suppose I'm technically trespassing at the moment... and you're lettin' me. I dinnae want to get you fired." She sipped on cold coffee. "Should I hide away here until dark?"

"I thought of that, but they lock the doors at night. You'd be stuck."

"How much longer till you get off work?"

Angus squinted out the window, looking at the sky. "Not much longer, by the sun. Pat will come by at the whistle and want to walk home together."

"Well then," Iris grunted, pulling herself to a stand, leaning heavily on her walking stick. "I'll need to be gone by then."

"What? You can barely walk! You cannae—"

"I'm much be'er, actually," she interrupted him. "That little sleep did me wonders. There's almost no pain in my leg."

"Are you sure?" He scanned her feeble frame doubtfully.

"Hey. I'm still Iris. I can function on caffeine and pure stubbornness. I think I'll make for the road with my stick here, and work my way to the village on my own. You walk with Patrick and do whatever it is you were *supposed* to be doing today... y'know, before you ripped a hole in spacetime." She gave him a mischievous wink.

"Arright, clever clogs. Have it your way." He shook his head.

"Gosh, you look so different, Angus," she marveled, still taking in the sight of his dark curls and brown scruff.

"I could say the same about you!"

"Hey now..."

"*Granny*," he teased.

"Whippersnapper!" She poked at him playfully with her stick.

"Arright, you win!" he laughed. "It's no fair, I'm unarmed! Besides, I'm a gentleman. It's not nice to tease decrepit little old ladies." Giggling, he scooted out of the way of her stick as she took another poke at him.

Angus went to the heavy door, slid it aside several inches, and peered out. He motioned her over with his arm. She seized her satchel off the workbench and hobbled up behind him. He budged over a few inches to let her look out, and pointed.

"See that chap in the bowler?"

"The one yelling?"

"Aye, that's Barclay, the foreman. Once he's gone round that corner, make a break for the trees. Then you can double back to the road. If you're pokey enough, we might overtake you on our way. If not, meet me at the pub, arright?"

Iris nodded, watching Barclay intently. As Barclay turned his back, she slung her satchel across her body and gripped her walking stick. As soon as his distant form disappeared around the building, she stepped forward. Angus made way, grabbing her hand and giving it a little squeeze. She turned back with a twinkle in her eye.

"See you soon," she whispered.

Patrick showed up thirty minutes later.

"What, no cuddle for me this time?" he teased as Angus donned his coat and hat.

"Why, d'you want one?" Angus chuckled.

"Eh, let's keep that to once a year. Maybe on Hogmanay, after I've had a couple. I've decided that was a friendship test, to see if I'd punch you. The question is, did I pass, or did I fail?"

Angus laughed, but didn't answer the question. "Fancy a stop at the pub? It's been a long day."

"Amen to that," Patrick agreed. "I could murder a plate of sausages right now."

The two men fell into stride, making easy conversation about nothing in particular. Angus had never appreciated his friend's company more than he did at this moment. Patrick delighted in the simplest things in life.

Where others would complain about the monotony of laying bricks all day, Pat would start a friendly competition with someone to see who could lay more in one shift. Where someone else might feel slighted by fate at becoming a breadwinner for two younger sisters at age nineteen, Pat would beam with pride at how capable and brilliant their little family had become in the past five years, despite everything. The man was a walking smile—the perfect complement to Angus's brooding nature and tendency to overthink everything.

Angus watched the road, looking for any signs of a crippled traveler, but found none. *She's makin' better time than I gave her credit for.*

They ducked into the noisy pub, cheeks rosy from the walk. Every table was occupied, every seat filled, save for two—at a corner table where a frail little woman sat alone, sipping a cup of tea. Angus tipped his chin in her direction, and she smiled sweetly at him, but didn't wave.

"Let's sit over there," he suggested.

"By that wee granny? She might not want a couple of smelly builders at her table, mate."

"Eh, it'll be fine. She looks like an interestin' person to talk to. Besides, there's nowhere else, unless you'd rather eat standin' up!"

Patrick gave a bewildered shrug and followed Angus.

"Are these seats occupied, madam?" Angus whipped off his cap with a flourish, addressing Iris with a slight bow and a quirky smile.

"Why *no*, young man, they're not!" Iris replied with dramatic hand over her heart and returned his silly grin. "Please *do* join me!"

Patrick raised an eyebrow, but removed his hat, took a chair, and extended his hand. "I'm Patrick Dawson. This is Angus Armstrong. Thanks for lettin' us intrude."

"Och, I'm glad for the company," Iris replied. "Pleased to make your acquaintance. I'm Iris."

"I dinnae think I've seen you about the village before, ma'am," Patrick commented.

"Aye, just passin' through," she said.

"From where?"

"Eh," she dismissed the question with a wave. "It's nae all that interestin,' laddy. Let's hear about you instead. What are you buildin'?"

Patrick's eyes widened. "How'd you know that? Are you a fortune teller?"

"Aye, that I am," Iris said, wiggling her wiry white eyebrows. "I can read the mysteries of the past from people's shirt fronts."

Patrick jerked his head down and pulled his shirt out in front of him. Realizing that he was covered in evidence, he let out a hearty laugh. "For that, you must allow me to buy your tea." He fished in his pocket and laid a coin on the table.

"That's kind of you!"

"My pleasure. Fine then, I'll admit it! I'm on the brick crew up the road at Ecclesgrieg. Angus here is a master joiner, craftsman... all around decent chap."

"So I'm in the presence of greatness!" Iris said sincerely. "Imagine all of the people who will visit that castle and marvel at it for years to come. It's inspiring!"

"Blimey, I'm impressed wi'myself now!" Patrick chuckled.

"Hello, boys!" said a boisterous, bassy voice.

Angus jumped. For months, he'd imagined catching just a glimpse of the golden-haired beauty who owned his heart... but instead, here stood her father.

"What can I getcha?" Gordon Mayfield asked.

"Hello, sir!" Patrick greeted him cheerfully. "Where's Gillian?"

"We're chockablock to the rafters, as you can see. She kicked me out of the kitchen, so I'm takin' orders."

"From her, or from everybody else?" Patrick laughed.

"Take your pick!" Gordon rolled his eyes.

"Tea for me," Angus said.

"Baps and butter, and a pint," Patrick added.

"Two ticks." Gordon disappeared.

Patrick looked Angus over. "Y'on a religious fast, or somethin'?"

"Left my money in my other trousers."

Patrick shook his head, fished another small coin out of his pocket, and slid it over to Angus.

"What a good friend you are, Mr. Dawson," Iris said.

In a moment of uncharacteristic candor, Patrick met her gaze and said simply, "He could have a million cups of tea off me and not even come close to owin' me."

The two men exchanged warm smiles.

Gordon returned with a mug of tea, a pint of ale, and three steaming plates of sausages, mash, and peas.

"Has Gillian forgotten how to read?" Patrick joked.

"She heard who the order was for, asked if Mr. Armstrong was with anyone, and then sent these out with a strongly worded message. Shall I repeat it?"

Angus's eyes widened. "I'm nae sure…"

"Let's have it!" Patrick hooted.

Gordon raised his voice an octave and repeated: "Tell that stubborn ox if he snubs one more dinner invitation, I'll not speak to him for a week!"

Patrick guffawed. Angus blushed. Iris giggled.

"On the house. Oh, and…" he pulled a parcel from his apron pocket. "That's for Marjorie. Send my regards," Gordon said, and bustled off.

"Blimey…" Patrick looked at Angus with a goofy grin, like he'd just overheard a secret.

Suddenly overwhelmed with ambition, Angus jumped up from his chair and followed Gordon into the back passage. He'd spent too long thinking he'd never have this chance. He wasn't about to wait another day.

"Sir?"

Gordon turned. "Everythin' arright, lad?"

"It's about Gillian…"

"Aye?"

Angus swallowed. *No turning back now.* "I've come to ask for your blessing. I intend to marry her, sir."

Gordon's mustache twitched. "Oh, son, I arready figured that much. You're the only man walkin' the earth, as far as she can see."

Angus's heart pounded, but he smiled at hearing that Gillian had made no secret of her feelings to her father.

"So… I'd have your blessing, then?"

"Of course!" Gordon beamed, and clapped Angus's shoulder. "I'd count it an honor to have you as my son! She could do no be'er."

"Thank you, sir! I figured I was in for a speerin, at least…"

"Well… I might have a bit of fun wi'ye later, but I know be'er than to stand in the way of an engagement. I'd never hear the end of it. Besides, you've already more than proven yourself. I know the kind of man y'are, so I know you'll do right by my girl."

Angus and Gordon shared a firm handshake. Angus gripped a little harder than usual to disguise the fact that he was trembling with excitement.

"Should I make the announcement now?" Gordon wondered. "Or…"

"Give me until tomorrow, if you would. I ought to speak to my mum first… and make certain Gillian actually says yes!"

"Hm. Arready seein' that you not take her for granted. I like that in a son in law!"

Angus beamed.

Angus could barely sit down after that. He returned to the table with a stupid grin, and sat picking at his food.

"What's gotten into you, mate?" Patrick wondered.

Angus shook his head and kept smiling at strange times, taking as many bites as he could manage.

After the meal, Patrick took his leave to get home and check on his sisters. Angus and Iris stepped into the cool evening air and turned toward the Armstrong cottage.

"You asked for her hand, didn't you?" Iris giggled.

Angus blushed, his shy smile revealing everything.

"Good on you," she nodded, remembering his anguish on the day she'd wished she could take back ever since—when she'd told Angus of Gillian's death. At last, this part of his life was being made right. "You deserve every minute of happiness there is, Angus."

"I'd have none of it, if not for you." He pulled her arm through the crook of his elbow, offering her extra support, and patted her hand.

"I'm excited to meet your mum," Iris said. "I hope she likes me."

"My mum likes everybody," he chuckled. "You'll be an easy sell. Although I've no idea what to tell her about you, and she can always tell when I'm lyin,' so I'll let you do the talkin.'"

When they reached the cottage, Marjorie Armstrong was seated on the front stoop with her leg propped on a small footstool. An ornately carved cane rested against her chair.

"Hello, son! Have you brought us a guest?" She rose and leaned on her cane.

Angus stood still, taking in the sight of her—wavy brown hair streaked with silver, simple brown work dress and striped apron, comforting smile. Her eyes were alight with kindness and years of laughter. Without a word, he strode up to her, enveloped her in a gentle embrace, and kissed her cheek.

"Well, now, where's all this comin' from?" She searched his face, smoothing his curls away from his brow. "Angus, lad, you look like you had a rough day."

"Be'er now," he said truthfully. "Mum, this is Iris! Iris, this is my mum, Marjorie."

"Hello, Iris! Pleased to meet you. What brings you this direction?"

Iris reached out her hand and gave Marjorie's a squeeze. "Happy to meet you as well! I'm just passin' through. I lived here in the village when I was a child. Had a notion to visit and see how it's changed."

"Surely you didnae walk?" Marjorie wondered, eyeing Iris's walking stick.

"Not the whole way, o'course. I was be'er off when I started, anyway. Managed to cut my leg. But your lovely young man helped me get it seen to. Made me this stick!"

"Och, I'm glad. He's a handy one, is he not? Well, I'd be happy to take a look when it wants attention again," Marjorie offered.

"Mum, I thought Iris could stay here with us for a few days whilst her leg heals. Silly to have her stay at the inn where she'd have to manage on her own."

"That's a lovely idea, son! Iris, how bout it? You could keep me and my gammy leg company."

"I'd be grateful, if it's nae a bother," Iris answered, relieved.

"Certainly not. You can take Angus's bed. Angus, be a dear... run to Mrs. MacDonald's and ask to borrow her cot. We'll set you up near the hearth, nice and cozy." She patted his cheek.

Angus smiled, kissed his mother's cheek a second time, and dashed across the lane.

"What will I do without that boy?" Marjorie murmured, looking after him fondly.

"Is he leavin'?" asked Iris.

"Well... he's not said, but I expect he will, any day. He's loved a lass all his life. Thought I might've heard them chattin' away this mornin.'"

"That sounds like a lovely business," Iris said.

"Aye, she's a wonder, that girl. Full of kindness and spirit. Angus'll grow fat on her cookin,' and never have a dull moment!" She turned and smiled at Iris. "Well, do come in. Rude of me to keep you standin' in the lane on your bum leg. We'll put the kettle on."

When Angus returned with Mrs. MacDonald's cot, the two women were deep in conversation like old friends. His heart warmed as he listened to them. He had never imagined seeing the two of them in the same room, but it was magical.

Iris fit in so easily here, so naturally. He wondered that God had put her in a different century.

Sensing that something was on Angus's mind, Iris excused herself to the privy so he could talk to his mother alone. When she returned, Angus was gone.

Marjorie sat by the fire with her needlework, a satisfied smile on her face.

"I was right!" she giggled. "He's off to get the girl!"

Chapter 28

Scotland ~ Present Day

Darrick MacCrann stood at the foot of the Great Hawthorn, his sharp eyes studying the newly replaced branch. The pieces were sealing together. In just over a day, the brilliant glow emanating through the cracks and seams of the limb had gradually dimmed, replaced by a dull glimmer that was only visible at night. Leaves and buds were beginning to form, out of season, as if the branch were having its own personal springtime. Darrick pulled a pen from behind his ear and jotted some notes into his leather pocket journal.

He crunched forward a few steps in the dry leaves, eyeing the blackened bones of the limbs that Angus and Iris had chopped away with his ax. He hadn't yet cleaned up the shattered remnants of Angus's jar because of how near they were to the fallen branches. Now, he was glad he hadn't attempted it—the heat radiating from the smoldering limbs had burned away the surrounding dead leaves and berries, and melted every shard of glass within two feet, leaving a trail of ash and shiny blobs sunk into the earth.

The tendrils of acrid smoke had finally stopped. The fallen branches were turning to powder—deteriorating as fast as the newly restored one was healing. He made another note.

◦ঌ৶ৄ

Scotland ~ 1844

Angus ran. The lightness in his soul pulled him upward, as though his feet were flying across the ground. He gave no thought to what he would say. He thought only of her. His heart ached once again, but this ache wasn't pain. It was hunger. Every weight of worry, every obstacle, had scattered like a flock of gulls. Iris was well, Mum was cared for, his heart was strong, he was home... and *Gillian was alive.*

He rounded the corner to the rear of the pub and knocked at the kitchen door. The old Angus would have stood there at least five minutes before knocking, considering what to say. But this Angus knew that the time for hesitation was long past. His heart leaped as the door opened.

Gordon Mayfield stood in the doorway, drying a pot with a linen towel. He smiled with satisfaction at the eagerness in Angus's face.

"She's gone for a walk, lad," he said. "Busy day today, so I told her I'd finish up."

"D'ye know which way she went?" Angus puffed, still catching his breath.

"Oh, down the beach, I expect," Gordon replied. "Had a lot on her mind."

"Thanks!"

Angus dashed off once again, a dagger of fear against his throat. *What if I'm too late? What if this was the day?*

In record time, his feet were on the little footpath that cut through the dune grass, down the bluff to the beach. Craggy black rocks lay scattered across the golden strand, casting the long, inky shadows of a late April sunset. Heart pounding, Angus scanned the shoreline.

Gillian stood ten yards away, eyes closed, facing the breeze as it ruffled her long curls and fluttered long blades of grass against her skirt. Just the sight of her sealed up the frayed edges of his tattered hopes, making them whole again. He closed the distance quietly, until he was five feet from her. She was humming to herself, and still hadn't seen him. She was more beautiful to him now than any image his memory had been able to summon.

Gillian finished the song and opened her eyes. Angus was afraid he might startle her, but when she saw him, her smile was peaceful.

"I was hopin' I might see you down here," she said.

"And I came down hopin' to find *you*," he replied. He covered the remaining distance between them and took her hand. He caressed the soft skin with his thumb, marveling at how delicate it was.

"Angus, about this mornin', I—"

He lifted her hand and kissed it, making her unable finish her sentence. Her eyes closed at the sensation of his lips on her skin.

"I still cannae believe I blurted all that out…" she tried to continue.

He took her other hand.

"What I mean is, I dinnae want you to think that just because—"

He kissed the other hand, locking eyes with her.

"What," he murmured, "has it been so long since I said I loved you that you've talked yourself out of believin' I meant it?"

She stood dumbfounded for a moment, then shook her head. "I just… I mean… would you have said it on your own?"

"To be honest, I'm not sure how long it would've taken me," he replied, still holding her gaze. "And I realize now, that was the greatest wrong I've ever done you. I've thought of nothin' but you for ages. I cannae stand the idea of ever bein' away from you. I should've said so. If I'd told you that when I first knew it, we'd have had this conversation ten years ago."

Her eyes widened in surprise.

"Please forgive me, Gilly."

"Of course I do," she whispered.

He embraced her, bending to press his cheek against hers. She wrapped her arms about his waist.

"You deserve to know, every moment, that I love you more than life," he said softly next to her ear. "You'll never be in doubt again, I swear it."

Her eyes shone with tears.

He released her, and reached into his trouser pocket for the silver claddagh ring his mum used to wear.

She covered her mouth with both hands as the tears spilled down her cheeks.

"I want to marry you, Gillian. I want to spend every day of my life growing old with you, keepin' you safe, givin' you everythin' I have. Please… will you be my wife?"

When she lowered her hands, her face was incredulous. She burst into joyous laughter. "I love you, Angus. I love you more than anything!" She beamed. "Of course I'll marry you!"

Angus placed the ring on her finger and took her in his arms. He kissed her with a sweet tenderness that told her every cherishing thought he'd ever had for her. They stood together, watching the sun sink into the North Sea until the light faded to twilight, her head against his heart. He looked to heaven and sent up his thanks in a silent explosion of joy and bewildered amazement. The prayer had no words in it, for none could be found.

Iris sat on Angus's bed, dressed in a nightgown that Marjorie had loaned her. The two of them had chatted away the evening as if they'd always been friends. Marjorie had given her a damp cloth and a clean bandage for her leg, and helped her brush the tangles out of her hair. Then she'd prayed for her, as naturally as if God lived there in the house with them. It had made Iris feel strangely warm. She had even opened one eye and peeked around during Marjorie's prayer, just to double check whether there was someone else in the room.

Iris could see where Angus had gotten his kind nature. She remembered how he'd instinctively held her hand after she'd had her hair yanked by a confused man at the nursing home, how he'd spent hours fighting to keep her warm as she came close to death. He had saved her life.

And now, he had gone after the one thing he'd always wanted—a life with Gillian. Iris felt that her heart would burst. On the one hand, she was overwhelmed with joy that her dear friend finally had his life back. But she could also feel a growing ache in the pit of her stomach. She would have to say goodbye to him soon.

Iris unwound the strip of linen that Ré MacCrann had wrapped around her cut. She used the bandage to peel back the layer of moss. Not only was the cut free of infection, it had completely sealed and formed a reddish pink scar. Incredulous, Iris touched the skin, testing it. No pain. *How did it heal so fast?*

She used the damp cloth to wipe away the remaining bits of moss and dried blood. She debated whether to put the fresh bandage on, since she didn't need it. But if she left it lying there unused, it might raise questions. She couldn't explain this dramatic improvement without bringing up the idea of time flowing all wrong because of mysterious tree sap.

Yeah, that won't do. She wrapped her leg loosely and tied the bandage in place.

She caught sight of her reflection in the glass above the little table in Angus's room. She gazed at the elderly lady staring back at her, and tried smiling at her. It was then that she had a sudden realization—she looked like Granny. She studied her eyes and mouth. Her smile made her want to smile even more.

I will be as pretty as Granny when I'm old! She giggled.

A strange color gleamed in the candlelight. She stood and crossed to the mirror, stooping for a closer look. It was her hair—it was turning back to ginger! A streak right in the middle of the thickest part of her hair had turned a pale strawberry silver ginger color. Quickly, she wound her hair back into a bun to hide it.

What is going on? If this aging is reversing as quickly as Angus's did, then Marjorie's not going to know who I am by morning! I might have to say goodbye sooner than I thought...

Iris peeked through the doorway curtain into the sitting room where Marjorie still sat by the fire, Bible in her lap. She approached, remembering to limp.

"Hello again," she said softly. "D'ye think it would be possible to write a le'er? If you had a pen and a bit of paper to spare?"

"Och, certainly, dear," Marjorie replied with a smile. "Everythin's in that desk. Help yourself."

Iris hobbled to the desk, admiring its beauty in the firelight.

"My goodness, this is a beautiful piece of craftsmanship," she commented. "Did Angus make it?"

"Nae, that was my John's handiwork," Marjorie replied, "but Angus did all the lovely ornamental bits across the top later. Not sure he makes furniture so much as works of art, that lad."

Iris agreed. Up until now, she'd only seen the mirror frame, but she found this work just as impressive. Angus clearly had a style. He mimicked nature as closely as possible, with stunning results.

Iris opened the desk drawer and found letter writing supplies, as well as a partial sheet of stamps... undoubtedly once attached to the very stamp she'd sold to get them here. Shaking her head, she drew out a quill, a bottle of ink, and a sheet of paper. She thanked Marjorie and went back into the bedroom.

She labored over the letter for the better part of an hour. When it was finished, she folded it, addressed it, and tucked it under the pillow. Then she rose from the bed and changed back into her dress, laying Marjorie's nightgown neatly across the headboard. She slung her satchel over her back, took her walking stick in hand, and snuffed her candle.

She waited, listening. She heard nothing besides the dying crackles in the fireplace. She poked her head out of the room. Marjorie had gone to bed, taking her candle with her. Angus's borrowed cot sat waiting near the hearth, unoccupied. Iris tiptoed across the room. Closing the door softly behind her, she ventured into the chilly night.

Angus had walked Gillian home at dusk. The two of them had shared their news with Gordon, who had clapped Angus heartily on the back and invited him in for a celebratory cuppa. He'd wanted to hear all of Angus's plans for his and Gillian's future home. Twenty minutes later, however, Gillian's eyelids were growing heavy. Because she was up at dawn every day getting her kitchen in order, staying awake this late was a losing battle, even with her two favorite men in the room. Angus had kissed her cheek and said his goodbyes, promising to see her in the morning.

He sauntered into the coolness of the evening feeling blessed beyond belief. He had a grin on his face that refused to go away, even though it was making his cheeks tired.

He approached the little cottage, seeing mostly darkness through the curtains. He knew that Mum would be in bed by this hour, but he was equally certain that Iris would be awake. She was used to the modern world where sunset had nothing to do with winding down for the day, it simply meant flipping a lightswitch. He deftly lifted the latch and let himself in, shutting the door with a soft click.

In trying to be quiet, he remembered the coins in his coat pocket as they clinked together. He placed old Mary, Queen of Scots back into her decorative box on the mantel. *Home at last.* Iris's three Georges went into the pouch with Victoria. The four of them, plus two more and some change at payday tomorrow meant not just rent, but a bit to put by. This job meant finally being able to provide.

I'm going to be a husband! he realized. The grin came back.

As Angus banked the fire, he considered the pillow and blanket waiting for him, but he was too excited to sleep... and a bit bothered. The fact that he'd be accepting full wages tomorrow, even though he'd spent most of today tending to Iris, had been niggling him, even though it couldn't be helped.

He decided to make up an hour or two tonight, since he was awake. He was going to have to carve a whole new mirror frame anyway, so he might as well get started. The perfect solution had presented itself during his walk home.

Forget fresh wood—even though I was completely right about the hawthorn being a magnificent choice—I dinnae have to use Mr. Grant's wood at all. Dad had a nice stash of cured limewood that would be perfect for this!

But before he could settle in to start the project, he had to tell Iris the good news about Gillian...

She said yes! He punched the air. Then he chuckled quietly to himself, realizing he must look crazy.

He stood at the partition curtain to his room, which was open a few inches.

"Iris!" he whispered. "Iris, you awake?" He waited several seconds. Shrugging, he turned, but caught a glimpse of the room through the opening of the curtain. The bed was made, undisturbed. A nightgown lay draped over the headboard. He frowned. *Why's it dark in there if she's not in bed?* He gingerly pulled the curtain aside a few more inches, letting in the growing firelight from the hearth. Her satchel was gone. He strode into the room now, looking around. *Where is she?*

A white corner sticking out from under the pillow caught his eye. He tugged it free. It was addressed to him. He walked slowly to his chair by the fire and unfolded the paper.

My dear Angus,

It's time to say goodbye at last. Remember what Darrick said about the secrets? I'm not sure how it works with letters, so I'll choose my words carefully, just in case someone else reads this. Remember how different you looked this morning? Something's changed for me, too, but it's happening slowly. Staying here would mean too many questions. I know you'd never lie, and I dinnae want to. That leaves only the truth. But I cannae bear the thought of you forgetting me and everything we've been through together. It's hard to describe what knowing you has meant to me. You're a miracle. I know that God allowed me to meet you so I could see that he's real. I meant what I said before, Angus... you really have changed my life. Thank you for saving my life, in so many ways. Thank you for helping me love who I am.

I'm not sure what's going to happen now. Maybe Ré will know. If I stick around, maybe I'll see you in the pub. If not, I'll see you in the history books. Either way, I'll never forget you, I promise. I love you.

Iris

P.S. I assume you're engaged now. CONGRATULATIONS!!

The last paragraph was smudged with a drop of moisture. Angus sat quietly, taking in the words. *So that's it, then? She's just... gone?* He read the letter again, then stared into the fire. *That cannae be it.*

He jumped to his feet, folded the letter, and stuffed it into his pocket. He grabbed his coat and hat, slid silently out the door, and jogged into the night.

He reached Woodstone Cottage completely out of breath, having run most of the two mile distance in the moonlight. He could hear voices inside, so he knocked. Ré MacCrann answered, looking both delighted and unsurprised to see Angus standing there.

"Welcome back, laddy! Come on in! I was just tellin' the young lady here about some interestin' developments with the Great Tree," Ré said.

Angus entered, taking off his cap. Iris stood by the fireplace. She no longer looked over eighty years old... perhaps closer to fifty. Her hair was mostly a pale ginger now, with silvery streaks through it.

"Iris..." Angus hesitated. "I got your le'er."

"Angus, I'm sorry I had to leave so suddenly, I—"

"No, it's arright. I understand… you did it for me." He stepped closer to her, amazed at the change in her appearance. "I dinnae ken why I ran all the way here. It's just…" He paused, trying to put his thoughts into words. A smile broke across his face and he grabbed her hands. "Iris, I'm getting married!"

She laughed, a joyous sparkle in her eyes. "Angus, that's brilliant!"

They stood together, hands clasped, in contagious delight.

After a moment, his face grew serious. "I wanted to tell you while I can…" Moisture collected in the corners of his eyes. "…that I love you. Always know that. You're the reason I've got a future again. If not for you, I'd…" He shook his head. "I'd be in a nightmare. I know be'er than anyone what it's cost you… I'm prayin' that God will pay you back a thousand times."

He pulled her into a bear hug. Iris returned his embrace, gratified beyond words to hear his heart beating strong and steady, to know that Angus was well and happy. His next words rumbled against her ear as he spoke them through tears.

"I'll not forget you, either. As much as I wish I could tell Gilly everything, I'll keep the secrets… so I never lose you."

Iris couldn't think of a single reply that would suit this moment. Although the future of their friendship was uncertain, its strength was not. He released her, and gave her hands a final squeeze.

"Well, I suppose I should…" he began, but stopped. He looked around the room with a quizzical frown, his eyes landing on Ré. "What's that sound?"

Ré's eyes widened and he gave a little shrug. He couldn't hear anything.

Iris listened intently. "I hear it, too…"

A melodic, buzzing hum was floating toward them on the wind, echoing down the chimney.

Iris and Angus looked at each other. "It's the tree!" they said at the same time.

Angus grabbed the lantern that Ré had set on the table, and he and Iris dashed out the door. Completely puzzled, Ré followed, hobbling behind them as fast as he could.

A minute's walk toward the Great Hawthorn only increased the sound. Once they stood at its base, they found the source of the hum. While the rest of the tree remained dark and vibrated at its normal volume, one branch was giving off a faint shimmer through the dark, like dying embers glowing inside of a cracked vase. The three of them stared at each other through the dim lantern light, eyes wide. The musical moan emanating from the branch was loud enough that Angus had to raise his voice to be heard above it.

"What's this mean?" he asked Ré.

"Not sure!" Ré shook his grizzled head, pondering. "Looks like the damage is reversing!"

"But I thought that on this side of the gap, Angus never even cut that branch!" Iris protested.

"The Great Trees dinnae pick sides!" Ré shouted. "They stand across all of time. Past or present, it's the same tree! It's workin' things out, is all!"

As Ré spoke, Iris could see strange, bright images beginning to appear all around her. It was as though she was seeing two scenes at once, like two film negatives laid on top of each other—small, dark trees over larger, lighter ones... Angus and Ré by the shadowy lantern, next to a third person standing in sunlight.

She shook her head. *Am I hallucinating?*

"Iris, what's wrong?" Angus asked, alarmed by the look on her face.

"I just..." She shook her head again. "I thought I could see..." She squinted. The third figure came into focus. *Darrick?*

"What did you see?"

She stared at Angus. His face was becoming dimmer. "I thought I saw Darrick!"

A look of realization crossed his features. He tried to offer her an encouraging smile, but his heart was heavy. "I'll miss you," he said. He faded away with the darkness.

Iris blinked. She was standing in overcast sunlight. The forest was quiet, except for a faint hum. She was still beneath the Great Hawthorn, in the same spot as before. Darrick MacCrann stood before her, holding a small journal, his pen frozen over the page.

"Welcome back," he said. "Nice dress!"

Angus stared for several moments at the vacant spot where Iris had stood.

With a final crescendo, the cracks in the glowing branch sealed off, releasing one last fiery flash of light. Then the Great Tree was quiet, enveloped in peaceful darkness.

"Blimey…" Ré muttered. "I remember it all now… *you* were the man who came with an ax, and… I was so… *afraid!*" He stared at Angus. "But you didnae do it after all. Both are true at the same time… It's just like you said!"

The two men stood in awe, trying to comprehend what they'd just seen. Angus could still hear a distinct hum, like a faraway song. He felt as if a small part of him had just disappeared. He bowed his head and let a tear fall, praying that Iris would be safe. "See you in the history books," he murmured.

Chapter 29

Scotland - Present Day

Iris was speechless. As she absorbed her surroundings, she was hit with the agonizing realization that she was home. Waxwings tweeted above her. Bright crimson berries twitched in the stiff December breeze. She sank to the cold, damp ground under a weight of tears as a piece of her heart was torn away. *Angus is gone. I'll never see him again.*

Alarmed, Darrick rushed to her side. "Iris! Are you arright?"

She nodded vigorously, even though her face was crumpled in anguish.

"You in pain?"

She shook her head.

"Your hair is…" Darrick began, but soon realized that she couldn't answer just yet. He knelt beside her on the ground as she cried herself out.

At last, she looked up, her eyes red and puffy. "It's just hard to say goodbye."

"I imagine so," he nodded, giving her shoulder a compassionate squeeze. "I've never seen a more extraordinary pair of friends." He looked her over with a fascinated expression. "You look so different!"

"I know…" she said glumly. "I look really old now. I'll never be able to explain it to my family."

"Well…" He cocked his head to one side. "I'd have said that five minutes ago, but now… what I mean is, you look different than when you got here."

"What d'you mean?"

"I mean you look like yourself again!"

Iris reached up and frantically unwound her hair from the bun, pulled it over her shoulder, and examined it. Pure ginger. She checked the backs of her hands. Smooth and slightly freckled. She looked at Darrick, apprehensive.

"How old do I look?"

He pursed his lips. "Nineteen… twenty?"

"I'm twenty-two!" she huffed.

"Arright! Twenty-two, then." Darrick smiled. "Except for the outfit."

"I got it from Ré MacCrann!" Iris giggled. "He really appreciated your le'er, by the way. It sure saved us a lot of explaining. Anyway, this dress belonged to your… many greats… great grandmother Eidith!"

"Well now," Darrick smirked. "Apparently this family's always been good for a costume!" He helped Iris to her feet.

She brushed herself off, looking around her. A pile of black, powdery ash littered the ground beneath Angus's branch, which stood solidly in place, covered in red berries. She gave Darrick a questioning look.

"That," he pointed at the ash, "is all that's left of what never should have been. And there…" he pointed at the tree. "Just ten minutes ago, that branch was covered in blooms and making quite the racket. When the berries appeared, it was like the branch had caught up to where it was supposed to be. The cracks sealed off, everything quieted down, and… there you were!"

"I had no idea where I'd end up," Iris said. "I guess…" Her shoulders slumped. "I guess everything's back the way it's meant to be."

"Aye, seems so." He smiled sadly. "C'mon back where it's warm. We'll have a pot of tea."

They wound their way out of the oak grove and through the wood to the clearing. Iris shivered. Her thin linen sleeves were little protection from the nip in the air.

"So… d'ye remember everythin' two different ways, like you thought you would?" she asked him.

Darrick stopped and closed his eyes, brows furrowed in concentration. "Aye," he nodded. "I can recall one quiet Christmas mornin' with just the family. Katie made pies. We had breakfast… and we went with the boys on a hike to the beach." He thought harder. "But I also remember the one where you and Angus came. I ran into the village to pick up a parcel… and then we nearly blew up half of Scotland." He opened his eyes and looked at her with an amused grin. "Obviously, the second one was meant to be."

"Clearly!" Iris laughed.

They arrived at the stone cottage, where Iris kicked off her boots and took a seat on the stone hearth, close to the fire. "How long was I gone?"

"Just over a day," Darrick replied, hanging up his coat and scarf.

"Huh…" Iris mused. "Same for me. What time is it now?"

He glanced at his watch. "About half three."

Darrick crossed the living room and sat in his leather armchair. He scratched his bearded chin, then pulled out his notebook and jotted a few things down. He looked up. "About the aging thing… any other symptoms? Was there extreme cold, like Angus experienced?"

"Yes! My gosh, I thought I was going to die! If not for Angus, I probably would have."

"Hmm. D'ye think it was the travel that caused it?"

"I dinnae think so," Iris replied. "Coming back didnae age me *or* make me cold. Angus and I had a theory that since we were both injured in a way that allowed the sap into our bloodstreams, it must've been like… Time Tree poisoning, or something."

"Interesting… that would make sense, actually…" Darrick became lost in thought. "Radiation poisoning causes burns… maybe Great Trees do the opposite," he muttered, staring into the fire. "Matter versus antimatter… radiation versus… what? Anti… radiation? Hmm…" He look up sharply at Iris as his mind suddenly came back into the room. "Was the aging temporary in his case as well?"

"Aye, he looked twenty-four again, almost right after we got there. It happened as his scar disappeared, so we thought maybe it was because the cut never happened, so the effects never did either."

"Good theory… but what about *your* scar? It definitely happened."

Iris frowned, suddenly curious as well. She lifted her skirt to the knee, and removed her bandage. The jagged, reddish pink mark was still there.

Darrick leaned forward and examined it. "Hmm… for a nasty ax wound that's only a day old, that's a pretty advanced state of healin.'" He scratched another sentence into his notebook.

"Well, time does flow all wrong around these trees, right?" Iris shrugged.

"No, that would not explain this, actually," Darrick replied. "You said it yourself… one day passed there, just as one day passed here." He studied her, twiddling his pen between his fingers. "Did you see anyone else besides Ré MacCrann? Any really tall men, perhaps?"

Iris's eyes lit up with a dim memory. "I... I thought I saw someone... in a green cloak. He was standin' over me, smiling..."

"Oh! Well that makes sense, then," Darrick replied, writing again. "Mystery solved."

"It is?"

"You saw your guardian. Sometimes people experience rapid healing when that happens."

"My... what?"

"Your guardian."

"I have a guardian?"

Darrick gazed at her for a long moment, thinking it an odd question. "Of course."

"Silly me," Iris muttered. "What's all this for, anyway? Why the twenty questions?"

"Oh, this entire thing is goin' into the central database after I write it up," he explained, finishing his notes. "Guardians are bound by oath to pass on their knowledge. Nowadays, we can share beyond just our families. Almost all the Guardians are gettin' their histories digitized. Thanks to the internet, we can read everythin.' Actually, it's because of that..." he smirked. "Well, let's just say the MacCrann name is a little... infamous."

Iris frowned. "Why's that?"

"Because this is the single greatest time disturbance in history... at least, of any on record. And it's because one of *my* ancestors made a right mince of things. But now it's been set right! I'm really looking forward to settin' the record straight. Plus, the knowledge we've gained is unprecedented. Other Guardians will greatly benefit from your experience."

Iris hung her head. "Well, I guess if I had to have a near death experience and come away from it with a giant scar on my leg and a gaping hole in my heart, at least it can *benefit* somebody."

Darrick's face softened. He closed his notebook and laid it aside. He knelt beside Iris with a serious expression. "I'm sorry if I'm comin' across very clinical about this. Guardians have to keep detailed records, but you're not just a case study. What you went through, it's… unfathomable. I can see how much you're suffering. Katie and I will always be here for you if y'ever need to talk to someone about it."

Iris nodded, fighting tears.

"Of course, you could always choose to forget all of this."

Iris looked up sharply, her eyes fiery. "*Never.*"

Darrick laid his hand on hers. "Okay. I understand. It's your choice. D'you want to stay here a night or two, with the family? Work through things a bit before you head back to real life?"

Iris sighed. "As lovely as that sounds, I cannae prolong the inevitable. I ought to face what I've got coming. I'm sure the police have picked up my car and the FBI have swarmed my apartment by now."

"And why would they do that?"

"Uh, because I'm a crazy kidnapper, remember?"

"Really now? Whoooom did you kidnap?"

"Angus…"

"Angus who? There's no Angus here." Darrick's eyes twinkled.

"But…" Iris's mind whirled. "You had Callum plant my car across from the—"

"Your car's right where you left it."

"How's that possible? Everything that's happened—"

"Never happened. Nobody remembers but us."

"So… that's it?" she gasped. "I'm not a criminal after all?"

Darrick laughed. He stood and retreated to his study for a few moments. He returned, still grinning at her, with something in his hand. "Here, I charged your phone," he said, passing it to her. "Text somebody if you dinnae believe me."

Iris stared at the screen, mind racing. She opened her messaging app. There was a new message from Granny. She pulled it up.

Sorry your flights were delayed, Poppet.
Looking forward to seeing you soon!
Anytime is great for us.

"I've not even been there yet?" Iris shook her head in disbelief. She decided to do a test. She pulled up Will's number and sent off a text:

How much $$ do I owe you?

A few moments later, her phone pinged with a reply:

Owe me for what? Gas money to the airport?
We talked about this. I told you not to worry about it!
It was my pleasure to drop you off.
Just bring me back something Scottish.

Iris was bewildered. "This is unbelievable. It's like I'm living in an alternate reality! How come so many things are different? How did all this happen without me knowing it?"

Darrick chuckled. "Well, I think—mind you, I'm just guessin' here, because this is totally new territory—but I think the same thing is happenin' to you that happened to me. Y'have two different versions of the past. Both are true, but only one is still in motion."

"But I cannae remember doin' any of this!"

"Because you dinnae have the memory of a Guardian!" Darrick laughed. "Dear me, that's gonna be awkward for a little while! Thankfully, the only changes you'll have to deal with will be from after the day you met Angus. But still… it might be best to let others fill in the gaps for you… just until you have a be'er idea what you've been up to."

Her phone pinged again. It was Will.

How do you think I'd look in a kilt? 🌚

She laugh-snorted and fired off a reply.

😂 *Let's find out!*

Darrick smiled. "Looks like you're arready gettin' on well in your alternate reality, as you call it."

Iris smiled. "Aye, I'll be okay, I guess. It's going to be so different without Angus, though."

"I know you'll miss Angus, but I'm sure he was so much happier in his own time. All the lives he was supposed to impact can now go on as they should have."

Realization dawned on Iris's face. "Darrick! We could look him up! Right?"

Darrick chuckled. "How about we get you into your own clothes and some tea down you? Or… here's a crazy idea— food? Katie's gettin' the messages but she'll be back in a few minutes. We can have some sandwiches, and then we'll look in the archives, arright? We'll see what old Ré had to say."

❧

Iris sat as patiently as she could through tea and sandwiches before Darrick finally relented and led her into the study. He offered to show her the transcripts of Ré's journals on his computer, but she wanted to see the actual pages he'd written. After some digging, he located the right volume and pulled it from the dusty shelf.

"Y'know, his bed actually stood right here," Iris motioned to the corner of the study. She smiled. "And his steamer trunk was on this spot where I'm standing. It's where he kept all of Eidith's old things."

"Yeah?" Darrick was fascinated.

"He was so in love with her," Iris went on. "You could tell by the way he talked about her, and how much he treasured her possessions. It must have been quite a sacrifice to take all of her stuff out of there and use it for storing wood scraps."

Darrick pondered that image for a few moments. "Thank you for tellin' me that, Iris. I have a lot more respect for him, knowin' he did that. He had quite the reputation for bein' proud and stubborn. But it sounds like he had a really good heart."

"Aye, he did." Iris nodded. "People can be many things at once."

Darrick set Ré's journal on the desk and turned the pages carefully, until he came to the entries marked April, 1844.

"I'll leave you to it," he said with a little nod, and left the room.

Iris was grateful to Darrick for giving her the space to experience this without having to hold herself together. She read through several pages of Ré's account of the time disturbance, including everything that had to be done to set it right. Even though Iris had been there, she was still fascinated to hear it from his perspective.

She turned the page. Two loose sheets were pressed into the book. She lifted them carefully and gingerly unfolded them. One was Darrick's letter to Ré, detailing her journey with Angus. The other was the letter she'd written to Angus.

Iris read the next journal entry:

Mr. Armstrong was loathe to entrust his precious letter to my care, but was persuaded at last that retaining it could draw the wrong eyes to it, thus leading to questions he was not prepared to answer. I convinced him that Eamon would see to its preservation. He has visited twice to read it again since that strange day. Whatever else is true, it is beyond doubt that he treasured his friend and misses her dearly.

"I miss you too," Iris whispered, eyes moist. The entry continued:

He has some idea that she may read this very page someday, and upon his last visit asked me to include the following notation, though I comprehended little of it. But essentially, Mr. Armstrong and his charming wife have, through many attempts in their kitchen, succeeded in building some sort of recipe which includes a flat dough, some tomato based preparation, and various cheeses, along with sundry meats. He was keen to pass that on. He brought some for me. I urged him to try it with smoked haddies on top. He strongly disagreed.

"Oh Angus!" Iris laughed until tears came. The bottom of the page even had a rust colored blob that could have been tomato sauce.

❧

After thanking the MacCrann family for everything and saying her goodbyes, Iris grabbed her backpack and made her way to the little white Kia. She sat in the driver's seat, feeling very much alone. She needed to get to Granny and Grandpa's soon, but there was one more thing she needed to do.

She made the short drive into the village, down the Beach Road to the old church. She parked, and tucking her tartan scarf around her head, ventured into the chilly wind. One of the creaking iron gates stood open, so she walked through, past the white cross in the kirkyard, and around the right side of the building to the path that led through a forest of gravestones.

Her direction was aimless at first. The wind buffeted her back as she tried to decide where to start. Almost instinctively, she aimed for a row of headstones nearest the church. She scanned the names as she walked by, hands stuffed deep into her coat pockets. Her cheeks stung.

Her heart leaped as the name "Armstrong" grabbed her eye. She stopped in front of a majestic obelisk with a stone cross at the top. It stood at the center of a plot of six grave sites. The engraved brass plaque on the front read:

ERECTED IN LOVING MEMORY OF

ANGUS JOHN ARMSTRONG
18 JULY 1820 ~ 20 AUGUST 1915
BELOVED HUSBAND, FATHER, AND FRIEND
WORLD-RENOWNED MASTER CRAFTSMAN

AND HIS BELOVED WIFE

GILLIAN FIONA MAYFIELD-ARMSTRONG
6 OCTOBER 1822 ~ 12 OCTOBER 1915
CHERISHED WIFE, MOTHER, AND CONFIDANTE
VILLAGE INN PROPRIETOR

"Wow, Angus," Iris murmured as she ran her fingers over the lettering bearing his name. "World-renowned, eh? I thought you said that poor people never make it into the history books." She did a bit of mental math, and shook her head in wonder. "Over seventy years with Gillian. Well done, you two."

She walked around the sides of the obelisk, awed by the ornate relief carving chiseled into the stone. The design was so intricate and captivating that it took several seconds for it to dawn on her what she was seeing. The entire thing was covered in irises.

Angus and Gillian's four children were buried nearby, each of them having lived until at least age eighty. Their firstborn, Iris Armstrong-Dawson, beloved mother, wife of Patrick Andrew Dawson, Jr., had lived until age ninety-two.

He named her after me! Iris smiled.

After some thought, she put the pieces together. Angus's daughter had married his best friend's firstborn son. She giggled to herself, thinking about how much fun that wedding must have been. *Angus and Patrick got to share grandchildren!* Iris was warmed to her toes.

She lingered among the stones until the light faded, piecing together the story of Angus's legacy and cheering him with every discovery. She wanted to cry because Angus was dead, but couldn't... because he had been *so alive*. He had forged ahead with abandon, carving out a rich life, filled with love and family. Just knowing she'd had a small part in the memories that surrounded her made it all the richer.

Chapter 30

Seattle, WA ~ Present Day

The Seattle sky was dark and drippy. Iris's legs felt numb as she shuffled along the jetway into the terminal. She checked her watch. Ten minutes to six. The flight from Dublin had been nine hours and forty-five minutes, and she'd managed to sleep for close to eight of those hours, in about sixteen different positions. Thanks to the miracle of crossing eight time zones, she'd landed only ninety minutes after she'd taken off.

That means I get to do this night all over again, she mused. *Another full night of sleep sounds amazing, especially since I've barely slept since 1844.* In her loopy state, the thought seemed extra hilarious. She giggled enough to draw a few strange looks. *Unless you count a short period of unconsciousness in a forest, an hour in someone's lap, followed by two completely sleepless nights, three restless nights, and a Hogmanay party watching people slinging flaming balls around.* She giggled again.

It had been so good to spend time with Granny and Granddad. They had no memory of meeting Angus. Conversing with them, while remembering to leave him out of it, had been good practice for when she went back to work at Rookwood. Angus had been her favorite person there. Pretending he didn't exist was going to be an ordeal.

But he *did* exist, right where he was supposed to be… which made something else start niggling her on her last day at Granny and Granddad's. She'd peeked into Granddad's workshop, and it had looked exactly the same as usual. All of his woodworking projects and commissioned pieces were still underway. But if she remembered their family story correctly, it had been the disappearance of Angus Armstrong in 1844 that had left the woodworking trade vacant in the village, launching a career change for Ewan Jacobs and giving rise to her family's long line of carpenters, contractors, and artisans. She had even done an internet search for her great uncle's company, Jacobs Construction. It still existed. Befuddled, she'd finally asked Granddad.

❧

"So… Granddad, I've been learnin' a bit about our family history," she began.

"Aye?" Liam looked up from the orange he was peeling.

"Is it true that we were not always woodworkers?"

"Well, Finn's not one, is he?" He grinned.

Iris giggled. "Aye, I think the gene might've skipped Dad."

Liam grunted. "I tried, lassie. Got him to make a couple of birdhouses, but he was always fonder of the library than he was the workshop."

"I love that about him." Iris thought fondly of her father's keen mind. "Must be where I get it. But I meant *way* back. Who was the first woodworker in the family?"

"Och, that'd be old Ewan. He had no fondness for his father's fishing business. When he came of age, a master craftsman livin' in the village took him on as an apprentice. Name was Angus Armstrong—you've heard of him, o'course."

Iris frowned, her stomach doing a tiny flip. "Should I have?"

"Well, most have! He's quite the name round here, what with the work he did with Prince Albert on the furniture suite at Balmoral…"

Iris's eyes widened. "Balmoral? Seriously?"

"'Tis common knowledge round here, lass. Put us on the map, so to speak. Y'really ought to read up more about the village you came from!"

"But how…" Iris was stunned. "Why would a craftsman from this tiny place get noticed by royalty?"

"Because of his work for the Grants, then some of their friends, and some of their friends… y'know how it goes, when money talks. His work came into high demand. Interesting, though… Ewan ne'er approached Armstrong for an apprenticeship. It was the other way round. Guess he'd heard how keen the lad was, and Ewan certainly had a knack! Armstrong brought him up in the trade at such a smart pace that he really came to rely on him. Put Ewan in charge of his shop here in the village when he moved his family to London for a time to join Holland and Sons. Retired back here, though. I have his biography, if you'd like to read it."

"I'd love that!" Iris almost shouted.

Liam chuckled at his granddaughter's sudden interest in woodworkers. He puttered into the lounge, scanned the bookshelves, and finally located his copy of *Roses to Royalty: A Craftsman's Journey* by D.M. Hawthorne. He handed it to Iris.

"I dinnae think much of this chap's other works… fictions, mostly. But this one's brilliant. It's even signed!"

Iris sat near the giant wall of windows in the central airport terminal, at the same table where she'd introduced Angus to burritos—or, as he called them, "food pillows the size of your heid."

She pulled the book she'd borrowed from Granddad out of her backpack and flipped through it. There was a whole section of black and white photos. Some featured Angus's most brilliant works, on display at the Crystal Palace Exhibition. There was even a portrait of him when he was quite a bit older, perhaps in his mid forties, wearing a smart suit and cravat. His piercing eyes were gazing at the camera with a serious expression, but with a hint of a suppressed boyish smile. He'd grown a magnificent beard and developed streaks of gray at the temples, but his curls were still dark.

She'd wanted to dive into reading this book at soon as possible. But first, she had to figure out how she was getting home.

In this version of her life, it seemed that Will had driven her to Seattle and dropped her off at the airport. *Did he really drive me three hours one way, just as a favor? That's quite the favor. That can't be right.*

Frowning, she dug through her wallet and located her stash of boarding passes from the journey. There were only four—two going, and two coming back. Seattle to Dublin to Edinburgh and back. Nope, she hadn't flown here from Portland. *Hmmm. So he dropped me off at this airport. Does that mean he's picking me up, too? Or did I book a train ticket?* She searched through her email for confirmation codes. Nope. No train tickets.

With a shrug, she composed a text to Will.

Landed safely. Looking forward to seeing you again.

Hmm. Vague enough… and true. Too flirty? Eh, whatever. I'm tired. She hit send. Her phone pinged back a minute later.

Off work a little late, sorry… be there by 6:30.
Looking forward to seeing you too.

Iris studied the words on the screen, letting them sink in. *Will is driving me home. That… is a flipping long way to drive. Again. Why, though?* She remembered his words when he had shyly asked her out for coffee… or noodles. *"I want to spend time with you, Iris." I guess he does in this version of reality, too.* She smiled, heart warming at the image of Will's face in her mind.

The problem was, she wanted to spend time with him, too. She'd liked him from the moment they'd met, and had been trying not to think about him that way ever since.

Her reasons for avoiding that kind of relationship with Will had seemed solid at first, but they were crumbling away little by little.

He had listened to her talk about her problems, cooked for her, supported her. He'd put himself on call for her, giving her his phone number without asking for hers in return. In one version of last week, he'd even been willing to commit grand theft and drop a four figure dollar amount on a rush shipment because she told him it would save someone's life. Even though the version of Will driving toward her now hadn't done it, she knew he would if she asked, because he trusted her implicitly. And he did all that while having feelings for her… and still agreeing to just being friends.

Why? Because *she* was scared… because some jerk in the past had betrayed her trust. But that wasn't Will. Will was the reason the wrongs of the past were able to be undone. Will was the reason Angus was home. And he was the reason she had a future again. She could never thank him for that, because not only was it a protected secret, it had officially never happened. *Still…* She smiled. *I think I might love him.*

෴

Vancouver, WA

"Waaaaaake uuuuup, sleepyhead!"

Iris opened one eye. "Oh my gosh, Charlie. What the heck…" she grumbled.

Charlie didn't bat an eye. She was used to Iris's morning brain. "Mmmm… smell that?" she coaxed. "Coffeeeee…"

Iris opened the other eye and squinted at the blue blur in front of her. "What is happening right now?"

"You, my dear roomie, have a wicked case of jet lag!" Charlie announced.

"Loud…" Iris moaned.

"Oh! Sorry…" Charlie lowered her voice. "What else, let's see… Your mommy called. She wants you over there for dinner tonight. Something about belated Christmas presents. There was another thing… oh yes, Will texted you like five times. I *really* wanted to read them, but I resisted. Also, your phone alarm's been going off in your backpack for like twenty minutes."

Iris sat up, hair sticking out in all directions. "What time is it?"

"Twenty after seven."

"No! No no no…" Iris was horrified. "I have fifteen minutes to get ready for work!"

"Yes, I know," Charlie said casually. "Any second now you're going to tell me I'm the best for waking you up."

"You're the best!" Iris dashed out of bed and threw herself into a frenzied whirlwind, pulling on the nearest jeans and sweater she could find. Doing her makeup consisted of removing yesterday's eyeliner rather that putting any on. She drank the coffee Charlie had made. Way too strong, with cream and sugar, just how they both liked it. She grabbed her phone, purse, and keys. Hand on the doorknob, she turned.

Charlie was in the kitchen, mixing three different cereals into one bowl. Today's hairstyle was a fabulous blue bouffant with pink highlights, gelled into a mohawk. She had a song in her head. Iris giggled quietly, watching Charlie play air guitar. Having Charlie in her life was like having a sister. Charlie would never know how much her loyalty had meant to her in the past weeks.

"Hey," Iris said.

Charlie turned and smiled. "Hey, yourself."

Iris crossed the kitchen and gave her a hug. "You really are the best, y'know?"

Charlie squeezed back. "Yeah, but it's nice when you remind me." Her eyes sparkled as she looked at Iris. "Y'know, that no-makeup look is really working for you."

"Think so? I thought I looked better when I looked older."

"Well... You can rock both looks. There's always time to look older... like, when you're older." Charlie grinned.

"Love you, friend."

"Love you more. Now go make the old people happy!"

⚘

Iris pulled into the employee lot. Miraculously, she'd still managed to get there by five till eight, and had broken no more than two traffic laws in the process. She pulled out her phone. *Good grief, he really did text me five times.* She clicked Will's name.

*(1/5) Thanks for the great discussion last night.
I think you're right. Slow is good.
(2/5) Also, thanks for the kilt. How the heck does it work?
(3/5) I think I figured it out.
What do dudes wear under these, anyway?
(4/5) Also, since you said it's ok, I'm going to
admit I'm still thinking about you right now.
(5/5) I know you're sleeping, but I just wanted to say
I'm looking forward to seeing you. P.S. I love
the accent you came home with. I hope you keep it.*

Iris smiled, her stomach fluttering at the idea of seeing Will today. A soft knock on her car window made her jump. *Speaking of...*

She opened the door.

"Did I scare you?" Will was all dimples, his sideways grin looking more vulnerable than she'd ever seen it.

"Well... it was a *good* scary." Grinning, she got out and locked the door. "Thanks again for the ride yesterday. And the one before that. And for... just, everything."

Will's cheeks flushed slightly. "It was my pleasure. Really. I didn't get you anything for Christmas, so..." He searched her face. "You look different today."

"No makeup," she shrugged. "Ran out of time."

He smiled. "That might be it. You always look... beautiful, but... today..." he struggled for words. "Today, it's amazing."

"I'm not sure how slow this is going to be, if you keep sayin' things like that."

Will's eyebrows went up. "Well, I could keep it to myself, but..."

Before he could backtrack too far, Iris took his hand. He was only startled for a second before giving her fingers an affirming squeeze. They started up the path, enjoying the warmth of each other's hands in the chill air. Iris could feel her heart pointing toward this man like a compass to magnetic north.

"What's up, guys?" James greeted them as they walked through the door. His eyes widened. "Ha! I knew it!" he hooted, pointing at their clasped hands. "Oh my gosh, does this mean you guys are dating now?"

"Yep, we're dating, James," Will replied, winking at Iris.

"But Iris, you said you don't date coworkers!"

"Changed my mind," Iris answered, without taking her eyes from Will's.

"Oh, okay cool. So then... Will, I guess this is the part where I'm supposed to tell you that you've been a worthy opponent, bro. And if you ever hurt her, I'll switch all your spice labels around."

"A noteworthy threat, good sir," Will said, with a slight bow at the waist.

"Welp, we coulda had a beautiful thing, Iris. You're missing out on these guns!" James flexed.

"I know, it's very sad," she nodded gravely at him, and then smiled back up at Will. "I'll make do somehow."

As Iris walked toward the Activities Office, she felt a gnawing in the pit of her stomach. Of all the changes she'd had to process since coming home, the one she'd been having the hardest time believing was that her last conversation with Candace hadn't happened. She felt a chill, remembering the disappointment and betrayal in her voice when Candace had told her she was fired, and that her best bet was to cooperate with the police.

Candace was a lot of things—fun, compassionate, full of wisdom, and sensitive to the pain of others because of all she'd been through. But Iris now understood that when it came to protecting vulnerable people, Candace was a force to be reckoned with—exactly as she should be.

Iris rounded the corner and found Candace sitting at her desk, shuffling forms with one hand while eating a bagel with the other. When she saw Iris, her eyes lit up.

"Iris!" She dropped her bagel and held out her arms. "Get in here, you bonny lass! It's been crazy around here without you!" Candace enveloped her in a motherly squeeze and then flashed her a brilliant smile.

"It's good to see you too, Candace," Iris said, flooded with relief.

"I want to hear all about your trip to Scotland on break, okay? Willy's making shortbread and I'm already positively drooling."

Iris giggled.

"But first, business. I'll have you set up the chapel for the hymn sing, then the canary cage needs attention, okay? You have thirty-two minutes! Readyyyyy go!"

With a laugh, Iris bounded out the door toward the chapel. She entered a bit out of breath, and began looking around for the stack of hymn books.

A movement caught her eye—her own reflection in a mirror hanging on the wall behind the piano. Her jaw dropped. The frame of the mirror was heart shaped, and covered in a spray of exquisitely carved irises. Ivy vines trailed down the sides, joining into a single rose at the bottom. She stepped slowly, reverently toward the mirror, her senses tingling.

Could it be?

Overwhelmed with curiosity, Iris gingerly lifted the mirror away from the wall, knelt, and laid it on the plush carpet. She ran her fingers over the realistic leaves and flowers, marveling at the skill with which they were brought to life. She was afraid of breaking the spell by turning the mirror over and finding just a commercial manufacturer's mark.

At last, she gathered her courage and gently turned the mirror on its face. A thin brass plaque attached to the wood backing read:

**BEQUEATHED TO ROOKWOOD ESTATE
BY MR. ANGUS ARMSTRONG
UPON HIS DEATH, 1915
TO BE DISPLAYED IN THE CHAPEL AT HIS REQUEST**

"Angus, you genius!" She ran her fingers over his name. "It's beautiful, friend. I love it."

Well, if Angus wanted it hung in the chapel, I'd better put it back up there.

As Iris grasped the sides of the frame to pick it up, her thumb felt a small poke. She lowered it back to the carpet and checked the spot where her thumb had been. There was the tiniest corner of paper sticking out between the backing and the frame, about a millimeter. She frowned. It wasn't like Angus to leave rough edges or untidy packing paper stuck in things. She rotated the turn buttons on the heart shaped wood backing and lifted it away from the frame.

An envelope was affixed to the inside of the wood by tiny tacks pressed through two of its corners. The envelope was addressed simply "Iris."

She gasped.

Iris pulled the tacks out to release the envelope. Behind it, nestled into a perfectly round, perfectly sized divot carved into the wood, lay a gold Victoria head sovereign. "What..." Iris covered her mouth.

She picked up the envelope, opened it gently, and drew out the letter inside. When she unfolded it, two black and white photos fell into her hand. The first was a wedding photo. Angus stood next to a delicate lady with a wildflower crown woven into fair, curly hair that fell around her shoulders. She was enchantingly beautiful in her wedding gown. He had an iris and a sprig of heather pinned to his lapel. They were looking into one another's eyes and smiling. The second was a family portrait. Angus stood in the center, as elderly as the day she'd met him, smiling under a mop of white curls. He had his arm around the same lady, but they were in their eighties. They were surrounded by four middle aged adults, all with happy smiles.

Iris half laughed and half cried, tears of joy flooding her eyes. She missed him dearly—and even across the centuries, he had sensed it. He had left her every assurance within his power that he'd been happy. She turned to the letter.

Iris—

What to say, dear friend? Plain words dinnae capture everything I wish I could say to you, but I'll try.

I hope this letter finds you as well and happy as I am. I'd not be here, were it not for you. I wish there was some way for me to hear from you, but time is a cruel master, always insisting on marching forward. Well... except that one time.

I've included photos of my Gillian, since you never got to meet her, and our children: Iris Fiona, John Angus, Marjorie Grace, and Gordon Henry. Our grandchildren and great grandchildren cannae fit into one picture, I'm afraid!

The sovereign is for your collection. Minted in 1841—I hope that's the one you were looking for.

I also left behind a lot of irises for you to find... you might've noticed. It's just my way of saying I've ne'er forgotten you or your love for me. You stood by me when no one else would. It meant everything.

I hope you point that fierce loyalty towards your Creator next, and let him show you what to do with it. I know that whatever you do with your life will change the world. I'm not just saying it to be kind, I know it in my heart.

A bit of advice from this old man—for that's what I really am now... Tell people what's on your heart as soon as you know it. Keep your head and heart full of gratitude. Run after the life you're meant to live—never be afraid you're not good enough to live it!

I've prayed for you since you left, and by the time you're reading this, I'll be praying for you from heaven.

Love and pizza,
Angus

P.S. This frame's not made of hawthorn!

The End

Epilogue

Iris's first full day back at Rookwood Senior Home had been peaceful, in a way that only a day full of canary droppings, unfamiliar songs, flying raisins, and cleaning glitter glue off of sixteen wrinkly people could be.

She walked out to her car, considering her day... and how she felt about having hundreds more just like it in her future. Being here without Angus was going to be tough at first, she knew that. Perhaps, after a time, she'd get used to it. She still loved the feeling of making the days brighter for these people. She had come to think of them as friends.

And knowing that Will was right downstairs made her heart skip.

But something had been different today. She'd been hoping to feel that same spark of fulfillment she'd felt before, when she'd finally started connecting with the people here. But as much as she enjoyed their smiles, her mind kept wandering to the six crimson roses lying where Irene's pillow had been. How many more friends could she stand to lose?

And it wasn't just that.

Meeting Angus had ignited her soul. What they had done together, been through together, had impacted more than just a handful of people like what she'd done today. It had changed history. It had changed *her*.

She had merely set out to reunite him with his family. Instead, she'd experienced a love that transcended everything she thought she knew about friendship—the kind of love that laid down its life, regardless of the cost, just for the sake of knowing another person would be safe. There was something so unexplainably *right* about that.

A whole new universe had emerged—more mysterious than Iris had ever imagined—its architecture framed on principles of physics beyond the understanding of the keenest human minds. An entire world of ancient spirit beings and Guardian families shared a responsibility to protect it, even though humanity remained oblivious to their existence.

Most stunning of all, it wasn't governed by random coincidence, as she'd first supposed. It was held by *Someone*. Angus had called Him friend. He had been sure that this Someone saw her, heard her… knew her… and was guiding her to a destiny she'd never imagined.

God, Angus said you'd show me what to do next. I know that helping these sweet people is a worthy calling… but is it mine?

She unlocked her car door and reached for the handle.

"Iris Jacobs?"

Iris whirled around. In front of her stood Jason Reynolds, her old science teacher.

"Mr. Reynolds, hi!" she breathed. "You startled me!"

"Sorry…"

"How did you know I was here?"

"It's in the database." He gazed intently at her. "I've come to talk to you on behalf of the Council of Guardians."

Her stomach fell into her shoes. She was afraid to speak. If he was talking about something else, and she said too much…

Jason laughed, his eyes merry. "I've freaked you out, I can see that. Iris, it's okay! Yes, *that* Council of Guardians. Your name's come up more than once in the central database. We find it interesting when someone gets a mention back in the nineteenth century, and then another one in the twenty-first."

Iris finally found her voice. "Uh... am I in trouble or something?"

He suppressed a smile. "Why would you be in trouble?"

"I cut the Great Hawthorn... with an ax?" She looked sheepish.

Jason shook his head. "Sounds like it was a good thing you did. We've all read the MacCrann diaries. Every detail's been recorded. According to them, you were the hero in that scenario. Iris, you *saved* the Great Hawthorn, and everyone within its reach... for all of time!" He searched her face. "Do you realize how many people that is?"

"A lot?"

"*Countless!* The Council is impressed with you. You're the first non-Guardian ever to stand in the midst of a massive time disturbance and not only live to tell about it, you can still remember it. Means you can keep a secret. That's valuable to us."

Iris processed his words in amazement. *Talk about secrets... this man has been a Guardian the whole time and never let on? He's good.*

"W-well..." she stammered, unable to decide on an appropriate response. "Tell them I said... thanks for the compliment?"

Jason chuckled. "They want to offer you a job."

To be continued...

Acknowledgments

The Three — Yahweh the Father, Jesus Christ his Son, and the Holy Spirit. May we stand in awe of your ways, ever seeking to know You with our minds and hearts.

Raymond — My favorite human. Thank you for making this book possible. I love you.

My wonderful kiddos — Thank you for always asking, "What happens next?" Reading this book to you chapter by chapter during its creation was nothing short of magical. I'll never forget that special time with you. I hope this story points you to Jesus, the first and best Person in the universe.

Mutzer — Your expertise as a fiction connoisseur was invaluable, while your enthusiasm for this story was contagious. I needed both!

To dear friends — Thank you for sharing this journey with me by contributing your time, influence, support, critique, and encouragement (and in some cases, inspiring a character!): Bellame Richardson, Leslie Conzatti, Christy Schmidt, Kileah McIlvain, Diana Moore, Jonathan Inabnit, Jeanette Finn, Ronda Butterfield, Evie Poythress, Valerie Krasner, Hannah Rothwell, Phoebe Wickliffe, Kara Stutheit, Jack Glasgow, Lauren Glasgow, Sarah Martin, Rhonda Bolling, and Kary Oberbrunner.

55306383R00257

Made in the USA
Middletown, DE
15 July 2019